COYOTE DESTINY

Books by Allen M. Steele

Novels

THE JERICHO ITERATION

THE TRANQUILLITY ALTERNATIVE

OCEANSPACE

CHRONOSPACE

NEAR-SPACE SERIES

ORBITAL DECAY

CLARKE COUNTY, SPACE

LUNAR DESCENT

LABYRINTH OF NIGHT

A KING OF INFINITE SPACE

COYOTE TRILOGY

COYOTE

COYOTE RISING

COYOTE FRONTIER

COYOTE CHRONICLES

COYOTE HORIZON

COYOTE DESTINY

COYOTE UNIVERSE

SPINDRIFT

GALAXY BLUES

Collections

RUDE ASTRONAUTS

ALL-AMERICAN ALIEN BOY

SEX AND VIOLENCE IN ZERO-G: THE COMPLETE "NEAR SPACE" STORIES

AMERICAN BEAUTY

THE LAST SCIENCE FICTION WRITER

Nonfiction

PRIMARY IGNITION: ESSAYS 1997–2001

COYOTE DESTINY

A Novel of Interstellar Civilization

ALLEN M. STEELE

ACE BOOKS, NEW YORK

THE BERKLEY PUBLISHING GROUP
Published by the Penguin Group
Penguin Group (USA) Inc.
375 Hudson Street, New York, New York 10014, USA
Penguin Group (Canada), 90 Eglinton Avenue East, Suite 700, Toronto, Ontario M4P 2Y3, Canada
(a division of Pearson Penguin Canada Inc.)
Penguin Books Ltd., 80 Strand, London WC2R 0RL, England
Penguin Group Ireland, 25 St. Stephen's Green, Dublin 2, Ireland (a division of Penguin Books Ltd.)
Penguin Group (Australia), 250 Camberwell Road, Camberwell, Victoria 3124, Australia
(a division of Pearson Australia Group Pty. Ltd.)
Penguin Books India Pvt. Ltd., 11 Community Centre, Panchsheel Park, New Delhi—110 017, India
Penguin Group (NZ), 67 Apollo Drive, Rosedale, North Shore 0632, New Zealand
(a division of Pearson New Zealand Ltd.)
Penguin Books (South Africa) (Pty.) Ltd., 24 Sturdee Avenue, Rosebank, Johannesburg 2196,
South Africa

Penguin Books Ltd., Registered Offices: 80 Strand, London WC2R 0RL, England

This is an original publication of The Berkley Publishing Group.

This is a work of fiction. Names, characters, places, and incidents either are the product of the author's imagination or are used fictitiously, and any resemblance to actual persons, living or dead, business establishments, events, or locales is entirely coincidental. The publisher does not have any control over and does not assume any responsibility for author or third-party websites or their content.

Copyright © 2010 by Allen M. Steele.
Map illustrations by Ron Miller and Allen M. Steele.
Calendar illustration by Allen M. Steele.
Text design by Tiffany Estreicher.

FIRST EDITION: March 2010

Library of Congress Cataloging-in-Publication Data

Steele, Allen M.
    Coyote destiny : a novel of interstellar civilization / Allen M. Steele.—1st ed.
      p.   cm.
    ISBN 978-0-441-01821-5
    1. Space colonies—Fiction.   2. Interplanetary voyages—Fiction.   3. Terrorists—Fiction.   I. Title.
    PS3569.T338425C6923   2010
    813'.54—dc22   2009047799

PRINTED IN THE UNITED STATES OF AMERICA

10   9   8   7   6   5   4   3   2   1

For Horace "Ace" Marchant

CONTENTS

DRAMATIS PERSONAE

Montero Family

Jorge Montero II, Lt.—officer, Coyote Federation Corps of Exploration

Susan Montero—naturalist, University of New Florida; Jorge's mother

Jonathan Parson, Col.—chief of staff, Corps of Exploration; Jorge's father

Wendy Gunther—former president, Coyote Federation; Jorge's grandmother

Thompson Family

Hawk Thompson (a.k.a. the *chaaz'maha*)—*Sa'Tong* spiritual leader

Melissa Sanchez—member, Order of the Eye; Hawk's partner

Inez Sanchez, Corp. (a.k.a. Inez Torres)—member, Corps of Exploration; Hawk's daughter

Sawyer Lee, Gen.—commanding officer, Corps of Exploration

Greg Dillon, Sgt.—member, Corps of Exploration

Hugh McAlister, Capt.—pilot, CFS *Gerardus Mercator*

Charles Edgar—president, Coyote Federation

Chris Levin—former chief proctor, Liberty

Tomas Conseco—Wendy Gunther's aide

Manuel Castro—Savant; Coyote Federation diplomatic liaison

Sergio Vargas—pilot, WHS *The Legend of Simon Bolivar*

Dominic Treece—*Bolivar* copilot

Kim Jewel—veterinarian

Jake Turner—stockyard employee

Kyle Olson—stockyard owner
Gary Smith—Olson's crony
Roland Black—commander, First Massachusetts Regiment, Provisional
    Army of the United Republic of America
Sam, Ted, Morse—Boston residents
Gerald Copperfield—mayor of Manuelito
Emma Stanley—chief proctor, Manuelito
Amy Atkins—lighthouse keeper
Erin Atkins—Amy's daughter
Jasahajahd Taf Sa-Fhadda—*hjadd* First Speaker of the Talus High Council
The *chaaz'braan*—*askanta* Great Teacher of *Sa'Tong*

COYOTE DESTINY

PROLOGUE

From eighty kilometers, Starbridge Earth was a small silver ring floating at its Lagrange point near the Moon, its surface reflecting the light of the distant sun. A portal to the galaxy, it seemed as if it were impatiently waiting for the stars to wake up and take notice.

"Does anyone know what's going on?" Seated on the left side of the *Bolivar*'s narrow cockpit, Captain Sergio Vargas listened to his headset as he studied the starbridge through the wraparound windows. Less than a minute ago, the ring had been filled by the coruscating flash of multispectral light, an indication that the wormhole had opened. Sergio was expecting to see a ship emerge from the ring. Instead, the wormhole had abruptly collapsed, without a vessel coming through.

"*Negative, Bolivar.*" Although the traffic controller aboard the nearby gatehouse remained calm, Vargas could make out other voices in the background; it wasn't hard to tell that they were as confused as he was. "*Stand by, please. We're still assessing the situation.*"

"We copy, Trafco. *Bolivar* standing by." Vargas tapped the mike wand to silence it, then looked over at his copilot. "Any ideas?"

"Haven't a clue." Dominic Treece was busy at his console, making sure that the freighter was keeping station. *The Legend of Simon Bolivar* was scheduled to be the next ship to go through the starbridge. Two other vessels were also in a holding pattern, each 160 kilometers apart from the others; if the *Bolivar* slipped out of position, the gatehouse controller would move the other ships to the front of the line. The delay would only be a few hours, but Sergio was acutely aware of the thirty-four refugees crammed into a passenger module within the freighter's hold. Most of them had never been in space before; his cargo master had already reported that many had become ill and that the module was reeking of vomit.

"It's probably nothing." Even as he said this, though, Vargas couldn't shake the premonition that something had gone seriously wrong. This would be the third time he'd taken the *Bolivar* through the starbridge, and usually everything went like clockwork. Once *Bolivar*'s AI was slaved to its counterpart aboard the gatehouse, the matter was out of his hands; the quantum comps would do the rest, automatically maneuvering the freighter until it reached the starbridge, then waiting until the precise moment when the wormhole opened and the ship would be launched through the event horizon for the harrowing, five-second jaunt to 47 Ursae Majoris.

With something as delicate as this, nothing was left to chance. Which was why AIs performed the fiendishly complex calculations; humans simply couldn't be trusted to complete a task that had such a low threshold for error. As a result, in the hundreds of times ships had gone through the starbridges since they'd been built, never once had there been an abort, let alone a major accident.

Until now.

"Something's wrong." Treece glanced across the center console at his captain. "Maybe they don't know either, or maybe they're not telling us, but . . ."

"Gatehouse to Bolivar, *do you read?"*

"Hold on." Vargas held up a hand, admonishing Dom to be quiet, then cracked his mike again. *"Bolivar* here. What's going on?"

"We have . . ." A moment's pause, just long enough for Vargas and Treece to share a glance. *"There's been a major malfunction on the other side of the interface. We don't yet know the exact cause, but there appears to have been an explosion aboard the inbound vessel."*

Vargas felt his heart skip a bit. "Please repeat, gatehouse. Did you say there was an explosion aboard the other ship?"

Another pause. When the traffic controller spoke again, there was a tremor in his voice that Sergio had never heard before. *"Affirmative, Bolivar. Last communication received from Starbridge Coyote stated that there was an explosion aboard the Lee just as it was crossing the event horizon."*

Before Vargas could respond, Treece tapped his own mike. "Gatehouse, please say again . . . do you mean the *Robert E. Lee?"*

It was a minor breach of protocol for the copilot to address Trafco without his captain's permission, but at the moment no one was about to make an issue of it. *"Affirmative. The inbound ship was the Lee."*

The fact that controller referred to the *Lee* in the past tense wasn't lost on either man. Vargas and Treece stared at each other, neither of them able to speak. The CFSS *Robert E. Lee* wasn't just the flagship of the Coyote Federation's fledgling navy; it was also one of the largest starships in existence, rivaled only by its sister vessel, the EASS *Magellan*. Its commanding officer, Anastasia Tereshkova, was almost a legend among spacers. Not only that, but there was no telling how many crewmen and passengers were aboard. Dozens, perhaps as many as a hundred . . .

"Christ preserve them," Treece murmured under his breath, his right hand forming a crucifix across his shoulders and chest.

Vargas wasn't a practicing Catholic, but he was also tempted to cross himself. "Do we have confirmation of this, gatehouse?" he asked.

"Negative. We have received no further word from either Starbridge Coyote or the Lee. All communications have been cut off at the source." Another pause. *"Please remain online. The CO would like to speak with you."*

Treece turned to him as Vargas muted the comlink. "'Cut off at the source'? What does that mean?"

"I'm afraid to know." The pilot felt something clutch at the pit of his stomach. Although the wormhole was periodically expanded wide enough for ships to pass through, it never completely closed. Instead, a tiny gap into hyperspace, no more than a few millimeters in diameter, was constantly kept open, thereby allowing a steady stream of laser pulses to be sent back and forth between the small space stations that served as gatehouses for the starbridges. In this way, near-instant communications between Earth and Coyote was continually maintained.

If Starbridge Earth was receiving no hyperlink transmissions from 47 Ursae Majoris, forty-six light-years away, then it meant that something had happened to Starbridge Coyote itself. And if that were the case . . .

Vargas did his best to remain calm. For the last several months, following the political meltdown of the Western Hemisphere Union, inhabitants of North and South America had joined the mobs of Europeans and Asians fleeing Earth in the aftermath of global environmental collapse. Although the WHU had extensive settlements on the Moon, Mars, and the satellites of the outer planets, they were already overcrowded; however, it wasn't until only recently that its citizens had been able to travel to Coyote. The Union's stubborn refusal to ratify the United Nations treaty recognizing Coyote's independence had prevented free trade or immigration, let alone the establishment of Union colonies. But when the Proletariat was overthrown, its Patriarchs and Matriarchs either executed or sent into hiding, those sanctions effectively became null and void. The cities of the Western Hemisphere Union were in flames, their individual governments struggling to contain the anarchy that had replaced social collectivism.

An interim agreement between the Coyote Federation and what remained of the Union had allowed for refugees to make their way to 47 Uma. When that happened, every person able to do so crowded aboard any space vessel capable of making the trip to Starbridge Earth. *The Legend of Simon Bolivar* was just one of dozens of Union Astronautica vessels that had been hastily refitted to carry immigrants to Coyote. Although the freighter had been designed to do little more than haul cargo from Earth to Highgate, the international space colony at Lagrange Five, it was capable of making hyperspace jumps once its navigation system was retrofitted with a starbridge key. So far, the *Bolivar* had transported nearly 70 people to Coyote; once this round-trip was completed, the total would be 102, almost as many as had been aboard the URSS *Alabama*, the first starship to reach the new world.

To be sure, this represented only the tiniest fraction of the multitudes seeking sanctuary. Nonetheless, Vargas took considerable pride in the fact that he'd saved so many lives. Only a couple of days ago, though, he'd promised his crew that this would be the last time that they'd return to Earth. On their next flight out, their own families would be aboard as well, then the *Bolivar* would remain at 47 Ursae Majoris once and for all.

But now it appeared that he might have waited too long.

"Bolivar, *this is Gatehouse Command.*" A new voice came through Sergio's headset, interrupting his thoughts. *"With whom am I speaking, please?"*

Vargas prodded his mike. "Command, this is Captain Sergio Vargas. I'm trying to get confirmation that . . ."

"Captain, I have bad news." Something in the way the CO spoke made Vargas brace for the worst. *"For reasons unknown, we've lost communications with Starbridge Coyote. We have reason to believe that the starbridge itself has been destroyed."*

From beside him, Vargas heard a sharp intake of breath. He shot Dom a stern look, silently warning him to shut up, then he leaned forward in his seat. "We copy, Command. I . . ." He hesitated, not quite knowing what to say. "I understand. That means the jump is aborted, doesn't it?"

This was obvious, of course, but he had to hear the words from the CO himself, just to make sure there was no mistake. *"Affirmative, Captain,"* the CO replied. *"We are requesting that all outbound vessels return to Highgate, where their passengers and crew will be asked to disembark. We will inform you if the situation changes, but for the time being, Starbridge Earth is no longer operational. Please acknowledge."*

"We copy, gatehouse." Vargas let out his breath, fell back in his seat. From the corner of his eye, he saw his copilot slam a fist against his armrest. "Thank you for telling us. I appreciate . . ."

"*I'm not finished yet. We have a request to make of you.*" A slight pause. "*According to our instruments, something came through the starbridge just a few moments before the wormhole collapsed. It's transmitting a wireless signal identical to that of an emergency transponder, and we have reason to believe that it may be a lifeboat.*"

Vargas sat up straight again. He glanced at Treece; the copilot was already bending closer to the console between their seats to examine the lidar screen. "Have you made contact with it yet?"

"*Negative. There's been no verbal response to our hails. However, our remote imaging leads us to believe that it may be a lifeboat launched from the* Lee."

"I have it," Treece murmured. "Bearing X-ray 42.1, Yankee -11.5, Zulu 01.1. Distance 51.4 kilometers and drifting . . ."

"Copy that, gatehouse. We confirm acquisition." As he spoke, Vargas reached up to the communications console above his seat. He flipped a couple of toggles, studied the screen: there it was, the steady and repetitive spike of something being received on the Ku band. "We're receiving the transponder signal, too."

"*Trafco reports that* Bolivar *is the closest available vessel. We request that you undertake the rescue effort before returning to Highgate and bring in the lifeboat and any persons who may be aboard to the colony. Are you able to do so?*"

"Affirmative." As if they had any choice in the matter. The *Bolivar* was the nearest ship, and international space treaties mandated that it render assistance; the thirty-four would-be immigrants in the passenger module would just have to wait a little while longer. "We're on our way."

"*We copy,* Bolivar. *Keep us informed. Gatehouse over.*"

"Wilco. *Bolivar* over and out." Vargas switched off the mike, then let out his breath. "Damn," he muttered. "Damn, damn, damn . . ."

"I can't believe it." Treece was staring straight ahead; he was still stunned by what they'd just heard. "First the *Lee*, then the starbridge . . . what the hell happened over there? They said there was an explosion, but . . . I mean, what . . . ?"

"Never mind that now." Vargas shook his head, then reached over to the nav console. Switching off the autopilot, he fed the lifeboat's present coordinates into the flight comp; once the *Bolivar* was close enough, they'd home in on the transponder signal. "Get Romas on the com, let him know what's going on, then tell him to get into the pod."

"Okay." The freighter was equipped with a small cargo pod. Normally used to load payload canisters into the cargo bay, it would serve as a salvage vehicle. As *Bolivar*'s cargo master, it was Caesar Romas's job to fly the thing. Treece started to tap his mike, then hesitated. "What about the passengers? Shouldn't we tell them . . . ?"

"Just give me a minute, all right?" Vargas tried to keep the irritation from his voice, but Treece winced all the same. "Sorry," he added. "I'm just . . . trying to get over this myself."

"I understand, Captain." The copilot was quiet for a moment. "Did you know anyone aboard the *Lee*?"

"No. Did you?" Treece shook his head, nor was Vargas surprised. Like most South American spacers, they were both Union Astronautica officers—or at least had been, until the Union collapsed; neither of them still wore UA insignia on his uniform—and thus had little interaction with their colleagues in the ESA, which was where most of the Coyote Federation's spacers originally came from. Not that it mattered, really. Regardless of which flag was painted on the hull of one's ship, everyone who worked in space belonged to a brotherhood. They all shared the same risks; whenever the dark claimed a life, everyone shared a bit of the pain.

And there would be no shortage of pain today.

"It's a black day," Vargas murmured as he finished entering the coordinates into the comp. "I'm afraid we'll remember it for years to come."

* * *

The lifeboat was a small, conical spacecraft, resembling an antique child's top that had somehow spun out into space. Slowly tumbling end over end by the time the *Bolivar* arrived, it took all of Romas's skill as a pod jockey for him to rendezvous with the tiny craft and use the pod's thrusters to stop its spin. Once this was achieved, though, it was relatively easy for the cargo master to maneuver the lifeboat into the freighter's cargo bay.

Treece took over from there. Leaving the cockpit to assist Romas, he stood at the rear-facing porthole of *Bolivar*'s lower deck and carefully used the freighter's remote manipulators to grasp the rungs on either side of the lifeboat's docking collar and guide it the rest of the way into the bay. Once the lifeboat was in place, grapples within the bay secured it to the other end of the passenger module. There was no way to reach the lifeboat from the *Bolivar*'s lower deck, but since the passenger module had an emergency airlock located at its rear, Treece was able to link the lifeboat directly to the module. Once this was done, it meant that they would be able to enter the small craft.

By then, Vargas had gone on the intercom to inform the passengers of the disaster. He'd kept his remarks brief and to the point, avoiding any speculation of what might have caused the loss of either Starbridge Coyote or the *Lee*. Nonetheless, as soon as he opened the module's forward hatch and pushed himself inside, he found himself surrounded by frightened, confused, and angry people, all of whom had questions he couldn't answer. The captain did his best to calm everyone as he used the ceiling handrail to pull himself through the module, yet he couldn't help but be relieved by the fact that they were all strapped down in their seats. It was easy to avoid the hands that reached up to grasp at his arms and legs, and by the time he reached the rear hatch, he'd stopped talking to anyone.

With one exception. Along the way, Vargas had checked the passenger manifest and discovered that there was a physician aboard: Dr.

Kim Jewel, late of Massachusetts. The fact that Dr. Jewel was a veterinarian more accustomed to treating dogs was a minor detail; she had more medical experience than anyone else on the *Bolivar*, including the crew, who'd only had Union Astronautica first-aid training. Sergio found her seated about three-quarters of the way back from the front of the cabin; Dr. Jewel immediately agreed to give Captain Vargas any assistance she could, then unbuckled her harness and followed him to the emergency airlock.

Twisting the hatch's lockwheel counterclockwise, Sergio pushed it open, revealing a closet-sized compartment with another hatch on the opposite side. Pulling himself into the airlock, he took a moment to check the pressure gauge; satisfied that there was an airtight seal on the other side, he undogged it as well. A faint hiss of escaping overpressure, then the hatch popped open.

Beyond the open hatch was the narrow crawl space of the docking collar. Vargas pulled a penlight from his jumpsuit pocket and shined it down the tunnel; the lifeboat's dorsal hatch was only a couple of meters away. The crawl space was frigid, the tiger-striped hatch crusted with ice, but there didn't appear to be any damage to the lifeboat's hull or its lockwheel.

Whatever fate had befallen the *Lee*, the lifeboat had somehow managed to escape unscratched. All the same, Vargas took no chances. Pulling a camera from his pocket, he snapped a couple of pictures of the lifeboat hatch before venturing any farther into the tunnel.

"What are you doing?" Floating in the airlock behind him, Jewel impatiently waited for Sergio to enter the lifeboat. "There may be wounded passengers over there."

"Covering the bases, that's all." There would eventually be an official inquiry into the disaster, and the review board would want all the physical evidence they could get. Not only that, but Vargas didn't want himself or his crew to be held culpable in any way for their role in the rescue effort; photos would prove the condition of the lifeboat when they found it. Putting the camera back in his pocket, the captain pulled himself into the crawl space. "Wait until I get this thing open before following me," he added. "I want to make sure . . ."

He winced and swore under his breath as his bare hands touched the ice-cold lockwheel. Nothing he could do about that, though, except rub his palms together to warm them, then try again. The lockwheel rasped as he yanked at it, and tiny bits of frost broke away, but the hatch yielded to his pressure and swung inward.

The lifeboat was dark, save for the faint glow of the red and blue diodes on its instrument panels. Pushing himself into the small craft, Vargas cast the beam around the interior. He'd expected to find it crowded with passengers, perhaps even a crewman or two; instead, he was stunned to find it nearly empty. All but one of its hammock seats were folded against the concave bulkheads; even the control console was still locked down. The lifeboat had been jettisoned with almost no one aboard.

Except for one person.

Grabbing hold of a bulkhead rung, Vargas pulled himself over to the lifeboat's sole occupant. Within the beam of his flashlight, he saw a young man, strapped into the seat, arms and legs dangling in midair. His eyes were shut, and for a moment Sergio thought he might be dead, until his flashlight caught the faint vapor of exhaled breath rising from his open mouth.

"Better get in here," he said aloud, and was startled when, in the next instant, Jewel's hand grasped his shoulder. The vet hadn't waited for the captain to give her permission to enter the lifeboat but had followed him through the docking collar.

"Let me see him." Grabbing hold of the back of the seat frame, Jewel turned herself around until she could look straight down at the unconscious passenger. "Do you think we could have a little more light in here?"

Turning around, Vargas unfolded the control console and used it to switch on the lifeboat's interior lights. As they flickered to life, he was able to see the young man more clearly. In his late twenties, he wore what appeared to be a hooded brown robe much like a monk's. His head was shaved save for a long, braided scalp lock dangling from the back of his skull; on his forehead, just above his nose and between his eyes, was a tattoo that resembled the Greek letter *pi* turned upside down.

Jewel gently pried open the young man's left eye, peered at the pupil. "Mild concussion. Probably caused when the lifeboat was jettisoned." She located foot restraints on the deck beside the couch and inserted her feet within the elastic stirrups; properly braced, she continued her examination, carefully flexing the passenger's limbs and prodding his chest. "Nothing broken. No ribs cracked. No signs of internal injuries. I think he's . . ."

The young man groaned, a soft sigh coming from his slack mouth, as his eyelids fluttered slightly. "Looks like he's coming out of it," Vargas murmured. "Think you can wake him up?"

"Give him a minute, all right?" Sensing the captain's impatience, though, Jewel gently massaged the passenger's wrist. "Hello," she whispered. "Are you with me?"

"Humm . . . huhh?" The young man's eyes slowly opened. Dazed, he gazed up at the two people hovering above him. "Whuh . . . who . . ."

"Captain? What's going on down there? Have you found anyone?"

Startled by Treece's voice in his headset, Vargas bit back a curse, then tapped his mike. "Affirmative," he replied. "We've found someone aboard . . . only one, but at least he's still alive. Stand by."

He clicked off again, then bent closer to the passenger. He was only semiconscious, but Vargas needed to talk to him as soon as possible. Dom was breathing down his neck for answers, and Vargas was all too aware that it wouldn't be long before everyone else would be as well.

"Can you hear me?" he demanded, raising his voice a little. "Do you know where you are?"

"Captain, please . . ." Jewel placed a hand on his shoulder, tried to push him back. "Give him a sec. He's been through a lot."

"Life . . . lifeboat." Apparently confused, the young man turned his head slightly, looking around himself. "In the lifeboat . . . I'm . . . where . . . ?"

"Yes, you're in a lifeboat." Vargas was trying not to lose patience. "The lifeboat was ejected from the *Lee*. You're the only one aboard. No one else made it. What happened to the ship? Why did it . . . ?"

"Captain, please!" Jewel insistently pushed him aside. "You're not helping." She turned to the passenger again. "Relax, you're okay. You made it through . . ."

"Ship . . . bomb on the ship . . . explosion . . ."

"There was an explosion, yes." Sergio bent closer to him again. "You say there was a bomb on the *Lee*?" The young man slowly nodded. "Who brought a bomb aboard?"

"Captain, please . . ." Once more, Jewel pushed him away. Then she turned to the young man again. "Can you tell me who you are?" she asked, as gently as she could.

The sole survivor of the *Robert E. Lee* was quiet for a moment, and Sergio was surprised to see tears glistening at the corners of his eyes, breaking off to form tiny spheres that floated away. Then he looked straight at both him and the doctor, and a soft smile touched the corners of his mouth.

"I'm God," he said. "And so are you."

Book 3

Sons and Daughters

The vast resources of the New World so liberated human potential that the imaginative mind felt a new relation with the universe—a new sense of control over destiny. But the consequent rise of the self-reflexive individual, severed from institutional contexts of identity, brought the loss of innocence that has made the reconquest of Eden the organizing image of the last half-millennium. If the Copernican expulsion from the literal center symbolizes this loss of larger meaning, then the leitmotif of the longing to return . . . has been the dream of spaceflight.

—WYN WACHHORST,
The Dream of Spaceflight

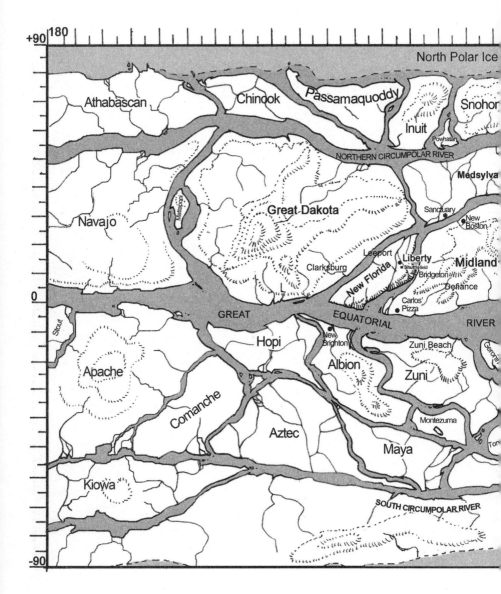

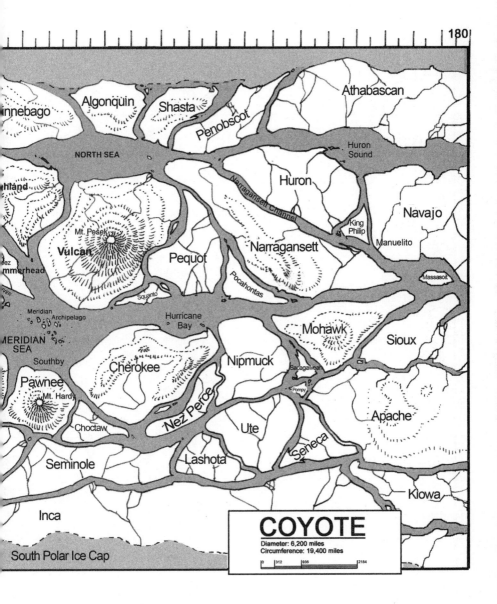

180

Winnebago Algonquin Shasta Athabascan

Penobscot

NORTH SEA Huron Sound

Highland Huron

Vulcan Mt. Pesek Navajo

Nez Hammerhead King Philip Manuelito

Meridian Archipelago Pequot Narragansett Massasoit

MERIDIAN SEA Squanto Pocahontas

Southby Hurricane Bay Mohawk Sioux

Pawnee Cherokee Nipmuck Sacagawea

Mt. Hardy Pompy

Choctaw Nez Perce Ute Apache

Seminole Lashota Seneca

Inca Kiowa

South Polar Ice Cap

COYOTE

Diameter: 6,200 miles
Circumference: 19,400 miles

0   312   936   2184

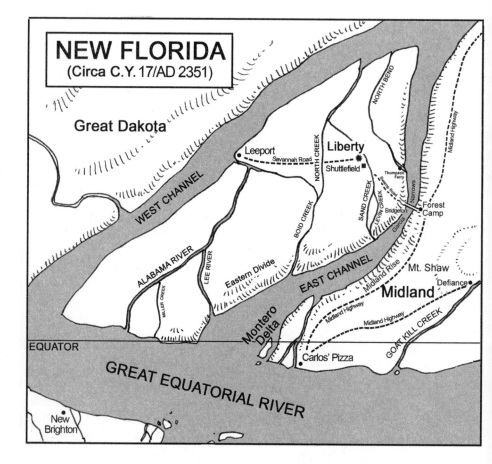

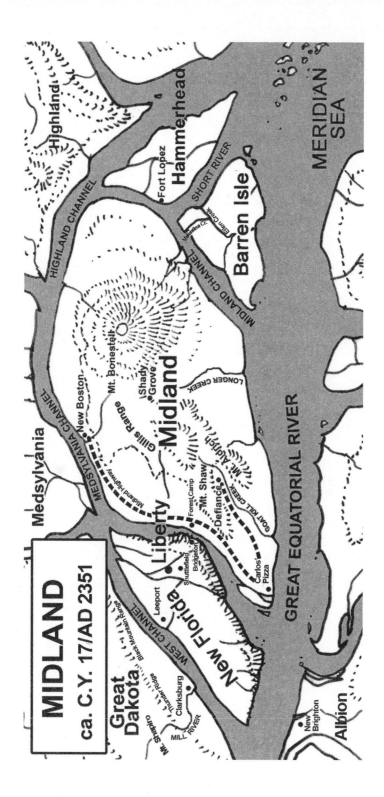

MIDLAND
ca. C.Y. 17/AD 2351

Highland

HIGHLAND CHANNEL

Fort Lopez
Hammerhead
SHORT RIVER

Ellen Creek
Valentina Cr.
Barren Isle

MIDLAND CHANNEL

MERIDIAN
SEA

Medsylvania

MEDSYLVANIA CHANNEL

New Boston

Mt. Bonestell
Shady
Grove
Midland

Gillis Range

LONGER CREEK

GOAT KILL CREEK

Mt. Aldrich

Midland Highway

Liberty

Forest Camp
Mt. Shaw
Defiance
Shuttlefield
Bridgeton
Carlos'
Pizza

GREAT EQUATORIAL RIVER

Leeport
New Florida

Great
Dakota

Black Mountain Range

Mt. Shapiro
Thunder Ridge
Clarksburg
MILL RIVER

WEST CHANNEL

New
Brighton

Albion

Part 1

THE CORPS OF EXPLORATION

The southern coast of Algonquin was a white and desolate expanse, its subarctic tundra hidden beneath the snows of winter. Beneath skies the color of dirty chalk lay a monotonous plain, with only the dark brown bluffs of the nearby mountains lending the slightest hint of color. Even the North Sea matched the landscape, its frigid blue waters concealed beneath a dense layer of ice. At first glance, it seemed as if this part of the world was utterly lifeless, save for the lonesome wind that picked up patches of snow and spun them away as miniature, short-lived twisters.

And yet, there was movement.

The polar cow and her family were almost invisible, their thick white fur allowing them to blend in with the snowpack. The cow had migrated down from the mountains, where, sometime last autumn, it had mated with one of the bulls that roamed its lower steppes. Now she was at the midpoint of an annual winter migration that would eventually take her across the frozen sea to the northern coast of Vulcan, a slightly warmer climate where she and her calves would find enough food to sustain them for the long, cold months ahead. She'd made this journey many times before, and even though her species was not terribly intelligent, she was doubtless aware that the most dangerous part of their trek still lay ahead.

Her children, of course, didn't know this. Seven in all—there had once been eight, but they'd lost one of their kin during a storm only a few days ago—most of them marched in tandem behind their mother, the footprints of their stumplike legs forming a deep trail that went almost all the way down to the frozen dirt beneath the snow. The cow carried the two smallest and weakest of her offspring upon her back, where they gently rocked back and forth with every step she took; they weighed at least a hundred pounds each, but their mother didn't seem to mind. Nine feet tall, weighing nearly a ton, her size was rivaled only by her close cousins, the shags that inhabited the equatorial continents of Midland and Great Dakota.

"Wonderful," Inez murmured. "Absolutely wonderful."

She lay prone upon the crest of a small hill, elbows propped against the snow-covered ground. In her gloved hands was a pair of binoculars through which she studied the herd from a distance of two hundred yards. Although she wore Corps winter gear, her maroon parka and snow pants were camouflaged by a solar-heated white cape that gave her additional warmth. Inez had pushed back her goggles in order to use the binoculars, but her voice was muffled slightly by the hood pulled up around her head.

"Aren't they?" Kneeling beside her, Jorge watched the polar cows with the naked eye—or rather, without the aid of binoculars; he was careful to keep his goggles in place, lest the ice-reflected sunlight damage his eyes. Which reminded him of something that might interest her. "Look closely," he added. "Do you see something peculiar about the way they walk?"

Inez was quiet for a few moments, during which Jorge stole a glance at her. Even though she wore thick clothes and was swaddled within the *arsashi* cape, he couldn't help but admire the arch of her back, the curve of her rump. It was a liberty he felt a twinge of guilt for taking, but Corps regulations only prohibited unwanted sexual overtures; there was nothing said about looking.

"I don't know what you mean." When Inez spoke again, there was an undercurrent of irritation to her voice. "What are you getting at . . . sir?"

Had she caught him looking at her? Once again, a tacit reminder that they were separated by rank, not to mention age. At six and a third by the LeMarean calendar, Corporal Inez Torres was a couple of years younger than Lieutenant Jorge Montero II. Nonetheless, he lay down in the snow beside her, close enough to feel the warmth of her cape. "Notice the way the mother moves. She keeps her head low, with her snout touching the ground, moving it back and forth. Almost like she's searching for something . . ."

"Food?" Inez looked away from the binoculars, her gaze briefly meeting his. Her eyes were beautiful; pale blue, solemn yet perpetually curious, as if always seeing the world for the first time. Jorge never got tired of looking at them.

"No. Not food. Not much of that around here. Besides, they're living on body fat. They probably haven't eaten in weeks. That's why they're migrating in the first place." He grinned, then pointed to the children. "Give you a hint. Look at her kids . . . the way they're following Mama, and what they're doing with each other, too."

Inez raised the binoculars again, peered through them. "All right, they're all walking one right behind the other, with their snouts touching against each other's backside. It's almost like . . ." Her eyes widened as the realization hit her. "They're blind!"

She spoke louder than she should have. The procession suddenly came to a halt as the mother's shaggy head swung in the direction of Inez's voice. Her large, tufted ears rose slightly, and her broad, lipless mouth opened to emit the bovine *mo-o-o-oah* that gave her species its name.

"Shh!" Jorge hastily reached forward to push Inez's binoculars into the snow so that the sun wouldn't reflect off their lenses. "Almost blind, but not entirely . . . and they've got very good hearing."

"Sorry, sir." Inez winced in embarrassment. But then she noticed Jorge's gloved hand still resting atop her own, and she hastily pulled her hand away. He was about to move closer to her again, but she rolled the other way, artfully putting a few more inches of distance between them.

"It's okay," he whispered, pretending not to notice her withdrawal. He remained quiet for a few seconds, waiting until the polar cow calmed down enough to continue moving, her calves in tow, before he spoke again. "No, they're not blind . . . but when they're traveling across ice and snow, they might as well be. They keep their eyes shut as much as they can, so that they don't lose their vision."

"So the mother uses her snout to feel her way along, and her calves use theirs to keep up with each other." Inez nodded, understanding now. "That's also why they walk in tandem, isn't it, sir?"

"Right. And also to fool predators." Before she could ask, he shook his head. "Not necessarily on dry land, no. But once they get out on the ice, they run a real risk of being ambushed by medusas. Traveling single file like that, they don't make as much sound. If they're lucky, a medusa won't swim beneath them at the wrong time."

Inez grimaced. She'd seen a medusa already during this expedition, when a couple of Corps naturalists had managed to capture one by planting a seismic device on the offshore ice that duplicated the vibrations a herd of polar cows would make. The monster that broke through the ice beneath the waiting net wasn't full-grown—which was probably just as well; it had taken eight men and women to haul the net onto the ice pack—nonetheless it was awesome to behold. Resembling a walrus of Old Earth save for the mass of tentacles around its mouth, medusas inhabited the waterways of northern polar regions. Although river horses and boids were still the most terrifying creatures on Coyote, an encounter with a North Sea medusa was nearly as scary.

"I guess that's why she has so many." Inez continued to study the cow and her offspring. "I read somewhere that it's unusual for large mammals to give birth to more than one or two at a time. But in this climate . . ."

"Right. The more children she has, the more likely she'll have survivors once she crosses the sea." Jorge smiled again. "They're really small when they come out, but once they fatten up on tundra grass and the lichen they scrape off rocks during the warm months, they'll get pretty hefty."

As they watched, the polar cows reached the edge of the shoreline. Once again, the mother stopped. Her head weaved back and forth for a moment, as if uncertain whether to proceed, then she carefully stepped out onto the ice. Her calves followed her, still keeping close to one another, and soon the procession was beginning its long march across the North Sea.

"Good-bye," Inez said quietly. "Good luck. I hope you . . ."

She was interrupted by a double beep in the headsets of their balaclavas, then a voice came over: *Algonquin Base to Sortie Two, do you copy?*

Rolling over on his side, Jorge reached beneath his cape to find the com patch attached to the outer shell of his parka. "Sortie Two to base, we read you."

"What's your present location, sir?" Jorge recognized the voice as belonging to Greg Dillon, his second-in-command for the expedition. He touched the left side of his goggles, activating its heads-up display. The holographic dial of an electronic compass materialized in front of his face, a range finder appearing just below it.

"Three-point-two miles southwest of base," he replied. "Just having a day at the beach."

His remark earned a fleeting smile from Inez, one that disappeared so quickly that he barely had time to enjoy it. It wasn't as if she lacked a sense of humor; she just seldom allowed anyone a chance to see it. *"Roger that,"* Greg replied. *"Hate to break up the party, sir, but we've just received a Priority One message from Fort Lopez. We need for you to return to base at once."*

Sitting up on the ground, Jorge pulled down his scarf to scratch absently at the beard he'd grown upon learning that he would spend the first four weeks of Gabriel in the subarctic. "What does the message say, Sergeant?"

"I have no idea, sir. As I said, it's Priority One, for your eyes only." A short pause, then Greg went on. *"It may only be a coincidence, but we've also received another message from Hammerhead, informing us that the* Monroe *is on its way up here to pick up someone."*

Another surprise. The *Dana Monroe* was the Corps of Exploration airship that had carried the expedition from the Corps garrison on Hammerhead to Algonquin only ten days earlier; however, it wasn't due to return for almost three more weeks. Although Jorge hadn't yet read the message, he knew that Greg was wrong; this couldn't be a coincidence.

"Understood, Sergeant. We're on our way home. Sortie Two out." He pressed the com patch again, then stood up from where he'd been sitting. "Hate to say this," he said to Inez, offering a hand to help her up, "but it's time to go."

"I'm sure there must be a good reason, sir." Ignoring his hand, Inez pushed herself to her feet. "Thank you for bringing me out here," she added, brushing snow off herself. "I appreciate it."

"The pleasure's all mine." He meant every word of it. His only regret was that he had so little opportunity to spend time with the young woman, or that his means of showing the affection he felt for her was so limited. Not that Inez ever seemed to notice . . . or if she did, she continued to be unwilling to reciprocate.

As they turned to walk back down the hill to where they'd left their skis, Jorge again found himself regretting that he'd ever joined the Corps of Exploration. There were a few reasons why he felt that way; unrequited love was near the top of the list.

Lieutenant Montero could have requisitioned one of the expedition skimmers to carry him and Corporal Torres to the seashore, but he'd decided to use skis instead. The practical reason, of course, was that skimmers made too much noise, and thus would have frightened away the polar cows. But the fact of the matter was that Jorge wanted an excuse to spend time alone with Inez, and a cross-country ski trip was the best way to accomplish this.

It took only a couple of minutes for them to fit the toes of their boots into the ski bindings. Picking up their poles, they shoved off, following the trail they'd broken earlier that morning. Jorge let Inez take the lead this time; although she had only recently learned Nordic skiing, he was impressed by how quickly she'd caught on. Besides, he enjoyed watching her body in motion, her long legs pushing first one ski forward, then the other, as she gracefully glided across the powdery snow.

Jorge knew that his infatuation was hopeless. Not only was it unseemly for a lieutenant to pursue a relationship with a corporal, but it was becoming increasingly clear to him that she felt nothing for him. Yet from the moment they'd met, when she had been assigned to 4th Company fresh out of cadet training, his emotions had threatened to overrule common sense. As beautiful as she was somber, with a face that reflected equal measures of sadness and joy, Inez had been noticed by every heterosexual male in the Corps. So far as he knew, though, she'd formed no relationships with any of them, nor was she attracted to any of the women. Corporal Torres was a reliable colleague, and that was all there was to it.

On the other hand, there was quite a bit about her that remained mysterious. Although Inez said that she was born and raised in New Boston, no one in the Corps who hailed from the same town had ever met her. She rarely spoke about her past, nor had Jorge ever heard her mention her family. He'd been told that she kept a printed copy of the *Sa'Tong-tas* on the bookshelf above her bunk in the barracks— not unusual, considering that more than half of the Corps were *Sa'Tong*ians—but she almost never said anything about this to anyone, apparently preferring to meditate in private.

Indeed, Jorge reflected, the only things that he really knew about

Inez was that she was grimly determined to succeed in the Corps of Exploration and that he was madly in love with her. Of course, this was probably the very reason why she was keeping him at arm's length. She probably realized that having an affair with a senior officer—particularly one who carried as much baggage as Jorge did— was a quick way of being expelled from the Corps. Which was why he hadn't pushed the issue. As much as he desired her, Jorge didn't want to do anything that would harm her chances of moving up the ranks, eventually to become an officer herself.

Nonetheless, there was nothing quite as painful as falling in love with someone who didn't feel the same way.

Deliberately looking away from her, Jorge concentrated instead upon maintaining the rhythm—right leg and arm forward, pull, coast, left leg and arm forward, pull, coast—that ate up the miles. The mountains lay directly ahead, and he could already make out Algonquin Base, a collection of blue-and-brown-striped dome tents clustered around a central area where the expedition vehicles were parked. The flags of the Coyote Federation and the Corps of Exploration fluttered from a pole set up in the middle of the camp. At midday, the base was nearly deserted: the geologists had gone off to the mountains to collect rock samples—they were searching for evidence to support the theory that the North Sea was an ancient crater formed by an asteroid collision that, in turn, might have been responsible for Coyote's chaotic terrain—while the cadets underwent arctic survival training with several other officers. Only Jorge and Inez had left the base on their own . . . and Jorge was aware that everyone had noticed the close attention Lieutenant Montero was paying to Corporal Torres.

Yeah, and so what if they do? he asked himself. *If I can't take advantage of the family name in such a small way, then I might as well drop out of the Corps.*

This wasn't the first time the thought had occurred to him. And he knew that it wouldn't be the last.

He followed Inez the rest of the way to the base, but once they entered camp he quickened his pace to catch up with her. "Go on ahead to your tent," he said. "I'll check us in."

"Thank you, sir." Inez glided away, heading toward the women's quarters. Jorge skied toward the headquarters lodge on the other side of the compound. He unfastened his skis and parked them upright in a rack beside the tent, then opened the plastic door leading to the vestibule. A moment to unzip his parka and remove his balaclava and gloves, then he opened the inner door and entered the dome.

The lodge was vacant save for a couple of duty officers seated at folding tables. The tent was warm enough that, despite the chill temperatures outside, they were stripped down to the brown waistcoats and blue unitards that were the standard Corps uniform. Jorge noted that they'd removed their boots and were wearing cat-skin moccasins instead; perhaps not the wisest thing to do, in case there was an emergency that would force them to run outside in a hurry, but he wasn't about to make an issue of it. After all, this expedition was largely a research-and-training mission; he could afford to let his people relax a little, and they seemed to appreciate the fact that their commander wasn't a martinet.

Greg Dillon looked up as Jorge came in. "That was fast," he murmured. "Didn't take your time getting back, did you, sir?"

"You made it sound important. When is the *Monroe* due in?"

"They're still an hour or so out. And don't ask who they're coming to get . . . you'll have to read the message to find out." Greg picked up a datapad. "I've already downloaded it. Just enter your code."

Taking the pad from him, Jorge sauntered over to a vacant chair and sat down. His thighs ached, so he stretched out his legs, absently massaging them with one hand to keep the muscles from cramping. The message had the familiar-yet-seldom-seen security header of a Priority One dispatch; everything below it was an encrypted mess of random numbers and letters. He typed in his six-digit security prefix, then his name. The message immediately unscrambled, allowing him to read it.

COEX PRIORITY ONE 1/11/23 10:47:34 CMT
To: Montero, J. Lt. (CO, 4th Co.)
Fm: Lee, S. Gen. (Cencom)
Grade: TS
Re: Withdrawal of Personnel

Request immediate removal from current Algonquin expedition of junior officer under your command: Corp. Inez Torres. Situation urgent & classified.

Further request that you accompany Corp. Torres. Relinquish expedition command to Sgt. Greg Dillon.

CES *Monroe* sent to Algonquin Base to retrieve both of you. Expect arrival soon. Briefing will be held en route.

Personal: Sorry about this, Jorge. I'll let you know what is going on when I see you.—Sawyer.

Jorge read the dispatch twice, not quite believing what he was seeing. He knew that it couldn't be a gag—he'd known the Corps' commanding officer since childhood, and General Lee wasn't inclined to make practical jokes—but nonetheless, there was a certain surrealism to this message that made him wonder, if only for a moment or two, whether he was suffering the effects of hypothermia and just didn't know it.

But, no, the message was real. Sawyer Lee had sent the *Monroe* all the way up here to fetch a couple of Corps officers who, by odd coincidence, had been out in the snow together less than a couple of hours ago. Watching polar cows, of all things . . .

"Lieutenant?" Greg's quiet voice broke into his train of thought. "Sir? Is something wrong?"

Jorge didn't respond at once. He encrypted the message again, then relayed it to his own pad before deleting it from the one the sergeant had given him. "No," he said, taking a deep breath as he stood up again. "Nothing wrong at all." He forced a smile. "Guess what? You're about to get your first field command."

"What?" Greg blinked in confusion, and the other officer in the tent turned around in his chair to look at both of them. "I . . . sir, what are you . . . ?"

"Word from on high. I'm being recalled. Flying out as soon as possible." He fumbled with his gloves, not quite knowing what to do next. "Call Torres, tell her to come here at once." He hesitated, then added, "And tell her to pack her gear. She's going, too."

The sergeant stared at him. "What in the world . . . ?"

"Damned if I know." Jorge felt a surge of irritation; this was the last thing he'd ever expected, and he hated questions that he couldn't answer. "Just do it, all right? And then get started on the paperwork."

Without another word, Jorge left the lodge, feeling the eyes of the two junior officers at his back. Inside the vestibule, he took a minute to collect his thoughts while he closed his parka and put on his gloves and balaclava again. Then he opened the door and marched back out into the cold, heading for his tent to pack his belongings.

A distant purr of turboprops, then what looked like an airborne catwhale emerged from the low clouds above the base. Nearly six hundred feet long, with an elliptical frame tapering to horizontal stabilizers at its stern, the CES *Dana Monroe* resembled a leviathan that had magically found a new home in the skies of Coyote.

The airship was coming in from the southwest; watching it approach, Jorge realized the *Monroe* must have set out from Hammerhead at first light this morning, the pilot keeping the engines at full throttle all the way across Highland and the North Sea. That was the only way the dirigible could have reached Algonquin so soon after the messages had been sent.

He stood at the edge of the landing field, stamping the soles of his boots against the ground to keep frostbite at bay. Knowing that he'd soon be returning to a slightly more temperate climate, he'd shucked most of his arctic gear while in his tent, relying instead on his Corps field uniform and an *arsashi* cape to keep him warm for the last hour or so that he and Inez would still be on Algonquin. Corporal Torres had done the same; beside him, the young woman huddled within her own cape, its hood pulled up around her head. Once again, Jorge was grateful for the alien technology that had given humans self-heating garments. The *arsashi* might look like the yeti of Earth legend, but they knew something about keeping warm.

Inez had said little to Jorge when she saw him again and had remained silent during the entire time they'd waited for the *Monroe* to arrive. Indeed, the girl seemed reluctant even to look at him; there was a tense air about her that Jorge had never seen before, as if she was anticipating bad news. Several times already, Jorge had almost given in to the urge to ask the obvious questions but had refrained from doing so. If this was any of his business, he'd learn soon enough.

The engines rose to a loud roar as the *Monroe* came to hover sixty feet above the ground. Doors beneath its underbelly opened, allowing mooring lines to drop. Corpsmen rushed to grab the lines; gathering them in their arms, the ground crew pulled the lines taut, then carefully walked backward as the airship slowly descended upon the landing field.

The ground crew was still lashing the cables around metal stakes hammered into the frozen ground when a forward hatch opened beneath the gondola. A gangway ladder came down, barely touching the snow. Although the airship's ducted turboprops had been throttled down, the pilot apparently wasn't shutting them off entirely; the *Monroe* was staying only long enough to pick up a couple of passengers and drop off a few supplies.

"All right, let's go." Jorge bent down to pick up the duffel bag at his feet, then led Inez across the field to the waiting airship. A cargo hatch near the stern opened, and a pallet loaded with crates was being winched down to the ground. A crewman came down the gangway; he wore only a light parka over his field uniform, and Jorge could practically hear his teeth chattering as he impatiently gestured for the two outbound Corpsmen to hurry up and come aboard. Jorge was barely able to keep from smiling as they passed the crewman. Probably a new recruit who hadn't yet undergone winter training; he'd get his chance next year, and if he wasn't lucky, he might draw an expedition to Inca instead. If he thought Coyote's northern subarctic regions were bad, just wait until he got a taste of the little-explored territory below the South Circumpolar River.

All the same, the warmth of the *Monroe*'s interior came as welcome relief. As soon as they climbed aboard, Inez threw back her hood and unfastened her cape, and Jorge did the same. They waited while the crewman came up the gangway behind them; cranking up the ladder, he knelt to slam the hatch shut, then stood up and touched his headset mike. "They're aboard, Captain. Forward hatch is sealed." He listened for a second, then turned to them. "Lieutenant, Corporal . . . this way, please."

As Jorge and Inez followed the crewman up a companionway from the gondola, then down a central passageway leading through the dirigible's interior decks, the engines throbbed a little louder and a vibration passed through the airship. Without notice, the *Monroe* had lifted off again. The crewman came to a halt before a pocket door marked WARDROOM; he knocked twice, waited a moment, then slid open the door. "Please go in," he said, stepping aside to let them pass. "You're expected."

The wardroom was a large compartment on the starboard side of the airship, with broad, louvered windows overlooking a polished faux-birch dinner table. The wardroom was vacant save for two individuals seated in armchairs at the far end of the table; they stood up as Jorge and Inez walked in, and Jorge was stunned to see that one of them was Sawyer Lee.

Middle-aged, with dark skin and close-cropped black hair becoming frosted with white, General Lee had been a constant presence in his life; because of that, Jorge had never felt intimidated by him, unlike other Corps officers. The other person was someone he'd never seen before: a woman wearing a dark brown robe, its hood pulled up around her head. In her midforties, by Gregorian reckoning, with a few strands of blond hair falling out from beneath the hood; her face was vaguely familiar, yet Jorge couldn't quite place it. Nonetheless, her cloak was familiar: it was the kind worn by the Order of the Eye, an enigmatic collective who had established The Sanctuary, a remote settlement on Medsylvania devoted to the study of *Sa'Tong*.

This was more surprising. Members of the Order were seldom seen outside The Sanctuary, but their existence was known across Coyote. It was rumored that they possessed the original *Sa'Tong-tas*, the holy book given to the *chaaz'maha*, which was the basis for the *Sa'Tong* spiritual movement. It was also said that they could read people's minds, and even though Jorge personally doubted this, unexpectedly finding himself in the company of one of them made him uneasy.

Jorge was about to say something when he heard a quiet gasp from behind him. Looking over his shoulder, he found Inez staring at the woman standing beside General Lee, her mouth fallen open in obvious shock. For a moment, there was only silence, then the woman reached up to lower her hood.

"Hello, Inez," she said quietly. "Good to see you again."

Another second or two passed, then Inez let her bag fall to the floor. She said nothing, but instead rushed across the wardroom. As she fell into the older woman's arms, Jorge realized that this was the first time he'd ever seen Inez express any unguarded emotions. Then she murmured the one word that explained everything:

"Mama."

My God, he thought, *that's her mother*. And then, another realization: *She's not from New Boston, is she? Not if her mother is from The Sanctuary . . .*

Even as these thoughts crossed his mind, Inez's mother raised her eyes from her daughter, and Jorge was startled to find her staring straight at him. A disapproving frown crossed her face, and he felt the hairs of the back of his neck begin to rise. Could she have . . . ?

"You must be Jorge," she said. "I've heard quite a bit about you."

"I . . . I didn't know she . . ."

Sawyer cleared his throat before Jorge could stumble through the rest of his reply. "By reputation, of course," he murmured, stepping around the end of the table. "You should be used to that by now."

Jorge felt his face grow warm; with stiff formality, he extended a hand to the Corps' commanding officer. As if he needed any more reminders of who his parents and grandparents were; it was something he'd spent his entire life trying to deal with. "Welcome to Algonquin Base, sir," he said, even though, from the corner of his eye, he could see through the windows that the *Monroe* had already left the camp far behind. "Sorry you couldn't have stayed any . . ."

"Been here before, son. Don't need to see it again." Sawyer Lee briefly clasped his hand. "My apologies for showing up without warning, but I knew I wasn't going to stay long, and I didn't want anyone to know that I was coming."

"Yes, sir. I understand." Jorge glanced at Inez and her mother. "Your message said that this is classified. Is this why . . . ?"

"It is, but . . ." Sawyer sighed, stepped back from him. "It's rather complicated and involves matters about which you haven't been informed."

"You need to tell him." Inez's mother had let go of her daughter, and now Jorge was surprised to see that Inez's face was as red as his own. "The time has come, I'm afraid, but he needs to know the truth."

"The truth?" Jorge caught Inez's eye, but only for a second; she quickly glanced away, as if reluctant to look at him. "What are you . . . ?"

"Let's take this a little at a time." Sawyer raised a hand, beckoning everyone to be quiet. "In fact, maybe we shouldn't do this when we're all in the same room. Melissa, if you could take Inez to your cabin . . ."

"No." For the first time since she'd come aboard, Inez seemed to assert herself. Moving away from her mother, she stared at Sawyer. "Sir, I've . . . forgive me, but I've picked up something from you. I'm not sure what it is, so you're just going to have to say it out loud." She hesitated. "This is about my father, isn't it?"

"'Picked up something'?" Jorge couldn't help himself; he was becoming more confused by the minute. "Would someone please tell me what's . . . ?"

"Lieutenant, shut up." Sawyer cast him a stern look. "I'll get to you in a minute." Then he turned to Inez again. "Corporal . . . Inez . . . yes, this is about your father." He took a deep breath. "We have reason to believe that he's still alive."

Inez's eyes widened, her mouth opening in a silent exclamation. She trembled, and for a moment it seemed as if her legs would give way beneath her. Melissa reached out to steady her, but instead she grabbed the back of the nearest chair. Inez took a deep breath; a furtive glance at the two senior officers, then she hastily ran the back of her hand across her face, wiping away tears that had appeared at the corners of her eyes.

"How do you know?" Her voice was low; she was plainly trying to keep her emotions under control. "Are you . . . are you sure?"

"To tell the truth . . . no, we're not. But something has happened that . . ." Sawyer shook his head. "Perhaps your mother should talk to you in private while I have a word with Lieutenant Montero."

"I think that would be best, yes." Once again, Melissa gave Jorge a discomfiting look, as if she knew things that he'd rather keep secret. "Come along, dear," she said softly, putting an arm around Inez's shoulders. "Let's go to our cabin."

Still wiping tears from her face, Inez nodded, then allowed her mother to lead her from the wardroom. As they walked past, Jorge remembered the duffel bag Inez had dropped. He picked it up and handed it to her. Inez took it from him, and for an instant their eyes made contact, yet there was something in her expression that he couldn't read. Then the two women left the compartment, closing the door behind them.

Sawyer Lee waited until they were gone before he spoke again. "Have a seat, Jorge," he said, patting the armrest of a chair as he turned toward the nearby galley. "There's some coffee in the urn, but it may be a few hours old . . . and I think there may be some bearshine stashed away somewhere."

It was a little early in the day for corn liquor, but Jorge noticed that Sawyer ignored the urn and instead was opening an overhead cabinet. "If you're drinking, sir . . ."

"Yes, I am, and I think we're going to need something stiffer than coffee." Sawyer located a small ceramic jug; pulling it down from the cabinet, he fetched a couple of water glasses from beneath the counter. "And knock off the 'sir' routine, all right? It's just the two of us now, and I'm putting rank on hold for the time being."

Jorge nodded. He had known Sawyer Lee since he was six Earth-years old, when the two of them had shared a cabin aboard the *Ted LeMare* during the First Exploratory Expedition. Jorge's parents and grandfather had led the ExEx, and Sawyer had been hired as a wilderness guide by Morgan Goldstein, the late founder of Janus Ltd., who had been the expedition's principal backer. The friendship between the hunter and the shy young boy Jorge had once been nearly ended when Jorge accidentally fired Sawyer's rifle in their cabin. This was Jorge's first brush with death, and his mother had retaliated by having Sawyer thrown off the expedition. In the years that followed, though, Sawyer had renewed his relationship with Jorge, eventually becoming his mentor after Jorge grew up to join the Corps of Exploration. Indeed, since the Corps had been brainstormed by Sawyer and Carlos Montero during their return from the ExEx—legend had it that the two men first discussed the Corps after crash-landing on Vulcan during a hurricane— it only made sense that the grandson of Coyote's most famous explorer would be taken under the wing of the Corps' founder and commanding officer.

So while the two men observed the priorities of rank while in public, when they were alone their respective insignia were ignored more often than not. Yet Jorge couldn't help but notice a certain reticence on Sawyer's part as he poured a couple of fingers of bearshine into each of their glasses. It was as if Sawyer, despite the many years he'd known Jorge, was having trouble expressing his thoughts.

"Jorge"—Sawyer hesitated, then let out his breath—"you know that I've always been candid with you, or at least about most things. And I think you've usually been honest with me."

"About most things, yes." Jorge hated to lie to him, but there were certain matters he'd never discussed with Sawyer, not the least of which was his growing reluctance to remain in the Corps.

Sawyer nodded as he walked over to the table and placed a drink in front of Jorge. "So you're going to have to trust me when I tell you that, even though there's one thing . . . well, maybe two . . . that I've always kept from you, it's only because I'd been sworn to secrecy about it, and so I couldn't tell anyone. Not you, not Jon or Susan, not the rest of the Corps . . . no one."

Jorge didn't pick up his drink. He could understand him not confiding in his mother—Susan Montero actively despised Sawyer Lee even though he was carrying out her father's legacy—but his father, Colonel Jon Parson, was Sawyer's chief of staff, and therefore the person Sawyer was supposed to trust the most. Jorge didn't say anything, though; instead, he toyed with the rim of the glass and let Sawyer go on.

"Let me ask you something," Sawyer said as he walked around the table to take a seat in front of the windows. "How do you feel about Inez?"

Jorge felt a chill. Of all the questions Sawyer could have asked him, this was the one he least expected. "She's . . . a very good Corpsman, sir." Sawyer's eyes narrowed at the uninvited formality, and Jorge realized that he'd inadvertently displayed his nervousness. "She's a capable explorer," he added. "Learns quickly and well. Has the makings of a senior officer . . ."

"Good to know, but that's not what I mean." Sawyer hesitated, then leaned forward to rest his elbows on the table. "I've heard scuttlebutt . . . not formal reports, mind you, but just hearsay . . . that you're . . . well, rather affectionate toward her. That you've been spending a lot of time with her since she was assigned to your company. Is this true?"

Jorge fixed his gaze upon the glass. He knew his face must be turning red, but there was nothing he could do about it. Sawyer was staring straight at him; if he lied, the old man would pick up on it in a heartbeat. "I like her, yes. Corporal Torres is a . . . well, she's very attractive. But I've been careful not to let my feelings get the better of me." He hesitated. "I've certainly never touched her, if that's what you're getting at."

Sawyer slowly nodded, but didn't respond at once. "Yes, that's exactly what I mean," he said after a moment. "And although I'm disturbed to hear that you're attracted to her, at least you've kept her at arm's length. That's going to make the rest of this . . . well, maybe a little easier for both of us."

Jorge looked up at him. "I don't understand. What does my relationship with Corporal Torres have to do with . . . ?"

"First, her last name isn't Torres. Or at least that's not the name she was born with. It's really Sanchez . . . Inez Sanchez. And as you've probably surmised by now, she isn't really from New Boston, but from The Sanctuary." He cocked his head toward the door. "Her mother came in from Medsylvania when we received the news about her father, and this is the first time the two of them have seen each other since she joined the Corps . . . against her mother's wishes, I might add, although that's another matter entirely."

"Melissa Sanchez." Something tugged at Jorge's memory. "I've heard the name before, but I can't quite place it."

"Haven't converted to *Sa'Tong*, have you?" Sawyer swirled the liquor around in his glass, sniffed it as if it were fine wine. "Neither have I. But if you had, you'd recognize the name at once. Melissa Sanchez was the *chaaz'maha's* partner . . . his common-law wife, really."

Jorge stared at him; it took several seconds for the knowledge to sink in. Sawyer waited patiently, a soft smile upon his face as he sipped his bearshine. "Oh, my god," he murmured at last. "You're telling me that Inez is . . . ?"

"Uh-huh. Inez Torres is really Inez Sanchez, and she's the daughter of the *chaaz'maha*."

Jorge sank back in his seat, stunned by what he'd just heard. In the six and a third Coyote years that had passed since the destruction of the *Robert E. Lee*, the *chaaz'maha* had become a martyr. Even though *Sa'Tong* wasn't a religion, he had become revered as a spiritual leader struck down in the prime of his life; in many ways, the story of his life and death had helped spread *Sa'Tong* across the new world, with countless inhabitants reading the *Sa'Tong-tas* and ultimately deciding to adopt it as their own philosophy. There were now more *Sa'Tong* schools on Coyote than there were churches or temples of traditional Earth religions; although priests and ministers of the older faiths initially distrusted or resented the introduction of the alien creed, they'd gradually come to realize *Sa'Tong* made allowances for other religions. Besides, speaking out against *Sa'Tong* was not in their best interests; after all, it had been a fanatical deacon from the Church of the Holy Dominion who'd smuggled a bomb aboard the *Lee*, and thus was responsible for the greatest disaster in recent Coyote history.

"But . . . the *chaaz'maha* is dead." Sitting up straight again, Jorge stared at Sawyer. "He was on the *Lee*, same as my grandfather. No one survived that."

"It's always been assumed that he was still aboard the *Lee* when it was destroyed, yes." Sawyer swiveled his chair around to gaze out the wardroom windows; the clouds had broken, allowing them to watch the frozen expanse of the North Sea as it passed beneath the airship. "Remember, though . . . just after the explosion, before the *Lee* collided with the starbridge, something was jettisoned from the ship. No one has ever been sure, but it's been thought that it might have been a lifeboat."

Jorge nodded. Like everyone else on Coyote, he'd seen the vid of the disaster, taken by a camera aboard the nearby gatehouse. Enhanced images of a few frames showed something that looked like a lifeboat being ejected from the doomed starship during the last seconds before the *Lee* slammed into the ring, destroying both the vessel and the starbridge. The meaning of these precious few images had been widely debated ever since, but even though a few eager *Sa'Tong*ians persisted in believing that the *chaaz'maha* had somehow escaped, most assumed that even if the object was, in fact, a lifeboat, it was probably jettisoned by accident, with no one aboard. After all, the last radio message sent from the *Lee* had given no indication that the ship was being evacuated, or that any effort had been made to send the *chaaz'maha* to safety.

"I always thought that was . . . y'know, wishful thinking." Jorge shook his head. "You're telling me it isn't? The *chaaz'maha* is still alive?"

"As I said, we have reason to believe that he survived, and that he's alive and well on Earth." Sawyer turned his seat back around. "That's the part of this whole thing that is still classified, and which I haven't received clearance to discuss with you quite yet."

Jorge raised an eyebrow. "Sir, you're the Corps' commanding officer. You're . . ."

"Sworn to silence until we reach Government House." Sawyer smiled slightly, apparently relishing the expression on the young man's face. "Oh, no, we're not heading back to Fort Lopez, if that's what you thought. It's straight to Liberty for us, for a private meeting with . . . well, you'll find out soon enough."

Jorge checked his watch. It was almost 1400; if the *Monroe*'s destination had been Hammerhead, he could have expected the airship to reach the Corps home base by late afternoon. But New Florida was much farther away; they probably wouldn't arrive until sometime after midnight. Not soon enough, so far as he was concerned.

"Guess I'll have to be patient," he murmured, leaning back in his seat again. Then a new thought occurred to him. "I don't get it. I can understand why you'd want Corporal Torres . . . Inez, I mean . . . to be there. But why me?"

Sawyer didn't respond at once, yet there was a quizzical look on his face. "You still haven't figured that out yet, have you?" he said after a moment. "Are you telling me you've forgotten your family history?" When Jorge shook his head, Sawyer let out his breath. "C'mon, son . . . think. What's the *chaaz'maha's* real name? The one he was given at birth?"

"He was . . . is . . . Hawk Thompson." Jorge hadn't forgotten. It was simply that this was something his family had always been reluctant to discuss. "He's my . . ."

In that instant, the revelation struck him with the force of a hammer. Unable to breathe, he sagged in his chair. The drink that Sawyer put before him had been untouched until now; all of a sudden, he found himself wanting it, yet when he reached out to take it, the glass slipped from his fingers, spilling bearshine across the fine-grained wood of the table.

"That's right." Sawyer's voice was low, sympathetic. "Hawk Thompson . . . the *chaaz'maha* . . . is your mother's cousin. Which means that Inez is your second cousin."

The *Monroe's* observation lounge was located on the upper deck above the gondola. Wide, downward-angled windows arranged in a semicircle afforded a sweeping view of everything below; the lounge was furnished with swivel-mounted armchairs, with a small telescope anchored to the floor between the seats. During expeditions, the lounge was frequently used by naturalists taking advantage of the dirigible's ability to hover silently above the terrain in order to study the wildlife below, but mainly it served as a place for crewmen and passengers to relax.

Jorge found Inez in the lounge, seated beside the telescope. The compartment was empty except for her, and she'd switched off the ceiling lights, allowing the darkness of the night to surround her. Bear had risen several hours earlier; at a quarter past midnight, the giant planet was at its zenith, its cool blue radiance the lounge's only illumination. She didn't look around when he came up the ladder, so at first he thought she hadn't noticed his entrance. But then she spoke, and he realized he should have known better than to believe that he could ever sneak up on her.

"Hello, Lieutenant." That was all she said: a simple acknowledgment of his presence.

"Hello, Inez." He hesitated. "Mind if I join you?"

She didn't respond with anything save a quiet nod as she continued to gaze out the windows at the dark landscape several thousand feet below. The *Monroe* was somewhere above Midland; when he came closer to the windows, Jorge saw that he was able to make out the northwest side of the Gillis Range, its snowcapped peaks resembling white papier-mâché beneath the pale blue bearlight. He'd never seen the mountains quite this way before. It was a stunning view, and yet he realized, too late, that he probably should have let her enjoy it on her own.

"Sorry to intrude," he said, not taking a seat. "If you'd rather be alone . . ."

"No, sir, that's fine. I think I'm ready for a little company, anyway." Inez was sitting cross-legged in the chair, her legs curled up beneath her and a mug of hot chocolate nestled in her lap. She wore only the blue unitard of her Corps uniform, apparently having decided to leave the waistcoat and boots in her cabin; Jorge noticed that she'd unzipped it to her sternum, exposing the white tank top she had on underneath, and quickly looked away. There were things about her that he couldn't allow himself to contemplate anymore.

"Thanks." Jorge settled into a chair on the other side of the telescope. "I didn't see you at dinner, and when I stopped by your cabin a little while ago, I found your mother had already gone to bed." He sighed in embarrassment. "I'm afraid I woke her up, but . . ."

"That's okay, sir. Mama's always been a light sleeper anyway." She smiled. "Let me guess . . . you were about to knock on the door when she called you by name and told you where I was."

Jorge looked at her sharply. Was that only a guess, or had she read his mind? "Yeah, that's pretty much what happened."

Inez took a sip of hot chocolate. "Members of the Order usually don't sleep very soundly. Too many distractions, especially if there's someone nearby." She gave him a sidelong look. "Never had that problem myself . . . but then again, I didn't inherit all of my parents' gifts."

Jorge didn't know quite what to say to this. "Umm . . . does that mean you're not . . . ?"

"Telepathic?" She shook her head. "No, sir. I'm what the Order calls a 'feeler' . . . a low-level empath. Which means I'm able to pick up on people's emotions but not their thoughts. Something I was born with, for better or worse, but since I've never been indoctrinated into the Order, mind-reading is something I can't do."

Thank God for that! Jorge tried not to show his relief, although she doubtless sensed it anyway. "So . . . ah, I take it that this was something you inherited."

"As I said, I got it from my parents, so I've had it since birth." Inez returned her gaze to the windows. "Shortly after my fifth birthday, the Order invited me to undergo the ritual that would've turned me into a high-level telepath." She glanced at him again. "And before you ask . . . no, I can't tell you what that is. That's a secret we keep in The Sanctuary that very few outsiders know about."

"That's all right. I don't have to know. But . . . you turned them down, I take it."

"Yes, sir. And they weren't happy about it. After all, I'm the *chaaz'maha's* only child. Some of them believed . . . and still do, I think . . . that I'm destined to follow my father's footsteps, become *Sa'Tong's* next spiritual leader. The new *chaaz'maha*, really."

"Uh-huh. That's what Sawyer . . . General Lee, I mean . . . told me." Jorge paused. "He also said that's the reason why you didn't join the Order. You wanted to find your own way in the world, so you left The Sanctuary and joined the Corps of Exploration instead."

"Uh-huh." She sipped some more hot chocolate, then lowered a bare foot to the floor and used it to swivel her chair around so that she could face him. "How much else did he tell you about me, sir?"

"I wish you wouldn't keep calling me 'sir' . . . or 'lieutenant' either, for that matter." Jorge looked away from her; perhaps he was trying to change the subject, but he couldn't help himself. "It's a surprise . . . to me, at any rate . . . that you're my cousin. Or second cousin, to be precise. I never knew that I had one, let alone that it was you. So this isn't making it any easier."

"Sorry. Old habits die hard." Inez sighed, shook her head. "He must have told you that I knew all along . . . that you and I are related, that is."

She was being persistent; Jorge knew that he had to confront the situation, as uncomfortable as it might be for both of them. "Sawyer told me that you'd changed your last name so that no one in Corps would connect you with your father, and that once you'd graduated from cadet training, he'd deliberately placed you under my command. Sort of a compromise he'd made with your mother since she was still reluctant about your joining the Corps in the first place." He paused. "He also said that, if it hadn't been for this, I would've never been told who you were."

"I'm sorry if I've embarrassed you, sir"—Inez corrected herself—"Jorge, I mean." A nervous laugh. "I'm going to have to get used to saying that, aren't I?"

He grinned. "That makes two of us. I'm going to have to get used to hearing it."

Inez nodded but didn't say anything for a moment. "I have a feeling that's not the only thing you're going to have to get used to. You really weren't expecting this, were you?"

Jorge shook his head. His family's relationship with the *chaaz'maha* had always been something that his parents didn't like to talk about. When Hawk Thompson was a teenager, he'd murdered his father . . . in part, he would later claim, to protect his aunt Susan, who'd only recently met Jonathan Parson, who in turn had been severely beaten by Lars Thompson's hired thugs. So Jorge's parents had always felt that they shared a certain measure of responsibility, if only indirectly, for that act of patricide. Even after Hawk had found personal redemption by discovering *Sa'Tong* and becoming the *chaaz'maha*, he'd continued to be a relative the family disowned. As a result, Jorge had never met Hawk; indeed, he'd been only scarcely aware that the *chaaz'maha* was his cousin.

"No, I wasn't expecting this," Jorge admitted, then changed the subject. "You've known the general for a long time, haven't you?"

"Not really . . . but he's known me since I was a baby." Seeing the puzzled look on his face, Inez went on. "When my father died, the first thing my mother did was take me to The Sanctuary. I'd been born only a few days earlier, you see, on Midland, and already people were regarding my father as some sort of messiah . . . something he never wanted, even while he was becoming known as the *chaaz'maha*. Very few people knew that he had a baby girl, and Mama wanted to spare me all the attention. Besides, by then they'd learned that a Dominionist minister had carried a bomb aboard the *Lee*, so there was still some question of whether there might be others who'd like to do us harm."

"Makes sense." He shrugged. "Could've been another fanatic out there who would have liked to get rid of you, too."

"Uh-huh. At any rate, Mama asked Sawyer if he'd get us to Medsylvania before anyone really caught on. He did so, then pretty much left us alone after that, except to check in now and then to see if we were okay. So I only knew Sawyer as a family friend who'd drop by once a year or so."

"So he didn't recruit you for the Corps?"

"No . . . or at least not directly." She shrugged, turning her face toward the window again. "But by the time I'd grown up to understand what was being expected of me, he'd formed the Corps, and I came to see it as an alternative to becoming the new *chaaz'maha*. So instead of undergoing the ritual and joining the Order, I asked the general if he'd let me in."

"The Order must have been furious when you left The Sanctuary."

"Some of them were, yes. Some still are. But they couldn't keep me there, and Mama knew better than to try." Inez let out her breath as she put her mug down on the floor. "Like I said, I owe you an apology. It was never my intent to deceive you, or lead you on in any way when you were . . ."

She abruptly stopped herself, but Jorge didn't need to be a mind reader to know what she'd almost said. If Inez could detect the emotions of others, then she must have been acutely aware of the intense sexual attraction he had for her.

Suddenly, it all made sense: the reason why she'd always been standoffish toward him, why she'd avoided even casual physical contact, why she'd sought to keep their friendship on a cordial, yet professional, level. They belonged to the same family, with only two degrees of separation keeping them from being brother and sister. Not only that, but old Colony Law, established seventy Earth-years ago, expressly prohibited marriage or sexual relationships between relatives, even if they were distant cousins. In the days when Coyote's population had numbered no more than a hundred, and the original *Alabama* colonists were starting to have children, this had been enacted in order to prevent birth defects that would have put future generations at risk. Although Colony Law was subsequently revised to form the basis of the Federation constitution, this particular statute had never been repealed.

So the facts were clear. Although he and Inez could be friends, they could never be lovers.

"No," he said. "Don't apologize. It's not your fault. You were only doing what had to be done." Jorge hesitated. "And I know what it's like to have a famous father, let alone a grandfather. My family wants me to . . ."

From the ceiling, the sound of a chime, then a voice came over the speaker. *"All hands, attention. We're on approach for landing at Liberty, with touchdown in twenty minutes. All members of the landing crew, please report to your stations. Repeat, we're on approach to landing at Liberty . . ."*

Jorge looked away from her. Unnoticed by either of them, the *Mon-*

roe had gradually lost altitude. As they watched in silence, the airship moved across the rain forests that lined Midland's western coast, leaving the mountains behind. Below them was the dark vein of the East Channel, the river town of Thompson's Ferry appearing as a small cluster of lights nestled upon the shores of New Florida. Farther inland, beyond the Eastern Divide, was the bright and shining sprawl that was Coyote's largest city.

"We better go." Rising from her chair, Inez zipped up the front of her uniform. As an afterthought, she bent over to retrieve her mug. "I'm glad we've had a chance to talk."

"Yeah. So am I." Jorge hastily reached down to pick it up for her. "Maybe we'll . . . um, I hope we do so again soon."

"So do I." Inez smiled as she took the mug from him. Their fingertips lightly brushed one another's, but this time she didn't immediately pull away. "See you soon . . . cousin."

He nodded, forcing a grin that he didn't feel, then watched as she padded barefoot across the deck. He didn't get up from his chair, though, but waited until she had walked down the ladder, heading for the passenger cabins on the lower deck. When she was gone, he sagged in his chair, letting out his breath as he buried his face in his hands.

Damn it. *Damn it!* He was still in love with her.

The *Monroe* descended upon the aerodrome on the western outskirts of Liberty. Spotlights painted the mammoth airship with shades of blue and silver as, ever so slowly, its prow nestled against the mobile mooring tower. A loud *clang* as the dirigible's bow hook mated with the tower, then the pilot throttled down the engines. By then, the ground crew had attached its lines to nearby tractors; once the crew and passengers disembarked, the *Monroe* would be towed across the field to an immense hangar, where it would await its next flight.

Sawyer Lee led the way down the ladder, followed by the other passengers. Jorge and Inez were back in uniform, including the field jackets and berets they hadn't worn while they were on Algonquin. In her brown robes, Melissa stood out within the group, or so it seemed to Jorge as he noticed the curious glances of the ground crew. Although the Order's existence was no longer secret, its members weren't seen very often in public, and it was unusual to see one coming down the gangway of a Corps airship.

Almost as soon as their feet touched ground, a coupe glided across the airfield, coming to a halt directly in front of them. Its rear passenger door canted upward, and Jorge was surprised to see a Militia soldier climb out, airpulse rifle slung over his shoulder. The blueshirt said nothing but simply gestured for them to get into the vehicle while casting a baleful eye upon the ground crew. Apparently realizing that curiosity was unwanted, the workers turned away. There might be some rumors circulating through town by morning, but with scant information to go on, it would be hearsay and nothing more.

It wasn't until everyone was in the coupe and the vehicle was in motion that Sawyer finally spoke. "We're going straight to Government House, where the briefing will be held. It's a little late for that, of course, so we'll be staying tonight in the guest quarters. I trust no one objects."

"Any chance I can see my family, sir?" It had been several months since the last time Jorge had visited his parents; besides, it would also give him an excuse to drop by his favorite tavern for a pint or two.

Sawyer shook his head. "Sorry, Lieutenant, not this time. In fact, I'm going to have to ask everyone to remain in Government House until further notice. Also, we're going to ask you to not wear your uniforms while you're here. For various reasons, we need for you to go incognito . . . you'll know why later. In any case, civilian clothes will be supplied to you." He gave Melissa a meaningful glance. "I'm afraid that applies to you as well, ma'am. Your robe . . ."

"I understand." Melissa pulled back her hood; again, Jorge was struck by how much she resembled Inez. "I don't like it, but I understand."

"I'm sure you do." Sawyer's voice was even, but something in the way he said this made Jorge aware again that Melissa probably knew more than she'd been told. There were few secrets that could be kept from a mind reader . . . and if Jorge had ever doubted that the Order was capable of telepathy, his conversation with Inez had erased his skepticism.

Inez said nothing but simply sat quietly beside Jorge, close enough that their shoulders touched. Only yesterday, he would have welcomed such contact, perhaps even taking the opportunity to casually drape an arm across the back of her seat. But that seemed ages ago, and much had changed in too short a time. Not only that, but he'd been made self-conscious by the cold way in which Melissa regarded him. She'd said little to him during the flight from Algonquin, remaining in her cabin for most of the trip, but Jorge had little doubt that she knew about the attraction he felt for her daughter.

In an effort to distract himself, Jorge gazed through the windows on his side of the coupe. By then, the hovercar had left the aerodrome behind and was crossing into Liberty's city limits; in the dark and silent hours between midnight and dawn, the sidewalks were empty, streetlamps casting a soft radiance upon the snowbanks along the curbs. Again, he reflected how much his hometown had changed in the last few years. When he was a boy, Liberty had still been little more than a large town, with packed-dirt streets meandering between wood-frame houses and the occasional adobe-brick structure. No building was more than three stories tall, and fish-oil lamps were still the principal source of lighting in most homes. It was even possible to see shags in the streets, tied up at hitching posts or pulling wagons from one place to another.

All that had changed. Once *hjadd* emissaries to Coyote assisted the Federation in rebuilding the starbridge, the colonists found themselves benefiting from increased trade with the other races of the galaxy. Although humankind apparently didn't have much to offer in terms of technology—aside from raw materials and certain cash crops, there was little that the *hjadd*, the *kua'tah*, the *morath*, or the *soranta* didn't already have, particularly in terms of technology—they were surprised to discover that aliens were fascinated by human culture. Music, painting, sculpture, even literature and vids: in all their variations, these art forms were as much in demand as wood, iron, or hemp, with the Talus races willing to exchange knowledge and tools that they'd long since taken for granted for things they'd never heard or seen before.

As a result, in the six and a third LeMarean years that had passed since Black Anael, human civilization on Coyote had undergone a distinct transformation. Liberty itself was a prime example; the older buildings, constructed of blackwood, mountain briar, and adobe, were vanishing, to be surrounded or outright replaced by amorphous, free-form structures that had been literally grown, from the ground up, by microassemblers that broke down the limestone-and-granite bedrock beneath the topsoil and used them as raw material. Even electrical fixtures were no longer limited to primitive wiring systems but now used embedded solar arrays and piezoelectric threads to supply and transfer power. The *hjadd* had used such advanced nanotech to erect their own embassy; now that they'd revealed its secrets to human-kind, the older methods of construction were rapidly falling into obsolescence, and it was only in the more remote settlements that carpenters and bricklayers still had steady jobs.

As the coupe entered the city center, the changes became more apparent. High-rise towers, more closely resembling enormous termite domes than the glass-walled skyscrapers of Old Earth, rose above broad avenues paved with native-stone compounds, their oval windows gleaming against the night sky. Within them were elevators that didn't rely upon cables and pulleys but instead used *kua'tah* null-gravity shafts. Delicate-looking but sturdy footbridges led from one building to another; below, maglev trams traveling upon elevated monorails had replaced wagons and carts as the principal means of transportation within the city. As the coupe moved past the limestone edifice of the Bank of Coyote, Jorge spotted a couple of proctors on graveyard-shift foot patrol. Even they were different; wearing *arsashi* cloaks, they carried *nord*-made airpulse rifles, nonlethal weapons that fired not bullets or fléchettes but energy-directed microbursts capable of knocking targets down without harming them.

Nor were the changes limited to Liberty. According to the most recent census estimates, Coyote's global population was around 6 million, spread across various provinces—no one but old-timers called them colonies anymore—along the Great Equatorial River. Almost as soon as the Corps mapped some previously unexplored island or subcontinent, boats and airships began to arrive, bearing homesteaders intent on staking a claim. The population was rising, sure, but there was still plenty of land available for those who wanted to make a new start.

Seventy Earth-years after the URSS *Alabama* had reached 47 Ursae Majoris, everything about Coyote was different. What had once been a remote colony world was now a full-fledged member of a galactic community. Every week, starships from Federation Navy's merchant marine departed from the New Brighton spaceport, bound for planets dozens of light-years away. Not only that, but a merchant marine ship had recently informed the Federation of its discovery of an artificial world, nicknamed Hex, that a reclusive race called the *danui* had built within their homeworld's system. If the cruiser's reports were to be

believed, Hex was two AUs in radius, comprised of trillions of cylindrical habitats forming an immense sphere around the G2-class star
HD 76700. Jorge found this hard to imagine . . . and yet, he'd seen the
pictures, and he knew it was real.

None of this would have been possible without the Talus, or the
hjadd's willingness to help humankind recover from the events of
Black Anael. But such gifts hadn't come without a price . . .

"Colonial for your thoughts?" Inez's quiet voice broke his reverie.

"Nothing, really." Jorge stifled a yawn behind his hand. "Just trying
to stay awake, that's all."

"We'll be there soon enough." Sawyer nodded toward the window
on his side of the coupe. "Trust me, the guest rooms are comfortable.
I've stayed there before."

By then, the coupe had passed through the city center and was
heading into Liberty's historic district. In the interests of preserving
Coyote's past, the University of New Florida had prevailed upon the
city council to set aside the original homes built by the *Alabama* colonists. There was a soft bump as the coupe left the pavement and
started traveling down unplowed dirt roads, passing houses, wood-
sheds, and chicken coops that university historians and volunteers
had managed to keep intact. Jorge caught sight of the log cabin his
grandparents had built. He'd lived there the first few years of his life,
until his parents decided to move to a new home on the other side of
the city; nonetheless, he had fond memories of the place. No one
resided there now, of course; even his grandmother, one of the few
surviving members of the *Alabama*, had long since moved to the outskirts of Bridgeton. Yet as antiquated as it was, the family home remained as a testament to the fortitude of the first settlers.

Government House stood at the edge of the district not far from the
Grange Hall, itself long since converted into a historical museum. Al-
though the original wood-frame structure was left untouched, with
Captain Lee's life-size statue still holding vigil out front, a couple of

years ago a limestone addition had been raised behind it, providing additional office space for the Federation's ever-growing government. The coupe entered a paved driveway beside the building and came to a halt in front of a rear door. Two blueshirts were waiting for their arrival; as the coupe settled upon its skirts, they assumed positions on each side of its passenger doors, their airpulse rifles at the ready. Jorge wondered whether they were simply an honor guard, or if someone seriously believed that an armed escort was necessary.

"Oh, hell," Sawyer muttered, plainly irritated by the Militia presence. "I was afraid of something like this." Stepping from the vehicle, he scowled at the blueshirts. "Thank you, gentlemen, but we don't need . . ."

"Sorry, General. President's orders." The soldier to the right made no move to leave. "We're to make sure nothing interferes with you . . ."

"Walking ten feet to the door. Right." Sawyer blew out his cheeks as an exasperated sigh. "Whatever you say, but I'm having words with the president the next time I see him."

Jorge almost laughed out loud. Only Sawyer Lee would have the nerve to stand up to the president of the Coyote Federation. On the other hand, since Sawyer had refused to publicly endorse Charles Edgar during the last election, he probably took it as his right to oppose the president. But Jorge wisely refrained from saying anything as he climbed out of the coupe, Inez and her mother behind him, and followed Sawyer and the two soldiers to the door.

The guest quarters were located on the third floor of the new wing, their limestone walls and floors disguised by faux-birch panels and shagshair carpeting. Everyone in the group had been assigned an individual room; after two weeks of sharing a dome tent with five other men, Jorge was ready for a little privacy, and although his room was hardly the luxury suite Sawyer had led him to expect, he nonetheless looked forward to sleeping in a bed instead of a cot. But when he saw the blueshirts take up positions at each end of the hallway, he couldn't help but feel that he'd been put in a velvet prison . . . and wondered why President Edgar had gone to such trouble to post guards.

Before they retired, Sawyer told the others that someone would come to fetch them first thing in the morning. Their briefing was scheduled for 0900 sharp, and they would be expected to be ready by then. Closing the door behind him, Jorge glanced at his watch. It was already 0147. Barely enough time to catch a few winks; he hoped breakfast would be provided.

No matter. It had been a long trip from Algonquin, and all he wanted to do just then was sleep. Civilian clothes had been laid out on the bed. Tossing them on a chair, he sat down on the bed to undress, but he had only just removed his boots when there was a quiet knock at the door.

"Yeah, come in," he growled. He expected that it was Sawyer, dropping by to discuss one thing or another, but when the door opened, he was startled to see Melissa instead.

"My apologies." She quietly shut the door behind her. "I know it's late, but I wonder if I could have a word with you?"

"Of course, ma'am." Jorge was instantly awake. He stood up. "Always happy to . . ."

"I rather doubt that, considering the hour, but I appreciate the courtesy all the same." A soft smile appeared. "And it's not necessary to call me 'ma'am.' I know we've never met until yesterday, but I *am* your cousin . . . in a certain sense, at least."

Despite the fact that he now knew Inez to be a relative, it was hard to think of this woman as belonging to his family. "I'll try to remember that."

A nod, then the smile vanished as quickly as it had come. "As you should. And you should also keep in mind something else." A tentative pause. "I'm aware of your feelings for my daughter. I think . . . that is, I'm sure . . . that you know that, too."

Jorge felt a chill. "Yes, ma . . . um, yes, I do." He hesitated. "There's probably not much you don't know about me, is there?"

Melissa shook her head. "Actually, there is. Contrary to what's often said about the Order, we don't make a practice of eavesdropping on other people's thoughts. In fact, much of our training involves learning how to stay out of another person's mind. Our talents are a gift, and as such shouldn't be abused. So your secrets are, by and large, still your own."

She let out her breath. "Having said that, though . . . yes, I know how you feel about her. That became obvious to me the moment I saw the two of you together. Before I was able to block your thoughts, I found something that I never expected . . . that you're in love with her."

Jorge's face became warm. As much as he wanted to deny what she'd just said, he knew that any lies he might tell would be futile. Instead, he sat down heavily upon the bed.

"Yes," he murmured. "You're right. I am."

Melissa regarded him with solemn eyes. "She knows this . . . and it's unfair that she wasn't able to tell you who she really is, if only because it would have spared you a lot of heartache and embarrassment. But the mistake has been made, and all you can do now is try not to make it worse. Jorge, your affection for her is misplaced. You may continue to love her as a cousin . . . but that's as far as it may ever go."

He shifted uncomfortably, unable to look Inez's mother in the eye. "I know that. And I . . . I'll try to keep that in mind."

Melissa nodded but didn't respond at once. He wondered if she was reaching into his mind; despite what she'd just told him, he didn't trust her to refrain from exploring his thoughts. "For your sake and hers," she said at last, "I hope that's true . . . because the two of you are about to go on a journey together that will test the limits of your relationship."

He looked up. "Pardon me? I don't . . ."

"No, of course not . . . and I've said too much already." Turning away from him, she stepped toward the door. "But you'll understand soon enough. Good night, Jorge."

Without another word, Melissa left the room. Jorge stared at the door for a while before he finally got undressed and put himself in bed. But even after he told the room to turn off the lights, it was a long time before he was able to fall asleep.

Jorge woke up at eight o'clock when a low but persistent chime from the ceiling succeeded in getting him to open his eyes. Climbing out of bed, he glanced through the window at nearby Sand Creek, where he saw a thin skin of ice reflecting the morning sun, then lurched to the bathroom. He emerged from the shower a few minutes later to find a covered tray on the dresser; someone had delivered a bowl of cereal, toast and marmalade, a glass of apple juice, and a small pot of coffee. He hadn't slept well; at least breakfast would help wake him up.

The civilian clothes he'd found on his bed the night before were his size: dark trousers, long-sleeve tunic, fisherman's sweater, socks, and a pair of moccasins. Nothing official-looking; again, Jorge wondered why he wasn't being allowed to wear his Corps uniform. As he got dressed, he listened to the morning news on the desk comp. Weather reports, local news, a feature story about a new settlement on Pawnee, followed by an interview with a well-known mystery writer . . . but nothing about the *chaaz'maha*, let alone the late-night arrival in Liberty of a group of Corpsmen and a member of the Order of the Eye.

He'd just finished breakfast when there was a knock at the door: Sawyer, summoning him to the briefing. Like everyone else gathered in the hallway, the general was dressed as a civilian. Jorge had never seen Inez in anything besides a Corps uniform, although he tried not to look as if he noticed her appearance. But Melissa seemed pedestrian without her robe; like Inez, she wore a hemp sweater and an ankle-length dress that made both mother and daughter look like a couple of university academics, while Sawyer could have been an ordinary bureaucrat.

The blueshirts stationed outside the guest quarters were still on duty. Without a word, the soldiers escorted them downstairs to the second floor, then led them to a conference room in the older part of Government House, a blackwood-paneled room downstairs from the president's office. President Edgar was already there, waiting for them.

"Gentlemen, ladies." The president rose from his seat at the end of the conference table. "Thank you for coming on such short notice . . . particularly those of you who were on Algonquin." He waved them to chairs on either side of the table. "I'm sorry to have interrupted your expedition, but . . ."

"That's all right, Mr. President." Sawyer took a seat beside him. "I'm sure Lieutenant Montero and Corporal Torres . . . Corporal Sanchez, that is . . . don't mind getting away from the subarctic for a while."

The president nodded as he sat down, yet he seemed uncertain whether General Lee was being sarcastic or not. A thin, rather ascetic young man in his early teens by LeMarean reckoning, Charles Edgar was the first president to come from the wave of immigrants who'd fled to 47 Ursae Majoris following the collapse of the Western Hemisphere Union. Although born on Earth, he'd adopted Coyote as his home and risen to high public office through the support of his fellow gringos—the old pejorative, now largely forgotten, for those who'd once lived in the New Brighton refugee camps. True, quite a few people detested having a leader who'd once been a WHU citizen; the scars left by the Union occupation had never quite healed, particularly among the old-timers who'd lived through those years. But Edgar was only a few Earth-years older than Jorge when his family had set foot on Coyote; he'd come of age in the refugee camps, and during his campaign his people had distributed an old photo of him shaking hands with the *chaaz'maha*.

Although Edgar had carefully remained neutral on the subject of religion, that image had gone far to gain him the support of the *Sa'Tong*ians. He'd won the election, but there were still quite a few people who regarded Charles Edgar as little more than an opportunist, and at best a political hack. Jorge was aware that his own grandmother, herself a former Federation president, openly detested him.

"Of course." The president looked away from Sawyer. "I'm certain you have many questions as to why you're here." A wary glance at Melissa; he doubtless knew that she belonged to the Order and probably wondered whether she was searching his mind. A quiet nod seemed to reassure him, and he went on. "General Lee has already been told that we've received an unconfirmed report that the *chaaz'maha* is still alive. Now it's time to let you know the rest."

Edgar reached forward to a comp embedded in the table's polished surface. His index finger caressed its keypad, and a holo glowed to life above the table. Suspended within it was a miniature of a rather primitive-looking spacecraft. Little more than a collection of fuel tanks arranged around a fusion engine with a cylindrical cargo module at its bow, the vessel was clearly a deep-space freighter, yet one so old that it probably should have been decommissioned a long time ago.

"This is *The Heroism of Che Guevara*," Edgar said, "a Jovian freighter registered to the Union Astronautica . . . and yes, it is an antique, isn't it?" As the miniature rotated on its axis, Jorge saw a Federation skiff attached to its port docking collar. "Two days ago, it made an unscheduled arrival through the starbridge . . . the reason being that it came from Earth."

The president had a politician's flair for the dramatic. Edgar allowed a moment for what he'd just said to sink in, savoring the shocked expressions of everyone in the room. Everyone except Sawyer, that is; from the corner of his eye, Jorge noticed that he was the only one who wasn't taken by surprise. Of course, the general would already have known about this; nevertheless, Jorge was amazed that Sawyer had managed to keep the news to himself.

But that was a minor distraction, compared to the bombshell Edgar had just dropped. It had been a little over six years—nineteen by the Gregorian calendar—since the last time a ship from Earth had come through Starbridge Coyote. Although the starbridge was reopened three years ago, no vessels from the Coyote Federation had been permitted to visit the birthplace of humankind. That was the stipulation that the *hjadd* had made for their assistance, a prohibition that the Talus had seconded. The aliens had no quarrel with Coyote, but they had come to believe that Earth was not mature enough to be allowed hyperspace access to Coyote or, by extension, the rest of the galaxy. The fact that the *Lee* had been destroyed by a member of a religious sect opposed to extraterrestrial contact was all the proof the *hjadd* needed to assert their claim that Earth was a danger to the Talus, and arguably even to Coyote itself.

So when Starbridge Coyote was rebuilt, the *hjadd* had been careful to reprogram its AI so that the starbridge wouldn't accept the hyperspace coordinates for Starbridge Earth installed in navigation keys used by human spacecraft. No ship could open a starbridge, regardless of where it was located, unless coded hyperlink signals were accepted by bridges at both ends; in this way, the Talus assured that its starbridges could only be used for peaceful purposes, not invasion or war.

Thus, while vessels from Coyote were permitted to journey first to

Rho Coronae Borealis, the *hjadd* home system, and later the other worlds of the Talus, travel to Earth was prohibited. And although Starbridge Earth probably hadn't been damaged by the destruction of Starbridge Coyote and subsequent collapse of the wormhole, there was also no way a vessel from Earth could reach 47 Ursae Majoris. Or at least not through hyperspace; a slower-than-light vessel might eventually get there, but it would be many years before it arrived.

"That's"—Jorge stopped himself before he said *impossible*—"incredible. The key system . . ."

"Would have prevented Starbridge Earth from opening a wormhole to 47 Uma." The president lifted a finger. "But that's not Earth's only means of hyperspace access, is it?"

"There's another?" Jorge glanced at the others. Inez and Melissa were just as bewildered as he was. Only Sawyer seemed to know what Edgar was talking about. "Sorry, Mr. President, but I never heard about . . ."

"KX-1." Sawyer's voice was vaguely amused. "Have you forgotten your history, Lieutenant?" Before Jorge could reply, Sawyer clasped his hands together upon the table. "Back in 2288, when the European Alliance was first experimenting with hyperspace travel, they built a prototype starbridge in orbit around Eris, a Kuiper Belt plutoid." Seeing the expression on Jorge's face, he rolled his eyes. "The region of dwarf planets on the outer fringes of Earth's solar system. Don't they teach you kids anything these days?"

Jorge let it go. Arguing with Sawyer was usually a no-win proposition. "I remember now," Inez said, speaking up for the first time. "Wasn't that the one used by the *Galileo* when it set out to explore Spindrift?"

"Right you are." Sawyer grinned, then nodded to Melissa. "You must have good schools in The Sanctuary." Melissa smiled back at him, and Sawyer went on. "Yes, that's the one . . . and, of course"—another glance at Jorge—"that's the expedition that led to our first contact with the *hjadd*."

"And the rest is history." Apparently annoyed to find himself momentarily forgotten, Edgar pointedly cleared his throat. "KX-1 was abandoned after that. After all, it was only an experimental model and didn't need to be used again. But it was still functional, and so . . ."

A pause, then he gave an offhand shrug, as if this was only a minor issue. "Well, it seems someone finally remembered it. And since the *hjadd* had only shut down access to Starbridge Earth, it was possible for the access code for our own starbridge to be modified, thereby allowing a ship to use KX-1 to make the jump to 47 Uma."

"Of course!" Jorge laughed out loud. "If you still have a key, then you could deconstruct the code, remove the coordinates for Starbridge Earth, and substitute the ones for KX-1. That way, you'd have a way of opening a wormhole between Eris and Coyote."

"Very good, Lieutenant." A condescending smile from the president. "Yes, that's exactly what was done."

Apparently Jorge had just saved the Corps' reputation, because he received an approving nod from Sawyer, but another thought occurred to him. "But . . . sorry, sir, I still don't get it. Why did it take so long for someone on Earth to figure that out? I mean, it's been almost twenty years."

"There's a reason for this, yes . . . and that brings us to the rest of the story." The president started to reach for the com patch on his shirt, then stopped himself. "Before we go on, though, there are a few things you should know. First, I want to remind you . . . just in case you've forgotten . . . that this matter is classified and should not be discussed with any outside this room."

"I've already informed them of that, Mr. President," Sawyer murmured.

"Very good." Edgar barely glanced his way. "Second . . . for the time being, at least, you're not to identify yourselves as members of the Corps of Exploration. This includes addressing one another by rank, calling each other 'sir,' anything like that. Until I say otherwise, you're here as civilian consultants, with no other governmental or military ties whatsoever." He looked at Melissa. "Same goes for the Order. For purposes of this meeting, it simply doesn't exist. Likewise, your special . . . um, talent."

"Understood, sir," Melissa said. "It won't be mentioned."

"Yes, but"—again, the president raised a finger—"I'd like for you to use them anyway. For the person you'll soon meet, that is. I want to know if he's telling the truth."

Edgar appeared reluctant to make this request. Jorge wondered if this was the first time he'd ever met someone from the Order of the Eye, let alone enlisted their aid. Melissa simply nodded, though, and the president went on. "Finally . . . and this is most important of all . . . I don't want you, or anyone else here, to acknowledge your relationship with the *chaaz'maha*."

"Sir?" Inez stared at him. "Mr. President, I don't know if you've been told this, but he's . . ."

"Your father." Edgar gave her an impatient nod. "I'm aware of that. And I'm sure you want to know whether he's still alive. But on this one point, you have to restrain yourself. The person you're about to meet must not know . . . or at least not for now . . . that you're his daughter. Am I perfectly clear?"

Baffled, the others looked at one another. No one objected, though, and that was enough to satisfy the president. He touched his patch. "Sergeant, please bring in our guest."

A few moments passed, then the door opened, and a blueshirt escorted a short, slightly overweight man into the room. In his midfifties by Gregorian reckoning, his short dark hair threaded with grey, he wore a Federation Navy jumpsuit that didn't quite fit; Jorge figured that it had probably been given to him sometime in the last couple of days. Although he appeared to have already met Edgar, he regarded the other people in the room with suspicion, uncertain of who they were or why they were there.

"Good morning, Captain. Please have a seat." Edgar gestured to a chair at the other end of the table. The blueshirt left, closing the door behind him. "Gentlemen, ladies . . . Captain Sergio Vargas of the Union Astronautica."

"Not anymore." A quick smile from Vargas as he sat down. "With all due respect, Mr. President, I haven't held that rank in many years . . . at least not since the Western Hemisphere Union collapsed."

"My apologies." Edgar nodded toward the hologram of the *Guevara*, still suspended above the table. "But your ship . . . doesn't it have WHU markings?"

"Only because someone neglected to remove them from the hull." Obviously nervous, Vargas fidgeted in his seat, not quite knowing what to do with his hands. "As I've already informed you and your people, sir, the Union Astronautica hasn't existed in nineteen years." He shrugged. "I took what I was able to get, and that was *The Heroism of Che Guevara.*"

"Interesting name," Jorge murmured. "Who was Che Guevara?"

Sawyer ignored him. "You stole your vessel?"

"Yes. The *Guevara* was a decommissioned Jovian freighter dry-docked at Highgate, on its way to a lunar junkyard. I managed to get it refueled, and once I transferred my nav key to its comp, I took off for Eris."

"You got all the way to Eris in that?" Jorge was hardly an expert in astronautics, but he knew just enough to be incredulous. "Pardon me, but I'm . . ."

"Mr. Montero." Edgar gave him an admonishing look, and Jorge shut up. The president returned his attention to Vargas. "Let me introduce you. Mr. Montero, Ms. Torres, Ms. Sanchez, and Mr. Lee are from the history and sociology departments of the University of New Florida. I've asked them to be here as consultants."

Jorge hid his grin behind a raised hand. His mother was a faculty member; she would've been amused to hear her son identified as a professor. The others managed to keep straight faces as they murmured greetings. Vargas appeared to accept Edgar's explanation although Jorge noticed that he gave Melissa more than a passing glance.

"Pleased to meet you all." Vargas looked at Jorge. "To answer your question . . . yes, I know it sounds hard to believe, but I did get to KX-1 in that craft. The *Guevara* is designed to make a round-trip to Jupiter and back without refueling. Eris is considerably farther away, of course . . . 70.5 AUs from Earth . . . but once I got the ship up to cruise velocity, I set the autopilot for automatic braking and rendezvous, then put myself in the emergency biostasis cell." A smug grin, as if all this had been easily accomplished. "Sixty-two days later, just before the ship reached Eris, the comp woke me up, and I went about reactivating the starbridge."

"Still, you must have taken a terrific risk," Sawyer said. "Even with a Jovian freighter, you must have exhausted your reserves getting there. Especially if you got it up to cruise speed."

Vargas nodded. "Yes, sir, that's true. I ran the main engine at its maximum rating of 200,000 ips to achieve a velocity of 2,000 kilometers per second . . . a lot to expect from the old bird, to be sure, and you're correct in that I used up all my fuel. But I knew I wasn't going home, though, so I figured I could do that."

"You meant to take a one-way trip?" Melissa raised an inquisitive eyebrow. "You must have been desperate."

"Yes, I was." Again, he stared directly at her . . . and this time, Jorge noticed it was Melissa's turn to become uneasy. "Excuse me, but who did you say you are?"

Before she could respond, the president butted in. "I understand that you managed to acquire a starbridge key, along with its hyperspace codes. How did you do that?"

Vargas reluctantly looked away from Melissa. "I've told you these things already, Mr. President, but I expect you want me to repeat it for the benefit of . . ."

"Yes, please. I figured that you could explain it better than I could."

"Very well." A shrug, then Vargas went on. "When I was in the UA, I was the captain of a lunar freighter . . . *The Legend of Simon Bolivar*, one of the vessels that brought Union refugees here." A wry grin. "So this isn't the first time I've made the jump to Coyote. In fact, it's my third trip . . . the only difference is that, this time, I used a different ship and didn't have any crew or passengers."

"So you used the key that once operated the *Bolivar*'s nav comp?" Sawyer asked.

"Yes. Before the *Bolivar* was grounded for good . . . that was after it failed to make the final jump to Coyote, the day your starbridge was destroyed . . . I removed the key and took it with me." Vargas let out his breath. "I'd learned what happened here before anyone else did, and although I figured that there was little chance your starbridge would be rebuilt, I decided to take the key on the off-chance that I might be able to use it again."

"Just a moment." Inez had been quiet until then. "Something you just said, about knowing what happened before anyone else did. What did you mean by that?"

Vargas regarded her with much the same curiosity he'd given her mother. "My ship . . . the *Bolivar*, that is . . . was scheduled to make the jump to Coyote when our starbridge went down. Because of that, my crew and I were the ones who recovered the lifeboat with the *chaaz'maha* aboard. So it was from him that I learned . . ."

A quiet gasp from Melissa. Her face had gone pale, and she clutched the armrests of her chair so hard that the knuckles of her fingers were white. "You . . . you actually spoke to . . . ?"

"Yes, I did. Along with a doctor who happened to be aboard, I was the first person to meet him." Vargas looked sharply at President Edgar. "Who *is* this woman?"

Edgar's mouth became taut. "As I said, she's from the university . . ."

"No." Vargas pointed toward Melissa. "You said her name is Sanchez.

The *chaaz'maha* has always said that he'd had a wife named Melissa Sanchez." His finger turned toward Inez. "He also said that, just a few days before he left Coyote, she gave birth to their daughter . . . Inez, if I remember her name correctly. Your age is about right, I think . . . would that be you?"

"Sir, you are mistaken." Edgar's face had gone pale. "Ms. Sanchez and Ms. Torres are . . ."

"No." Inez's voice was quiet, yet it interrupted the president as surely as if she'd shouted. "You're right. I'm Inez Sanchez, and this is my mother, Melissa . . . and yes, she's the partner of the *chaaz'maha*, and I'm his daughter."

The president scowled but didn't say anything. Caught in a lie, he apparently realized that further denial was pointless. Sergio Vargas stared at the two women; although he'd been proven correct, he was unable to speak. Indeed, he appeared to be awestruck by their presence.

"Thank you for telling us that Hawk . . . the *chaaz'maha*, that is . . . is still alive," Melissa said. "And I'm grateful to you for having rescued him." As she spoke, she took her daughter's hand. "For the last nineteen years, we've assumed that he perished aboard the *Lee*. I'm glad . . . we're glad . . . to learn otherwise."

Vargas sank back in his chair, nodding but remaining silent. Inez stared at him. "I don't understand," she said after a moment. "You're not pleased by this, are you? In fact, your feelings about my father are rather hostile."

"Inez . . ." Sawyer began.

"So that part's true, too." Vargas finally found his voice; his eyes narrowed as he returned Inez's stare. "We've known for a long time that the *chaaz'maha* is a telepath, and he told his followers that his wife was, too."

"I'm not his wife, but rather his partner." Melissa smiled slightly. "I'm glad to hear that he considered me as such, though."

"Yes, well . . . you know that already, don't you?" There was a bit-
ter undertone in Vargas's response. "What else have you two found
out about me? Or should I even ask?"

"My daughter isn't a telepath. I can read minds, but only when I
care to do so." Melissa shook her head. "When I tell you that I haven't
probed your thoughts, you can believe that I'm telling the truth."

Jorge didn't know whether she was lying, but although there was
still distrust in Vargas's eyes, the pilot slowly nodded. "I suppose I
don't have a choice, do I? And I suppose it would be unfair of me to
blame either of you for what the *chaaz'maha* has done." His gaze flickered toward Inez. "Particularly not you. You never knew him at all."

"What are you talking about?" Her eyes widened.

"Oh, c'mon." Vargas closed his eyes, shook his head. "Do you think
I stole a freighter and risked my life coming all the way out here just
because I felt like it?" He looked at Melissa again. "I'm sorry to say
this, but if I could do it all over again, I would've left that goddamn
lifeboat where I found it. Maybe even rammed it."

Melissa hissed beneath her breath, while Inez gazed at him with
astonishment. "Mr. Vargas, you're way out of line," Sawyer growled.
"If you don't shut up . . ."

"Why should I?" Vargas barely looked his way. "I don't know what
you people think of the *chaaz'maha*, but where I come from, he's
been nothing but trouble. That damned religion of his has been the
worst thing to happen to us since . . . well, everything else that's
happened . . . and we would have been better off if he'd never set foot
on Earth." He hesitated. "Of course, I'm partly to blame for that," he
added. "Not only did I rescue him, but I actually helped bring him
home. Was that a mistake . . ."

"Why?" Jorge couldn't help himself; he had to know the reasons
for this man's hostility.

"And who are you? Another one of his followers?"

"No." Jorge felt the president's eyes upon him, but there was no point in keeping up the charade. "My name's Jorge Montero, and I'm Hawk Thompson's . . . the *chaaz'maha's* . . . cousin." Before Vargas could reply, he went on. "What's he done that's caused you to hate him so much?"

Vargas gazed around the table, studying his inquisitors as much they studied him. "Look," he said at last, raising his hands, "I'm not trying to pick a fight. All I'm saying is that, back where I come from, the *chaaz'maha* took a bad situation and, just when we were beginning to pull ourselves out of it, made things worse. Hell, he's even withdrawn our colonies from the outer planets, brought everyone back to Earth. That's why I had to steal the *Guevara* . . . no one's going out past Mars now, let alone Eris."

"So that's why no one used KX-1 until now?" Jorge asked.

"That's right." Vargas shook his head. "Oh, no, it wasn't forgotten, just as Starbridge Earth is still usable. It's only that the *chaaz'maha* told everyone to leave them alone."

"Sounds as if his word carries a lot of weight," Edgar murmured.

"You could say that, yes." Vargas's voice was dry with sarcasm. "Not that we needed a messiah, but that's exactly what he set himself up to be. Now he's got a whole lot of people believing this crap . . ."

"*Sa'Tong*, you mean."

"I mean *Sa'Tong*." Vargas's lips curled in distaste. "Started as a cult . . . and if it had only stayed that way, I wouldn't have any problem with it. But now it's become a full-blown religion, with more people getting involved with it every day, and that's just the last thing we . . ."

"Where is he?" Melissa was becoming impatient with him. "Where is the *chaaz'maha*?"

"You want to find him, don't you?" A humorless smile crossed Vargas's face. "Good. Maybe you'll go back and get him. That would be a blessing . . ."

"Cut it out." Sawyer was also losing patience. "Just tell us where he is."

"Last time I heard, he was in Boston." An indifferent shrug, as if Vargas couldn't have cared less. "He gets around a lot, so no one is ever sure where he's going to show up next, but I understand that he's spent a lot of time there."

"That's rather vague, isn't it?" Edgar asked.

"Best I can do . . . but don't ask me to lead you there." Clasping his hands together, Vargas leaned back in his seat. "It took years for me to pull off my getaway, and I'm in no hurry to go back. Especially not to Boston . . . not the safest place in the world, if you know what I mean."

"Regardless, it's in our interests to find him." Edgar turned to Sawyer. "This is your area, General," he continued, apparently abandoning the pretense that anyone in the room was affiliated with the university. "I want you to see about sending an expedition to Earth as soon as possible, with the express purpose of locating the *chaaz'maha* and bringing him back home." He nodded toward Vargas. "I'm sure our guest will be willing to provide you with whatever assistance you need . . . won't you, Mr. Vargas?"

Vargas seemed dubious about this proposal, but apparently he'd realized that his future rested upon cooperating with the government; he nodded, albeit reluctantly. The president turned to Inez. "No doubt you'll be interested in participating in such an expedition, Corporal"— she quietly nodded as well—"so I'll put you under the general's command. You'll be relieved of all other . . . um, assignments . . . for the time being."

"Sir?" Jorge raised a hand. "I'd like to be in on this, too, if I may." He glanced at Sawyer and Inez. "Unless you have any objections, that is."

Inez smiled, and Sawyer did as well. "I think we have our first two volunteers," he said to the president, then he pushed back his chair and started to rise. "If there's nothing else for now, I'd like to . . ."

"Actually, there is." Edgar looked at Vargas again. "There's one other thing you mentioned to me when we met earlier that I think would interest my people." Vargas appeared to be at a loss. "About the destruction of the *Lee*," the president added, prompting him. "What the *chaaz'maha* told you after you rescued him . . ."

"Right." Vargas snapped his fingers. "On the way to Highgate, where he was questioned before I took him to Earth, I had a chance to talk to him about what happened. He told me that the *Lee* was destroyed by a bomb that had been brought aboard by a Dominionist deacon. Someone named Alberto Cosenza . . ."

"We know that already." Sawyer resumed his seat; impatient to get started on his new assignment, he glanced at his watch. "I don't see how that . . ."

"He also said that he knew who built the bomb." Vargas scowled. "We didn't know it then, but that was the first indication anyone had that he could read minds. Apparently he learned this while he was in telepathic contact with . . ."

"Wait a sec." Sawyer stared at him. "Did you just say that someone else put together the bomb? Someone besides Cosenza?"

The others glanced at one another. In the years that had passed since the destruction of the *Robert E. Lee*, it had been rumored that another individual had been involved. A government investigation turned up an eyewitness who claimed that, a couple of hours before Cosenza boarded the passenger shuttle that transported him to the starship, he had seen him in a cafe in New Brighton, speaking with someone who'd brought in a suitcase that the deacon had carried out of the cafe. Yet no one else had seen that individual, let alone identified him, and in the end the official report had concluded that, if only for lack of corroborating evidence, Cosenza had probably acted alone, even though there was nothing in his background to indicate that the deacon had any prior expertise in bomb making.

"Yes," Vargas replied. "He said that the bomb was made by someone named David Laird." He paused. "Why, does that mean something to you?"

Sawyer's expression became grim, and there was cold fury in his eyes. Jorge didn't have to ask why. Although the general seldom spoke about it, everyone who knew Sawyer well was aware that he'd had a close friend aboard the *Lee*: a woman whom he'd deeply cared about, who'd been on her way back to Earth. Indeed, that very morning, he'd tried to persuade her to stay on Coyote, even move in with him. Jorge had lost his grandfather, and Melissa and Inez had lost both partner and father, but Sawyer's loss was probably the most tragic of all, if only because he could have prevented it.

"Yeah . . . yeah, that means something to me." Sawyer slowly exhaled. Then, without another word, he shoved back his chair, stood up, and stalked out of the conference room. The slam of the door behind him was like a gunshot.

No one spoke. Vargas stared at the door. "I'm sorry, but . . . what did I say?"

"Enough," Melissa murmured. "Perhaps too much."

Jorge didn't see Sawyer again for the rest of the day. Once the briefing was concluded, the blueshirts escorted him, Inez, and Melissa back to their rooms, where—much to their annoyance—they were told that, on presidential orders, they were confined to quarters until further notice. Jorge didn't know where Vargas was staying, but it was a safe bet that the former UA captain was being held by the Militia in some location where he'd have minimal contact with anyone. Edgar was taking no chances with word leaking out that a ship had recently arrived from Earth, and it was obvious that he didn't trust his guests to keep their mouths shut.

So Jorge spent the day reading, napping, and pacing. Early that evening, a proctor arrived with a dinner tray. By then, Jorge was beginning to feel like a prisoner, and it didn't help that the meal he'd been brought—boiled chicken, spongy potatoes, limp greens—was the sort of thing he would have been fed in a jail cell. But he'd just finished picking his way through dinner when there was a knock at the door. Before he could get up to answer it, Sawyer came in.

"Got a few minutes?" he asked, leaving the door open behind him.

"Yes, sir. More than a few." Jorge noticed that, although Sawyer was wearing the same clothes he'd had on that morning, he'd put on his boots and was carrying his Corps parka over his arm. "I take it you managed to get out of here."

A brief nod. "Grab your boots and jacket," he said quietly. "We're going for a walk."

That was the best thing Jorge had heard all day. Sawyer waited as he put on his gear, then escorted Jorge out into the hallway, quietly shutting the door behind them. There was no one in sight save for two blueshirts standing watch at each end of the corridor; the soldier at the far end of the corridor took a sudden interest in his belt buckle, while the one watching the stairs gave the general a quick nod before raising his eyes to study the ceiling. Apparently Sawyer had persuaded them to look away for a few seconds while he and Jorge left the building.

Night had fallen, and with it, a thin shower of snow, carried by a cold wind from the northwest. Everyone who worked in Government House had left for the day; most of the windows were dark, and there was no one on the street. Once they were outside, the two men paused to put on their berets, then Sawyer led Jorge away from the building. He didn't speak until they were on the raised wooden sidewalks of the historic district, and even then it was in a subdued voice.

"Sorry I didn't come earlier," Sawyer murmured, "but I've been busy all afternoon." A faint smile. "Figured you'd like to stretch your legs . . . and besides, this way we can talk without being overheard."

"You think our rooms are bugged?"

"No, not really . . . although I wouldn't put it past Edgar." Sawyer glanced back the way they'd come. "Melissa is my main concern. I don't know what her range is, but I'm not taking any chances."

Jorge gave him a wary look. "You don't trust her?"

Sawyer raised his jacket collar against the wind. "Oh, I trust her, all right. She's an old friend. It's just that . . . well, for the time being, it would be best to keep this between the two of us. There's something I'd like to show you."

Once they were a safe distance from Government House, he deliberately slowed their pace to a leisurely stroll. The sidewalks hadn't been cleared; their boots crunched against the fresh powder, their voices muffled by the soft hiss of the falling snow. "I spoke with Melissa just a little while ago," Sawyer went on. "As I suspected, she'd lied when she told Vargas that she wasn't searching him during the meeting. She was . . . and according to her, he was telling the truth the entire time. Or least he believed that what he said was true."

"He believed . . . ?" Jorge shook his head. "Sorry, sir, but I don't understand."

"Melissa says that one of the things you learn once you become a telepath is that truth is seldom an absolute value. People perceive things in different ways, so they interpret what they see and hear according to their individual mind-sets. So when Vargas says the *chaaz'maha* is a menace, that he's become a religious tyrant, that's the truth as he sees it . . . but that doesn't necessarily mean it's really true." Sawyer paused, then added, "That's something you'll have to find out for yourself, once you get to Earth."

That stopped Jorge in his tracks. "Does that mean you're not coming with us?"

"Yes, it does." Sawyer halted to turn toward him. "I thought I was going to lead the expedition, but that changed the second Vargas told us who was responsible for the bomb being aboard the *Lee.*" Jorge couldn't see his face clearly in the darkness, but from the tone of his voice, he knew Sawyer was angry. "Damn Edgar. He could've let me know about David Laird, but he didn't. Instead, he let Vargas drop that on us while we were all in the same room. That's why I had to leave. I was too pissed off to . . ."

"I understand." Jorge hesitated. "Why do you think he did that? Not warn you in advance, I mean."

"We don't like each other very much. I think he just wanted to show me who's in charge around here." Sawyer stamped the soles of his boots against the snow. "I'm glad your grandfather didn't live long enough to see someone like him become president. Your grandmother knows him, of course, but she doesn't . . ."

His voice trailed off. Not that he needed to finish his thought. Wendy Gunther, Carlos Montero's widow and Jorge's grandmother, had become a recluse since her husband's death. One of the last surviving members of the *Alabama* party, she spent her days at Traveler's Rest, the home she and Carlos had built on the Eastern Divide just outside Bridgeton. Jorge hadn't seen her in nearly a year, but his parents had informed him that her health was in decline. And although Wendy herself had served two terms as president, she was no longer involved in politics. If Edgar had ever met her, it was probably in the most perfunctory way: perhaps only a courtesy call after he'd been sworn in as president.

"So you're not coming with us?" Jorge asked, trying to get the conversation back on track.

"No." Turning away from him, Sawyer continued down the sidewalk. "First, I'm going to visit your grandmother. She deserves to know, and I don't want her to get the news from Edgar . . . if he even bothers to tell her." He paused. "And then I'm going to track down Laird."

Jorge wasn't sure he liked the sound of that. "Then what? If you find him, I mean?"

Sawyer pretended as if he hadn't heard the question. "So I'm putting the expedition under your command. Edgar won't like it, of course . . . but the Corps is mine, and it's my prerogative as to who gets assigned to individual missions. So I'm putting it on you to find the *chaaz'maha* and bring him home."

"Sir?" Caught by surprise, Jorge stumbled, almost losing his footing in the snow. "Are you sure you . . . I mean, that I'm ready for this?"

"What, you think you can't handle this?" Sawyer didn't look around. "Lieutenant, I can make that an order . . . but if it comes to that, I'd be just as happy to find someone else to take charge and relieve you from the expedition entirely. Do you really want me to do that?"

"No, sir, I don't. It's just that . . . are you sure I'm capable of . . . ?"

"You're a Montero." Sawyer's voice was gruff, almost threatening. "Get used to it."

There it was again, the same thing Jorge had heard all his life: the Montero legacy, and how he was expected to continue it. His great-grandfather, one of the so-called dissident intellectuals who'd helped steal the *Alabama* from the Western Hemisphere Union, only to become the first colonist to die on Coyote. His grandfather, explorer and war hero, the first president of the Coyote Federation. His parents, instigators of the rebellion that had sealed Coyote's independence from Earth, and later the leaders of the First Exploratory Expedition.

A family history of pioneer fortitude and bravery. It had always been assumed that Jorge would carry on the tradition. There was never any question that he would join the Corps of Exploration or that he'd be groomed for a leadership role, yet no one ever asked him what he wanted out of life, nor was he ever given a choice to find his own destiny. He was a Montero, and he had to get used to it . . . whether he liked it or not.

"Sure," Jorge muttered. "That's what I always do."

"What?"

"Never mind." Again, Jorge changed the subject. "How are we . . . how am *I* . . . going to get back to Earth? We could use KX-1, but that's . . ."

"Seventy AUs from Earth," Sawyer said, finishing his thought. "A long way to travel, yes, even if you use one of our own ships and not that beat-up wreck Vargas used to get here. But if he's right, and Starbridge Earth is still active, then you can use it instead. It'll save you a lot of time."

"It would . . . but won't the Talus object?"

"Edgar says he's going to take it up with the *hjadd* ambassador, see if they'd be willing to make an exception. After all, your cousin is the *chaaz'maha* . . . they'll probably want to have him returned to Coyote just as much as we do." Again, Sawyer looked at him askance. "Don't be surprised, though, if you have to first make a trip to Rho Coronae Borealis and plead your case before the High Council. They'll have the final say, y'know."

Hearing this, Jorge took a deep breath. "So now I'm going to have to play diplomat, too." *This is getting worse all the time,* he silently added.

"No . . . no, you're going to have a little help there. We'll probably send the diplomatic liaison with you." Sawyer grinned. "Quite a unique individual. I think you'll be interested to meet him." His grin faded. "I hate to say it, but you're going to have Vargas along for the ride as well."

"But he said he wasn't . . ."

"I know what he said. But he's been told that, unless he wants to be put on trial for piracy, he's going with you back to Earth." Sawyer gave Jorge an apologetic glance. "That's just an excuse, of course. I don't like him very much either. I'm not even sure how much we can trust him. But you're going to need a native guide, and since he's the only person around who's been on Earth in the last nineteen years . . . ah, here we are."

By then, they'd reached the Grange, the two-story wood-frame building that had been Liberty's town hall during colonial times. Jorge was surprised when Sawyer began heading toward its entrance. As they tramped up the snow-covered front steps, the general reached into his parka and pulled out a key ring.

"Borrowed this from the curator," Sawyer said quietly as he picked out a key. He glanced around to make sure no one was watching them. "So long as we lock up on the way out and turn off the lights, she doesn't mind if we sneak in for a peek."

"Why?" Like everyone else in Liberty, Jorge had visited the Grange dozens of times. "Nothing here I haven't seen before."

"I'm sure there isn't." Sawyer selected a key and fitted it into the front door. "But there's still something I'd like to show you."

Sawyer unlocked the door and pushed it open. The place was dark save for the cold radiance of streetlights, filtered by snowflakes, that slanted in through the tall windows. He fumbled along the wall for a few seconds until he located the switch for the ceiling lights that had been retrofitted into the building, replacing the fish-oil lanterns that once hung from the rafters. Fluorescent panels glowed to life, illuminating the large main room where colonists had convened for town meetings.

Although the Grange Hall had been restored to its original appearance, most of the faux-birch benches and tables were gone. In their place stood glass-covered shelves and tables, holding artifacts university historians had recovered from attics, basements, and storage sheds throughout the provinces. On display were handmade farm tools, ceramic goat's-milk jugs, and homespun garments, along with fléchette rifles and ancient datapads brought from Earth. Handwritten journals lay open for public view; Jorge spotted his grandmother's original diary, the basis for the memoirs she'd later write. Dominating one wall was an enormous watercolor mural depicting the *Alabama*, hand-painted by some forgotten artist just before the Union occupation. Below it, sealed inside a glass sarcophagus, was the single-masted cat-skin kayak that Carlos Montero had used to sail alone down the Great Equatorial River.

Yet Sawyer ignored most of the items. Instead, he sauntered across the bare wooden floor to the elevated stage at the far end of the room. "There," he said, pointing to the wall above the stage. "Here's what I want you to see."

Within an airtight frame was one of the museum's oldest and most valuable artifacts: a large flag, thirteen horizontal red and white stripes next to a blue field containing a single white star.

"You know what that is, don't you?" Sawyer asked.

"Sure." Jorge shrugged. "Who doesn't?"

It was the flag of the United Republic of America, presented to Captain Robert Lee the day the *Alabama* left Earth. A placard affixed to the wall at eye level told the story that every schoolchild knew by heart: Lee refused to let it be flown above the colony, but he'd also resisted demands from some of the colonists to burn it. Instead, he had it displayed in the meeting room of the original Colonial Council as a reminder of the totalitarian government from which they had fled.

Sawyer gazed up at the flag. "When Melissa probed Vargas's mind, trying to discover whether he was telling the truth, she kept finding this image. Particularly when he was talking about your cousin. She couldn't get anything more than that, though, and she thinks maybe he figured she was searching him and was deliberately blocking the thoughts from his mind." He was quiet for a moment. "Strange thing to find in someone's head, isn't it? After all, the URA has been dead and gone for . . . how long? Three hundred years?"

"Something like that." Jorge swallowed what felt like a stone. "Yes, sir, it is strange. Think it means anything?"

Sawyer said nothing for a moment. "I think it means you better be careful," he said at last. "There's something going on back there that we don't know about."

Then he turned and began walking back toward the front door. "Come on. You've got a lot to do before you leave for Earth."

Part 2

TRAVELER'S REST

(from the memoirs of Sawyer Lee)

On occasion, there comes a time in a man's life when—suddenly, without warning—the road ahead becomes clear. In that instant, his mind is focused upon achieving a single objective; all other considerations are secondary at best. When that happens, a man knows he must do this one thing, or else risk losing his honor and self-respect, perhaps even his soul.

The Corps of Exploration gyro circled the Eastern Divide before the pilot found a place where we could safely touch down. It wasn't easy; when Carlos and Wendy built Traveler's Rest, they made sure it would be as inaccessible as possible, and that included not furnishing an aircraft landing pad. I'd been there before, though, so I knew that the ridge wasn't completely covered by trees; about a hundred yards from the manor was a level spot suitable for a small, two-man gyro, and that was where I told the pilot to put us down. He clenched his teeth, but he knew better than to argue with me. The rotor nacelles swiveled to horizontal position, and we managed to land without colliding with one of the stunted faux-birch trees clinging to the snow-covered granite bluff.

My arrival wasn't unexpected—I knew better than to pay a visit without first calling ahead—but that didn't mean I was welcome. Susan Montero had seen us coming, and even before the pilot lowered the landing gear, she'd left the house and walked down to meet us. The rotors had barely stopped spinning before she marched out to the gyro. One look at her face, and I knew that I was the last person she wanted to see, that day or any day.

"Morning, Susan," I said, once I'd opened the side hatch and climbed out. "Good to see you again."

That was a lie, of course. We'd never gotten along very well. Her husband was my chief of staff, so she had to put up with me. This was her family home, though, and my coming there constituted a breach of privacy that she could barely tolerate.

"Hello, General." Her arms were folded across her chest, her gaze as cold as the Gabriel winds buffeting the ridgeline. She glanced past me; the pilot was climbing out of the gyro, buttoning up his parka with one hand as he removed his helmet. "Sorry," she added, "but he can't come in."

Damned woman; the older she got, the more inhospitable she became. Not that you could tell that she was sixty-six by Gregorian reckoning; she'd opted for somatotropin therapy a few years ago, bringing her apparent age down to about forty. Indeed, she now looked a decade younger than I. But the reversal of age was only skin-deep; inside, she was a cranky old lady who neither forgot nor forgave, and her grudge against me was nearly two decades old.

I looked back at the gyro. The pilot had heard her: a shrug, then he shoved his gloved hands in his pockets and leaned against the fuselage. He'd be patient and wait for me. "That's all right," I replied, starting to step past her. "I'm not planning to stay long."

Susan wasn't happy about any of this, and for a moment I thought she was going to block my way. But someone must have told her that I was permitted to visit her mother because she moved aside. A wise decision; I was in no mood to argue with her.

"How is the president . . . your mother, I mean?" I asked, once we were walking together to the house. "Doing better, I hope."

I tried to phrase it as a polite question, but it was also something that genuinely concerned me. What I was about to tell her would come as a surprise, perhaps even a major shock, and I didn't want to cause any harm. Susan seemed to recognize this, because when she spoke again, her attitude softened a bit.

"All right, I suppose," she murmured, keeping her voice low. "Her doctor gave her a physical just a few weeks ago, and said that she's as well as could be expected." She hesitated. "For a woman who's 315 in Earth-years, that is. If she'd taken therapy . . ."

Her voice trailed off. She didn't need to finish the rest. Although rejuvenation treatment had been available to Federation citizens for quite some time, it hadn't worked for the original colonists who'd tried to take it. No one had yet learned the exact reason why the procedure wasn't successful for them, except that it probably had something to do with the fact that they'd been in biostasis for nearly 230 years during the *Alabama*'s long voyage from Earth to Coyote. Apparently their bodies, constantly repaired at the cellular level during that time, rejected subsequent efforts once they'd resumed the normal aging process.

In any case, the small handful of *Alabama* colonists who'd tried to become young again had died during the procedure, leaving the others with no recourse but to live out the rest of their biological existences the way nature intended. The last person from that group to die trying to extend his life was Barry Dreyfus, whom I'd met when he was the *LeMare*'s pilot during the First Exploratory Expedition. He'd been almost Wendy's age when he passed away. But I didn't miss him as much as I did one of my closest friends, Dana Monroe, who had been the *Alabama*'s chief engineer. She died four years ago, during one of the first attempts to sustain the life of an original colonist. I'd scattered her ashes beneath the apple trees she'd cultivated in her backyard in Leeport, and christened a Corps dirigible in her memory, but there wasn't a day that went by that I didn't miss her. Susan was facing that same loss now.

"I know." Again, I tried to be as diplomatic as possible. "At least she's comfortable." A glare from her, and I realized that I'd picked the wrong words. "That is, she's got you and the rest of her family . . ."

"I'm here, yes. And Marie has come by, although she's no longer fit to travel." Marie was Carlos's younger sister, nearly as old as Wendy herself. I'd been told that she'd become senile, barely recognizing anyone from her own family. "Jon would be here more often," she added, "but you keep him busy, don't you?"

Another stab. Susan was clearly in the mood for a fight. I didn't reply, though, instead turning my gaze toward the manor. Constructed of blackwood imported from Great Dakota, with a cantilevered roof and broad windows overlooking the East Channel, Traveler's Rest was the retreat Carlos Montero and Wendy Gunther had built for themselves following their retirement from politics. Few people were allowed to visit them once they'd gone into seclusion; I'd been here only a couple of times before, when Wendy, Jon, and I had met to make plans for carrying out Carlos's last wishes by forming the Corps of Exploration.

A beautiful place for an old woman to spend her final years. No doubt she'd once thought Carlos would spend them with her. The fact that this wasn't to be lent a sadness to Traveler's Rest; the wind that moaned through the bare tree branches sounded like the utterances of a ghost who'd never left the premises.

Susan didn't say anything until we reached the wooden steps leading to the veranda, but then she stepped in front of me. "All right," she demanded, "before I let you see my mother, I want to know why you're here."

"I told you on the phone. I have something important to tell her . . ."

"Tell me first."

"I'd rather tell you both at the same time." She started to object, but I brushed her aside as gently as I could. "Look, I know you're trying to spare your mother's feelings, but this is something she's going to hear anyway. It's better that it come from me, in person, and not from someone else." I decided not to let her know that person might be President Edgar; for all I knew, she might actually prefer it that way. "Besides, there's something I need to talk to her about."

Susan was hesitant to trust me, but she also knew that I wouldn't lie to her. It had been many years since we'd been on the ExEx together, and although she'd never gotten over the gun accident that nearly killed Jorge, she'd also come to realize, however reluctantly, that I'd never meant harm to her or her family. She looked me straight in the eye for another moment or two, then slowly exhaled a small cloud of vapor.

"All right," she murmured. "You may see her. But you can only stay for a few . . ."

She was interrupted by a high-pitched bark. An instant later, a small dog with shaggy grey-black fur trotted down the steps, its stubby tail wagging in consternation. He stopped a few feet from us and regarded me with suspicion, a soft growl rising in his throat.

"Hush, Campy. It's all right." Susan bent down to stroke him behind the ears. The dog looked like a mixed-breed, perhaps a Lhasa-terrier, and he was definitely wary of strangers; although he calmed down a bit, he didn't take his eyes off me. "Mama's dog," Susan explained. "He isn't used to . . . "

"Susan? Is there a problem?"

Unnoticed by either of us, a back door had opened, and someone had walked out onto the veranda to peer down at us from the railing. For a second, I thought it might be Tomas, Wendy's lifelong aide. Instead, I saw an older gentleman whom I recognized. Nearly Wendy's age, with a trim build and a white mane of hair, nonetheless he appeared younger, as if the years hadn't quite touched him.

"No . . . not really." Susan stood up, letting Campy come over to carefully sniff at my ankles. "Just talking, that's all." A glance in my direction. "General, this is . . ."

"We know each other." The older man smiled. "Good to see you again, Sawyer. Been a while."

"Yes, it has, Chief." I returned the smile. "Nice to see you, too."

It had been a few years since the last time I'd seen Chris Levin. Not since his retirement party, at least, when he'd stepped down as Liberty's chief proctor. He and I had never been close friends, but when

I'd moved my wilderness outfitting business from Leeport to Liberty, not long before I helped form the Corps, I'd gone to him to acquire a firearms permit, and he'd taken the opportunity to tell some stories about the times he'd humped the boonies himself. I always thought that, if Chief Levin hadn't been a lawman, he might have made a pretty good wilderness guide; as another original colonist, he was no stranger to Coyote's unexplored regions.

Susan seemed surprised that we'd know each other; I bet she was wondering if the chief had ever run me in. And indeed, there was a time, many years ago, when I'd tried to stay off his radar. But my days of hard drinking and cheating at poker were long behind me, and I'd given them up for the Corps before I had a chance to enjoy the questionable comforts of the old town stockade.

Chief Levin—it was hard for me to think of him as anything else— gave me a brief nod, then looked back at Susan. "If you're done, perhaps you ought to come in. Wendy's waiting to see him . . . and since she's due to take her medicine soon, I don't know how much longer she'll be awake."

"Sure . . . of course." Another brief glance in my direction, then Susan turned her back on me and started walking up the stairs. Apparently Campy had determined that I was harmless, because he let me follow her without further protest. Chief Levin didn't say anything, but when I reached the veranda, he gave me a wink and a pat on the shoulder.

He'd probably been standing there for a minute or so before he'd let his presence be known, quietly eavesdropping on our conversation until coming to my rescue. I nodded my silent thanks, then followed him and Susan into the house, with Campy leading the way.

Tomas met us at the door. He shooed the dog into a side room and shut the door behind him, then took our jackets and hung them in the vestibule closet before pulling out a pair of soft moccasins and silently offering them to me. As I sat down on a bench to remove my boots, once again I found myself marveling at Tomas Conseco and his reasons for being there. A quiet, middle-aged man who, as a child, had been among the first wave of immigrants to come to Coyote from the Western Hemisphere Union, he'd been Wendy's aide when she was president. Rumor had it that she and Carlos had tried to persuade him to enter politics, but apparently his first loyalty was to them. In any case, Tomas never left their side, and once Wendy became a widow, he'd moved into Traveler's Rest to take care of her, assuming the role of a surrogate son.

The manor's main room was magnificent, its vaulted ceiling rising high above tall windows that looked out over the East Channel, the blackwood walls decorated with Wendy's oil landscapes, painted before she'd grown too old to wield a brush. Mounted above the mantel of a fieldstone fireplace was the lacquered skull of the boid Carlos had shot when he was a teenager; I wondered whether the historical museum in Liberty, which I'd visited only the night before, had ever approached the family about acquiring it, and decided that it probably had but been turned down. Nonetheless, there was a lot of history in this place . . . and like the museum, it was uncommonly quiet.

I didn't spot Wendy, though, until Susan led me across the room to where she was sitting, beside a window overlooking the Garcia Narrows Bridge. As we came closer, I was astonished by how frail she'd become. Seated in a faux-birch wheelchair, a fleece blanket draped over her legs, she barely resembled the strong young woman who'd once led the Coyote Federation. Her hair, once thick and pale blond, was now sparse and the color of dirty snow; her skin had become almost waxen, the flesh shrunken around her eyes and mouth. It seemed as if it took all her effort just to sit upright; whatever strength she still had was being held in reserve, rationed out a bit at a time just to get her through the day.

No wonder Susan was so protective. It didn't matter what the doctors said; her mother was dying.

I'd just come to regret being there when Wendy turned her head to look at me. "Sawyer," she said, her voice little more than a dry rustle. "How pleasant to see you again. What brings you here?"

Her body was in a state of terminal breakdown, yet one look at her eyes, and I knew that her mind was as sharp as ever. Although it had been over three years since my last visit, she recognized me at once and realized that this wasn't a social call.

"Good morning, Madam President." I forced a smile. "I . . ."

"Please. Not 'Madam President.'" She closed her eyes, shook her head ever so slightly. "I wish people wouldn't call me that anymore. They mean well, but"—a quiet sigh—"I'm Wendy, and that's all I want to be called."

"Wendy . . . as you wish." From the moment we first met, the day the *Lee* was destroyed, I'd never called her anything except "Madam President." I was uncomfortable about using her first name, but I wasn't about to make an issue of it. "I've come to tell you something you may want to know . . . and also ask your advice."

"Advice?" A raised eyebrow: she was both intrigued and skeptical. "Oh, dear, I hope not. I'm so tired of people asking me what to do." She might have been joking, but I couldn't tell for sure. "Please, sit down," she added, then raised a liver-spotted hand to gesture toward a nearby ottoman. "Would you like something? Perhaps a cup of coffee? Tomas . . . Susan . . . somebody, please get Sawyer some coffee."

Before I could object, Tomas walked off. Susan wasn't about to leave us alone; without a word, she sauntered over to an armchair. From the corner of my eye, I saw that Chris Levin had taken a seat on a couch, far enough away not to be intrusive while still being able to listen to what I had to say. I hadn't expected to speak to anyone except Wendy, but there was no diplomatic way to ask the others to leave us alone. I'd just have to hope that they'd have the common sense to keep what they heard to themselves.

"Now," Wendy went on. "You've something you'd like to discuss?"

"Yes, ma'am." I took a deep breath, then began to relate the events of the past few days. The unexpected arrival of a ship from Earth, with a former Union Astronautica captain aboard. The revelation that the *chaaz'maha* had survived the *Lee* disaster. The knowledge that he was alive and well, and apparently living somewhere in North America, possibly in Boston. That President Edgar had instructed the Corps of Exploration to send an expedition to Earth, and also that he was currently negotiating with the *hjadd*, requesting permission for us to reopen the hyperspace passage between Coyote and humankind's homeworld. And finally, with no small reluctance, that I'd informed Jorge and his cousin Inez of what we'd learned, and had enlisted both of them to join the expedition.

The last part caused Susan to rise from her seat. "Oh, no, you don't!" she snapped. "You're not sending my son to . . . !"

"Susie. Be still." Wendy had been quiet throughout all of this, her face showing little or no emotion. Her eyes darted toward her daughter, and although Wendy didn't raise her voice, that simple, understated command was sufficient to make Susan sit down again. "Go on, Sawyer. Tell me . . . why do you want to send my grandson on this mission?"

By then, Tomas had returned with a cup of coffee. He placed it on a table beside me, then quietly took his place next to Wendy. I ignored the coffee and went on. "Inez needs to go because the *chaaz'maha* . . ."

"Hawk." A small frown. "I know what he was . . . what he is . . . but here in this house, my nephew's name is Hawk."

"Yes, ma'am. Of course." Another glance at Susan, who remained silent but angry, then I started again. "Inez is Hawk's daughter, so the reason for her being on the expedition is obvious." Wendy nodded; she understood. "But she's still only a corporal, so she doesn't have the experience for such a . . . such an advanced mission."

"Dangerous, you mean."

There was no double-talking her. "Yes, ma'am," I said. "It will be dangerous. That's why I'm sending Jorge, too. Although he's only recently learned that they're related, he's been her commanding officer ever since she joined the Corps. They work well together, and I think . . . I believe . . . that he can protect her from any harm."

Wendy nodded again. It had been many years since Black Anael, but she obviously remembered the decision, made that night in the New Brighton consulate, to hide Melissa Sanchez and her newborn daughter from the rest of the world. Even before I spirited them away to Medsylvania, we'd also decided that Jorge would never know that he had a second cousin who was the *chaaz'maha's* only child. The boy was just too young to be trusted with the secret, and even after he grew up, it had been to our advantage never to reveal Inez Torres's true identity to him. Not even Susan and Jon were aware of this; of Jorge's family, only Wendy knew that he had a younger relative serving with him in the Corps.

"So you've finally told him the truth." Wendy closed her eyes, let her head fall back against the chair. "I'm glad. Perhaps it's for the best . . . especially since he's going with her."

"Mother!" Susan was aghast. "I can't believe you're actually . . . that you'd even think of letting Jorge do this!"

I didn't know whether to laugh or sigh; instead, I just bit my lip. Apparently the news that Susan had a cousin she'd never known about was completely lost on her; as usual, her primary concern was only herself and her immediate family. I'd been told that she hadn't always been so self-centered, but it was hard for me to believe.

"Oh, please . . ." Wendy sighed, opened her eyes again. "Susan, I love you very much, but you're far too protective. Jorge is a very capable young man, and you know it. He doesn't need you shielding him." Again, the knowing smile. "There's a lot of your father in him, even if you can't see that for yourself."

Susan opened her mouth as if to protest, then closed it again. Wendy had her there, and she knew it. The Monteros were very proud of their family tradition: three generations of leaders and explorers, going all the way back to the earliest years of the colonies. Susan herself was

the first child born on Coyote, and before motherhood had made her
overly cautious, she'd been the first naturalist to study *chirreep* tribes
in the wild. Claiming that her own son wasn't ready to undertake a
hazardous assignment would be a betrayal of blood heritage, and she
knew better than to say that in her mother's presence.

"She's right." Perhaps I was being opportunistic, but I needed to
have Wendy on my side. "Jorge is ready for this. That's why I've also
asked him to be expedition leader."

Susan stared at me, not quite believing what I'd just said. Before
she could speak, though, Wendy raised her hand again. "I think . . . I
know you've got faith in him. So do I. But I'm just curious why you're
not doing this yourself. After all, you were born and raised on Earth.
He's never left Coyote."

I let out my breath. Here came the hard part, the real reason why I'd
commandeered a gyro in Liberty and flown all the way out there. "Because of something else we learned from Captain Vargas . . . something
I have to take care of here at home. We know who built the bomb that
destroyed the *Lee*."

No one spoke for a second or two. Susan regarded me with disbe-
lief, while Tomas's mouth fell open. The chief rose from the couch,
moved closer.

Wendy sat up a little straighter. "We already know who was responsible. That priest"—she sought to remember his name—"Cosenza.
You're telling me . . . ?"

"Yes, ma'am. Another person was involved. The *chaaz'maha* . . . Hawk,
I mean . . . said so himself, according to Vargas." I paused. "Or at least
that's what Hawk told him after he was rescued."

"And how would Hawk know this?"

"He got it from Cosenza's mind. Apparently he had some close contact with him just before . . ."

The chief pointedly cleared his throat, interrupting me. "I know about
David Laird. His name was in proctor files for a while . . . a suspected

terrorist who had migrated to Coyote about a year earlier. Apparently he once belonged to the Living Earth movement. Hawk helped nail him at the spaceport, back when he was working there as a customs agent. But the magistrates didn't have enough evidence to convict him on anything other than a weapons-smuggling charge, and since they couldn't deport him because of the unrest back on Earth . . ." He shrugged. "Long story. At any rate, he was put on probation, and once he served his time, the proctors had no choice but to let him go."

"That's it?" I couldn't help but be astonished by this admission. "You had a possible terrorist, and you let him loose?"

The chief glared at me. "Do you have any idea how many suspected criminals were coming here during the immigration crisis? If we'd tried to lock 'em all up, we would've had to build a prison the size of Midland." As he spoke, he wandered over to the windows. "Laird didn't slip away overnight. He remained in New Brighton for a while after the bombing. That's how I know about him."

"You were involved in the official investigation team, weren't you?" Susan asked. "Was Laird someone you checked out?"

"Yes, I was . . . and yes, Laird was a suspect, at least for a little while." Hands clasped behind his back, the chief studied the bridge far below. "We'd heard that Cosenza had been seen talking to someone in a cafe a few hours before he boarded the *Lee*, and that this person had apparently brought him a suitcase. Since there was nothing in Cosenza's background that indicated that he had any previous demolitions experience, and Laird was thought to be connected to the bombing of the New Guinea space elevator, naturally he was someone we wanted to interview. But Laird had an alibi. He was wearing a parole bracelet that should have interfered with any attempt at violence . . . Hawk wore one like it, too, for a while . . . and since our eyewitness couldn't be positive whom he'd seen in the cafe, we were unable to connect him to Cosenza. Or at least not enough to convince the magistrates to indict him on conspiracy charges."

"So where is he now?" Susan asked.

"I don't know." The chief looked over his shoulder at me. "Do you?"

I shook my head. "I put out a call to the New Brighton proctor's office, but they told me that he left Albion many years ago and hasn't been seen there since."

"Which means he could be anywhere." The chief folded his arms together, turned his back to the window. "If he is who we think he is . . ."

"I'd say that it's pretty certain that he built the bomb," I added. "Vargas didn't just pick his name out of a hat. He told us that he'd heard Hawk say that Laird was the person responsible. In fact, he let us know this on his own accord . . . we didn't have to ask him."

"Then he's probably gone as far away as he can get." The chief sighed, shook his head. "Laird was probably afraid that someone would eventually put two and two together, so he disappeared as soon as he thought he was no longer under the microscope. In any case, he's had a nice, long head start. Good luck catching up with him . . . if that's what you mean to do."

And that was the crux of the matter. I turned to Wendy. "That's what I wanted to talk to you about. Cosenza was the person who killed your husband, along with everyone else . . . almost everyone else . . . who was on the *Lee*, but Laird was the man who built the bomb. Still, it's been over six years . . ."

"Are you asking if we should go after him?" When Wendy looked at me again, her eyes had gone cold. She might have been an old lady, but in that instant, I saw the woman who'd once fought alongside her late husband in the Revolution.

"No, ma'am." Again, I found myself wishing that this conversation was between only the two of us, with no one else in the room. That couldn't be helped, though, so I went on. "That's not the question. I'm going to find him, even if I have to do so by myself. In fact, that's probably what I'll have to do. The Corps can't get involved in this . . .

we're under the auspices of the Militia, but law enforcement isn't part of our charter. So I'm going to have to take a sabbatical from the Corps if I'm going to track him down."

"The proctors . . ." Susan began.

"They won't be able to help, either." Chief Levin shook his head again. "Regardless of what Vargas may have told you, I know that the magistrates won't accept that as anything but hearsay. And without an arrest warrant from the maggies, the proctors can't touch him."

"All the same, I want Laird." I looked Wendy straight in the eye. "I also lost someone aboard the *Lee*. Do you remember?" Gazing back at me, she slowly nodded: yes, she remembered Lynn Hu, although she'd not known her as well as I did. "So here's my question, ma'am . . . if I find him, what do you think I should do with him?"

Again, the room went quiet. Everyone knew what I was saying, even if I didn't come right out and say it. The law couldn't touch David Laird; from there on, any actions I might take would be my own, without any legal authority. Yet if I was going to be an avenger, I wanted to know whether I had Wendy's blessings.

For a long time, she said nothing. Then she closed her eyes and slowly let out her breath. "I think . . . I think you should do whatever you believe is best," she said, in what was little more than a whisper.

"Yes, ma'am," I said. "I understand."

Wendy nodded, then opened her eyes again and looked up at Tomas. "I'm very tired, and I think it's time for my medicine. Would you help me, please?"

Tomas quietly moved behind her to grasp the handles of her wheelchair. Before he took her away, though, Wendy reached out to clasp my hand. Her fingers were fragile, yet her grip was surprisingly firm.

"Thank you for coming to see me, Sawyer," she said. "When the time comes, I know you'll do the right thing . . . for both Carlos and Lynn."

I nodded. There was no need for me to say anything, because nothing more needed to be said. We understood each other perfectly.

Tomas wheeled her away, leaving me with a question that had been answered and a task to be performed.

Susan followed Tomas and her mother from the living room. She didn't bother to say farewell, and judging from the look on her face, it was all too clear that she was relieved to see me go. Truth be told, I was ready to leave. A little more than an hour had passed since my arrival, and my pilot was probably getting cold. Besides, I had a lot to do back in Liberty.

I was halfway to the vestibule when Chris Levin stopped me. "Could I have a word with you?"

"Sure, Chief. What's on your mind?"

A wary glance toward the back of the house. "Perhaps we ought to talk outside," he said, keeping his voice low. "This should be between the two of us."

I nodded, and he followed me to the vestibule, where I took off the moccasins Tomas had loaned me and retrieved my boots and parka from the closet. Once the chief put on his coat, we stepped outside. The sun was a little higher in the sky, spreading the false warmth of a winter's day across the divide; the wind had died down a bit, and it was easy to pretend that springtime was just around the corner rather than three months away.

As we walked across the veranda, I waited for the chief to say what was on his mind, but he didn't speak until we had trod down the steps and were on the path leading back to the gyro. Another glance over his shoulder, as if to make sure that we weren't being overheard, then he began.

"I think I can help you. In fact . . . and I know this is abrupt . . . I'd like to come along."

It *was* abrupt, so much that I halted in my tracks. "I appreciate what you're saying, Chief, but . . ."

"Stop calling me that." A fleeting smile. "I know it's something you're accustomed to, but I haven't been chief proctor in quite a while. Besides, it'd probably be better if you don't. So just call me Chris, all right?"

"All right, Chris." I hesitated, then went on. "Look, I could use any assistance you can give me, but this is something I'd rather do on my own. And it'll be better if no one else gets mixed up in this."

I turned to continue walking down the ridgeline, but Chris remained at my side. "I understand that. But if you're going to find Laird, you're going to need more than a little help. In fact, you're going to need a *lot* of help."

"I don't see how you can . . ."

"Just hear me out, all right?" He laid a hand across my forearm, gently stopping me again. Reluctantly, I paused to listen to him. "I may not be chief proctor anymore, but I still have a lot of contacts in the law-enforcement community. There isn't a proctor in the provinces I haven't talked to at one time or another, and most of them owe me favors. So I can lay my hands on info that . . . well, with all due respect, you're just not going to get."

I was skeptical of his claim and didn't try to hide it. "Chief . . . sorry, Chris . . . I have a hard time buying that. As head of the Corps of Exploration . . ."

"You've got pull, sure . . . but you said yourself that the Corps isn't in the business of tracking down criminals. Proctors have resources that you won't have, particularly not if you intend to do this as a private citizen."

"And you would, even though you're retired?"

He nodded. "It would mean calling in a few debts. But you're better off having me along than trying to go at this alone."

He had me there, yet I was still unconvinced. "It's not going to be easy. In fact, I imagine this could take some time. No telling how far Laird might have gone in six years, or where he's holed up. So it's probably going to be a hard road to wherever he . . ."

"If you're trying to say that I'm too old for this sort of thing . . . well, you're wrong." He glanced back at the house again. "Wendy and I are about the same age, but my health is a lot better than hers. I'm not going to try to claim that I could pass Corps basic training, but I've done my best to stay in condition. I can still run five miles, and every morning I work out by chopping firewood. My doctor tells me I've got the body of a fifty-year-old . . . which makes me a little younger than you, all things considered."

He was exaggerating, of course, but I couldn't deny that Chris was in pretty good shape for an old guy. He would've had to do so in order to stay on the job for as long as he had. So that was another argument I was bound to lose, short of challenging him to arm-wrestle me . . . and somehow, I had the feeling that he'd probably pin me in ten seconds.

"Why would you want to do this?" I glanced over at the gyro. The pilot had been keeping warm by returning to the cockpit; now that he saw me coming, he'd climbed out again, and was impatiently stamping his boots against the packed snow. "I've got my reasons to go at it alone. I don't see how you have anything at stake."

"You lost someone on the *Lee*, sure . . . but so did I." Chris hesitated. "Look, Carlos Montero was my best friend. In fact, at one point in my life, he was my only friend. Wendy and I go back a long way, too."

I knew the story; indeed, I was surprised that I'd forgotten it. When Carlos, Wendy, and Chris were teenagers, during the earliest years of the Liberty colony, the three of them ran away to explore Coyote, using a couple of handmade kayaks they'd built in a boathouse near Sand Creek. Chris's younger brother, David, had been on the trip, too, as had Barry Dreyfus. The only adult to go with them was Kuniko Okada, the *Alabama*'s chief physician and Wendy's adoptive mother; the boys didn't know it then, but Wendy was pregnant with Susan, and Dr. Okada had insisted on joining them in order to keep an eye on her adopted daughter's condition.

The trip had ended in disaster. The whole thing had been Carlos's idea, but he hadn't thought things through as well as he should have.

By the time they reached the Great Equatorial River, their rations had run low, prompting David to attempt shooting a passing catwhale. The creature attacked the boats, destroying one of them, and David lost his life. Chris blamed Carlos for his brother's death, and when the Western Hemisphere Union subsequently invaded Coyote, Chris betrayed the other colonists by taking sides with the Union. It wasn't until the Revolution that the two young men ended their feud, with Chris rejoining the colonists and, later, participating in the Liberation Day assault on Union Guard strongholds in Liberty and Shuttlefield.

The tale was recounted in Wendy's memoirs, and had become a well-known chapter in Coyote history. Only the night before, I'd seen Carlos's kayak in the museum. Yet I'd overlooked the fact that, without Carlos, Chris might have remained an outcast and possibly been sent back to Earth along with the surviving Union Guard soldiers. So it was no wonder that he wanted to find Laird as much as I did; the old man had his own score to settle.

"So you figure you owe him," I said.

"I owe them both." Chris's mouth tightened. "For the last few months, I've been coming out here once a week, just so that she'll have someone besides her daughter and Tomas to be with her. And the toughest part has been knowing that there's nothing I can do to save her. Getting the man who helped Cosenza kill her husband won't do anything about that . . . but with any luck, at least she'll die knowing that his death has been avenged."

I understood what he was trying to say. Nonetheless, I remained reluctant to bring him along. "You realize, of course, that even if I manage to track him down, it may not . . . well, may not be possible to put him under arrest." I didn't look him in the eye as I said this, but instead raised my hand to let the pilot know that I wouldn't be there much longer. "The maggies . . ."

"I know what the maggies said." Chris continued to stare at me. "I can't condone . . . well, whatever it is you may have in mind . . . but there's nothing wrong with acting in self-defense." He paused. "And accidents sometimes happen, y'know, particularly when it comes to apprehending suspected felons. Either way, you'd do well to have a witness. Just in case any questions are raised about your conduct."

I looked at him again. He said nothing but simply nodded. Without saying as much, we both knew what each of us had in mind. It was entirely possible that David Laird would never be put under arrest, or that he'd never face the magistrates in a court of law. If that happened, any justice he'd receive would be of the frontier variety, from the barrel of a gun or at the end of a rope.

"All right, then. You're in." I let out my breath. "Unless you hear from me again before then, be at Fort Lopez a week from today. We'll set out from there. Pack light, but be prepared to rough it for a while."

"Not a problem." Chris raised an eyebrow. "I take it, of course, that my equipment should include a gun?"

"A gun, sure . . . but no badge or uniform. Once we leave Hammerhead, we'll be private citizens. You won't be a chief, and I won't be a general. Understood?"

He smiled. "Understood. Besides, I gave up my badge and uniform when I retired."

I nodded, then he silently extended his hand to me. I shook it, then turned to walk the rest of the way to the gyro. A few minutes later, I was airborne again; looking back at Traveler's Rest through the passenger window, I saw Chris standing where I'd left him, watching me go.

For the next week, I'd be helping Jorge and Inez prepare for their expedition to Earth. And then we would undertake a mission of our own.

Part 3

THE HOUSE OF THE TALUS

Cape pulled around himself for warmth, hands shoved in his parka, Jorge watched as the spacecraft was towed from its hangar on the government side of the New Brighton spaceport. He didn't like what he saw. "You're sure the Corps couldn't have gotten us something better?" he asked his father.

"Oh, we could have." Jonathan Parson studied the small vessel as well. "But Sawyer thinks that anything more sophisticated would draw attention, and that's something you don't want." A shrug. "He has a point. Take a ship with null-gravity drive to Earth, and any local who happens to see it is going to know that you're not from around there."

The reasoning was sound, but it didn't make Jorge any more confident in what his expedition had been given. The CFS *Gerardus Mercator* was a Vespucci-class shuttle designed for sorties between Earth and Lagrange-point space colonies. Sixty-five feet long, with stub wings jutting from each side of its cylindrical hull, its main engine was powered by an indigenous-fuel nuclear reactor. Funnel-like airscoops on the upper fuselage tapered back to ramjets mounted on either side of the vertical stabilizer, while its narrow cockpit rose above a conical bow. The shuttle was more than twenty-five Earth-years old, and hopelessly obsolete in comparison to the newer vessels of the Federation Navy, most of which had been retrofitted with reactionless drives derived from *hjadd* technology. Dents and blackened scars of atmospheric friction along its hull and wings only deepened Jorge's impression that it was an antique that had been mothballed until only a week ago.

Jorge turned to the Navy pilot standing beside his father. "Not to make an issue of it, but . . . how long has it been since the last time you flew this thing?"

"Two days, if you must know . . . and once every three months before that." Hugh McAlister, the former European Space Agency spacer who'd flown the *Mercator* to Coyote nearly twenty years ago, scowled as if he'd been personally insulted. "It may not look like much, Lieutenant," he added, his voice an irate Scottish burr, "but it'll get us where we need to go. And I'll thank you not to . . ."

"I'm sure he didn't mean anything, Hugh." Jon gave his fellow ESA veteran a mollifying smile. "Jorge has just never seen a craft which has had as much service as yours." As he spoke, the colonel glanced at his son. *Watch your tongue,* his expression said. *Pilots take comments about their craft rather personally.*

"My apologies, Captain." Realizing that he'd said the wrong thing, Jorge sought to make amends. "I wasn't trying to . . ."

"Of course you weren't." Standing behind them, Sergio Vargas regarded him with amusement that bordered on contempt. "You're just a kid. Probably never seen anything before that wasn't made before you were born." He prodded McAlister's shoulder as if sharing a joke with an old comrade. "Count yourself lucky. Compared to the heap I stole to get here, this is the height of space technology."

If Vargas's last remark had been intended to ingratiate himself with the pilot, it didn't work. McAlister didn't look his way; instead, a frown appeared beneath his trim mustache. McAlister wasn't one to keep his opinions to himself, and he'd already let his superiors in the Navy and the Corps know how he felt about having a former Union Astronautica officer—particularly one who'd hijacked a freighter, even one that had been decommissioned—as a passenger. Although there had never been any actual hostilities between UA and the ESA, it was a known fact that spacecraft of both services were frequently armed, with their crews undergoing space-combat training.

Jorge wasn't crazy about having Vargas in the expedition, either, but there was little choice in the matter. They needed someone who'd recently been on Earth—particularly the East Coast of North America—to act as a native guide, and Vargas was the only person who qualified. Yet when Jorge glanced back at him, he noticed that Inez seemed to be keeping her distance as well. Only a couple of days earlier, while the two of them were taking a break from weapons practice on the Corps' small-arms range outside Leeport, Inez had confided in him that there was something about Vargas that she didn't trust.

"I can't read his mind," she'd said, "but I don't think he's told us everything. He's holding something back."

Jorge didn't trust Vargas, either . . . which was another reason why he'd recruited Greg Dillon to the expedition. The sergeant had been Jorge's right-hand man in the Corps for a while, and Jorge needed someone reliable to keep an eye on Vargas. So, although Greg's ostensible purpose for being on this mission was to back up Jorge, his real job was to watch Vargas's every move and clamp down on him if he did anything even remotely suspicious.

The tractor had finished wheeling the *Mercator* out of its hangar. The driver detached its tow cable, and a couple of ground crew moved in, dragging the fuming hoses of hydrogen fuel lines behind them, while another pad rat ducked beneath the shuttle to open its underbelly hatch. "Time to get aboard," Jorge said, bending over to pick up his pack. "Gentlemen, Inez . . ."

"Not so fast." Laying a hand on shoulder, his father stopped him. "You've still got one more passenger . . . and I think that's him now."

Jorge looked up, saw a small coupe approaching from the direction of the airfield. Whoever it was, he must have flown into New Brighton on a different gyro than the rest of the crew. He'd forgotten that the Federation liaison to the Talus was supposed to be going with them to Rho Coronae Borealis, where he was to assist Jorge in negotiating with the High Council of the Talus. This person wouldn't be accompanying the expedition—provided, of course, that the Council granted them permission to visit Earth—but instead would return to Coyote aboard another ship.

"You haven't told us who this gent is, Colonel." McAlister watched as the coupe glided to a halt between them and the *Mercator*. "I hope he's not some run-of-the-mill . . ."

Whatever he was about to say, it was left unfinished, for at that moment the coupe's rear door canted upward, and a tall figure in a black robe emerged. Jorge caught a glimpse of titanium-alloy feet, then two multifaceted red eyes within a metallic, skull-like face peered at them from the raised hood.

"Oh, for the love of God." Vargas's voice was an angry mutter. "You can't be serious."

Jorge said nothing, though he couldn't help but stare at the newcomer. Since childhood, he'd heard his parents' stories about Manuel Castro. Once the lieutenant governor of the colonies during the Occupation, Castro had been one of the Savants—posthumans who had sought immortality by having their brains scanned and downloaded into quantum comps encased within artificial bodies—who'd come to 47 Ursae Majoris aboard the first Western Hemisphere Union starships. Thought to have been killed during the Revolution, Castro was left behind when the Union was forced off Coyote; a few years later, he'd met Jon and Susan and become part of their short-lived rebellion against the early colonial government.

Few people had seen Castro since then. For a long time, he was believed to be a hermit living in the Black Mountains, studying the *chirreep* tribes of Great Dakota. But when Jorge was a teenager, he and a couple of friends had hiked into the mountains, hoping to catch a glimpse of the last Savant on Coyote. Apparently Aunt Marie had once been a very close friend of his, because she had a hand-drawn map pointing the way to the one-room cabin he'd built near an abandoned logging site; when she wasn't looking, Jorge had copied the map, and the boys had used it to find the cabin. But Castro's home had been long since abandoned, its roof rotted and on the verge of collapse, its only room infested with birds' nests and skeeters. No one knew where Manuel Castro had gone, and over the years he'd gradually become a figure of myth and legend.

Jon ignored Vargas's remark as he walked over to the Savant. "Hello, Manny," he said, extending a hand. "Thanks for coming."

A rasping burr from the grille of his mouth that might have been laughter. "The pleasure is all mine," Manny replied. A four-fingered claw appeared from the folds of his robe, grasped Jon's hand. "Any opportunity to visit the *Talus qua'spah* is one I'll gladly accept."

"I see you finally got your left eye fixed."

"Left eye, and much more." The Savant opened his robe, exposing a robotlike body that dully reflected the winter sun. "Seems that the *danui* have a lot of experience with cyborgs. The last time I was there, I managed to talk some of their representatives into upgrading my . . ."

"Wait a damn minute!" McAlister was staring at Manny with undisguised loathing. "You're not telling me . . . you didn't say . . . !" He pointed at the liaison as if he was a monster. "He's a Savant!"

Manny let his robe fall back in place. "You're the pilot, correct? I hope your skills match your keen grasp of the obvious."

His immobile face and strange eyes displayed no emotion, yet Jorge thought he detected the slightest twinge of sarcasm in Manny's voice. From behind him, he heard a stifled laugh; peering over his shoulder, he saw Inez clasping a hand across her mouth.

"As you've so wisely pointed out . . . yes, he is." Jon glared at McAlister and Vargas as he stepped aside. "Allow me to introduce you to Manuel Castro, the Federation representative to the Talus. I hope you'll afford him the same respect and courtesy as you would any government official . . . particularly one who's a senior diplomat."

"But . . ." McAlister shook his head, both bewildered and irate.

"Hell's bells, Colonel, how can you expect us to trust someone . . . something . . . like . . ."

"Captain, you're out of line. Savant Castro . . ."

"Captain, with all due respect, my loyalty and trustworthiness are not at issue here." Apparently unwilling to let Jon defend him, Manny approached the pilot, the bottom of his robe whisking softly against the concrete. "The last four presidents have entrusted me with the task of speaking on behalf of the Federation . . . and indeed, not just the Federation, but all humans on Coyote. No one has ever complained about my service, although I'll admit that my role has been circumspect. I'm sure, however, small-minded individuals might object."

Jorge understood McAlister's and Vargas's feelings about Manny, even if he didn't share them himself. Long ago, when the Savants had shared power with the Patriarchs and Matriarchs in the Western Hemisphere Union, their inner circle had secretly plotted to ease Earth's population crisis by eliminating one-third of the population. The conspiracy had ultimately been exposed, but not before tens of thousands of persons were killed; those Savants who weren't captured and destroyed fled from Earth, eventually taking up residence in the farthest reaches of the solar system. Manny had never been involved in the plans; nevertheless, those who remembered the Savant genocide automatically despised his kind.

"Goddamn right I object." McAlister started to take a step back, but not before he found himself staring Manny straight in the eye. "I can't believe the president would allow something like you to . . ."

"If you don't believe it, then you're welcome to take this up with President Edgar. I can link directly to Government House . . . would you like for me to do so?" Manny waited. When McAlister didn't reply, he went on. "Your objection has been noted. However, I'll remind you that your job is not to pass judgment on me but to transport us to *Talus qua'spah*, where I'm to carry out my official duties, as mandated by the president. Are you clear on that?"

"Yeah." McAlister was still simmering, but he reluctantly nodded. "Yeah, I . . ."

"'Yes, sir' is the proper response to a senior official, Captain." Manny paused. "Furthermore, in the future, I'll thank you to refer to me as 'someone' and not 'something.' Are we clear on that as well?"

"Yes, sir." The pilot's face had gone red, and he seemed to be having trouble keeping his upper lip from curling. "I understand, Savant Castro."

"'Mr. Castro' will do. My friends call me 'Manny.' Either one is acceptable, since I no longer use my former term of address." Manny turned toward Vargas. "Do you have anything you'd like to add, Mr. Vargas?"

Vargas appeared to be shocked that the Savant would know his name. Unwilling to challenge a senior diplomat the way McAlister had, though, he shook his head. A dismissive nod, then Manny strolled over to Jorge.

"Lieutenant Montero, I presume?" Again, the clawlike hand appeared from within his robe. When Jorge grasped it, he found Manny's touch to be cold, yet surprisingly gentle. "Very pleased to meet you after all these years. Your grandfather and I were on opposite sides during the war, but later we became friends."

"So I've been told." Jorge glanced at his father, who nodded but said nothing. For an instant, he considered telling the Savant about his attempt to find him, then decided against it; perhaps later. "I've heard a lot of stories. My grandfather always spoke well of you."

The staccato buzz that sounded somewhat like a laugh. "Happy to hear this . . . even though, as I said, we'd had our differences. In any case, I'm proud to have assumed his old position as diplomatic liaison. I only hope that I'll be able to serve you as well as he would have."

"Thank you." Jorge began to say something else, but before he could, Manny turned to Inez. This time, though, he didn't offer his hand, but instead bowed slightly, his hands clasped before his chest.

"*Sa'Tong qo*, Corporal," he said, his voice now low and oddly reverent. "It's an honor to meet you. Your father's teachings have meant a great deal to me."

Oh, my god, Jorge thought, *he's a* Sa'Tong*ian!* The expression Manny had just used was *hjadd* in origin. Literally translated, it meant "Follow the wisdom of *Sa'Tong*," but it could also have different meanings, depending on the circumstances: "hello," "good-bye," and "good luck" were but a few. Nonetheless, it was something only a devout *Sa'Tong*ian would be likely to say. Inez seemed to be surprised as well, because her eyes widened and her mouth fell open. Yet she recovered quickly and reciprocated with the same bow and formal clasping of the hands. "*Sa'Tong qo*, Savant . . . that is, Mr. Castro. I'm pleased to learn that you've received the wisdom of the *chaaz'maha*."

Jorge thought they'd go further, but apparently that was all that needed to be said. Manny briefly introduced himself to Greg, who accepted the Savant's handshake despite a moment of obvious reluctance, then Castro turned to McAlister again. "Captain, I believe the time has come for us to leave. If you will . . . ?"

"Right." The pilot bent over to pick up his bag. "If you'll follow me, please . . . ?"

Hoisting his own bag across his shoulder, Jorge started to join the others, but then his father stopped him. "Just a moment, son. If I could have a word with you . . ."

Knowing what was coming, Jorge halted. Jon waited until the rest of the expedition members were out of earshot, then he went on. "Look," he said quietly, "I know you don't want a speech from the old man, but . . . well, I just want to tell you how proud I am of you. If I could've come along . . ."

"I know." Jorge was aware of the fact that his father had tried to pressure Sawyer into adding him to the expedition, arguing that he was a more experienced pilot than McAlister. Sawyer had turned him down, though, saying that Jon was too old for this sort of thing; besides, he was uncomfortable with the notion of sending both father and son on such a hazardous mission. "Don't worry about it. I'm sure he'll get us there and back again."

Jon nodded, and Jorge was surprised to see a trace of redness in his father's eyes. Jon was trying to force back tears; in all the times they'd seen each other off, for one Corps expedition or another, never before had his father been so emotional. "Give Mama my love," he added. "Tell her I'll see you both as soon as I get back."

"Sure. I'll do that." For a second, Jorge thought his father would embrace him. But they both knew that would be embarrassing—as expedition leader, it wouldn't do for him to be seen being given a fare-well hug by his father—so instead they formally shook hands. "Good luck, boy," Jon said. "Take care of yourself . . . and the others, too."

"Thanks. I will." Then Jorge turned and followed the others to the *Mercator*.

The shuttle's interior wasn't spacious, but it was suitable for their purposes. The belly hatch led to the middeck passenger cabin, where four couches were arranged on either side of a center aisle and their supplies tucked into cargo nets behind them. Inez, Vargas, Manny, and Greg were buckling themselves into their seats when Jorge came aboard. He raised the ladder and closed the hatch, making sure that it was dogged tight before moving forward. Apparently Inez sensed his emotions, because she turned to give him a sympathetic smile; Jorge patted her fondly upon the shoulder, then went up a short flight of steps to the flight deck.

The cockpit was even smaller than the cabin, with two couches crammed nearly shoulder to shoulder within a wraparound array of control panels. Although Jorge knew nothing about flying a space-craft, as expedition leader he'd nonetheless been assigned to the right-hand copilot seat. McAlister was already going through the prelaunch checklist, his hands roaming across the various toggle switches and buttons as he activated the shuttle's major systems. The pilot grunted as Jorge straddled the center console to fall clumsily into his couch, and Jorge felt McAlister's eyes upon him as he struggled to untangle the harness straps and attach them to the six-point buckle at the center of his chest.

"Ever been up in space before, Lieutenant?" he asked.

"Yes, I have." Jorge wasn't about to admit that his previous experience was limited to two suborbital training sorties. "Just . . . remembering how to do all this, that's all."

"Hmm . . . well, fortunately, I've done this a few times. Sir."

Jorge glanced at McAlister. Although there was a hint of irony in his voice, the pilot's expression remained neutral. Jorge only hoped that his attitude wasn't a permanent fixture, or there would be problems.

Instead of responding, he gazed through the cockpit windows. As the ramjets took on the low moan of its warm-up procedure, he saw the ground crew moving away, dragging the fuel lines behind them. He spotted his father standing just beyond the edge of the flight line. Jorge briefly raised a hand, but apparently Colonel Parson didn't see him because he didn't respond in kind.

McAlister finished the checklist. He slipped the datapad into a web above his console, then took a deep breath as he laid his right hand upon the center-mounted bars for the VTOL thrusters. "All set back there?" he called over his shoulder. Hearing affirmative responses from the passenger cabin, he grunted, then touched his headset mike. "Flight Seven Six Zulu Tango to tower, requesting permission for takeoff." He waited a moment. "Affirmative, tower, thank you," he added, then he looked over at Jorge. "Want a countdown, Lieutenant, or . . . ?"

"Ready when you are, Captain." Jorge pulled on his own headset, too late to hear the other half of the exchange.

"Very well, then." McAlister slowly pushed the bars forward, and as the moan rose to a deep-throated snarl, he pulled back on the yoke. A shudder passed through the shuttle, and Jorge felt something push him back in his seat as the *Mercator* rose upon its VTOL thrusters. Once the small craft was five hundred feet above the runway, the pilot tilted the prow upward, then pushed the throttle bar forward. An immense roar, then the *Mercator* lunged toward the cloudless sky.

They were on their way.

McAlister might have had a less-than-soothing temperament, but he was an excellent pilot; the ride to orbit was smooth, with hardly any jarring along the way. Nevertheless, shortly after the blue skies of Coyote were replaced with the star-flecked blackness of space, Jorge unbuckled his harness and pushed himself out of his seat. Now that the main engine had been engaged, the trip to the starbridge would take ten hours; the less time he spent in the cockpit, the better he'd get along with McAlister.

Everyone had endured the launch and ascent well, save for Greg, who'd become violently ill almost as soon as the *Mercator* reached space. The shuttle was too small to contain a Millis-Clement field generator, so weightlessness was a fact of life they'd have to deal with. Fortunately, the sergeant had managed to restrain his urge to vomit until he reached the small zero-g toilet in the rear of the passenger compartment, leaving the others to gaze out the portholes at Coyote.

Seen from above, the world was a vast hemisphere, its snow-covered plains and mountains broken by the deep blue of its myriad rivers and channels. Leaning forward to peer through the small window above Greg's vacant seat, Jorge watched as the *Mercator* crossed the daylight terminator east of Narragansett. A last glimpse of the tiny lights from coastal settlements along the Great Equatorial River, then there was a brief surge as the shuttle's main engine fired again. Coyote began to drift away as the shuttle headed out for the starbridge in trojan orbit around Bear.

"Too bad we couldn't have stayed longer," Inez murmured. "I was enjoying the view."

Jorge looked around at her. She was seated in her couch, calmly gazing through another porthole. She seemed a little pale, but otherwise was holding up. "We'll be back soon enough," he replied. "Besides, we'll be seeing more interesting things than this before then."

"Your opinion." Vargas was seated behind her, across the aisle from Manny. He didn't look very happy to be there. "Personally, I'd rather stay behind."

Jorge suppressed a sigh. He'd heard Vargas gripe enough already about his role in the expedition. Not that he could blame him; after all, the last thing the former Union Astronautica spacer had ever expected was to be returning to Earth, let alone so soon after making good his escape. But that was an argument he'd already lost, and Jorge was getting tired of hearing it again.

"Oh, but then you'd have missed one of the most interesting sights in the galaxy." Manny turned his glass eyes toward him. "Feel honored, my friend . . . you'll be one of the few men from Earth to visit *Talus qua'spah*."

"I'm not your . . ."

"What should we expect once we get there?" Jorge hastened to cut off an insult. "I mean, I know we're supposed to be meeting with the Talus High Council, but other than that . . ."

The toilet door slid open, and Greg floated out of the tiny compartment, grasping a ceiling rail for support. He was still a little queasy, but apparently he'd managed to empty his stomach without causing a mess, because he gave Jorge a wan smile.

"I'm not entirely sure," Manny went on, as Jorge pulled himself aside to let Greg resume his seat. "I've visited the House of the Talus many times, and have met with the High Council twice before. Each occasion has been a bit different, though, and none have ever been quite like this. All I know for certain is that, before we're allowed to make the jump to Starbridge Earth, we'll have to make our case to the Council."

"Yes, well . . . that's the part I still don't get," Vargas said. "I mean, you've got a nav key already programmed for Starbridge Earth, right?

And I've told you the bridge itself is still functional, even if it hasn't been used since the *Lee* blew up. So why do we have to ask anyone's permission to go home?"

"Your home," Inez said quietly, without looking at him. "Not mine."

Jorge nodded but allowed Manny to continue. "When the *hjadd* stepped in to help us rebuild Coyote's starbridge," the Savant said, "they stipulated that it could be used to reach only Rho Coronae Borealis and other Talus systems. It was their opinion that Earth was a hostile planet, and that further contact with it would pose a hazard not only to the Federation but to the Talus as well. The High Council backed this decision, and since then our access to Earth has been denied."

"But you could have gone back . . ." Vargas began.

"Not without disobeying the High Council, no. Technically speaking, it's Coyote that's become a member of the Talus, not humankind. Our trade and cultural ties to the other races of the galaxy are too valuable for us to risk losing. Like it or not, we have to get permission from the Council to do this."

"Christ . . ."

"You needn't worry, Mr. Vargas. In my communiqués with the Council, they've expressed no desire to speak with you . . . only Jorge, Inez, and me."

"They want to see Inez and me?" Jorge was surprised. This was the first time he'd heard that.

"Yes." Manny turned his head to look at him and Inez again. "You needn't worry, though. I'm only going to be there as liaison, and you're only attending as expedition leader. The person whom they really want to meet is Corporal Sanchez."

"Because I'm the *chaaz'maha's* daughter," Inez said, her voice low and reserved.

"Correct." A slight nod of Manny's skull-like head. "They were unaware that the *chaaz'maha* left behind a child. Naturally, they're curious about you . . . which means that, for better or worse, it may be up to you to persuade them to relax their prohibition against traveling to Earth."

Inez slowly let out her breath. "That's a lot to ask."

"I know. But that's the way it is."

The hours crawled by. They chatted, snacked from the freeze-dried rations stocked in the galley, took naps, gazed out the windows. Once Jorge returned to the cockpit, he finally found something to talk about with McAlister that was a little less incendiary: namely, the upcoming soccer playoffs between the Liberty Patriots and the Clarksburg Loggers. And in the meantime, Bear grew larger, its vast rings gradually gaining dimension, the superjovian's swirling cloud bands more distinct.

Finally, just as everyone was reaching the limits of their patience, they reached Starbridge Coyote. It was bigger than the one that had been destroyed on Black Anael; the first starbridge had been converted from the diametric-drive torus transported to 47 Ursae Majoris by the EASS *Columbus* in c.y. 13, while its replacement—using materials mined from Bear's closest satellite, Dog, and assembled with *hjadd* technology—was designed to allow larger vessels to pass through it. Even the gatehouse was new; the original station, converted from the *Columbus*'s primary hull, had been dismantled several years earlier, and in its place was a wheel-shaped collection of modules that also served as a port of call for the vessels of those aliens who found Coyote to be uninhabitable.

"Gatehouse Traffic," McAlister said, "this is CFS *Gerardus Mercator*, on primary approach. Request permission to initiate hyperspace transit to Rho Coronae Borealis." The pilot typed an eight-digit string into the nav comp. "Standing by to transmit key code, on your mark."

A short pause, then a voice came over their headsets. *"We copy, Mercator. Ready to receive key code. Mark."*

Without a word, McAlister took a small black cartridge from his vest pocket, slid it into a slot within the comp. This was the *Mercator*'s starbridge key, programmed with the hyperspace coordinates for the starbridges in both 47 Ursae Majoris and Rho Coronae Borealis. Without it, hyperspace travel would be impossible: the AIs that controlled access to the starbridges would not permit a wormhole to be opened, thus prohibiting a ship from passing through. In this way, the Talus was able to operate its galaxywide system of starbridges in peace.

Another pause, then the gatehouse traffic controller spoke again. *"Key code received and confirmed,* Mercator. *Please transfer navigation control to local AI."*

"Roger, Trafco." McAlister reached up to the communications panel, flipped a couple of toggles, then pushed a red button on his console marked PILOT AUTO. "Control transferred. Awaiting your signal." Cupping his hand around his headset mike, the pilot glanced at Jorge. "This is the part I hate."

Jorge nodded. He understood what the pilot meant; the shuttle's main comps were now slaved to the gatehouse AI, which in turn had been interfaced with the AI aboard the distant starbridge. From that point on, control of the *Mercator* was out of McAlister's hands. The AIs would do the rest. No pilot liked to surrender his craft to a machine, but it had to be done; the calculations necessary for a successful hyperspace jump relied on split-second decisions too rapid for human reflexes.

A few seconds went by, then they heard from the traffic controller again. *"Mercator, you're clear for transit. Final approach and insertion in T-minus sixty seconds. Abort window closes in T-minus fifty seconds. Good luck. Coyote gatehouse over."*

"We copy, gatehouse, thank you. *Mercator* over and out." McAlister muted the comlink, cocked his head toward the aft cabin. "One minute to go. Make sure you're strapped down . . . and if you're prone to vertigo, I'd suggest you shut your eyes."

Stretching his shoulders against his harness, Jorge peered back at the others. They were all in their seats, their straps holding them immobile. The only person who appeared calm—save for Manny, inscrutable as always—was Sergio, who'd been through this more than a half dozen times before. Both Greg and Inez were plainly nervous, though, with Greg clutching his armrests and Inez staring anxiously at the porthole above her seat. Jorge noticed that her lips were moving soundlessly; he guessed that she was reciting one of the *Sa'Tong-tas*'s many poems, probably the one meant to calm followers in times of peril.

It was times like this when he envied her for her beliefs. Even though their training for this mission had included a ride in a Navy flight simulator, Jorge knew that it would do little to prepare them for the real thing.

A few seconds later, there was another surge as the shuttle's main engine automatically fired. Through the cockpit windows, he saw the starbridge gradually expand until there was nothing else in sight. As the *Mercator* hurtled toward the giant silver ring, there was a brilliant flash from within its cavity: white at first, then multispectral, as if all the colors of visible light had been split apart by an immense prism, swirling together to form a funnel-like kaleidoscope.

Gravity tugged at him, pulling his body against his straps. "Hold on!" McAlister shouted. "We're going in!" Then he looked at Jorge. "Shut your eyes, you fool."

Jorge did so, and an instant later the *Mercator* plunged into the wormhole.

For the next five seconds, he felt as if he had been thrown into a maelstrom. No, worse than that: something indescribable by terms of any previous experience. As the spacecraft spun along its major axis, he had the sensation of being physically stretched, as if he'd become a string of saltwater taffy; there was no pain in this, yet reality itself seemed to have been warped. From behind him, he heard a scream—he barely recognized the voice as Inez's—and yet the sound was distorted, coming to him from some great distance. He struggled to breathe, but even that seemed impossible.

And then, just as he was wondering how much longer the ordeal would last, it was over. Like a rubber band being snapped, reality abruptly resumed its proper state. He could breathe again, although only as a ragged gasp that burned his lungs. When he opened his eyes, he saw that the cockpit was just the same as he'd last seen it.

"Fun, huh?" Beside him, McAlister was grinning, albeit ruefully. Sweat stained his collar and underarms, formed tiny beads that broke free from his face and drifted away. "Maybe I should've said that *this* is the part I hate the most."

"Yeah . . . whatever." Jorge felt a wave of nausea; fighting the urge to vomit, he closed his eyes again, took deep breaths.

"Right." The pilot cranked his seat back a few inches, then looked over his shoulder again. "Everyone okay back there? No casualties, I hope."

A few murmurs from the cabin prompted Jorge to open his eyes once more. The nausea was gone, and it didn't appear as if anyone had become sick, although the others also looked as if they'd been pulled through a laundry wringer. Only Manny seemed unperturbed. For the first time, Jorge found himself wishing that he was a Savant.

"Better get used to it," McAlister muttered. "This won't be the last time." He nodded toward the cockpit windows. "Unless, of course, you'd like to make that your permanent residence."

At first, Jorge didn't understand what he was saying. Then he followed McAlister's gaze and saw the House of the Talus.

At first sight, *Talus qua'spah* resembled an immense snowflake that had, in defiance of every natural law, formed in high orbit above an Earth-sized planet. Roughly circular in shape, a little more than two hundred miles in diameter, it was massive yet strangely delicate, its latticework giving it a fragile appearance despite its enormous size.

As the *Mercator* came closer, Jorge perceived the reason for this illusion. *Talus qua'spah* wasn't one single structure but rather a vast collection of habitats in different sizes and shapes—spheres, cylinders, hexagons—connected to one another by a complex web of cables, struts, and bars, with a central torus as its nucleus. Spacecraft of nearly every description moved around its outer fringes; a giant rhomboid, speckled with windows and larger than any vessel in the Federation fleet, glided past the *Mercator*, carefully avoiding the tiny shuttle as it headed for the nearby starbridge.

"When the *hjadd* agreed to play host for the rest of the Talus," Manny said, "their first challenge was designing a colony suitable for the requirements of many different races." The Savant had left his seat in the aft cabin and floated up to the flight deck, where he clung to a ceiling rail. "Their solution was to build a support structure in geosynchronous orbit above their homeworld, then invite the other member races to bring their own habitats and attach them to it. This way, each race has its own hab . . . sometimes a few, in fact . . . containing native environments that they don't have to adapt for the needs of others."

"Nice to know," McAlister said, "but that doesn't tell me where I'm to dock."

"Coyote has a hab. The *hjadd* converted a vacant sphere for our purposes shortly after humans made contact with them." Manny paused. "However, I'm not sure we'll be docking there. The Council may have other plans for us. We're close enough . . . may I use the ship's wireless, please?"

McAlister hesitated, then started to remove his headset, apparently intending to pass it to the Savant. "Thank you, but that won't be necessary," Manny added. "I have my own comlink." As if to demonstrate, he reached to his chest, slid open a recessed panel, and pulled out a small prong along a slender cord. "Lieutenant, if you'd be so kind as to insert this in the com panel . . . ?"

Jorge tried not to smile as he took the prong from Manny and pushed it into an auxiliary port on the communications panel. McAlister didn't bother to hide his amusement. "Do you also come with a can opener?" he murmured.

"And a knife sharpener, too." If Manny was insulted, he showed no indication. "Please adjust the frequency to 1,120 kilohertz, Lieutenant."

Manny waited until Jorge did this, then he spoke again, this time in the series of sibilant hisses, clicks, and croaks that Jorge recognized as the *hjadd's* spoken language. For the first time, he realized why Manuel Castro had been asked to serve as Coyote's liaison to the Talus. So far as he knew, no one else had mastered more than a few words of the *hjadd's* native tongue. It was nearly unpronounceable by humans, but apparently the Savant vocoder was able to replicate it without effort. Indeed, Jorge wondered how many other languages Manny had learned over the past few years.

There was a brief pause, then Jorge heard a response through his headset: the same language, apparently spoken by a *hjadd*. It lasted for a minute or so, then Manny made a brief reply before looking at McAlister again. "Just as I suspected . . . we won't be docking at our own sphere but somewhere else. It seems that the High Council has chosen a different site for our meeting."

Jorge and McAlister exchanged a worried look. "Is this good or bad?" Jorge asked.

"I couldn't tell you because I don't know. There is one bit of good news, though. Given the fact that we'll be here for so short a time, the Council has allowed us to forgo the usual decontamination procedure, provided that we have our own air supply."

"Not a problem." As a precaution, the Navy had furnished the expedition with five airpacks. Previous experience with the *hjadd* had shown humans the wisdom of being prepared to cope with the aliens' native atmosphere, with its lower pressure and higher nitrogen content. "But that still doesn't tell us where we should . . ."

"I was coming to that." Manny tapped McAlister on the shoulder, and apparently didn't notice that the pilot flinched at his touch. "Interface the nav system with the comlink, then return to autopilot. The local traffic network will guide us to whatever berth the Council wants us to use. Once we've arrived, you may resume manual control and commence docking maneuvers as usual."

"'As usual,' he says." McAlister reached forward to enter a new command into the comp's keypad. "I should've never volunteered for this damned mission."

Talus qua'spah steadily grew in size until it filled the cockpit windows for as far as the eye could see. As Manny said, the *Mercator* was on full autopilot, guided in by the traffic-control net. As the shuttle reached the colony's periphery, its reaction-control thrusters fired on their own accord, putting the spacecraft on a new course that swung it along a shallow arc above the vast construct.

Dozens of habitats moved beneath them, with thousands of lights gleaming within their portholes. Every now and then, they caught a fleeting glimpse of an alien figure, as if a member of one extraterrestrial race or another had paused for a moment to watch the approach of the tiny craft. Along the thick cables that linked *Talus qua'spah* together, Jorge spotted small, lozenge-shaped cars moving at breakneck speed within transparent tubes: obviously a rapid-transit system, providing access from one hab to another. *Talus qua'spah* was called a house, but in fact it was a city, one larger than any ever built by humankind.

The *Mercator* began to lose altitude, gradually dropping to a couple of hundred feet above the colony, until it headed directly toward a geodesic sphere five hundred feet in diameter. As the shuttle approached the hab, a rectangular hatch opened just above its equator; light spilled out, revealing what appeared to be a small hangar. The thrusters fired again, this time to brake the shuttle, then the *Mercator* slipped into the bay.

As soon as the shuttle was past the doors, Jorge felt weight return; apparently their craft had just entered a local gravity field. At that moment, the master alarm rang, signaling that that the autopilot had been disengaged. Caught by surprise, McAlister swore under his breath; he grabbed the yoke and pulled back on it, firing the thrusters one last time to complete the braking maneuver. He reached up to snap a row of toggles; a bump from beneath their feet as the landing gear was lowered, then the pilot slowly brought the craft down. A hard thump as the *Mercator* made its touchdown, and the pilot let out his breath.

"They might have warned us," he said to no one in particular, as his hands moved across the console, shutting down the engine and thrusters. That done, he craned his neck to peer aft through the cockpit windows. "All right, they've closed the door. Let's see if it's okay to leave."

Jorge was already ahead of him. Gazing at the environmental control panel to his left, he studied the readout for the outside atmosphere. The gauge slowly rose, indicating that the hangar was being repressurized. "Coyote-normal," he said at last. "Same for gravity. Looks like they're expecting us." He looked back at Manny. "We may not need those airpacks after all."

"Wear them anyway. This is only the hangar, after all. We'll be going . . . well, somewhere else." The Savant leaned forward to activate the wireless again. Once more, he said a few words in the *hjadd* language. This time, though, there was no response, only an expectant silence. "I believe that means they're waiting for us. Shall we?"

Jorge unfastened his seat harness, then climbed over the center console and followed Manny into the passenger cabin. The others had already unbuckled their own harnesses; Inez had risen from her seat, but Greg and Vargas remained where they were, staring out the portholes at the hangar. "Don't see anything else out there," Greg said, looking up at Jorge as he entered. "You'd think there'd be other ships."

Jorge shrugged. Just then, that was the least of his concerns.

"Manny says we might need the airpacks," he said to Inez, then another thought occurred to him. "Weapons, too?" he asked, turning to the Savant. "Or would that be considered an insult?"

"More than an insult," Manny replied. "Weapons of any kind are prohibited on *Talus qua'spah*. Fortunately, we'll be here for so short a time that no one will ask to inspect our ship and its cargo. Otherwise, we could expect to have them impounded."

Jorge had expected as much. "All right, then . . . no guns." Inez nodded, then walked aft to the cargo nets and found the equipment case containing the airpacks. He turned to Greg and Vargas. "I don't know how long this will take, but until we get back, you're to stay put. No wandering around, no exploring . . ."

"Aw, c'mon, Lieutenant." Sergio looked at him askance. "Can't we just get out and stretch our legs? We've been cooped up in here for eleven hours now."

"That shouldn't be a problem," Manny said before Jorge could respond. "Just make sure that you don't leave the hangar . . . and under no circumstances should you reveal any weapons."

Greg nodded, and once again he and Jorge gave each other a knowing glance. The sergeant was to keep an eye on Vargas. And perhaps McAlister, too, for that matter; Jorge wasn't sure how much he trusted their pilot.

By then, Inez had removed the airpacks from their case. She handed one to Jorge, and they took a couple of minutes to put them on: a small pack, about the size and shape of a knapsack, that they each carried on their backs with a small harness. Once activated, the packs would filter oxygen and nitrogen from the ambient atmosphere and turn them into breathable air. Two elastic tubes led to a half-face airmask, which was also fitted with a mike and amplifier; a pair of goggles went with it. Inez and Jorge pushed the goggles up on their foreheads and let the masks dangle beneath their chins.

Once they were ready, Jorge knelt to undog the belly hatch. A faint hiss of escaping pressure, then the hatch opened. He lowered the ladder, then stood up. "Ladies and Savants first," he said, making a polite gesture.

"No." Manny shook his head. "As expedition leader, you're expected to be the first to exit your craft."

Something in the way Manny said this caused Jorge to pause at the hatch. "You think we're being watched?"

"From the moment we came through the starbridge. And believe me, Lieutenant . . . the Council, and particularly the *hjadd*, take great stock in even the most casual of actions." He looked at the others. "Remember that when you get out to stretch your legs."

Jorge swallowed, but there was no point in arguing. Bending forward again, he climbed down the ladder, with Inez and Manny just behind him. Ready or not, they were about to enter the House of the Talus.

They had just emerged from the shuttle when a circular door within the hangar's far wall opened like a sphincter. A robot came through, or at least that was what Jorge assumed it to be; spherical, about the size and shape of a spacecraft oxygen tank, it scuttled forward upon four multijointed legs resembling those of a spider. The machine moved toward them so quickly that both he and Inez instinctively stepped back. Manny remained where he was, though, and waited until it stopped in front of them.

"Greetings," he said, hands at his sides. "I am Manuel Castro, diplomatic liaison to the Talus from the Coyote Federation. With me are Jorge Montero and Inez Sanchez, both of the Coyote Federation Corps of Exploration."

As he spoke, a slender arm detached itself from the sphere's base and extended toward them. At its end was a pair of lenses that rapidly telescoped and retracted as the arm twitched back and forth, inspecting each of the three visitors in turn. At the same time, a panel near the top of the sphere opened, allowing something that looked disturbingly like a gun barrel to protrude. If it was, indeed, a weapon of some sort, then it was aimed straight at them.

Manny had barely finished when the machine responded in a high-pitched chitter that sounded somewhat like that of a grasshoarder. Whatever its language was, it clearly wasn't *hjadd*. Manny listened for a moment. "Yes, we're here to see the High Council regarding a matter of some urgency." Another outburst. "We've been invited, yes," Manny continued. More chittering. "I assure you that we're unarmed, and that my friends will abide by the protocols. Now, please, escort us to the meeting place."

A pause, then the gun barrel disappeared, and the machine began to retreat, returning to the door from which it had appeared. "Come along," Manny said quietly, not looking at Jorge and Inez. "My friend has agreed to take us there."

"Some friend." Jorge followed him, with Inez right behind. "A security 'bot, I take it?"

"Not exactly." Manny kept his voice low. "You're right about her job, but she isn't a robot. She's a *danui* . . . or at least that's how she was born. Since then, though, she's become their version of a Savant. The difference is, in her case, her brain was physically transplanted into a machine body, thereby allowing her to become a very efficient sentry."

Inez stared at the *danui* cyborg. "Why?"

"Why not?" The buzz that signified Savant laughter. "The *danui* are naturally suspicious, and this particular one loves nothing more than interrogating new arrivals. Believe me, if I weren't with you, you'd have been here for hours, arguing with her just for the sake of her amusement."

The cyborg led them into a broad, steel-walled tunnel; the door behind them swirled shut as they walked down the corridor to an identical door. The sentry halted before it, her eyestalk twitching toward Manny. Once again, she voiced another demand. "I understand,"

Manny replied, then he looked back at his companions. "My friend informs me this is both an airlock and also a sterilization area. Although we won't have to undergo full-body decontamination, the Council does want to make sure that our clothes aren't carrying any contagious microorganisms. So you'll need to put on your masks and goggles once we go in."

"Understood," Jorge said. Manny responded to the *danui* in her own language, and a second later the door irised open, revealing a small, circular room. To Jorge's surprise, the sentry didn't follow them inside but remained in the corridor.

"She decided we're harmless," Inez said, as the door closed behind them.

"I had much the same impression, yes. Otherwise, she would've joined us." Manny watched as she and Jorge donned their masks and goggles. "Just out of curiosity . . . the way you said that leads me to wonder if you picked up on her emotions."

Inez didn't respond for a moment. "In a manner of speaking," she said at last, her voice distorted by the mask's amplifier. "She might look like a 'bot, but her brain is organic. That was how I was able to pick up on her. It was . . . well, weird . . . to be able to sense an alien's emotional state, but it was surprisingly human. Or humanlike, at least."

"I see." Manny was quiet for a few seconds. Panels within the ceiling turned red, and Jorge felt a subtle rise in temperature. He guessed that the room was being bathed in ultraviolet radiation. "But you can't do that with me, of course."

"No. Your intelligence is contained within a quantum comp, and so it's inaccessible to me."

"Interesting. I'd never thought of that." Manny paused. "Still, I'd refrain from doing that during our meeting with the Council. Some of its members are empathic by nature, and I understand a few of them have some strong cultural taboos against uninvited sensing."

"I'll keep that in mind." Looking at Jorge, she gave him a wink through her goggles. "I have plenty of practice in shutting out strong emotions of those around me."

Jorge said nothing, but he was suddenly glad that the air mask hid his expression. How many times in the past had he entertained fantasies about her before he'd known that they were related? Again, he was uncomfortably reminded that she had been aware they were kin long before he was, and had been shutting out his feelings toward her.

A few seconds later he felt his ears pop from the lowered atmospheric pressure, then the ceiling resumed its former appearance. "We're done," Manny said. "Remember . . . the atmosphere we're now in isn't necessarily fatal, but you'll pass out if you try to breathe it. So keep your mask on at . . . ah, here we go."

Jorge turned to see two curved sections of the wall behind him split in half, sliding open to reveal a doorway that he hadn't realized was there. On the other side of the door was a broad, elliptical chamber, its floor a smooth expanse of fine-veined black marble, its walls reflective black glass. The ceiling was a concave dome just a dozen feet above the floor, with indirect lighting from around its rim. No furniture of any sort, although there appeared to be a keyhole-shaped door on the opposite side of the room.

"Ever been here before?" Jorge asked, as he and Inez followed Manny into the cold and featureless chamber.

"No. This is new to me." Jorge couldn't be sure, but he thought he detected nervousness in the Savant's electronic voice. "My previous meetings with the Council or its individual members have always been in . . . well, other places."

Their footsteps echoed softly off the black walls as they walked farther into the room. A faint sigh from behind them; Jorge looked back, saw the door sliding shut. All of a sudden, he felt as if he'd stepped into a trap. No way out . . .

"It's okay," Inez murmured, coming up beside him to touch his hand. "There's no reason to be afraid."

A reluctant nod as he took a deep breath, tasting the antiseptic flavor of his pack's air. Whatever happened next, he could only hope that she was right . . .

All of a sudden, they were no longer alone.

The surrounding walls, once empty black glass, now displayed the images of aliens: not holograms, but nonetheless forms three-dimensional enough that it seemed as if they were silently peering in at them from behind plate-glass windows. Nearly two dozen extraterrestrials, no two of them alike. Jorge recognized a few—a fur-covered, wide-eyed *arsashi*; a four-armed, blue-skinned biped with an elongated skull that he tentatively identified as a *soranta*; an emaciated-looking quadipod that was probably a *kua'tah*—but most were unfamiliar to him, with some so weird that he wouldn't have even believed that they were sentient creatures if he hadn't known better.

The High Council of the Talus was all around them, their virtual presence both shocking and humbling at the same time. Jorge realized where they were: a conference room where the aliens could gather to meet with aliens—he and his companions, in this case—whose environments were unlike their own. Yet if this were so, then why was it that the room hadn't been furnished with an atmosphere suitable for humans?

Jorge was about to ask Manny about this when the answer became apparent. The keyhole door split apart at the center, allowing a *hjadd* to enter the room. Slightly shorter than a human, heshe somewhat resembled a tortoise that lacked a shell and walked upright on two stumpy legs, but with a fin rising from the top of hisher sloping skull. The alien wore the iridescent, togalike garment favored by hisher kind, and as heshe walked toward them, hisher slitted eyes moved independently of each other, as if examining the three humans before himher.

"Greetings, and welcome to *Talus qua'spah*." When heshe spoke, they heard two languages at once: the hissing, almost reptilian tones of hisher own voice, and Anglo, coming from the pronglike translation device heshe wore against hisher lipless mouth. Heshe formally raised hisher left hand, six webbed fingers spread apart, as a gesture of goodwill. "I am Jasahajahd Taf Sa-Fhadda, First Speaker of the High Council. For purposes of conversation, you may call me Taf Sa-Fhadda, or First Speaker."

When heshe said this, Jorge immediately knew who heshe was. Many years ago, Jasahajahd Taf Sa-Fhadda had come to Coyote as the *hjadd's* Cultural Ambassador, a role intended to help humankind better understand the aliens who'd recently built an embassy on their world. Yet Taf had done far more than that; upon arrival at the New Brighton spaceport, heshe had given a *Sa'Tong-tas* to the young customs inspector who, along with Jorge's grandfather, had come out to greet himher. That person was Hawk Thompson; the rest was history.

Jorge was unaware that Taf had since returned to Rho Coronae Borealis, or that heshe had apparently been promoted to a more senior diplomatic position. Which was not surprising; even after all these years, the *hjadd* on Coyote still kept to themselves, although they'd continued to maintain their embassy in Liberty. So while it was surprising that Taf would be there today, it nevertheless made sense; not only did heshe have previous experience with humans, but heshe had known Hawk Thompson before he'd become the *chaaz'maha*.

"Greetings, First Speaker Taf Sa-Fhadda." Manny returned the gesture, his four-fingered claw appearing from beneath his black robe. "I am Manuel Castro, diplomatic liaison of the Coyote Federation to the Talus." No doubt this was only a formality; Jorge knew that Manny was no stranger to either Taf or the Council. The Savant extended the same hand toward him and Inez. "Allow me to introduce my companions . . . Jorge Montero, an officer in the Coyote Federation

Corps of Exploration, and Inez Sanchez, also a member of the Corps."

As he spoke, Jorge was aware of subtle movements from the aliens observing them: heads moving back and forth, or weaving to and fro; mandibles silently clicking; pinchers, paws, or tentacles making discreet motions. He could hear nothing from them, but he assumed that the Council members were receiving translations of the conversation, and these little movements were the equivalent of nodding, perhaps even a smile or two. Or so he hoped.

"Welcome, Jorge Montero and Inez Sanchez." Facing each of them in turn, Taf repeated the same left-handed gesture. Inez reacted before Jorge did, raising her left hand and making a slight bow; Jorge hastened to do the same. "What matter do you wish to bring to the attention of the High Council?"

Manny didn't say anything. Instead, he half turned toward Jorge. His face was incapable of human expression, yet Jorge was suddenly aware that he was being called upon to speak. Jorge hadn't expected this; his face grew warm, and for an instant he was tongue-tied. There was no way out of this, though. The time had come for him to address the Council.

"Umm . . . ah, yes, thank you, First Speaker, and . . . uh, other members of the High Council." He hesitated, praying that he hadn't committed a faux pas. He had to assume that his words were being translated by some hidden device within the room; otherwise, everything he said would be nothing but babble. The *hjadd* continued to regard him with expectant eyes, and Manny gave him a small nod of encouragement. "I have come here today . . . that is, we have, Inez and I . . . to request the permission of the Council to take an expedition to Earth, in order to find a member of our race whom we believe to be there. This person is . . ."

"My father, Hawk Thompson, the *chaaz'maha* of humankind." Inez took a step forward, addressing both Taf and the aliens around them. "We've lately received news indicating that, contrary to our previous belief, he is still alive and somewhere on Earth. Jorge and I belong to his family, and we therefore request permission to return to our homeworld in order to find him and bring him back to Coyote."

At first, Jorge was annoyed by the interruption, until he realized that Inez was far better suited to address the Council than he was. There was no reticence in her manner or voice; when she spoke, it was with utter self-confidence, almost as if she'd been practicing for this moment. And perhaps she had, if only in her imagination. After all, Manny had warned her that the Council would be more interested in her than Jorge; she'd waited until her second cousin had broken the ice, then come forth to take the lead.

"This is quite interesting indeed." Taf's right eye twitched toward her as hisher hands folded together within the bell sleeves of hisher toga. "I met your father, if only very briefly, when I made a gift of a *Sa'Tong-tas* to him."

"I am aware of this, First Speaker . . . and on behalf of the members of my race who've embraced its wisdom, I thank you." Clasping her hands together, Inez bowed again, holding it for a little longer this time. "I never knew the *chaaz'maha* myself. I was only a few days old when he was presumed to have been killed. For this, I envy you."

The *hjadd's* fin rose a little higher, and heshe uttered a stuttering hiss that Jorge thought might be a sign of irritation. "You honor me, daughter of a *chaaz'maha*. Yet I'm still confused why neither myself, in my former role as an emissary to your race, nor this Council as a whole, as fellow disciples of *Sa'Tong*, was ever informed that the *chaaz'maha* of your race had a child. Why was this knowledge kept from us until now?"

This time, it was Manny who answered the question. "As you and the Council doubtless recall, our *chaaz'maha* was aboard a starship that was destroyed by a bomb while en route to Earth. Although the person who set off the bomb was also aboard the same vessel, for a long time it was unknown whether he acted alone. The *chaaz'maha's* family . . . that is, his partner and a few of his relatives and friends . . .

decided that, in order to keep his daughter safe from any other ene-
mies, her existence should be kept a closely guarded secret."

"I . . ." Jorge nervously cleared his throat. "Pardon me. I wasn't
aware that Inez was a relative . . . that is, my second cousin . . . until
only a few days ago. Until then, she was only a friend who happened
to be serving with me in our Corps of . . ."

"I understand now," Taf said, cutting him off. "Thank you, Jorge
Montero and Manuel Castro, for your explanations." Heshe seemed to
disregard both him and Manny as heshe returned hisher attention to
Inez. "However, this raises another question. I respect the fact that the
human *chaaz'maha* is your father and that you wish to find him . . .
and yet your companions admit that he was parted from you by a
violent deed performed by a member of your own race. Indeed, it was
for this very reason that the Council has forbidden the inhabitants of
Coyote from having further contact with Earth. Therefore, why should
we allow you to visit your homeworld, when there is precedent to
suggest that such contact may present a hazard not only to your own
kind but also the other races of the galaxy?"

Inez was ready with an answer. "Because the other races of the
galaxy . . . those who have adopted *Sa'Tong* as their spiritual philosophy, that is . . . each have their own *chaaz'maha*. Ours was taken from
us. We thought he was dead, but now that it turns out he's alive,
it's important for us to find him." She paused, then added, "Besides,
he's also my father. I wish to meet him. That's why I volunteered for
this expedition."

Taf's head rose slightly upon hisher neck. "Neither is a sufficient
reason. Other races have lost their *chaaz'maha*, some quite long ago,
and have continued their practice of *Sa'Tong* despite the absence of a
teacher. By much the same token, while I respect your desire to be
reunited with your father, bear in mind that many races don't put as
much stock in knowing their parents as humans do. For example, the
soranta are parted from their parents shortly after birth and raised by
their communities, while the *danui* lay their eggs as far from home as

possible and never think about them again. Humans are among the minority of races who actually care for their offspring long after they're born."

Inez started to reply, but Manny raised a hand. "All this is true, First Speaker, yet in asserting this, aren't you also denying humans the right to conduct their own affairs as they see fit? If so, then you're violating one of the main principles upon which the Talus was formed . . . tolerance for the customs and traditions of all races, regardless of how strange they may seem."

Taf didn't respond at once. Instead, hisher head cocked to one side, as if listening to a voice only heshe could hear. From the corner of his eye, Jorge noticed small, discreet movements from the Council members. Apparently Manny had scored points with that last comment, for the aliens appeared to be discussing it among themselves.

"The issue you have raised is valid," Taf said after a few moments. "However, the fact remains that Earth has caused numerous problems for its colony world. Your own history is testament to this. If the star-bridge were to be reopened to Earth, for whatever reason, then there is a danger that the same thing could happen again. And this time . . ."

Heshe was interrupted by a loud, abrupt *bong!* that echoed through the chamber, as if an unseen bell had just tolled. Taf's fin rose to its full height; hisher throat sacs inflated, and hisher eyes widened. The First Speaker had obviously been startled by the sudden sound, and when Jorge glanced at the walls, it seemed to him as if the other Council members were similarly taken aback. Taf didn't continue what heshe was saying, but again cocked hisher head to listen to something.

"What's going on?" he whispered to Manny. "Why did he . . . ?"

"Hush." The Savant didn't look at him, yet his voice was so low, Jorge could barely hear it. "Whatever happens next, don't say anything. Understood?"

Bewildered, Jorge quickly nodded as Taf turned toward them. "I have been informed that another individual wishes to attend this meeting," heshe said. A pause, then hisher eyes swiveled toward Inez. "He wishes to speak to you personally, here in this chamber. Is that acceptable?"

Inez hesitated. "Who? I don't . . . I mean . . ."

"Don't ask," Manny murmured. "Just say yes."

"Yes." She reluctantly nodded. "That is acceptable."

Taf's head swung back and forth, the *hjadd* affirmative, then stepped aside. "By your grace, then . . . please welcome the *chaaz'braan*."

Again, the keyhole door bisected, this time to allow the arrival of an extraterrestrial unlike any other attending the meeting. Slightly taller than a human, swaddled in a brightly colored robe whose elegantly brocaded train dragged across the floor behind him, the alien faintly resembled an enormous, bipedal bullfrog, a once-commonplace Earth creature that Jorge had seen only in pictures. Fleshy jowls hung from either side of a broad, thick-lipped mouth, while two eyes—one of which was half-shut and slightly askew—glittered deep within an enormous head whose white hair was thin and sparse. As the alien slowly walked into the silent room, shoulders hunched forward as he rested his weight upon the staff in his right hand, Jorge was given the impression of great age. This being was very old, perhaps by a matter of centuries.

Jorge didn't know much about *Sa'Tong*, but he knew who the *chaaz'braan* was. The last surviving member of the *askanta*, an extinct race whose planet had been wiped out by the rogue black hole called Kasimasta, he had been sent to safety just before the end of his world. In doing so, the *askanta* had preserved that which they held most dear: their philosophy, *Sa'Tong*, as represented by its Great Teacher.

In the many years that followed, the *chaaz'braan* had brought *Sa'Tong* to the starfaring races of the galaxy. Race after race had come to embrace its teachings, with *chaaz'mahas* like Hawk Thompson learning the wisdom of the *Sa'Tong-tas* and passing it along to others of their kind. Although the Talus itself was largely established upon its principles, the *chaaz'braan* held no formal position within its government. Nonetheless, the last of the *askanta* was the most revered being in the Talus . . . and only a small handful of humans had ever seen him in person.

Noticing that Taf, Manny, and Inez had all bowed, Jorge quickly did the same. The *chaaz'braan* didn't seem to notice his tardiness; indeed, he didn't appear to notice Jorge's presence at all, nor that of either Manny or Taf. Instead, he slowly walked toward Inez, not stopping until he was only a couple of feet away. When Inez raised her head again, Jorge could see that she was trembling.

The *chaaz'braan* solemnly regarded her in silence, not saying anything but instead appearing to study her closely. When his mouth finally opened, though, the others in the room heard nothing but a faint, almost subaudible burble. Yet his words became known as finely scripted, luminescent lines of Anglo text that were superimposed upon the walls around them, wrapping themselves around the circumference of the room.

Sa'Tong qo, *Inez Sanchez of Coyote.* **It is a pleasure to meet the child of a chaaz'maha.**

Inez glanced at the walls, reading the transcript of what the *chaaz'braan* had to say, before returning her gaze to him. "*Sa'Tong qo, chaaz'braan.* It is an honor to meet you as well."

A soft grunt, as if the *chaaz'braan* was satisfied by her response. *I have been listening to this exchange with great interest. Although it is not my custom to interfere with the Council's deliberations, I have decided that I would like to question you personally. Is this acceptable to you?*

"Yes . . . yes, please," Inez stammered. "It would be my honor."

Are you a follower of **Sa'Tong?**

"Yes, I am."

A slow nod of the great head. *Very good. I would not have expected otherwise. Is the* **Sa'Tong-tas** *that* **Jasahajahd Taf Sa-Fhadda** *gave to your father still in your possession?*

"It now belongs to the colony where I was raised, where it remains in safekeeping." Inez paused, then added, "I have studied it myself."

Very interesting. Another nod. *And yet you did not follow your father's example and become a* **chaaz'maha** *yourself. May I ask why?*

"I . . ." Inez hesitated. "With all due respect for my father's legacy, I decided that my path . . . my destiny . . . lay elsewhere. So I became an explorer instead."

Again, very interesting. So your world does not currently have a **chaaz'maha**, *but instead relies solely upon the* **Sa'Tong-tas** *as the basis of your people's understanding of our philosophy.*

Again, Inez hesitated. "Not entirely. In the short time that my father was actively teaching . . . before his presumed death, I mean . . . he spoke with enough of my people that he subsequently became something of a legend. So when those among my kind turn to *Sa'Tong*, very often they do so because they've become fascinated with my father's story, even though they never met him personally.

So your father is now regarded as a messiah?

Inez's face colored. "In some ways, yes."

The *chaaz'braan* didn't respond for a moment, but instead lowered his head and began to slowly walk around her, as if contemplating what she'd just said. After a few moments, his words scrolled across the walls again. **Sa'Tong** *is philosophy and not a religion. Because of this, we try to discourage* **chaaz'mahas** *from being regarded as messiahs.*

"I'm sorry, *chaaz'braan*." Inez seemed to have trouble looking at him. "I . . . we never intended for that to happen."

The *chaaz'braan* stopped, turned toward her. *No reason to apologize. I realize that this can sometimes occur, particularly with races such as yours that embraced theistic beliefs for so long. Nevertheless, it means that, although* **Sa'Tong** *has been accepted by many of your people, it may yet become a religion, and thus risks becoming misinter-*

preted. In order to avoid this, it still needs a **chaaz'maha** *. . . a role which you yourself have refused to perform.*

Inez took a deep breath. "Is this . . . what you'd like for me to do?"

The *chaaz'braan* didn't reply for a moment, but instead gazed at the black-marble floor. *Tell me, please . . . what is the First Codicil of* **Sa'Tong***?*

"I am God, for God is a creation of the self."

What is the Second Codicil?

"Since I am God, then so is everyone else, and therefore I must treat all others as manifestations of God, with the same reverence and respect as I would give to myself."

The Third Codicil?

"In order to adhere to the Second Codicil, one must never take any actions that will harm myself or others."

The Fourth Codicil?

"One must never fail to take action that will prevent harm to myself or others."

And the Fifth Codicil?

"Wrongful acts must be atoned for with righteous acts of equal or greater proportion."

Very good. You have learned well. Now, tell me, please . . . how does your desire to find your father fit in with the Five Codicils?

Inez opened her mouth to reply . . . and then stopped. A puzzled expression crossed her face as she weighed the question. For several seconds, she said nothing. Then she closed her eyes and slowly shook her head.

"My apologies, *chaaz'braan*," she said, very quietly. "I don't know the answer to this."

The *chaaz'braan* peered at her with what seemed to be both sadness and sympathy. *No, I do not think you do. Which is all the more reason why you should undertake this mission.*

He turned to Taf. *First Speaker, it is my opinion that these people should be permitted to return to their homeworld, in order to find their* **chaaz'maha** *and, if possible, return him to the place from which he came. There are risks to this endeavor, true, but I believe that they are outweighed by the potential benefits.*

Taf's fin rose, yet hisher head slowly moved back and forth. Glancing around the room, Jorge saw that the other Council members appeared to be reacting to what the *chaaz'braan* had just said, all in their own ways. Taf cocked hisher head, as if once again listening to the voices in hisher translation device. Several minutes went by, during which no one in the room spoke, then heshe turned toward the humans standing before himher.

"Upon the recommendation of the *chaaz'braan*," Taf said, "the High Council has agreed to accept your request. Our starbridge will be opened to allow your spacecraft to journey to Earth. Furthermore, you will be permitted to return to Coyote via hyperspace once your mission is complete. Your ship's starbridge key will be temporarily adjusted to allow for this one-time use. However, any future access to Earth will depend upon the outcome of your expedition."

Jorge slowly let out his breath. Glancing at Inez, he saw relief upon her face as well. "Thank you, Taf Sa-Fhadda," Manny said, bowing ever so slightly. "I appreciate the Council's decision."

The *hjadd's* only response was to bow to the *chaaz'braan*. The ancient *askanta* started to leave, but then he paused to turn toward Inez again.

Sa'Tong qo, *daughter of a* **chaaz'maha.** *I hope you find what you're looking for.*

"*Sa'Tong qo, chaaz'braan.*" She pressed the palms of her hands together. "You honor us with your actions, and I will tell my father of our meeting once I find him."

A soft grunt, as if the *chaaz'braan* was amused by what she'd just said. *You misunderstand me. Your father is only your objective. What you're looking for is something else entirely.*

Then the Great Teacher slowly walked away, leaving Jorge to wonder what he'd meant by that.

Part 4

DEFIANCE

(from the memoirs of Sawyer Lee)

Once we got to Defiance, it took less than a day for Chris Levin and me to learn David Laird's whereabouts. But that knowledge cost us dearly.

We came into town aboard the steam sledge that made twice-weekly trips up into the Pioneer Valley. That time of year, deep snow covered the Midland Highway as it led into Gillis Range, making it impassable to any ground vehicles that weren't hovercraft or equipped with plowheads. Goat Kill Creek was frozen over, so a ferry was out of the question, and although I could have requisitioned a Corps skimmer, that wouldn't have fit the low profile we were trying to maintain.

So we caught the twin-deck sledge when it stopped at Carlos's Pizza, using cash instead of credit chits. It wasn't the most comfortable of rides; the seats were little more than plastic benches crowded together in the lower-deck compartment, and we were crammed in there with a dozen other passengers, mostly farmers and stockmen returning from New Florida or Albion. The rumble of the steam engine made conversation nearly impossible; whenever someone stood up, they'd have to grasp handrails or risk being thrown to the floor by the sledge's constant rocking upon its skids. I was just happy that Chris had had the foresight to buy box lunches before we left Carlos's Pizza; otherwise, we would've been starving as well as sore by the time the sledge arrived in Defiance.

We had both been there before, of course, yet it had been many years since the last time Chris had set foot in the town. That was during the war; he was a young man then, reunited with his family after making peace with Carlos Montero. In those days, Defiance was a small mountain village where the original colonists had fled following the Union occupation of New Florida: little more than a collection of tree houses nestled within the boughs of a blackwood grove, hidden from the searching eyes of Union Guard satellites.

Chris hadn't been back since the Revolution, so he was only vaguely aware that Defiance had become a large and prosperous agricultural community. The tree houses had vanished, replaced by wood-frame houses along tidy streets, with enormous greenhouses and livestock sheds on the outskirts of town allowing the locals to continue their livelihoods during the long winter months. When the sledge went west again, its hold would be packed with crates of corn, potatoes, sugar beets, tomatoes, and waterfruit, its refrigerator compartment stocked with beef, lamb, and chicken. The town proclaimed itself to be "the Breadbasket of the Provinces," and the fact that it had once been the sanctuary of the *Alabama* colonists was a source of civic pride as well.

Chris and I disembarked from the sledge at the depot and, carrying our packs over our shoulders, went in search of a place to stay. We had plenty of choices; Defiance had a lot of visitors, many of them businessmen like those we were pretending to be, so accommodations ranged from a large and fairly luxurious hotel in the town center to third-rate boardinghouses that catered mainly to migrant workers. We settled for a small inn located on a side street: not so fancy that our arrival would draw attention, but neither so seedy that we'd stand out. The innkeeper booked us into two rooms with a connecting door and a shared bathroom; we stayed just long enough to put away our bags before going out again to get a decent bite to eat and, not incidentally, begin our search for David Laird.

Or rather, for Peter Desilitz. Laird had disappeared the moment he'd left New Brighton, but when Chris searched government census records for Peter Desilitz, it came up as belonging to someone who, up until at least three years ago, had an address in Defiance. That surprised me; Desilitz had been Laird's alias when he was busted at the New Brighton spaceport, so I would have assumed that he'd have adopted a different pseudonym. When I mentioned this to Chris, though, he'd only grinned and shook his head.

"One of the things you learn when you're a proctor," he said, "is that there's no such thing as a 'criminal genius.' People who make a career out of breaking the law are usually too dumb to make an honest living . . . and dumb people tend to do the same dumb things over and over again."

"But still, using the same alias when you're trying to go underground . . ."

He shrugged. "He probably had a whole set of phony IDs under that name which would've been good enough to establish his bona fides while renting an apartment or getting a job. Not everyone makes background checks, y'know. He probably figured that, so long as he didn't do anything that would give a proctor a reason to search the provincial database, he could get away with it. In any case, the guy we're looking for isn't Laird, but Desilitz."

It made sense, or at least it does if you've got a lawman's mind-set. Once again, I realized that I'd made the right decision by letting Chris join me. Having a former chief proctor as a partner in a manhunt has its advantages. Nonetheless, as we stepped out onto the snow-packed streets of Defiance, I wondered how long it would take for us to track down Laird.

Indeed, I'd begun to have second thoughts about the whole thing. Early that morning, while we were waiting in Carlos's Pizza for the sledge to arrive, I'd checked in with Jon Parson. He'd told me that the *Mercator* had just lifted off from New Brighton and was on its way to Rho Coronae Borealis; I guessed that the expedition had probably gone through the starbridge by then, and my people would soon be meeting with the High Council. I had nothing but confidence in Jorge

Montero, and yet, at the same time, I kept wondering whether I should have led the expedition myself instead of taking a leave of absence from the Corps in order to look for someone I might never find.

Although we were hungry, Chris and I decided to postpone dinner until we'd found the place where Peter Desilitz was last known to have stayed. A rickshaw cab took us to a run-down tenement building near the outskirts of town. It looked like the sort of flats that itinerants would rent, but the foyer mailbox didn't have a card for either Desilitz or Laird. Chris rang the bell for the manager's apartment; when her voice came over the intercom, Chris claimed that he was an old friend of Peter's who happened to be passing through town, and asked if he was still around. A minute later, a door down the hall opened and the manager herself came to speak with us. The old crone was suspicious at first, but Chris turned on the charm, and she eventually told us that Desilitz had moved out about three years earlier. In fact, he'd left overnight, leaving behind his furniture and apparently taking only a couple of bags; he'd also stiffed her for a month's rent, which the landlady had collected by selling his belongings.

"So he's not in town anymore?" Chris feigned regret. "That's too bad. I was looking forward to having a drink with him."

"Not so far as I know." The landlady rubbed the tip of her blue-veined nose; it looked like she probably spent a sizable portion of her tenants' rent on bearshine. "Looked high and low for him, but even the boys at the bar don't know where he's gone." A crooked grin. "Or if they do, they ain't telling me."

"Yeah, could be." Chris shrugged. "Well, maybe if I talked to them, they might know something. Which bar did he usually hang out at?"

Her eyes narrowed as she pulled at an earlobe beneath her frizzled grey hair. "Y'know, it's right on the tip of my tongue, but I can't quite remember . . ."

"Maybe we can help out a little." Chris gave me a knowing wink.

"Seeing how we're old friends of his, the least we can do is pay the rent he stuck you for."

He'd already warned me that we might have to grease a few palms. I reached into my trouser pocket, pulled out my money clip. The manager's eyes glittered when she saw the cash. "Well, that's awful nice of you. I think it was . . . oh, three hundred, if I remember correctly."

I doubted that she did—in Liberty, C300 would be the monthly rent for an entire house—but she'd already figured out that we probably weren't who we were claiming to be, so there was no point in arguing with her. I peeled off a few bills, and her memory improved the moment they were in her callused hand. "Ah, yeah, now it's coming back to me . . . the Alabama Tavern, over on Pleasant."

"I know the place. About four or five blocks from here, right?" She nodded, and pointed in its general direction. "Thanks. Anyone there you think we should talk to? Maybe someone who'd know Peter?"

An indifferent shrug. "Just about any of the regulars, I reckon. He was there almost every night, after he got off work at the stockyards." Her gaze searched us. "That's what he was doing, y'know. Working in the barns, shoveling manure and the like . . . but I guess you already know that, don't you?"

"Sure. Just been a while since we've last seen him." Chris smiled. "Thanks again for your help. And, hey, if we catch up with him . . . anything you want us to tell him?"

"Not really." She was already counting the money in her hand. "Just that if he shows up around here again, he'd better find another place to stay. Ain't gonna be here."

Night was falling by the time we made our way to the Alabama Tavern. I hadn't been lying when I said that I knew the place. Back when I was a wilderness guide, it had been a bar I'd frequented when I'd found myself in Defiance. Provided, of course, that I was down on my luck and looking for a cheap watering hole; it wasn't the sort of nightspot where I'd take a client. And in the years that had passed since then, the tavern didn't look like it had changed very much.

We paused on the sidewalk across the street, gazing at yellowish light gleaming through its frost-rimmed windows. "This can be a rough place," I said quietly. "Sure you don't want me to handle this on my own?"

Chris looked at me askance. "You think I've never been in a bar before?"

"No, but . . ." I stopped, not knowing how to say what was on my mind. Chris Levin was a tough old boid, but nonetheless he was in his eighties by Gregorian reckoning. I wasn't anticipating any trouble, but in a dive like this, it paid to expect the unexpected.

"Never mind me." He opened his parka halfway. "If things get hairy, I've always got backup."

A Union Guard fléchette pistol was tucked into a shoulder holster beneath his left armpit, an antique that he'd kept in prime condition ever since he picked it up during the Revolution. I was carrying a Corps airpulse pistol, but Chris disdained nonlethal weapons: bad guys didn't take you seriously, he said, unless you were packing a gun that they knew could put an end to their lives. We weren't trigger-happy, but neither were we under the illusion that all our problems could be solved by sweet talk and a roll of cash.

We walked across the street, pushed open the heavy blackwood door. The Alabama Tavern was the same badly lit, smoke-filled beer joint that I remembered, with tough-looking men and women seated at tables or throwing darts near the fireplace. It was still early evening, so the room was only half-full. A few people looked up as we came in, but otherwise we didn't attract much attention. Which was what we wanted; nevertheless, I kept my hat on. There was always a chance that someone might recognize one of us, and the last thing we needed was to have word circulate through the bar that a Corps of Exploration senior officer and Liberty's former chief proctor had dropped in for a drink.

There were two vacant stools near the end of the bar. We took them, and Chris ordered a couple of pints of ale. The bartender seemed to do a double take; he might have vaguely remembered my face, but if he'd matched it with a name, he didn't say so. I sipped my beer while I glanced over the menu. Pretty much your usual tavern fare—sandwiches, stew, chili—but at least we'd get a bite to eat. If we were lucky, the cook might have bothered to wash his hands.

Chris and I ate in silence, pretending to ignore the regulars while letting them get used to the presence of a couple of strangers. More people began showing up, and it wasn't long before we had company. We made small talk with the locals, not giving our names but letting them know that we were sales reps from the Thompson Wood Company who'd come to town in hopes of landing new customers. After a little while, Chris got up from his stool and sauntered over to the dartboard; I remained at the bar, nursing my beer while commiserating with a couple of farmers about the hard winter we were having that year.

It wasn't all idle chatter, though. As I went from one conversation to another, now and then I'd mention Peter Desilitz, ever so casually saying that he was an old friend and wondering if anyone had seen him lately. As his former landlady had told us, he was well-known in the Alabama Tavern; whether he was well liked, though, was another matter entirely. It appeared that he was someone whom several people had known, yet almost no one had known well; he'd drifted into town a few years earlier, stayed for a while, then abruptly moved on again, leaving behind a string of unpaid debts. More than a few people scowled when I mentioned his name, and one guy went so far as to hit me up for the five colonials Pete had sponged from him the day before he disappeared.

This was all very interesting, but it wasn't getting me any closer to finding out where he'd gone. At one point, Chris walked past, giving me a quick tap on the shoulder as he headed for the men's room. We met there a couple of minutes later and, after quickly making sure that the stalls were vacant, quietly discussed what we'd learned. Which amounted to almost nothing, except that our quarry had split town almost as suddenly as he'd appeared, without even bothering to quit the job he'd been holding down at the stockyard.

"That's significant," Chris said. He was standing at the urinal, his back turned to me. "People don't vanish overnight unless they've got a good reason."

"Sounds to me like someone was after him for money." I glanced at the door. "From what I've been told, he was carrying enough IOUs to buy drinks for everyone out there."

"Maybe." He zipped his fly, turned toward the sink. "Or maybe someone learned who he really was, and he figured that it was time to leave before the truth got around." He gave me a stern look. "If that's the case, we'd better be careful."

"How come? If there's someone here who knows this . . ."

"Then they're keeping it to themselves . . . which means they could be as dangerous as he is." Chris finished rinsing his hands in the sink; he eyed a filthy towel hanging from the rack beside it and decided instead to wipe his hands on his trouser legs. "Just be careful, all right?"

Returning to the barroom, I bought another ale, then wandered over to the dartboard. A few minutes later I managed to pick up a game, and it was then that I got lucky.

"Yeah, I know Pete." The young guy with unwashed blond hair who'd consented to throw a few turns with me wore the mud-caked field jacket of someone who spent his days in the stables. "We worked together at Olson's . . . that's the stockyard a little ways from here. Why?"

"Oh, nothing." I took aim at the board, did my best to sink a dart into the bull's-eye. "Just that I haven't seen him in a long time, but from what I've heard, he left town in a big hurry."

"Yeah, well . . ." The kid shrugged, picked up the pint of ale he'd brought with him from the bar. "Think he had a reason to get outta here. And if you know him half as well as you say you do, you'd know what that is."

I tried not to look at him too sharply. This didn't sound like the usual gripe about an unpaid debt or a mooched drink. "I said I knew him. I didn't mean we were best friends, though. Why, is there something about him I should know?"

My companion didn't reply at once, but instead took a sip from his drink. From the corner of my eye, I noticed a couple of men standing near the fireplace. They were leaning against the mantel, apparently doing nothing more than observing our game; somehow, though, I had the feeling that their interest in us was more than casual.

"Maybe." The kid waited until I threw the last dart in my hand, then walked over to the target. He paused as if to study the arrangement I'd left on the board; I moved closer to join him. "Depends what you wanna know," he went on, dropping his voice to a near whisper. "You a proctor or something?"

I shook my head. "No . . . just someone who wants to find out where he went."

He slowly plucked the darts from the board, taking his time. "I can help you there," he muttered, "but it'll cost you."

"I can do that."

A faint smile. "Kinda what I thought." He juggled the darts from hand to hand, careful not to let the spears jab his fingers. "Finish the game, then we'll go. Not safe to talk here."

We left the tavern a few minutes later, by ourselves. That wasn't the way I wanted to make our exit, but when I'd looked around the crowded room, Chris was nowhere to be seen. The kid was nervous enough already that I didn't want to leave his side to go searching for Chris; the young man was our best shot at finding out what had happened to Laird, and I was afraid that, if he became aware I wasn't working alone, he'd disappear.

So we departed the Alabama Tavern without my letting Chris know where I'd gone. As we trudged down the snow-covered sidewalk, I glanced over my shoulder to see if we were being followed. Bear had begun to rise over the mountains, casting a cold blue radiance that made everything stand out; there were few streetlights in this part of town, with plenty of shadows in between, but the bearlight was bright enough to reveal anyone who might have left the tavern after we did. No one else was in sight, which made me feel a little better. All the same, though, I remembered Chris's warning; when the kid's back was turned to me, I quickly shifted my gun from my shoulder holster to the right pocket of my parka. No sense in taking chances . . . or at least no more than I was taking already.

The kid's name was Jake Turner, he told me as we walked to the stockyard, and he'd lived in Defiance all his life, born and bred in Midland to parents who'd come to Coyote during the last great immigration wave. I figured that he was about Inez's age, give or take a few months. When he was old enough to bring money into the house, he'd dropped out of school to go to work in the stockyards, where he'd done the sort of menial tasks a not-so-bright kid would do: feeding the animals, pitching hay, mucking out the stables, and so on. It was there that he'd met Peter Desilitz, who'd been hired to do much the same thing.

Jake didn't tell me more than that, though, until we reached the stockyards. We walked a short distance down an unlighted side street until we reached a row of long concrete sheds beside a fenced-in paddock. The sign hanging above the front gate read OLSON BROS. LIVESTOCK; the gate was locked, but Jake fished a key from his jacket pocket and used it to let us in. He led me past the first two sheds, then opened the side door of the third one in the row. The interior was dark and warm; I could smell hay, manure, and the strong aroma of animal fur.

Jake didn't turn on the ceiling lights, but instead found a lantern hanging from a post near the door. He switched it on, and within the circle cast by its wan glow I saw wooden stalls arranged in three long rows beneath the open rafters of a mountain-briar ceiling. Within the stalls were sheep: curly white Cotswolds, black and tan Suffolks, black-fleeced Romneys. They bleated when the lantern came on, and a few rose from their straw beds to approach the chest-high sides of their stalls, thinking perhaps it was time to be fed. Jake stroked the heads of the nearest ones, shushing them with a few soft words, then turned to me.

"Say you got money?" he asked, his voice low.

"Uh-huh." I reached into my pocket, pulled out my clip. "Fifty do you?"

He snorted. "C'mon, man . . . you can do better than that." He placed the lantern on a workbench beneath the windows, and I couldn't help but notice the pair of large and very sharp-looking shearing scissors that lay upon it. Jake probably didn't intend for them to be menacing, but nonetheless I was intimidated enough to be thankful for having moved my gun to a pocket where I could easily reach it.

"All right," I replied. "A hundred." Jake hesitated, perhaps wondering if he could bargain for more, then slowly nodded. A hundred colonials was probably more than he made in four weeks. I pulled five C20 bills from the clip, handed them to him. "Let's have it, then. What do you know about Desilitz?"

He took a moment to count the money, his lips moving silently, then shoved the cash in his pocket. "Couple'a years ago . . . naw, more than that, more like three or so . . . I was working here late, hosing down the shearing pen." He nodded toward a fenced-in oval near the center of the shed. "We'd spent the day collecting fleece, and the boss don't like it when we leave a mess. Some of the ladies get nervous, y'know, so there's always a lot of shit on the floor after . . ."

"Desilitz." I didn't want to sound impatient, but I hadn't come there to hear the details of the wool business.

"Yeah, okay. I was coming to that." Jake shifted from one foot to another; when he glanced out the window, I could tell he was nervous about being there. "Anyway, I'm working late, hosing down the place, when I hear some people talking out back. They're laughing a bit, and one of them says something about opening another jug, so I figure it's some'a the guys having a little get-together. We do that here sometimes, after we get off work. Break out the booze, light up a smoke, just, y'know . . ."

"Unwind. I understand."

"Right. So anyway, I put down the hose and walk over to the back door"—he cocked his head toward the other end of the barn—"but I stop before I go out 'cause . . . well, when I get there, I see through the window that one of 'em's Kyle Olson. That's the boss's son, and me and him never really got along all that good, if y'know what I mean."

I nodded, and he went on. "They're sitting around a trash-can fire, two or three guys with a couple'a jugs of bearshine between them, and even though I know all of 'em, I know they won't let me drink with them. I was still a kid then, y'know, and Kyle . . ."

"You and he don't get along. You told me."

"Yeah, right. But they're all pretty loaded, so I figure that, if I stick around long enough, maybe I can grab one of those jugs once they move on, help myself to whatever's left in it."

I smiled at that. Jake hadn't yet reached the age when he could walk into the Alabama Tavern, but he'd learned little tricks of stealing liquor from adults without getting caught. Something a bored stable boy would do. "So you decided to wait and see if they'd forget to take a jug with them."

"Yeah, that's it." Encouraged, he went on. "So I park myself on a hay bale where they can't see me through the window and listen in for a while. Now, one of 'em's Pete, and he's already pretty ripped and gettin' drunker by the minute. And, y'know, I liked him well enough, but . . . well, he'd never talked much about himself, except to say that he'd come from Earth 'bout the same time my folks did, and he'd been trying to get by ever since. This time, though, he gets to talking, telling the other guys a little more about who he is and why he's here and all that."

"And what did he say?"

Jake hesitated. "That he once killed a man."

That was all? I almost asked. David Laird had told the truth, yes . . . just not all of it. Indeed, he must have been stewed to admit that much. "I see. And who did he say he killed?"

"I dunno." The kid shrugged. "He didn't say his name . . . just that it was someone who'd done something wrong to him, and so he had it coming." Jake seemed to think it over, then added, "I kinda got the idea that the other guy mighta been someone big, 'cause he said that the proctors really wanted him bad. 'They're not gonna give up till they get me,' was what he said."

"Did he say that Peter Desilitz wasn't his real name?"

Jake's eyes widened. "You mean it isn't? Who is he?"

I let that pass, at least for the time being. "Never mind. So what happened then? How did the other guys take it?"

"You mean, did they get pissed off or something?" Again, a non-committal shrug. "Nah. Kyle's never been totally on the up-and-up, and neither has his ol' man. Ever since his uncle died . . . his dad's brother was the one who started the business . . . the two of 'em have been getting into some pretty sleazy stuff. Things that don't have too much to do with the family business." Jake shook his head. "Look, what the Olsons do ain't none of my business. I'm just sayin', if Pete . . . or whatever his name is . . . wanted to tell someone else that he was wanted for murder, then he couldn't have picked anyone better than Kyle and his buddies."

"What do you mean?"

"Well, Kyle tells him that he understands where he's comin' from, and that if he ever needs any help, he'd be willing to give him a hand." A knowing smile. "Maybe that sounds weird, but you gotta understand, Pete and Kyle had been pretty tight ever since Pete showed up. This ain't the first time I seen 'em been drinking together, so maybe it was just a matter of time before Pete fessed up. And like I said, the Olsons don't have any particular fondness for proctors."

A picture was beginning to form in my mind. Perhaps Laird hadn't been careless after all but rather quite cunning. After making his way to Defiance and establishing himself as an itinerant worker, he'd deliberately sought out others on the wrong side of the law. He must have figured that, sooner or later, the full truth about his involvement in the *Lee*'s destruction would come to light, and when that happened, the proctors would begin searching for him again. If he was going to remain one step ahead of the authorities, he'd need help . . . and that meant confiding in someone who'd be in a position to do so.

As luck would have it, one of those people happened to be the very person who was paying his salary. Kyle Olson might be a sleaze, and so was his father, but the fact of the matter was that they owned a stockyard in a large farm town. Not only did they have money, but also connections on both sides of the law. Just what Laird needed if he was going to make a clean getaway.

Chris was wrong. There might not be such a thing as a criminal genius, but you didn't need to be a genius to use someone to your own advantage. Just able to lie with a straight face.

"So what then?" I asked. "Did Pete ask him for a favor?"

"Yup." Jake nodded. "He asked him to . . ."

From somewhere beyond the open door, a new sound: the quiet crunch of footsteps against the snow. Jake froze, stopping himself in midsentence. We listened for a moment, and although we didn't hear anything, I suddenly realized that we'd made a mistake. The lantern was too close to the window. Anyone walking by outside would be able to tell someone was in here.

"Put out the light," I murmured.

The kid was just beginning to reach for the lantern, though, when we heard the footsteps again, much closer this time. An instant later, a figure appeared in the doorway, his features visible in the lamplight.

"Hello, Jake," he said. "What brings you out here so late?"

I recognized him immediately: one of the two men who'd been near the fireplace when I'd met Jake in the tavern. As he stepped into the shed, I saw his companion just behind him.

"Uh, ah . . . hi, Kyle." If I had any doubts about who the first person was, they were eliminated by Jake's stammering voice. "Not . . . I mean, not much. Just thought I'd . . . y'know, check on the animals, make sure they weren't . . . y'know, that they had enough water and . . ."

"They've got enough water. I had you fill the troughs this afternoon, remember?" Olson peered at him, his hands shoved in his jacket pockets. "Or is there some other reason I should know about?"

By Gregorian reckoning, Kyle Olson was in his midforties, a thickset man whose goatee framed a humorless mouth. His friend was tall and wiry, with the sort of face that reminds me of a horse. Both wore wide-brimmed hats pulled low over their foreheads, as if to hide their faces as much as possible.

"Well . . . uh, yeah." Seeing a possible excuse, Jake grabbed for it. "Actually, my friend here . . ." He glanced at me and stopped, suddenly realizing that I'd never told him my name. "He said that . . . um . . ."

"George Johnson," I said, picking up the thread. "I'm with the Thompson Wood Company. Jake said that you might be interested in purchasing a supply of faux-birch for refurbishing your stalls, and I figured I might come out here to take some . . ."

"No." Olson shook his head. "No, that's not true. Not from what Gary and I heard you talking about in the Alabama . . . and it sure as hell wasn't what we heard Jake tell you just a second ago."

We'd been followed from the tavern; that much was obvious. Perhaps I hadn't seen them, but these two men didn't need to shadow us to figure out where Jake was going to take me. All they'd needed to do was see a dim light within the window of one of the livestock sheds and approach quietly enough to be able to eavesdrop on our conversation.

As casually as possible, I slid my hands into my jacket pockets. Yet my fingertips had barely touched the pistol grip when Olson's right hand jerked from his own pocket. The lean barrel of a fléchette pistol was pointed straight at my chest.

"Whatever you got there," he said, "just take it out nice and slow and drop it on the ground. And then we're going to"—a pause, as his mouth stretched into an ugly grin—"talk some more."

By then, I was having serious regrets about not having told Chris where I'd gone. Yet there was no question that I was on my own; Jake was cowering beside the workbench, his hands half-raised from his sides even though the other two men weren't paying much attention to him. So I did as Olson said and carefully withdrew the airpulse gun from my pocket and tossed it on the floor between us.

Gary bent down to hastily snatch it away from me. "Hey, what is this?" he muttered, turning it over in his gloved hands. "Ain't seen nothin' like it before, have you?"

Carefully keeping his pistol trained on me, Olson glanced sideways at him. "I know what it is," he said after a moment. "That's"—his eyes narrowed as he sought for the right word—"an airpulse gun. Beakheads make 'em." He looked at me again. "The only people who carry 'em are blueshirts and proctors. Is that what you are?"

Beakheads was a racial slur for aliens; some of the backwoods gentry thought all extraterrestrials looked like the *hjadd*, so the word was applied to ETs regardless of their origin. "No, I'm not," I replied. There was no purpose served by hiding my identity any longer; I was in a tight spot, and these yokels ought to know the truth. "I'm General Sawyer Lee, commandant of the Corps of Exploration."

Olson's mouth fell open, and for a moment his pistol seemed to waver. Nor was he the only one surprised by what I'd said. "I . . . I didn't know!" Jake blurted out, taking a step forward. "I swear, he didn't tell me who he . . . !"

"Shut up." Olson glared at the kid, and he shrank back against the bench, raising his hands even higher. Jake had seen too many vids; he wasn't armed, so there was no point in keeping his hands up. Gary was staring at me, my gun still in his hands. "Lemme see that thing," Olson said. "Here . . . switch with you. But don't let him outta your sights."

Gary nodded, then the two men exchanged weapons, neither of them looking away from me for even a second. I remained passive as they made the trade; once my gun was in Olson's hands, he seemed to relax a little, studying the *nord* weapon with admiration. "Nice . . . very nice," he said after a moment. "I hear these things shoot nuthin' but air. Is that so?"

I didn't like the way he was handling it, so I kept quiet. Perhaps I should have said something, because Olson's curiosity was matched only by his cruelty. "Let's see if that's true," he said, then he leveled the pistol at Jake and squeezed the trigger.

A soft *whomp!* of discharged air, then an invisible fist slammed into the kid's chest. At such close range, the shot was particularly violent; Jake was lifted off his feet, thrown against the bench behind him. The back of his head connected with the table edge; the lantern rocked upon its base, and the shearing scissors fell off the bench, but not before Jake slumped to the floor and lay still.

"Wow! That's really something!" Olson laughed like a brat who'd just found a new toy and hadn't wasted any time using it for malicious purposes. "This is a keeper!"

"You didn't have to do that." I glanced at Jake; the kid was unconscious, and I could only hope that he hadn't been more severely hurt.

"No? Well, I'm not done yet." Olson pointed the gun at me. "Wonder what it would do if I got even closer . . ."

"Kyle . . ." Gary was clearly unnerved by what he'd seen and heard. "Man, didn't you hear what he just said? He's a general. Not just that, but he's also in charge of the Corps. You don't screw around with . . ."

"Put a clamp on it, willya?" Olson was unimpressed. He had my gun; in his mind, that was his trump card. "No one knows we're here, and no one has to find out either." His grin became repulsive. "We got some big ol' sows in the next barn, and they're not too picky about what they eat. Not when it's all nice and chopped up for 'em."

He might have only been bluffing, but I couldn't take that chance. "Kyle, if anything happens to me, someone will find out. Count on it." I kept my voice even, trying not to show that I was beginning to fear for my life. "So far, all you've done is knock out the kid and hold me at gunpoint. Let it go at that, and no one has to . . ."

Olson's forefinger curled around the trigger again. "What you can count on, General whatever your name is, is becoming pigshit unless you tell me why you're lookin' for Pete."

"You want the truth?" I stared back at him, ignoring the gun as much as possible. "All right, then . . . your friend Pete isn't who he said he is. His real name is David Laird, and he's responsible for the bomb that destroyed the *Robert E. Lee* nineteen years ago. It's taken a long time for us to find out who built it, but now we know, and that's why I'm searching for him." I paused, then added, "And if you've got any sense, you'll put that gun down and tell me what Laird asked you to do for him."

Olson said nothing for a second or two. The gun didn't move an inch, but it was clear that he was thinking it over. Gary was convinced, though, because he started to lower the fléchette pistol. "He's not foolin', Kyle. This is way over our heads. Maybe we should . . ."

"Point that goddamn gun at him!" Olson snapped, and Gary jerked to obey his order. "He's lyin'! I knew Pete, and so did you, and if all he did was kill a proctor . . ."

"He was lying," I said. "He killed a lot more people than that . . . everyone aboard the *Lee*, including the *chaaz'maha* . . ."

"Well, hell . . ." His expression became a smirk. "No loss there, so far as I'm concerned. I can't stand those damn *Sa'Tong*ians." He shook his head. "And even if what you say is true, no Olson ever rats out a pal. Me and Pete hoisted a few jugs together. As far as I'm concerned, that makes you nothin' but a—"

"Drop the guns!"

I couldn't see Chris, but his voice from somewhere in the darkness beyond the shed's open door was the best thing I'd ever heard. Olson's back was turned to the door, so someone yelling from behind him caused him to jump . . . and then Gary whipped around, raised his pistol, and fired blindly in Chris's general direction.

Bad mistake. His fléchettes did little more than splinter some wood from the doorframe. An instant later, there were two soft *whufts!* from outside. Gary grabbed at his chest; a red blotch had already begun to spread beneath his fingers as he sagged and fell forward. He'd barely hit the floor when Chris called out again.

"Drop it! Or you get the next one!"

For a second, I thought Olson was going to take his chances. But apparently he thought better of it, because he slowly extended his right arm away from me and opened his hand, letting my gun fall from his grasp.

"Kick it away," Chris demanded, and Olson obeyed by nudging the airpulse pistol with the toe of his right boot. That was enough for me; I reached down to retrieve my weapon, careful not to take my eyes off him. Olson had just enough common sense, though, to know better than to try to jump me. He'd seen how quickly his friend had been dropped, and whoever was outside the barn doubtless had a dead bead on the back of his neck.

Once I had Olson covered, Chris stepped into view. He cautiously entered the shed, his fléchette pistol gripped in both hands, carefully looking around to make sure no one else was waiting to ambush him. "Are they the only two?" he asked.

"Uh-huh. Just them and the kid over there." I nodded toward Jake, who still lay on the floor near Gary. "Where the hell did you come from?"

"I spotted you leaving the bar, and I was about to catch up with you when I saw these two guys tailing you. Had a hunch they were up to no good, so I followed them here." He frowned at me. "Next time, don't take off on your own like that."

"Sorry, but . . ." I let it go. We could argue about it later. Instead, I waited until I was sure that Chris had Olson under control, then I hurried over to Jake. Kneeling beside him, I took off my left glove, rested my fingertips against the side of his neck. His skin was warm, and I felt a pulse. Good. I was afraid that he might have broken his neck.

Gary, on the other hand, was all but dead. The razor-sharp barbs had ripped through the front of his field jacket and penetrated his chest. He was bleeding out from his lungs; his face had gone white, and bright pink bubbles foamed around his mouth with every ragged breath he took. Whatever life was left in him was fading fast. As I stood over him, I saw his eyelids flutter, then he coughed up some blood and was still.

"This one's gone," I murmured.

"Son of a bitch." Kyle's hands were raised above his head, and he trembled with fury as he watched his friend die. "He didn't mean no . . ."

He didn't get to finish whatever he was about to say, because Chris came forward to bring the butt of his pistol down against his forehead. Kyle cried out and staggered backward; reaching for the ugly welt that had opened above his right eye, he lost his balance and toppled to the floor, landing on his ass between Jake and Gary.

"Don't worry about him." Chris bent down to grab him by his jacket collar and throw him against a bench leg. "Worry about yourself, or so help me, I'll . . ."

"Chief. Stop." I saw what Olson saw: the murderous expression on the old man's face, the utter lack of sympathy. One man was dead already; I was afraid there would soon be another. "He . . ."

"Take care of the kid," Chris snarled, his eyes never leaving Olson's as he squatted in front of him. "Let me handle this one." The younger man was shaking; there was no ignoring the gun barrel that hovered only inches from his face. "Talk! Tell me what you did with David Laird!"

Olson hastily shook his head. "I don't . . . I don't . . . who's . . . ?"

"You called him Pete, and you damn well know where he went!" Chris yanked him forward by his collar, slammed him against the bench again. "He didn't tell you that stuff for no reason! He was looking for help! Now tell me what you did, or . . . !"

"I sent him away!" Olson's voice became a terrified whine. Where there had once been a bully was now only a coward quivering. "I . . . he said he had money . . . money he'd stashed away, and all he needed was a way out of town. Some place where no one would find him. So I got him on a boat . . ."

As he spoke, I heard Jake groan. Looking around, I saw him begin to stir. The kid was coming to; no doubt he was in considerable pain. Turning away from Chris and his captive, I knelt beside him again. "Easy, boy," I murmured, putting down my gun to help him roll over. "Relax. You're going to be all right . . ."

"A boat to where?" Another thud from behind me; Chris had just slammed Olson against the bench again. "Where did you send him?"

"Nava . . . Navajo." Olson was trying hard to remember something he'd done three years earlier. "Yeah, that's it. Manuelito, I think. Some town in Navajo where we . . . my dad's company, I mean . . . ship breeding stock. I took his money, got him a ride out there . . ."

Suddenly, what everyone who'd met Peter Desilitz had told us about him was beginning to make sense. All the unpaid debts, the rent he'd skipped: he wasn't pissing it away on ale but was squirreling away money to buy passage aboard a freighter that would take him to the other side of the world. A frontier settlement on Navajo, as far from the central provinces as you could possibly get.

"What . . . ?" Jake opened his eyes, peered at me with bleary confusion. "Who's . . . how did you . . . ?"

"It's all right." I reached around to the back his head. He had a lump the size of a grasshoarder egg, but I didn't find any blood. He'd have a bad headache, but that was all. "We got help, that's all. You're going to be . . ."

"Manuelito?" Chris demanded. "Are you . . . ?"

He abruptly stopped, and in the next instant I heard a sudden, agonized gasp. Looking around, I saw him rear back on his haunches, his left hand reaching up to grab at something that Olson had shoved against his chest. There was an evil leer on the stockman's face as he thrust his arm forward, but it wasn't until Chris fell back that I saw what the object was: the shearing scissors, its long blades protruding from Chris's heart.

Twisting away from Jake, I snatched at where I'd carelessly left my gun on the floor beside me. Olson saw me; kicking Chris aside, he made a grab for the old man's fléchette pistol. This time, though, he didn't have the advantage of surprise. I got off a shot before he was able to lay a hand on Chris's weapon. The pulse knocked the gun away from him; another shot threw him headfirst against the wall and made him lie still.

I scrambled on my hands and knees over to Chris. He lay on his back, left hand loosely wrapped around the scissors. I knew better than to pull them out, but even if I had, it wouldn't have made any difference. Blood, dark red in the wan light of the lantern, pumped from around the edges of its blades and seeped from the corners of his mouth, and when I crouched beside him, I saw the color fading from his face.

"Get . . . him . . ." he whispered. Then he closed his eyes.

That was the last thing he said.

I sent Jake to find a proctor, making sure that he'd tell him to bring a doctor as well. Chris was beyond medical assistance, but I knew that someone would have to officially pronounce both him and Gary dead.

Jake appeared reluctant—all he wanted to do was put as much distance between him and the stockyard as he could and never come back again—yet one look at my face, and he knew that he'd better do as he was told.

Once he was gone, I found an old blanket lying across one of the stalls and used it to cover Chris. Gary didn't get the same courtesy. I removed the scissors from my friend's chest, careful to wear my gloves as I did so, but otherwise left the scene undisturbed. The proctors would want to know everything that happened, and although I'd have Jake to back up my version of the events, I didn't want there to be any lingering doubts whether I'd killed either of the two men.

Nonetheless, I found myself standing above Kyle Olson for a few minutes. There were two fléchette pistols within easy reach; either of them could put an end to his existence before he even woke up, and I doubted that anyone besides his family would mourn his death. But I didn't have it in me to commit murder, so I found a roll of twine and used it to bind his hands and feet. He remained unconscious throughout, unaware of my deliberations.

I sat on the floor beside Chris for a while. He'd come with me to this place to find the man who'd killed his best friend, only to meet his own fate. A lousy way to die, stabbed to death by a punk in a foulsmelling sheep shed. He'd been a good man, one of the last of the original colonists. He deserved better than this.

It was hard to look at him, so I pushed myself to my feet and, for lack of anything else to do, walked over to the pens to see how the sheep were doing. Remarkably, they'd remained quiet during the entire thing. Most of them were asleep, and the few who'd witnessed the killing of two men had done so in silence, passive observers who cared little about what humans did to one another in their little world. I envied them.

With no one except the animals to keep me company, I walked over to the door and leaned against the frame. The stars were out, with Bear high in the night sky. As I waited for someone to show up, though, I found myself looking to the east. Toward Navajo, where David Laird had gone.

I remembered Chief Levin's last words; I knew what he'd meant. And I also knew that I had one more death to avenge.

Book 4

The Homecoming

We won't find anywhere as nice as Earth unless we go to another star system . . . It is important for the human race to spread out into space for the survival of the species. Life on Earth is at the ever-increasing risk of being wiped out by a disaster, such as sudden global warming, nuclear war, a genetically engineered virus, or other dangers we have not yet thought of.

—STEPHEN HAWKING,
speech at Hong Kong University of Science and Technology, June 2006

Part 5

THE LOST CITY

Like a silver wedding band lost from the finger of some celestial giant, Starbridge Earth hovered in its Lagrange-point orbit near the Moon. Infrequently visited by the maintenance crews who came out every so often to repair micrometeorite damage and check long-dormant electronic systems, the hyperspace portal hadn't been opened in nineteen years. All but forgotten, it was a silent reminder of a brief time when people from Earth had traveled to the stars, only to have the door slammed in their faces.

A hundred miles away, the gatehouse was just as silent. A spindle-like collection of modules and solar vanes, its only sign of life were the blue and red navigational beacons that flashed at each end; its windows were dark, and the air inside was stale and cold. Yet the station was not entirely dead. Electricity trickled through its circuits, maintaining the low-power current necessary to keep the comps from decaying. Many years had passed since the last time the station had been occupied, though, and no one knew whether it would ever be used again.

There had been suggestions over the years that both the starbridge and its gatehouse should be dismantled, its components auctioned off as scrap metal. After all, the starbridge led in only one direction, and that way was now closed, for reasons unbeknownst to those who'd been left behind. Yet individuals with long memories and foresight had prevailed; there was always a chance, however remote, that Starbridge Coyote might become active and a ship might yet emerge from hyperspace. When that day came, the mystery would be solved; for that reason alone, they argued, the starbridge should remain operational, its gatehouse ready to accept and respond to a signal transmitted by an incoming vessel.

So Starbridge Earth stayed where it was, the nearby gatehouse its only companion. In the darkness of the eternal night, their comps murmured to each other like an old married couple muttering in their sleep. Day after day, week after week, year after year, they dozed among the stars, waiting to be awakened.

And then, all of a sudden . . .

On a flatscreen within the gatehouse control room, a red light flashed. It blinked several times, the only source of illumination in the dark compartment, before it was replicated by other lights on other screens. A few seconds later, lines of type began to scroll down the screens, unread by human eyes yet nonetheless significant to the artificial intelligence that had stood vigil for nearly two decades. Within moments, various comps were roused from their diagnostic subroutines, each performing automatic procedures programmed in their memories; one comp was dead, its systems decayed beyond self-repair through years of disuse, but relays were hastily rerouted, and its chores were quickly assumed by its companions. In the meantime, the master AI performed the series of rapid and inhumanly complex calculations that only a quantum computer was capable of making without error.

Ten seconds after the first light glimmered on the comp screen, a command was sent to the starbridge. Deep inside the ring, comps responded to instructions they hadn't received in decades. Zero-point energy generators stirred, sending power through the hundreds of miles of wires packed like ganglia inside the giant torus. Within moments, starbridge was fully awake, its interior quietly humming with anticipation.

Almost as an afterthought, the gatehouse AI sent a signal to the

Moon. A brief and simple message, to be received by a comp within the space-traffic control station at Copernicus Centre. Yet the message went unheeded; the room was unoccupied at that particular moment, its most recent shift having gone to bed several hours earlier, and so the transmission from Starbridge Earth wasn't noticed for quite some time, and even then only after a technician chanced to glance at the automatic logbook and spot an anomaly. By then, many other things had happened.

Light swirled within the center of the starbridge, quickly becoming a kaleidoscopic funnel opening into hyperspace. A brilliant flash from the depths of the wormhole, then a small vessel plunged forth from the spacetime rift.

Jorge opened his eyes, took a deep breath. His second jaunt through a starbridge hadn't been as bad as his first, but he still wasn't accustomed to its violence. This time, at least, McAlister hadn't needed to warn him not to look when the *Mercator* went through the wormhole; Jorge still felt a touch of vertigo, but he knew that it would pass.

"Glad to see we got through," he murmured.

"You didn't think we would?" From the left side of the cockpit, McAlister gave him an amused glance. "Believe me, if this starbridge weren't operational, we'd still be in orbit around Hjarr. There's no way we could've made the jump." He reached up to snap a couple of toggles on the overhead console. "I'm just surprised that it's still functional. I would've bet that someone would have shut it down by now."

"You didn't say that before we left."

"Didn't want to jinx the mission." The pilot gave his console a quick inspection, then turned his head toward the passenger compartment. "Everyone all right back there?"

"We're fine," Greg replied, raising his voice to be heard. "Just don't do that again anytime soon, okay?"

McAlister laughed out loud, but Jorge was no longer paying attention. Through the cockpit windows, he caught sight of something that, until little more than a week ago, he never thought he'd see with his own eyes. Just off the port side was a broad, silver-grey crescent, its sunlit side marred by craters, rills, and vast basalt plains. The Moon . . . and beyond that, in the far distance, a blue-green orb, flecked with bands and swirls of white, that vaguely resembled Coyote save for its enormous oceans.

Earth.

He'd seen pictures of it throughout his life, but even though it was a world his father and grandparents had known well and told him about, somehow he'd always thought of it as a mythical place, no more a part of his daily experience than a bedtime story he'd heard in childhood. And yet there it was, as tangible as the seat in which he was sitting, more beautiful than he'd ever expected.

"Nice, huh?" McAlister murmured, and Jorge looked around to see that the pilot was following his gaze through the windows. "It's been a while for me . . . but this is your first time, so I can only imagine what it's like for you."

"Uh-huh." Jorge couldn't think of anything else to say. Words failed him.

"Yeah, well . . . we've got a long way to go, so let's get to work." McAlister rested his left hand upon the keyboard between their seats and, studying the comp screens before him, began entering navigation coordinates. "Get on the com, see if you can pick up any chatter. Try the K*u* band . . . that's the one most commonly used by local space traffic. Even if Vargas is right, and there's no one on the gatehouse, someone must have noticed our arrival."

Jorge nodded as he turned toward the communications panel. Switching the frequency finder to the appropriate channel, he slowly turned the knob first one way, then the other. Distant voices, rendered almost unintelligible by static, came through his headset, yet he heard nothing that sounded like a message being sent to an unknown spacecraft that had just emerged from the starbridge.

"Not getting anything," he said. "At least, not anything that's meant for us."

"I'm not surprised," Vargas said from behind them, and Jorge looked around to see that he'd left his seat to come forward. The former Union Astronautica pilot floated in midair behind him and McAlister, holding on to a ceiling rung as he gazed over their shoulders. "Even if the AI transmitted a signal to Copernicus, there's only half a chance that anyone's even listening."

Jorge didn't miss the irate expression on McAlister's face. He clearly didn't like to have passengers visit the cockpit uninvited, and Vargas even less so. Vargas was the mission's guide, though, so there was little McAlister could say about his presence. "What, you think their traffic controllers are asleep or something?"

"I wouldn't doubt it. There's just not as many spacecraft out here as there used to be, and the ones that are follow pretty rigid schedules." With his free hand, Vargas pointed to the local-time chronometer just below the center window: it read 0232 GMT. "That's the wee hours of the morning at Copernicus. Five bucks says the graveyard shift is sacked out."

Jorge had no idea what bucks were, but it didn't sound like a bet he was willing to take. He looked at McAlister. "If he's right, then no one knows we're here. I'd like to keep it that way."

"You're not going to contact anyone?" Vargas asked.

"I'd rather be discreet, at least until we have a better idea of where things stand. Someone may eventually figure out we're here, but . . ."

"Oh, I'm sure someone *will* figure it out, sooner or later. But until they do . . ." Vargas shrugged. "Yeah, you'd do well to maintain radio silence. With any luck, we'll be a long way from here before anyone gets around to trying to locate and track us."

"My thoughts exactly," McAlister said. While the other men were talking, he had finished entering the coordinates into the nav system.

He pressed the key marked EXEC, and luminescent figures appeared on the center screen. "All right now, hold tight . . ."

"Hey!" Vargas snapped. "How about a little warning?"

McAlister grinned, the only sign that he wasn't ignoring him. Grasping the yoke with his left hand, the pilot gently pushed the throttle bar forward. A hollow thrum from the rear of the spacecraft as its main engine ignited, then Jorge felt himself being pushed back into his seat. Vargas yelped as he grabbed another ceiling rung for support; reaction-control thrusters fired to adjust the shuttle's trajectory, and an instant later the view through the cockpit windows changed as Earth and the Moon gradually shifted positions.

Their next stop was Earth.

Once the *Mercator* achieved cruise velocity, it would take a little less than seven hours for the shuttle to reach its destination. McAlister fired the nuclear main engine until the shuttle reached 1-g. This used up most of the shuttle's fuel, but since he was counting on replenishing the hydrogen tanks from Earth's atmosphere once they arrived, there was no point in holding anything in reserve beyond what he'd need to make a safe landing. Besides, if someone on the Moon was alerted to the *Mercator*'s presence, the additional speed would make it harder for the shuttle to be located and tracked.

Yet there was no need to worry. While everyone except McAlister and him slept, Jorge had continued to monitor the space communications network, roaming across the different radio bands as he sought to detect any conversations that might indicate that someone had become aware of an unusual event that had occurred at Starbridge Earth. All he had heard, though, was normal comlink chatter, and remarkably little even of that. It was as if traffic between Earth and the Moon had become a fraction of what it had once been. Indeed, he and McAlister spotted only one other craft: a distant, starlike object that went by in the other direction, probably a lunar freighter making a routine outbound flight.

"After the bridge went down, that was pretty much it for the off-world colonies," Vargas explained. He lounged in his seat in the passenger compartment, his outstretched legs crossed together and floating in the center aisle. Now that the shuttle was no longer accelerating, its interior had returned to free-fall conditions. "It was . . . well, the last straw, I guess you could say. The Western Hemisphere Union had collapsed, the European Alliance was barely holding together, the Pacific Coalition was in ruins, and just about everything else was a mess. Without access to 47 Uma, there was nowhere for refugees to go. It wasn't long before the lunar and Martian colonies became overcrowded, and after a while the various governments back home got tired of supporting them when they were having so much trouble feeding their own people."

"So they pulled out and left the colonies to fend for themselves?" Jorge shifted restlessly in his seat. Although he'd taken a break from monitoring the comlink to catch a nap in the passenger compartment, the larger couch wasn't much more comfortable. "I suppose that makes sense."

"But Copernicus Centre is still there." Inez shook her head, not quite understanding what Vargas had said. "So are the Mars colonies . . . or at least that's what you told us before."

"Oh, sure, they're still there. So's Highgate, for that matter." Vargas shrugged. "But when the governments pulled out, their own economies collapsed. It wasn't long before most people there decided that enough was enough." A grim smile. "Life on Earth might be tough, but at least you didn't have to pay for the air you breathed or the water you drank . . . and everyone had forgotten how much those had been subsidized by the Earth governments."

"So the colonies emptied out?" Jorge asked.

"Pretty much, yeah." Vargas took a sip from the water bulb in his hand. "They're still self-sufficient, more or less . . . a little more so, now that they don't have so many of their own mouths to feed . . . but some of the smaller settlements have become ghost towns, and even Highgate only has half the population it once did." A wry grin. "Another reason why I was able to steal the *Guevara* so easily. Hardly anyone left in the Jupiter colonies, y'know, so no one really gave a damn about a freighter on its way to the junkyard."

"Hard to believe that people aren't leaving Earth anymore," Inez said. "When I was a little girl, I was taught that humankind became a spacefaring race several centuries ago. And most of the Talus races were traveling the galaxy long before that."

"Yeah, well . . ." Vargas crushed the empty bulb within his fist. "You can thank your dear old dad for this. Once he set himself up as a messiah, he managed to convince a lot of people that they didn't belong out here." He absently batted the bulb back and forth between his hands. "That's how the whole thing got started . . . him preaching about how we all needed to convert to *Sa'Tong*, come home from the Moon and Mars, start raising corn and beans . . ."

"I don't believe you." Inez stared at him. "A *chaaz'maha* would never insist that anyone convert to *Sa'Tong*. It's not a religion, and we don't have messiahs. And my father wouldn't . . ."

"Uh-huh, sure." Vargas regarded her with patronizing contempt. "And when was the last time you talked to your old man?"

"That's enough." Jorge said. "Leave her father out of this. Your only job is to help us find him."

Vargas glared at him, and for a moment Jorge thought the former pilot was going to challenge him. But then Greg moved a little closer; floating in the back of the compartment, the sergeant had been quiet throughout the conversation, but he was clearly prepared to back up the expedition leader. Vargas noticed Dillon hovering nearby; apparently realizing that he was outnumbered, he slowly raised his hands.

"Calm down, Lieutenant." An easy smile appeared on his face. "Not trying to start anything." He glanced at Inez. "My apologies. No offense intended."

Inez didn't respond, but instead turned back around in her seat. Jorge was about to tell Vargas to keep his opinion to himself when he heard McAlister call down to the flight deck.

"We're about an hour away from ETA," McAlister said. "I'll be commencing braking maneuvers soon. Jorge, I'm going to need you here. The rest of you, stow everything that's loose."

"Thanks, Captain. On my way." One last look at Vargas, then Jorge unbuckled his seat harness and, pushing himself down the center aisle, headed for the cockpit.

Night lay heavy upon the North Atlantic, the first light of dawn just reaching the Azores, as the *Mercator* entered the atmosphere midway between Europe and America. As the shuttle's wings sliced into the thin air of the ionosphere, its hull trembled, and a reddish orange corona began to form around its bow. Jorge felt himself being pushed back into the copilot's seat as never before; every breath demanded a conscious effort, and his body seemed to weigh a ton. He didn't realize that he was groaning, though, until McAlister said something about it.

"I'd appreciate it if you'd cut that out." The pilot had the yoke gripped tight with both hands, his gaze fixed upon the translucent prism of the heads-up display. "This is"—a sudden jolt—"hard enough as is, and you're distracting me."

"Sorry." Jorge clenched his teeth and tried not to think about the glowing plasma sheath that had wrapped itself around cockpit windows, rendering invisible the darkened limb of the planet. Glancing at the heads-up display, he saw the tiny holographic circle that jiggled within a slightly larger square. Most of the shuttle's major systems were under comp control at this point, but McAlister had told him that the trick to getting the *Mercator* safely through the atmosphere lay in keeping the circle within the square. It seemed easy, almost like a child's pad game, but the pilot's knuckles were white, the tendons of his wrists and hands clearly visible.

The spacecraft shook and rattled for a few minutes longer, then abruptly everything calmed down. Looking up again, Jorge saw that the fiery glow had disappeared, leaving behind a slightly curved horizon only a bit darker than the star-flecked sky above. McAlister let out his breath. "There . . . that's the worst of it. We're in the upper stratosphere now." He reached forward with his right hand, snapped three switches set in a row, then flipped open the safety cover above a fourth switch and snapped it as well. A muted roar from somewhere behind them, and the shuttle trembled slightly before settling down again. "Main engine off," he added. "We'll ride the rest of the way in on the jets."

"Sure . . . okay." Jorge felt his tension begin to ease. Unfortunately, his weight didn't do the same, or at least not by much. The sluggish sensation he felt was no longer being caused by engine thrust but by Earth's own gravity, a little more than one-third higher than Coyote's. *How can anyone live like this?* he thought.

"Good. Now make yourself useful and pull up the charts. I'd like to get a fix on where we are and where we're going." When Jorge hesitated, McAlister impatiently reached over to type a command into the nav comp. Its screen changed, displaying a false-color map of the northern hemisphere; a tiny crosshatch above the Atlantic marked the *Mercator*'s present position. "Use the trackball to zero in on us," he said, returning both hands to the yoke, "and tell me when we're on course for Massachusetts."

Jorge moved the trackball as McAlister indicated. The display expanded, with the crosshatch becoming larger. He peered at the lines of type that appeared beside it. "Umm . . . we're at 39.5 degrees North, 49 degrees West, altitude 42.8 miles."

"Very good," McAlister said. "Now give me the coordinates for Boston. You don't have to be precise, or at least for now . . . just enough so we don't end up somewhere in North Carolina."

Jorge turned the trackball to the left, changing the screen until he located the Massachusetts coast. "Boston is . . . um, 42.3 degrees North, 71 degrees West."

"Excellent." Watching the eight ball in the center of his console, McAlister carefully twisted the yoke to the right, making a slow starboard turn. "Thank you. Now keep watching the screen and give me a readout on our position and altitude every few minutes."

Navigating turned out to be easier than Jorge thought it would be. He reported the shuttle's coordinates as the *Mercator* continued to shed altitude and airspeed. Glancing through the windows, he saw that the darkness was no longer as intense. Raindrops tapped lightly against the thick glass as the shuttle passed through a cloud layer; looking down, he could make out the ocean a couple of dozen miles below, a black expanse tinted silver here and there by the first light of the rising sun.

The miles peeled away, the shuttle shaking every so often as it penetrated the thicker layers of Earth's atmosphere, until Jorge saw that they were approaching the American coast. By then, the *Mercator*'s altitude was less than twenty thousand feet, yet he could see nothing through the windows except a vague hump low upon the horizon. The shuttle was moving faster than the coming dawn, he realized.

"It'll still be night down there by the time we arrive," Jorge said.

"I can land on instruments only," McAlister replied. "The only question is where." He turned his head slightly. "Sergio? You're on. Come up here and tell me where to go."

A minute passed, then Vargas entered the cockpit. "Lost?" he asked, his smirk irritatingly fatuous.

"I know perfectly well where we are, thank you," McAlister growled. "What I want to hear from you is where we should touch down. You told us in the briefing that you know the area. Time to prove it."

Vargas moved a little farther into the cockpit, bending low so that he could peer through the windows. "Like I said, much of the city is still flooded, so you've got only a couple of options. Your best shot is probably Port Logan. Last time I heard, the waters had subsided from the runways. You may be able to put down there."

"What's Port Logan?" Jorge asked.

"The old international spaceport on the other side of the harbor." McAlister looked up at Vargas again. "Anyone still using it? I don't want to take a chance on colliding with . . ."

"No." Vargas shook his head. "It's been abandoned for twenty years, at least." He smiled. "Of course, if you'd like to get closer, you can always try landing on the Boston Common. I wouldn't recommend it, though. Not if you're trying to keep a low profile."

"No. We'll do that only if Logan is still underwater." McAlister paused. "Okay, be straight with us. You said there are still people living in Boston . . ."

"A few, yes. Not many. Squatters, mainly."

"Uh-huh. So what are the chances of them seeing us?"

"I don't know." Vargas was quiet for a moment. "Anyone who's down there is probably still asleep. And since you're landing across the harbor, they might not wake up. But it's been a long time since anyone's used Logan. A shuttle touching down there . . . yeah, it might attract some attention."

"Better that than the Common." McAlister glanced at Jorge. "Way

I see it, our only other choice is finding some place to land beyond the city . . . Cambridge, maybe, or even the western suburbs . . . and hiking the rest of the way in. A little less risky, but it would also mean having to travel farther from the ship."

"No." Jorge shook his head. "I'm with you. Let's try for the space-port. We can cross the harbor from there."

McAlister nodded, then returned his attention to his controls. Var-gas said nothing but continued to watch through the windows. For the first time, Jorge found himself regretting the fact that Inez wasn't fully telepathic. He would have liked to know what the former Union Astronautica pilot was thinking.

When the shuttle reached the coast, they discovered that it was hidden beneath a thick blanket of clouds. Following McAlister's in-structions, Jorge typed a command into the nav comp that pulled up a map of the Boston area. Once he had the exact coordinates for the spaceport, McAlister activated the lidar; watching the screens closely, he began a slow, spiraling descent, using the shuttle's VTOLs to make the final approach. But the clouds extended all the way to the ground; even after McAlister switched on the landing floods, the halogen beams barely penetrated the dense fog.

"At least we've got dry ground down there," McAlister murmured, one eye on the lidar display. He reached over to the landing-gear con-trols and pulled down the bars; there was a hollow thump as the wheels and landing probe lowered from their bays. "All right, we're going in," he said, gently pushing the yoke forward. "Give me an al-timeter readout, Lieutenant."

Jorge stopped looking out the windows, concentrated on the digi-tal display. "One hundred and twenty feet . . . one hundred . . . ninety . . ."

An alarm went off, a shrill *beep-beep-beep* that startled them. "Oh, hell," McAlister hissed, pulling back on the yoke to stop the descent. "Metal contact. Lidar picked up an obstruction just below us."

"Might be something on the field." Vargas craned his neck to peer through one of the side windows. "Can't see a damn thing."

"Yes, well . . . I have a solution for that." McAlister moved the yoke a few degrees to port, maneuvering the shuttle away from its vertical line of descent. The alarm stopped, and he nodded. "Okay, I think we're going to miss it, whatever it is."

Again, he pushed the yoke forward, and Jorge continued his recital. "Eighty feet . . . seventy . . . sixty . . . fifty . . ."

"I see ground!" Vargas snapped. "Looks like dry pavement, all right."

"Good," McAlister murmured. "Let me know if that changes."

"Forty . . . thirty . . ." Jorge glanced up from the controls. The fog was still too thick for him to see anything clearly, yet it appeared as if the floodlights were reflecting off a flat surface directly below. He prayed that it wasn't water. "Twenty . . . ten . . . nine . . . eight . . ."

The roar of the descent thrusters increased in volume, nearly drowning out his voice. McAlister throttled back, easing the shuttle toward the ground.

"Seven . . . six . . . five . . ."

Another alarm went off. "Probe contact," McAlister said as he continued to pull back on the thruster bars. "Hang on."

An instant later, there was an abrupt bump as the *Mercator's* wheels came to rest. McAlister immediately yanked the thrusters down to their lowest position, then reached up to snap a row of switches. "All right, we're down," he said, as the engine noise slowly died. "And that was the second-most scary landing I've ever made."

Jorge let out his breath. "I won't ask what the scariest was."

"I'll tell you another time." The pilot clicked a few more toggles. "It's okay to thank me. Really. I don't mind."

"Thank you." Jorge settled back in his seat, feeling the tension begin to ease. "I mean that."

"Couldn't have done better myself," Vargas added.

McAlister didn't reply, but his expression told Jorge that he was neither complimented nor amused. "Right," he muttered, then began to unclasp his seat and shoulder straps. "Well, then, let's see what we can see."

Which wasn't much, or at least not through the cockpit windows. The floodlights penetrated only a couple of dozen yards in any direction, and all they could make out was a flat expanse of battered concrete. But when Jorge climbed the ladder down to the passenger compartment—moving slowly, his joints creaking with every step he took—he found Inez and Greg staring through the starboard portholes.

"There's something out there," Greg said, pointing to the window beside his seat. "Can't quite make out what it is, but it's big."

Jorge bent down, followed Greg's gaze. Just beyond the range of the floodlights, all but swallowed by the predawn darkness and fog, was an enormous hulk of some sort. "Probably whatever it was that we had to avoid while coming down," he said quietly.

"Only one way to find out." Pushing past Jorge, Vargas headed for the aft hatch. Squatting beside it, he grasped its lockwheel with both hands and started to turn it.

"Not so fast," Jorge said. "We need to get ready first." Vargas gave him a querulous look, but obediently backed away from the hatch as Jorge moved toward the rear of the compartment. "Inez, Greg . . . help me break out the gear."

"What about the parkas?" Inez carefully rose from her seat. Like Jorge, her shoulders were slumped as if she were carrying a full pack. Earth gravity was something everyone except Vargas would have to get used to; even McAlister, who'd been away from Earth for two decades, would have to adjust. "Looks cold out there."

"I wouldn't doubt it." McAlister was the last to come down from the cockpit; while the others were gazing out the windows, he'd been activating the atmospheric conversion system that would replenish the

Mercator's fuel tanks. "It's mid-November, by the Gregorian calendar." The Coyote natives gave him a blank look, not understanding what he meant. "Think of it as early Hanael," he added. "Late autumn, just before the first snowfall. So, yeah, it may be a bit nippy today."

"Okay," Jorge said. "We'll need parkas, caps, heavy boots, gloves . . ."

"Guns?" Inez asked, her voice low.

Jorge hesitated. Vargas nodded, and Greg did the same, but it was hard to miss the reluctance in Inez's eyes. Although she'd received firearms training from the Corps, carrying a weapon was something that went against *Sa'Tong*ian principles. "We should take precautions," he went on, picking his words carefully. "Just in case we need to protect ourselves."

Inez nodded. Couched in those terms, his decision was nominally acceptable; the Fourth Codicil clearly mandated that one should act to prevent others from being harmed. Nonetheless, Jorge noticed that, when she unpacked the weapons from their case, she chose an airpulse pistol while the others took rifles. A nonlethal weapon was as far as she was willing to compromise.

The parkas were Corps-issue, as were the caps. Their insignia had been removed, though, just in case the expedition encountered any inhabitants who might be hostile toward visitors from Coyote; only their unitards had Corps markings. They left most of their gear behind, though, for the time being; the first order of business was seeing exactly where they were. Once everyone was ready, Jorge gave Vargas permission to open the hatch. He turned the lockwheel counterclockwise; there was a faint hiss as the hatch was undogged, then he pulled it open and reached down to unfold the ladder. Vargas was about to climb down; then he seemed to remember his place in the expedition and instead stood aside to let Jorge be the first to leave the shuttle.

The air outside was cold, although not frigid, and thicker than he anticipated. Jorge had known that Earth's atmospheric density was greater than Coyote's, but his first few breaths made his lungs ache. As he stepped out from beneath the *Mercator*'s fuselage, he felt as if he'd just run a couple of miles; his legs were rubbery, and his lower back was sore. Jorge was suddenly grateful for the intense physical training that he, Inez, and Greg had undergone just prior to leaving Coyote; without it, they would have been crippled. Even so, he realized that, until their bodies adapted to the higher gravity and pressure, they would tire easily, with fatigue a constant enemy.

Yet all this was forgotten as soon as he looked around. To the east, the sky was beginning to turn a few shades lighter, and although a dense fog still lay about them, he began to make out some details. The *Mercator* had touched down on a concrete landing strip much like those on New Brighton, but it was obvious that it hadn't been used in decades; floodwaters, only recently receded, had eroded the surface. Long cracks ran through it, with weeds and grass sprouting from the fissures. From somewhere nearby, there was the odor of salt.

Turning around, he got a better view of the object Greg and Inez had spotted. Although it was still indistinct through the haze, he now perceived that it was a spacecraft that had apparently crashed during takeoff. Judging from its size and shape, Jorge figured that it had probably been an orbital passenger transport. Yet it was little more than a blackened skeleton; its port landing gear had buckled, causing its hull to smash down against the concrete, and fire had done the rest, reducing the vessel to a burned-out ruin.

"You can only imagine how that happened." McAlister had come up beside him. He, too, was staring at the wreckage. "Something must have caused the pilot to panic, make some sort of error . . ."

"A lot of people were panicking back then." From behind them, Vargas's voice was low; Jorge suddenly realized that this was the first time the former UA pilot had shown any real regret for what had happened to his world. "Everything was falling apart. No one was thinking straight. It was like"—a long pause—"I dunno. The end of the world or something."

Jorge didn't want to think how many lives had been lost. It seemed impossible that anyone could have survived the crash. Looking aside, he saw that Inez had deliberately turned her back on the demolished spacecraft, her arms crossed tightly across her chest as if to ward off the cold. He had little doubt, though, that what she saw and heard had given her the chills much more than the weather.

"All right," he murmured, "what's done is done. Let's see about getting out of here."

Although they couldn't yet see the sun, the new day was coming; with the fading of night, only the early-morning fog was left behind. It soon became apparent that the *Mercator* had landed a few hundred feet from the edge of the small peninsula on which Port Logan was built. Just past its steep embankment lay the inner harbor; beyond that, still lost in the thick haze, was Boston itself.

Jorge put his team to work unloading the rest of their gear: backpacks, a case of food, two tents, and a portable stove. And most important, an inflatable boat, complete with collapsible paddles and a small outboard engine, which had been included in the expedition's equipment just in case they had to cross water. He and Greg got their morning exercise by lugging its container bag to the embankment; although the boat weighed a little less than a couple of hundred pounds, they had to stop and rest a few times before they finally reached the weed-grown shore.

After they unpacked the boat, Greg went about inflating it with a portable air compressor while Jorge went back to the shuttle. Inez and McAlister were setting up the tripod-mounted parabolic antenna for the expedition's long-range transceiver. It had already been determined that McAlister would remain at Port Logan, where he would guard the shuttle while maintaining radio contact with the exploration team. If there was any trouble from which they couldn't extricate themselves, the pilot would take the *Mercator* aloft and come to their rescue. Likewise, if or when they managed to find Inez's father, Jorge would have the option of asking McAlister to pick them up.

The fog was beginning to dissipate when the expedition rested for a few minutes to have breakfast: fruit bars and cereal sticks, eaten while sitting on their packs and boxes. About a mile away, they could make out the port's terminal and its adjacent control tower; both were in ruins, with the tower little more than a broken pylon, its cupola a heap of twisted metal and shattered glass that lay beside it. The crashed transport was the only other spacecraft in sight; it had been many years since anything had flown out of Port Logan. And in the far distance was Boston, little more than a vague silhouette shrouded by the haze.

There seemed little else left to say or do except make their way there. A brief radio check to make sure that everyone's headset was on the same channel, then Jorge shook hands with McAlister before leading the others to the boat. Once their gear was loaded into the amidships cargo area, Greg and Vargas took their places in the bow, then Jorge and Inez waded through the cold shallows to push the craft into the water before climbing aboard themselves on either side of the engine. Jorge made sure everyone was comfortably seated, with his map case in his lap and their guns not far from their hands, then used a paddle to shove the boat the rest of the way from shore.

The engine started without effort, its hydrogen cell supplying all the power the motor would need. After one last look behind, Jorge grasped the tiller and twisted its handle. The prop churned water, and the small boat purred away, heading for the lost city.

Before the expedition had left Coyote, a senior officer from the Corps of Exploration quietly visited the University of New Florida, where he consulted archivists from the history department. As he'd hoped, the university database included maps of the North American continent; some that had been aboard the *Alabama* dated as far back as the United Republic of America. Among them were maps of the East Coast, including the greater Boston area. Although the most recent was from the early twenty-fourth century, it was not so old as to be unusable; it clearly showed the streets and major buildings of downtown Boston, along with the inner harbor and the nearby Charles River.

Without explaining why, the Corps officer requested that the map be downloaded into datapads. The pads were later issued to the expedition, but just to be safe, a waterproof chart was also prepared by the Corps, if only for the sake of redundancy.

As the boat moved across the mile of water that separated Port Logan from Boston, Jorge silently thanked that nameless Corps officer back home for his foresight. With his left hand on the tiller, he wasn't able to use his pad easily; for that, he'd need to have both hands free. Instead, he took a few moments to open the cylindrical map case, pull out the chart, and spread it across his lap, using his rifle barrel to keep it from being blown overboard. With the fog still thick upon the inner harbor and visibility reduced to a few dozen yards, only the map and Inez's compass would prevent the expedition from veering off in the wrong direction.

The sun had started to burn away the mist, though, and by the time the boat was more than halfway across the harbor, they were able to see Boston more clearly. Jorge hadn't known quite what to expect, but he was nonetheless stunned by what he saw. Where there had been a great city was now a decayed and abandoned ruin; towers once sleek and graceful were in a state of slow disintegration, their windows shattered, their elevated walkways collapsed, their arches and lower floors covered by creeping vines. Once gleaming in the sunlight, they'd become dark and burned-out hulks; uncontrolled fires had devastated many of the skyscrapers, with only their concrete inner cores preventing them from collapsing altogether. Even so, one building had fallen against its closest neighbor; they precariously leaned upon each other like a couple of drunk titans, threatening to eventually crush the smaller buildings beneath them.

No one said anything as the boat approached the waterfront. The horror of what they saw was beyond words, and the air reeked of ash and putrescence. Jorge had originally planned to make landfall at one of the harborside piers, but as they came closer, he saw that this would be impossible. Long Wharf had vanished, with only a few barnacle-encrusted wooden posts left in its place; as they came closer, they made out the upended stern of a sunken ferry, rotting seaweed dangling from its rusted propellers. The waters had begun to recede, but they still hadn't returned to the levels where they'd been before the catastrophe.

Consulting the map, Jorge decided to head for the Charles River; perhaps they'd find a way to go ashore once they left the harbor. He turned the boat to the north, and they slowly moved along the waterfront, passing harbor-view condominiums whose lower levels were now submerged, their upper balconies overrun by tangled brush and vines that had somehow managed to take root. Cabin cruisers and catamarans, the pleasure craft of the rich, lay capsized or half-sunk along the adjacent piers; Jorge wondered why they had been left behind, and decided that their owners must have believed that the boats would remain afloat even while the rest of the city drowned. Whether they had ever returned to discover the results of their foolishness, he had no idea.

They passed the spire of Old North Church, built over six centuries ago yet miraculously intact despite the fact that its white paint had peeled away and the steeple cross was missing, and circled the city's North End until they approached the mouth of the Charles River. Before them lay what the map identified as the Charlestown Bridge.

The floodwaters had devastated its ironwork, causing the roadway to topple into the river, but its center trestle, supported by an enormous, drumlike rotary pedestal, had been moved aside, forming a gap that would allow sailboats to pass beneath the bridge. Perhaps port-authority engineers had decided, in the last days of the city, that doing so would save the historic old bridge from destruction. The river lapped against the pedestal as Jorge maneuvered the boat through the gap. As they moved under the bridge, he noticed a rusting sign dangling from the trestle: SLOW NO WAKE. He would have liked to smile, but he just wasn't in the mood.

Just past the Charlestown Bridge were the Gridley Locks, two artificial canals set within a concrete dam that had been built across the river, with a series of iron-reinforced wooden gates leading from one section of each canal to the next. The locks had been installed to control tide levels in the Charles River Basin, yet they had never been designed with global catastrophe in mind. At some point, the waters had risen above flood stage, demolishing the gates and sweeping away the lampposts and guardrails atop the canal walls. A capsized boat blocked the entrance to the one on the right; the canal to the left, though, was clear of obstruction. Yet as they passed through the locks, he noted that, although the water stopped just below the thirteen-foot line on a tide marker, brown stains along the top of the wall showed where it had once risen much higher than that.

Just past the locks, they encountered their first major obstacle. The Bunker Bridge, which had once carried cars and a maglev rail across the river, had collapsed, causing both the roadway and an eight-car train to plummet into the water. The river was blocked by debris; rusting coupes and railcars stuck up from the water between enormous chunks of concrete and twisted coils of bridge cable. There was no easy way through; Jorge turned off the engine and raised its prop to prevent it from getting fouled by the half-submerged cables, then he and Inez picked up paddles and carefully maneuvered the boat close to the southern shore, where the debris seemed a little less dense. Even so, they found their way blocked by pieces of the fallen bridge; ultimately, they were forced to paddle over to an overturned support pylon, where all four of them climbed out and portaged the boat across the pylon before climbing aboard again. A slow and hazardous diversion, but at least no one slipped and fell into the water.

The river became narrow at that point, leading to a second, much older dam, upon which Boston's science museum and planetarium had been built. The dam had survived, but at some point the flood-waters had spilled over its top, breaking through the museum windows and inundating its ground floor. As the boat moved into the narrow canal leading through the dam, Jorge spotted a pair of slender, four-legged creatures placidly grazing on the high grass that had grown up on the riverbanks. They stared at the boat for a couple of moments, then turned and bounded away.

"White-tail deer," Vargas said. It was the first time he'd said much of anything since leaving Port Logan, and he seemed to be as surprised as anyone else. "I'll be damned . . . I thought they'd become extinct."

"So that's what they look like." Jorge tried to catch another glimpse of the animals, which he'd only read about in books brought from Earth, but they'd vanished within the thickets of an overgrown park. "I guess nature finds a way."

"Sometimes it does," Inez murmured. "It's humans who have problems with change."

This small moment of wonder seemed to break the spell. Up until then, the ruined city had weighed heavily upon everyone, silencing them with its oppressive darkness. Yet the sun was beginning to pierce the clouds, dissipating the last of the fog; the day was becoming warmer, and they gradually opened their parkas and removed their gloves. As the boat moved through the final canal and entered the river basin, they were able to see more of the city. To the right, on the other side of the river, lay Cambridge, the dome of the Massachusetts Institute of Technology covered with vines but still visible above the low buildings along the shore. To the left, closer to them, was a massive white edifice that the map identified as Massachusetts General Hospital. The hospital appeared to be intact, and as they slowly cruised past it, Inez spotted something floating on the river just in front of a nearby embankment.

"I'm not sure," she said, keeping her voice low, "but that looks like a dock."

Jorge throttled down the engine to idle, and Greg pulled out a pair of binoculars. "It's a dock, all right," he said. "I see several boats tied up . . . two or three sailboats, some canoes, a skiff or two. Nothing big."

"Anyone in sight?" Jorge asked.

Greg shook his head. "No . . . but there's something on the river-bank that looks like a sandbag wall. If that's the hospital, then it makes sense that someone would've tried to protect it."

"That's not all." Vargas pointed toward the low buildings just south of Mass General. "Look . . ."

Raising a hand against the sun, Jorge searched for what Vargas had spotted. Two thin tendrils of smoke rose from some area not far from the hospital; they could have been wildfires, yet they looked too small for that.

"There's someone living over there," Inez murmured.

"I told you there were squatters," Vargas said. "At least that's what I'd heard." He nodded toward the smoke trails. "That's Beacon Hill, if I remember correctly."

Jorge studied his map, closely examining its topographical gradient lines. "Looks like the highest point of land. Makes sense for someone to set up camp there, especially if the rest of the city was flooded."

Greg turned to look back at him. "What about it, chief? Go ashore and see if we can find them?"

Jorge considered the question for a moment. "I'd like to go a little farther," he said. "Just to see if there are any other signs of habitation. If we don't find anything, we can always circle back."

"That might be our best shot, Lieutenant." Vargas continued to gaze at the smoke. "We ought to take it."

He had a good point, and Jorge was about to agree when he felt Inez's hand on his knee. Glancing sideways at her, he saw her silently shake her head. He didn't know why, but something in her expression made him think that she might have sensed something that he didn't . . . or couldn't.

"No . . . no, I'd like to explore the river a little more," he said slowly. "Just to be sure we don't miss anything."

Vargas frowned but didn't argue as Jorge throttled up the engine again. But as soon as the boat was in motion once more, Jorge leaned over to Inez. "What's going on?" he said as quietly as he could, using the engine noise to cover his voice.

"He's nervous," she whispered, putting her face close to his. "I can't be sure, but I think he's hiding something."

"Like what?"

Inez shook her head; she didn't know. Yet Jorge decided to trust her feelings. His doubts about Vargas had never subsided; once again, he was wondering how much faith they should put in their guide.

The river broadened as the boat traveled upstream, and a few minutes later they came upon a massive stone bridge that looked as if it had been built several centuries ago. The map identified it as the Longfellow Bridge, and although three of its outer spans had fallen, the ones near the middle were still standing. The boat passed below the bridge, giving them a chance to look at the ornate scroll carved into the stone just below its center support; most of its Latin inscription had eroded away, but the words *Bostonia Condita AD 1660* remained legible within the shield at its center.

"Eight hundred years," Inez said quietly. "Almost eight hundred years, this city has been here." Gazing at the scroll, she shook her head in sadness. "Gone, all gone . . . and it didn't need to happen."

Past the bridge, the Charles River become nearly as wide as one of the smaller channels back home, and it was there that they sighted the Back Bay area. The urban neighborhood near the river had reverted to swamp, its brownstone town houses and mansions long since lost to water, mud, and brush. Farther inland rose the massive edifice of the Hancock Hub, the eighty-story arcology that had once straddled six square blocks. Fire had ravaged the giant building, turning it into a colossal black skeleton that loomed over the smaller buildings around it. Hawks circled the remains of the Hub's twin towers, searching for prey in the streets below.

There were no signs of human presence, though, and Jorge estimated that they'd traveled a little more than three miles by water since leaving Port Logan. Time to check in with McAlister. The radio crackled with static, its signal marred by the tall buildings between the river and the spaceport, but Jorge was still able to hear McAlister's voice. He gave the pilot a brief description of where they were and what they'd found so far.

"Copy that," McAlister said. *"Be careful, and let me know if you run into anyone."* A brief pause, then he went on. *"Incidentally, I'm seeing a bit of life out here, too. There are a couple of boats in the harbor, and it looks like they may be heading this way."*

Jorge raised an eyebrow. "That's hardly what I'd call incidental. Think they've seen you?"

"No idea. Hard to tell from here . . . just two small boats with a few guys aboard. I didn't see where they came from. Probably only some fishermen. I'll let you know if I make contact."

"Do that. We'll do the same if we find anyone here. Over and out." Jorge prodded his headset, switching it off, and looked at the others; they'd listened through their own radios. "Well . . . appears this place isn't as deserted as it seems."

"We're wasting time." Vargas was becoming impatient. "If you're serious about finding Thompson, your best bet is to go back the way we came, find whoever it is who set those fires."

Jorge and Inez traded a quick glance. "You're pretty sure about that, aren't you?" she asked. "What makes you certain they'd know where my father is?"

"Your *chaaz'maha* isn't just anybody . . . I've told you that already. If he's been in the city again lately, people would know about it. They may even know where he is right now." Vargas gestured toward the Back Bay area. "You're not going to find anyone here, that's for sure. Nothing there except birds, squirrels, and rats."

Jorge had to admit that he was probably right. Not only that, but it didn't look as if they'd be able to travel much farther upstream. Not far away was yet another Charles River landmark, marked on the map as the Harvard Bridge. It appeared to have collapsed entirely, with its remains blocking their way. And although they might be able to make landfall in the Back Bay, that would mean having to hike through swamp-infested neighborhoods until they reached the higher ground of Beacon Hill.

"You've got a point." Jorge throttled up the engine again, pushed the tiller so that the boat began to make a slow turn. "But let's play it safe and not really announce ourselves until we actually meet someone."

Vargas didn't reply, instead turning back around in his seat. Greg gave Jorge a questioning look, though, and Jorge responded by silently raising two fingers to his eyes, then pointing at Vargas's back: *Keep an eye on him.* A mute nod from the sergeant, then he patted the stock of his rifle. It was clear that Greg didn't trust him either.

Jorge hugged the shore as he steered the boat back down the river. Keeping the engine at half throttle, he managed to pick their way through the fallen spans of the Longfellow Bridge without colliding with any debris. Once past the bridge, they were able to make out Beacon Hill a little more clearly, with the gold dome of the Massachusetts state capitol building at its crest. Yet it wasn't until they reached the floating dock again that they saw anyone.

Three figures stood upon the dock: two adults, and what appeared to be a child. None of them noticed the boat until it was only a few dozen yards away; squatting beside a small sailboat tied up at the pier, they appeared to be working on its furled sail. Yet when the smallest of the three—a boy, no more than ten years old—finally glanced upstream, he raised his voice and pointed toward the approaching craft. Jorge couldn't hear what he said, but it was enough to get the others' attention. The others stood up and quietly watched as the boat came closer. Greg raised a hand as a friendly greeting, but no one on the dock responded in kind.

"Good morning," Jorge called out once they were within earshot and he'd throttled the engine down to neutral. "Mind if we put in here?"

It was now clear that the two adults were both men, one considerably older than the other. The younger man gave his companion a sidelong look; he stuck his hands in his pockets, stepped away from the sailboat.

"Don't mind at all," he called back, "so long's you got something to pay for it."

"The dockmaster, most likely," Vargas said quietly, turning to Jorge. "And he probably means barter. I doubt anyone uses money around here anymore."

Jorge nodded, then returned his attention to the dockmaster. "Got a little extra food, if that's what you mean. We don't have much else." He hoped that the lie wasn't too obvious, but he was unwilling to give up any of their equipment.

"That'll do," the dockmaster replied, "so long's it's not spoiled." The younger man laughed, and Jorge took that to be a good omen. "Pull right up here," he added, pointing to a vacant space between the sailboat and a tarp-covered canoe. "Kill your motor first, then toss me a line."

Jorge remembered the SLOW NO WAKE sign he'd seen on the Charlestown Bridge. Some things hadn't changed. He shut off the engine, then he and Inez paddled the rest of the way in while Greg located a hemp rope stowed beneath his seat. Once they were close enough, Greg threw the coiled end of the rope to the dockmaster. He caught the line in midair and used it to haul the boat against the dock; he knelt to lash the rope around a post, then offered Greg a hand.

"Nice boat you got there," he said. "Haven't seen one like it in a long time. Where y'all from?"

"Down south." Grasping the dockmaster's hand, Greg took the high step that put him on the dock's weather-beaten planks. He gave Jorge a quick glance as he turned to help the others climb out of the boat: *What do I say next?*

"Long Island," Jorge supplied as he crawled over the equipment cases to reach the dock's edge. It was the alibi he'd decided to use in case just that sort of question came up. "Decided to take a little trip up north, see whatever there is to see."

"Long Island, New York?" The younger man sounded dubious. With greasy brown hair and a coarse beard, he looked like someone hardened by years of living in the ruins. "Didn't know anyone was living down there. Last I heard, most of it was still underwater."

"Most of it, sure . . . but there's a few parts where people have been coming back to live lately, now that the water's going down." Remembering his promise, Jorge unstrapped the case containing the expedition rations, hoisted it onto the dock. "That's where we found the boat . . . in a store down there."

"Uh-huh." The young man remained skeptical, and Jorge became conscious of just how different he and the other expedition members were in comparison to the people they'd just met. Their parkas were not the patched and threadbare overcoats the two men and the boy wore; their boots were clean and new, while the men wore old shoes that looked as if they were being held together with tape. The younger man openly stared at Jorge's headset, and Jorge suddenly realized that he should have removed it. His story about finding the boat, and by implication everything they had, was thin indeed.

The dockmaster, though, had little interest in their boat or clothes. He nodded toward the food container. "So . . . what do you have for me?"

Jorge climbed onto the dock and helped Inez out of the boat, then bent over the case and unlatched its lid. "Not much in the way of anything fresh," he said, revealing the foil-wrapped rations stacked within, "but we've got a lot of freeze-dried stuff. Meat, fruit bars . . ."

A low whistle from the young man, and Jorge looked up to see the astonishment in his eyes. "Damn. I ain't seen anything like that in a long time . . . not since I was his age, at least."

He meant the boy standing nearby. The kid stared at the case with naked avarice, and Jorge easily imagined his mouth watering.

"Are you with the TC?" the boy suddenly asked.

Jorge had no idea what he meant by that. It wasn't something Vargas had mentioned during his previous conversations with the other expedition members. Before he could muster a response, though, Vargas came forward.

"No, we're not," he said, "but we're searching for someone who is . . . the *chaaz'maha*."

The dockmaster had squatted on his haunches to sort through the rations. When Vargas said this, he looked up sharply. "Is that why you're here? You're trying to find him?"

The dockmaster wasn't the only one to be surprised. Jorge wanted to know how Vargas apparently knew what the TC was. Yet there was no way to ask him without prompting more unwanted questions from the locals; no choice but to bluff. "Uh-huh," he said. "We've heard that he's been here recently. If you know where he is . . ."

"Nope. No idea." As quickly as he'd become distracted, the dockmaster returned his attention to the food case. "I'll take ten of these for one day's rent on a slip," he said, lifting a handful of packets. "Throw in another five, and I'll let you have it for two."

Ten to fifteen ration packs represented nearly four days of food for the expedition. It was a hard bargain, but Jorge didn't see that he had much choice; they'd have to leave the boat behind while they went into the city. "And you'll watch our belongings while we're gone?"

The dockmaster grinned, revealing gaps in his teeth. "Yup. These people trust me with their boats, so I reckon you can trust me with yours."

That sounded like as good a promise as they were likely to get. "All right, then," he said, and extended a hand. Apparently this was one custom that hadn't been forgotten, because the dockmaster shook it, sealing the deal.

"If you're looking for the *chaaz'maha*," the young man said abruptly, "I might be able to help you."

Inez peered at him. "You know where he is?"

"No, but I know someone who does." He cocked his head in the general direction of Beacon Hill. "Fellow over on Irving Street has something to do with the TC. I think he's even met the *chaaz'maha* himself a couple'a times when he's been in town."

Again, that phrase: the TC. Jorge suspected that it was significant, but he refrained from betraying his ignorance by asking what it meant. "The *chaaz'maha* isn't here now?"

"Oh, he comes around every now and then." The young man's expression hardened. "Like whatever he has to say means a damn. But he has his followers, y'know . . ." His eyes narrowed. "You're not some of 'em, are you?"

"No." Greg smiled. "Just interested in meeting him, that's all."

The young man nodded but didn't say anything. The dockmaster glanced at him. "Ted and me will work on your boat, Sam, if you want to take 'em up to Irving. I think we can get that sail stitched up by the time you get back."

"Sounds good." Sam—who Jorge now realized was probably a fisherman and most likely Ted's father as well—gave the boy a swat on the shoulder. "You stay here with Mr. Morse. I'll be back in an hour or so."

Ted nodded. He was still staring at the boat that was like none other he'd ever seen. Jorge was tempted to leave someone behind to guard their property, yet he knew that he couldn't spare anyone for that task. He needed Vargas as a guide, as untrustworthy as he might be, and Greg to watch Vargas. Inez had to come along, too; after all, the purpose of the expedition was to find her father. So he had little choice but to leave their boat and equipment in Morse's care and hope that everything would still be there once they returned.

However, he wasn't about to set out on foot without taking precautions. Climbing back into the boat, Jorge picked up their rifles and passed them to Greg and Inez. Neither Morse nor Sam raised any objections; apparently it wasn't unusual to see armed men in the streets of Boston. Jorge paused to fold the map and shove it in the left pocket of his parka, then he rejoined the others on the dock.

Sam waited until everyone was ready to leave, then, without another word, he turned and started walking toward the moored end of the floating dock. A long, steep flight of wooden steps, nailed together from pieces of wallboard, led up and over the sandbag emplacement; on the other side of the embankment was a mud-covered street, its cracked asphalt worn but reasonably dry. Followed by Inez, Greg, and Vargas, Jorge let the fisherman lead them into the ruins of Boston.

Not far from the embankment were the remains of a four-lane highway that once ran alongside the Charles River. Weeds and brush had found root in the cracked asphalt, and a half-fallen overhead sign identified the road as Storrow Drive; sometime in the past, someone had climbed up one of its poles to paint over the "t." A bad joke, Jorge reflected, but not unjustified.

Once Sam led them across Storrow, he turned right and began taking the group down a side street leading away from the river. The hospital was now behind them, and although most of the buildings around them were several stories high, none seemed to have suffered significant damage above ground level. Yet their windows were either broken or boarded up, with storefronts barred by rusting metal grates that seemed to have been hastily welded into place. Jorge figured that landlords and shop owners must have had just enough time during the city's evacuation to make an attempt at protecting their property before they were forced to flee. Very few vehicles were parked at the curbs, and those that remained had been stripped bare of everything usable.

Sam walked slightly ahead of them, occasionally glancing over his shoulder as if to make sure they hadn't fallen behind. Only Vargas was able to keep up with him; the rest were still getting used to Earth gravity, and Jorge felt as if he had a fifty-pound bag on his back. But it was Sam's silence that bothered him the most. Perhaps the fisherman was laconic by nature, but his silence unnerved Jorge almost as much as that of the buildings around them. Although he obviously knew his way, it seemed as if he was searching for something. At the end of each block, Sam would pause for a moment to glance warily in all directions before continuing onward, and once they'd turned a couple of corners, Jorge realized that the river was no longer anywhere in sight.

"I'm not liking this," Greg murmured. He'd fallen back a step to join Jorge and Inez, and Jorge noticed that he had unlimbered his rifle from its shoulder strap. "I know he's taking us somewhere, but I'm not sure . . ."

"If it's any place we'd want to go?" Inez finished. Greg nodded, and she looked at Jorge. "I agree," she went on, keeping her voice low. "He's nervous about something . . . and so is Sergio."

Jorge didn't respond for a moment, then he cleared his throat. "Hey! Sam! You want to hold up for a second?"

Sam came to a halt, as did Vargas. They waited until the rest of the group caught up with them. By then, they'd reached a broad, four-lane avenue. A bent-over signpost identified the intersection as Cambridge and North Grove, with the latter continuing past Cambridge as Grove Street, which sloped upward into a hillside residential neighborhood.

"What do you want?" Sam was impatient, no longer quite as willing to wait for them as he'd been back at the dock.

"Nothing . . . just a minute to catch our breaths, find out where we are." Jorge was sweating beneath his parka, and he saw that Greg and Inez were panting as well. He nodded toward Grove Street. "Is that Beacon Hill just ahead?"

"Uh-huh."

"So where's this place you're taking us? Irving Street, you said . . ."

"Just a few more blocks. We'll be there soon." A sardonic smile as Sam looked them over. "Little out of shape, huh? We ain't gone all that far."

"Just not used to hiking through a city, that's all." Jorge peered past him at Grove. Brownstone buildings, most of them no more than three or four stories in height, lined both sides of the street; judging from their bay windows and columned doorways, they appeared to be old apartment houses, their ground-floor windows either shattered or covered with plywood. Not far away, he saw smoke rising from rooftops a few blocks up the hill. "Is this where most people live now? On Beacon Hill?"

"Uh-huh." Sam continued to study him. He said nothing for a moment, then slowly shook his head. "Y'know, I got a feeling you ain't been straight with me."

"What do you mean?"

"You're not really from Long Island, are you?" A corner of his mouth ticked upward. "In fact, I don't think you're even from New York."

Jorge felt something cold run down his back. "What gives you that idea?"

"Your clothes are too nice to have just been found. And that boat of yours . . . I ain't seen no inflatables since I was a kid, let alone one with an outboard." Sam lowered his voice. "Tell me the truth, now . . . you're with the TC, ain't you?"

"No, we're not. I promise." Jorge hesitated. "But you're right . . . we're not from Long Island, or even New York. We're from . . . well, somewhere much farther away, let's just put it that way."

Sam mulled this over a few moments. There was distrust in his eyes, but also a certain cunning that Jorge didn't like. Before he could add more, though, Inez stepped forward. "Look, where we're from isn't really important. All we want is to talk to someone who can tell us how to find the *chaaz'maha*. That's all."

"Yeah . . . yeah, okay." Sam appeared to have made up his mind. "Awright, let's go. I'll take you to my friend on Irving. He'll help you out."

He turned around, began crossing Cambridge. Vargas started to follow him, but before Jorge and Greg could join them, Inez tapped Jorge on the arm. "He's lying," she whispered. "I don't think that's the way we should be going."

"Wait a second!" Jorge called out. "Are you sure we . . . ?"

Sam suddenly broke into a run. Before Jorge could stop him, he bolted across Cambridge and continued running up Grove. Jorge started to go after him, but gravity slowed his muscles, made his reactions sluggish. Sam ducked into an alley between two boarded-up apartment houses; within seconds, the fisherman had disappeared from sight.

"Damn!" Jorge stopped in the middle of the weed-grown avenue. "Damn it to hell!"

"Not your fault." Inez came up from behind him. "I think he was planning this all along."

Jorge glared at her. "Then why didn't you . . . ?"

"Because I didn't know what he was going to do until—" She stopped herself, shook her head. "I'm sorry, but I can't predict the future, you know. There's a limit to what I can tell from people's emotions."

"Okay, all right." Jorge let out his breath. No, it wasn't her fault; indeed, he was angry at himself for having been misled. "Sorry I snapped at you like that."

"So what do we do now?" Greg caught up with them. "Our native guide is gone." He looked at Vargas. "Unless you have any idea where we are . . ."

"No." Vargas shook his head. "I've never been in this part of town."

"You're not telling us something." Inez turned to look him straight in the eye. "I'm not saying that you're lying, Sergio . . . but there's also something you've been keeping from us."

Vargas didn't respond. He turned away from her, refusing to meet her gaze. "Never mind," Jorge said. "Right now, the first priority is figuring out where we are and what to do next."

Kneeling in the street, he pulled the map out of his pocket and unfolded it. Borrowing Inez's compass, it took him only a minute to get a fix on their location. As Inez had deduced, Sam had been leading them away from Irving Street, which lay three blocks farther down Cambridge, east of Grove. It also turned out that they were only a couple of blocks west of the Longfellow Bridge. For some reason, Sam had taken them the long way from the Charles River, yet it also appeared that they could return to the dock within minutes, if they chose to do so.

"Perhaps we should go back." Squatting beside him, Greg peered over Jorge's shoulder at the map. "If that guy was giving us the runaround . . ."

"He may have been taking us somewhere other than where he said he was." Inez crouched between them, studying the map as well. "But I didn't sense that he was lying when he said that there was someone on Irving Street who might be able to help us."

"How can you be so sure?" Greg stared at her. "I mean, how do you know whether he was lying or not?"

Inez didn't answer this, and Jorge remembered that Greg hadn't been informed that she possessed empathic abilities. "She's . . . got a certain knack for this sort of thing," Jorge said, then he folded the map and stood up. "I'm going to check in with the ship," he went on, prodding his headset. "See what Hugh has to say about this."

Again, the reception was poor, the tall buildings between them and Port Logan interfering with his signal. Nonetheless, he was able to get through to the pilot. *"Sounds like you've got a situation,"* McAlister said, once Jorge let him know about all that had happened. *"Maybe you ought to come back. We can try again, in some other part of the city."*

"No." Inez had been quietly listening in, and she emphatically shook her head. "This is our best chance . . . maybe our only chance . . . to find my father. If there's even the slightest possibility that there's someone around here who knows where he is, then we have to make the effort to find him."

"That's too much of a risk," McAlister said.

"Then we're just going to have to take it." Jorge glanced at Inez, and she nodded. "Look, we always knew this might be dangerous, but it's something we're just going to have to accept."

A long pause from McAlister. *"All right, then,"* he said at last. *"I'll stand by and wait for your word. If you run into trouble, let me know. I'll pick you up in the park."*

Jorge knew that he meant the Boston Common. Although it was on the other side of Beacon Hill, he'd seen from the map that it was only about ten blocks south of their present location. A long trek, given their problems coping with gravity, but still their best point of retrieval if it came to that.

"Wilco," he replied, then something else occurred to him. "Has there been any more activity from those fishing boats? Have they spotted you yet?"

"Negative. I've been keeping an eye on them, but they're still out in the harbor. Looks like they've dropped anchor, and they're just floating there."

"Affirmative." Jorge felt a twinge of relief. At least that part of their mission was still according to plan. "We'll be in touch. Over and out." Clicking off the headset, he turned to the others . . . and suddenly realized that there was one less person in their group than there had been only a couple of minutes ago.

"Where's Vargas?" he demanded.

Greg's mouth fell open. He quickly turned about, looking first one way, then another. "Oh, hell! How did he . . . ?"

"He must have slipped away while we were checking the map." Jorge glanced in both directions down Cambridge, then toward North Grove. Vargas was nowhere to be seen. "Inez, you didn't . . . ?"

"I'm sorry. I wasn't paying attention to him either." She let out her breath, shook her head in embarrassment. "I sensed panic when I confronted him, but I didn't think it was enough to make him run off."

Jorge ignored her but instead scowled at Greg. "My fault, I know," the sergeant muttered. "It was my job to keep an eye on him, and I screwed up." He gritted his teeth as he hefted his rifle. "So help me, when I catch up with him . . ."

He started to walk away, obviously intent on pursuit, but Jorge hastily grabbed his arm. "No. Whatever we do, we can't let ourselves get separated. Besides, if he's hiding from us, he'll make sure that we can't find him."

Greg sighed, reluctantly nodded. There was no need for him to apologize further; the self-recrimination was plain to be seen. "So what do we do now?" he asked.

Jorge looked back at Inez. She remained quiet, having already let her opinion be known. "Same thing we were about to do," he said. "We keep going, and hope for the best."

They saw no one on Cambridge Avenue except for a feral dog who growled at them from the doorway of an abandoned pharmacy, but just before they reached Irving Street, they were surprised to see a young woman on a bicycle pedal through the intersection ahead. She barely glanced in their direction, though, but kept on moving, her knapsack bumping against her back. Besides the two men and the boy they'd met at the dock, she was the first person they'd seen since entering Boston.

When they reached Irving and began to walk up the narrow, sloping street, they saw more signs of current habitation. The first two buildings on the block were boarded up, yet there were a couple of bicycles chained to a signpost in front of an apartment house, along with a small electric cart parked in an alley between the next two buildings. Greg noticed that the cart appeared to be in good shape and that it had been rigged with a small photovoltaic array. Although most storefronts were still shuttered, a secondhand clothing shop appeared to have been reopened for business, as was a hardware store across the street. Looking up, Jorge observed that the second-story bay windows had glass in their frames, and he could see light from within. Smoke rose from the rooftop chimney of the next building on the block, and more bicycles were chained to a rack next to its front steps. The sidewalks were clear of garbage and debris, and there were no abandoned vehicles at the curbs.

Clearly, there were people living on Irving Street, and although it was still a little too early in the morning for most of its residents to be

up and about, it wasn't long before they began to spot various individuals. A middle-aged man sweeping the front steps of an apartment
house. A couple of teenagers smoking cigarettes in an alley. An old
lady feeding her cat on the third-floor landing of a fire escape. None
of them were dressed in rags or seemed to be on the verge of starva-
tion; they regarded the newcomers with aloof interest, and while no
one called out to them, neither did they run for cover or reach for
guns.

But it wasn't until Jorge, Inez, and Greg reached the end of the
second block of Irving that they found the heart of the neighborhood. At the intersection of Revere Street, they came upon an
open-air market. On both sides of the street were rows of tents and
kiosks; wooden tables and bins had been set up within them, with
local merchants and craftspeople setting out their wares. A couple of
kids helped an adult unload crates of fresh vegetables from a cart;
nearby, a thickset man with a long beard draped homespun shirts
and sweaters upon a rope suspended above his table. From somewhere close by could be heard the clucking of chickens; a woman in
a calf-length skirt carried a small wicker basket filled with eggs away
from a stall. A pig was being slowly turned upon a spit above a bar-
becue grill, with a young man carefully basting it with sauce from a
tin can.

"Could be home," Inez said quietly as she leaned against the side of
a building at the street corner. Like Jorge and Greg, she needed to
catch her breath again; although the street they'd just walked up
wasn't particularly steep, none of them were yet accustomed to Earth
gravity. At least Revere seemed level; above the rooftops, Jorge was
able to make out the dome of the state capitol building. "If I didn't
know better," she added, "I'd say we were in Bridgeton, or maybe
Defiance."

Jorge nodded but said nothing as he studied their whereabouts. As
before, their arrival hadn't gone unnoticed. Several residents were
glancing in their direction. He already knew that their clothes would

get attention; he now became aware of the fact that no one on the street was armed.

"We'll probably have some questions before long," he said. "Maybe we ought to start asking a few of our own." He looked at Greg, who was still carrying his rifle in his hands. "It'd probably make things easier if you put that away. I don't think we're going to have any trouble here."

Greg reluctantly slung the rifle by its shoulder strap, although he kept its stock under his arm, with its trigger within easy reach. Jorge made sure that his own rifle was less obvious; as an afterthought, he pulled off his headset and tucked it in his jacket pocket. "We've made that mistake once already," he said, gesturing for the others to do the same. "No sense in doing it again."

"You want to go on pretending that we're from Long Island?" Greg gave him an incredulous glance. "That didn't work before."

"Better than telling the truth, don't you think?" Jorge shook his head. "I'd rather not do that until it becomes necessary. Right now, I'd just like to see if we can learn anything useful."

They began to make their way down Revere, strolling through the marketplace as if this were something they did every day. By then, the street had become a little busier, as neighborhood residents began to show up to do their morning errands. Jorge and the others were unable to buy anything, even if they'd wanted to, but they went through the motions of looking over the various items on display. As they did so, Jorge noticed something else; trade wasn't being done entirely by barter, as Vargas had claimed. Now and then, he saw money exchange hands, paper bills that, at first glance, appeared to have been recently printed. Apparently a system of currency had recently been reintroduced to Boston society, such as it was.

They went from stall to stall, making small talk with the various sellers and craftsmen, finally asking the questions that were foremost on their minds. *Do you know where we can find the* chaaz'maha? *Do you know anyone who would know how to find him?* The queries themselves seemed to raise little attention—at least no one asked whom they meant, or objected to being asked—but neither did they gain any useful information. Yes, the *chaaz'maha* had been seen in Boston, and more than once. In fact, he'd visited this very neighborhood, although that had been quite some time ago. But, no, he wasn't there now, nor did anyone seem to know where he was.

It wasn't until they reached the corner of Garden and Revere that they got their first solid lead. An elderly gentleman maintained a book stall on the street corner; his tables and shelves were lined with printed books, all old and often read, a few missing their covers. He was putting an ancient cookbook out for display when Inez asked if he'd seen the *chaaz'maha* lately. His eyes became sharp behind the scratched lenses of his glasses, and he peered at her with sudden interest.

"Yes . . . yes, I've seen the *chaaz'maha*," he replied, his voice low. "In fact, I spoke to him myself, not long ago." A grey eyebrow cocked upward ever so slightly. "And who may you be, if I might ask?"

Noticing that the bookseller seemed cautious in the way he spoke, Jorge moved closer. "We're from out of town," he said quietly. "We'd like to find the *chaaz'maha* very much. He . . ."

"There's no reason to be alarmed," Inez said, interrupting Jorge but keeping her voice low as well. "But it's very important that we find him. A matter of some urgency."

"Oh, indeed?" The old man shifted from one foot to another as he scratched at the potbelly beneath his frayed sweater. "If it's enlightenment you seek, I can help you there. No need to talk to him personally."

Bending beneath the table, he opened a box that was just out of sight. When he stood up again, in his hand was a small black book, clothbound and not much larger than his palm. There was no title or author's name on the cover. "Everything you need to know is here," the old man murmured, placing the book on top of the others on the table. "Read it, and it will speak to you."

Jorge didn't have to pick up the book to know what it was. Inez took the book from the table, opened its cover. "You realize, of course, that a *Sa'Tong-tas* is never to be sold, but only given away."

The bookseller gave her a sharp look. "Then you're already familiar with it?"

Inez smiled as she closed the book and handed it back to him. "'The truth is always self-evident so long as . . .'"

"'. . . You have the courage to search for it.'" The bookseller returned the smile as he completed the quote. "You're a follower, yes?" She nodded, and his expression became quizzical. "Then I take it you're with the TC"—he shook his head—"but if you are, then why would you be searching for the *chaaz'maha* since you'd already know where he is?"

Jorge glanced at Inez. She said nothing, but only nodded. "We're not with the TC," Jorge said. "In fact, we don't even know what that is. We're . . . well . . ."

The bookseller suddenly looked away from them. "Trouble coming," he whispered, then he clamped a hand over the *Sa'Tong-tas* and made it disappear beneath the table. "I'd make yourself scarce, if I were you."

From the corner of his eye, Jorge saw four men moving through the crowded marketplace. They were headed in their direction, each of them with his right hand in his coat pocket. As they came closer, he realized that one of them was Sam.

"That way," the old man said softly, cocking his head in the direction of the street behind them. "Second alley to the right. Go down it till you reach the courtyard. Plenty of ways out from there. Now scram."

Jorge didn't need any more prompting. Taking Inez by the hand, he quickly walked behind the bookseller's stall, with Greg hard on their heels. For a moment, they had the bookshelves between them and Revere Street; Jorge dropped Inez's hand as they darted for Garden Street, dodging a couple of pedestrians as they put the marketplace behind them.

They hadn't fooled Sam and his companions, though. Looking over his shoulder, Jorge saw the four men turn the corner and come after them; they were only a couple of dozen yards away. "Don't run until I tell you," he whispered to the others as he sought to keep a steady, unhurried pace. "Just keep walking, and don't use your guns unless . . ."

"Take 'em!" Sam yelled.

Running footsteps from behind them, and Jorge looked back to see the four men charging toward them. Their hands had appeared from their coat pockets, and he could see the pistols they carried.

"Move!" he shouted, then he and Inez broke into a run. But they hadn't gone ten feet before he realized Greg was no longer with them. Glancing back, he saw that the sergeant had turned, stopped, and dropped to one knee.

"Dillon . . . *no!*" he snapped, but Greg was already bringing up his rifle barrel. Yet he was a second too slow; two loud cracks of gunshots that reverberated off the brick walls of the buildings around them, and Greg sagged forward, his rifle still clutched in his hands.

"Greg!" Inez screamed. She skidded to a halt, and Jorge realized that she meant to go back for him. But one glimpse of the blood on the sidewalk beneath the sergeant's body told him that doing so would be pointless. Grabbing Inez by the arm, Jorge pulled her away while at the same moment unlimbering his own rifle. The men were still running toward them when he squeezed the trigger, not bothering to aim but instead firing from the hip.

His shot didn't hit anyone, but it was enough to make his pursuers drop to the sidewalk or press themselves against the walls. "Go, go!" he yelled, turning to shove Inez ahead of him. "Keep running! Don't stop."

Another gunshot rang out behind them as they dashed down the sidewalk. Jorge was tempted to stop and return fire, but then he saw that they weren't alone. Across the street, two teenage girls huddled together in a doorway; a little farther away, a man and a small boy were crouched behind a bicycle rack. Any one of them could be caught in the cross fire or hit by a ricochet; he couldn't risk a firefight, even though Sam and his pals didn't share the same reluctance. Their only remaining choice was to keep running.

An alley appeared before them, and Jorge and Inez dove into it. Within seconds, though, he realized that they'd made a mistake. The old man had told them to take the second alley to the right; this one ended in the rear wall of a building, with no courtyard or escape route ahead.

Doors led into the buildings on either side of them. Jorge jiggled the knob of the one to the right, found that it was locked. He was about to try the one to the left when he heard footsteps at the mouth of the alley. Whipping around, he started to raise his rifle, but before he could, he heard a hollow *whump!* from behind him.

Glancing over his shoulder, he saw that Inez had flattened her back against a wall. She'd unholstered her airpulse pistol and, with her arm straightened level with her shoulder, was taking aim at the alley entrance. Someone darted across the sidewalk and she fired again, but her pursuer had managed to take cover before the invisible bolt did little more than knock dust from the bricks.

The door to the left was locked, too. A fire escape rose above it, but the bottom rung of its iron ladder was too far overhead for him to reach. Crouching beneath it, he started to aim the barrel of his rifle at the alley when he heard a familiar voice.

"Hey, in there!" It was Sam, calling to them from just around the corner of the building to their right. "Give it up, or you're gonna get the same thing as your bud!"

Jorge didn't respond. With his free hand, he fumbled for the headset in his pocket. Not bothering to put it on, he held its earpiece and mike prong to his face. "*Mercator*, come in," he said, keeping his voice low enough so as not to be heard by anyone outside the alley. "Emergency . . . come in!"

"Look, I know you've got guns," Sam went on, trying to sound reasonable, "but so do we, and more than you do. And forget about anyone coming to the rescue. People around here know better than to mess with us."

"*Mercator*, do you read?" It was hard to handle the headset and his rifle at the same time; Jorge braced the stock against his knee as he kept talking. "Hugh, come in! We've got an emergency!"

Nothing but static from the earpiece. Jorge was about to repeat himself when a hand clutching a pistol thrust itself into view from around the left corner of the alley. Jorge barely had time to duck before another shot was fired. The bullet missed him by several feet; a quick glance at Inez confirmed that she hadn't been hit either, but he knew that the shot had only been meant to remind them just how precarious their position was.

"That's your last warning!" Sam yelled, still unseen yet far too close for comfort. "We can turn this into a firing squad if you don't give up." A long pause, then he went on. "And if you don't think we can do it, listen up!"

A shrill whistle from above them, and Jorge looked up to see that two of Sam's men had taken positions on the rooftops overlooking the alley, one on each side. Their guns were trained on both him and Inez.

"Last chance!" Sam shouted. "Put your guns down and kick 'em away, or . . ."

"Jorge," Inez said. "They mean it. They'll kill us."

There was fear in her eyes, even though her expression remained stoical. And even if he managed to reach the shuttle—why the hell wasn't McAlister responding?—there was no way the pilot could rescue them before they were shot to death.

Jorge took a deep breath, let it out . . . then he put the rifle down, stood up, and shoved it away with the toe of his boot. "All right," he said as Inez tossed her pistol into the alley. "Have it your way."

Another whistle from one of the men on the rooftop, then Sam and the fourth man entered the alley. They said nothing as they marched toward Jorge and Inez, but when they reached them, Sam pulled back his fist and threw it straight into Jorge's stomach.

Jorge doubled over, the wind agonizingly knocked from his lungs. He started to rise, but Sam's fist came down again, this time against the back of his neck. He fell forward, his face scraping the cracked asphalt of the alley. He heard Inez cry out in pain, but when he started to push himself up on his elbows, a heavy foot came down upon his back, forcing him to lie still with his face against the ground.

"Don't move," Sam snarled from above him, "and you won't get hurt."

Jorge didn't care what happened to him. "Inez . . . !"

"I'm . . . !" Then she yelped, this time more loudly.

"Shut up!" another voice demanded. A second later, Jorge heard footsteps running into the alley; Sam's other men had come down from the rooftops. He couldn't see anything except the worn-out toes of someone's boots, though, as someone else grabbed his hands and yanked them behind his back.

Coarse, heavy twine was quickly wrapped around his wrists, yanked tight. A flapping sound, then a black canvas bag that smelled like potatoes came down around his head. A moment later, something came down against the back of his head. A flare of pain, then it was over.

Consciousness returned as a headache like none he'd ever had before, and with it the awareness that he was no longer where he'd last been.

The bag had been removed from his head; nonetheless, it took a few moments for Jorge's eyes to become accustomed to the dim light of the room in which he found himself. He lay upon an old mattress that was bare except for a small pillow and the brown-wool blanket that had been thrown across him. His parka, cap, gloves, and boots were missing, leaving him with only the clothes he'd worn underneath. At least his hands had been untied—he discovered this when he sat up to look around—and he wasn't alone.

"Are you all right?" Inez sat on another mattress a few feet away, her own blanket pulled up around her shoulders. "They said you weren't badly injured, but I've been worried. You've been out for a while."

"I'm . . . okay." Jorge raised a hand to the back of his head, winced as his fingers found the large bump that something—he presumed it had been a gun butt—had left behind. A small adhesive bandage had been placed over the scrape he'd received on his face. "How about you?"

"I'm good . . . except for a headache where they hit me, that is." A wan smile. "I expect you've got the same thing."

Jorge nodded painfully as he looked around. The room was small and cold, and empty save for the little battery-powered lamp that had been placed on the concrete floor near their feet. No windows in the redbrick walls, only a narrow air vent. A single door—heavy wood, reinforced with iron strips, lacking a knob or handle—rested within the wall to the left. There was a thin sliver of light beneath it, but he couldn't hear anything from the other side. He suspected that they were in a basement—perhaps the place had once been a storeroom—but if so, then it could be anywhere.

"Have they said anything? Told you who they are?" Sitting up a little straighter, he patted the pockets of his vest and trousers. Nothing in them, nor was he surprised. If their captors had removed their winter gear, they would have also taken the precaution of taking away their headsets, utility knives, and datapads. The last was probably the worst, he realized; there was a lot of information in them that could be useful to whoever had kidnapped them.

"No, but I've got an idea who they are. Look behind you."

Trying to ignore the pain shooting through the back of his neck, Jorge carefully turned his head and saw that the room wasn't as unadorned as he'd first thought. A flag had been draped across the wall above their mattresses: crude and obviously handmade, it had thirteen red and white horizontal stripes beside a dark blue field, at the center of which was a single white star.

He'd recently seen one much like it, among the historical exhibits at the Grange Hall: the banner of the United Republic of America. He stared at it for a few moments, remembering what Sawyer Lee had told him that night in New Florida. "This . . . isn't a good sign," he said at last.

"No. It's not, is it?" Inez hesitated, then lowered her voice to a near whisper. "My mother told me that, when she searched Sergio's mind, she found . . ."

"I know. Sawyer said the same thing to me." He sighed, looked away from the flag. "I guess . . . or at least I think we can guess . . . what Vargas's role in all this has been. He set us up."

Inez's eyes narrowed as she shook her head. "We can't assume that. If he'd been hiding something like this, my mother would have found out. She . . ."

From just beyond the door, footsteps. Jorge placed a forefinger against his lips, but Inez had already fallen silent. A key rattled in a lock, then the door swung open on creaking hinges and, one at a time, two men walked in.

Jorge recognized the first man as belonging to the group who'd captured them on Beacon Hill. He carried a small wooden chair, which he silently placed on the floor on the other side of the lantern. The other man was a stranger: thickset and squat, with grey-flecked hair combed back from a jowled and pugnacious face. They were dressed in what appeared to be military-style field jackets and dungarees; both wore black armbands upon which a small URA flag had been stitched.

"That'll be all," the older man said. "I'll knock when I'm done." His companion nodded before leaving the room, shutting the door behind him. The visitor remained standing; he quietly regarded Jorge and Inez for a moment, then a humorless but not unkind smile stretched across his face.

"We waited until we thought you might be awake." His voice was hoarse, like someone accustomed to speaking more loudly than he was now. "I imagine you're hurting a little."

He stopped, clearly expecting an answer. Jorge didn't reply, though, and neither did Inez. "Well . . . I'll take that as a yes," their captor said, then he reached into a breast pocket. "Here," he went on, pulling out a small plastic bottle and tossing it to Jorge. "It's not much, but it might help a bit."

Jorge didn't try to catch the bottle, instead letting it fall to the mattress between his feet. Something rattled inside. "Go ahead," the older man said. "It's just ibuprofen. Two for each of you." He paused. "We don't have much to spare . . . hard to come by, when we can get them . . . so if you don't take 'em, I'll have to ask that you give it back."

Jorge hesitated, then picked up the bottle, unscrewed the cap, and shook out two small pills. "Good," the older man said, waiting until Jorge had passed the bottle to Inez before he sat down in the chair. "Sorry we don't have any water for you yet, but that'll be brought to you soon. Along with food, or anything else you might need."

Jorge was tempted to ask for their headsets, weapons, and the rest of their clothing and gear, but he knew that was pointless. So he swallowed the ibuprofen and sat back on the mattress, folding his legs together as he silently waited to see what their visitor would do or say next. But he seemed to be just as capable of patience; knitting his hands together across his broad stomach, he studied them with a gaze that was both curious and unrevealing.

"All right, then," he said after a few moments, "let's start by getting better acquainted. I'm Major General Roland Black, commander of the First Massachusetts Regiment of the Provisional Army, United Republic of America. Which means that I'm in charge here, if you haven't guessed already." A smug and self-important smile. "And, of course, we already know who you are . . . Lieutenant Jorge Montero, of the Coyote Federation Corps of Exploration, and Corporal Inez Torres, also of the Corps of Exploration."

Despite his relief, Jorge managed to keep from smiling. The fact that Black referred to Inez by her last-name alias meant that he'd pulled their identities from their pads; if he'd called her Sanchez instead of Torres, then it would've meant that Vargas had told him who she really was, and that could've meant even more trouble than they were already in.

But why didn't Sergio let him know? he wondered. *He knows that Inez is the* chaaz'maha's *daughter. Why didn't he inform his people of this?*

Again, Black seemed to be anticipating a reaction. Upon receiving none, a slight frown betrayed his disappointment. He crossed his legs and went on. "I regret to inform that one of your team, Sergeant Gregory Dillon, was killed during the effort to detain you. As with you yourselves, we discovered his identity through the pad he carried on his person. His body has been retrieved, though, and it will be given a respectful burial in accordance with his standing as . . . ah, a war casualty." Another pause. "On the other hand, you'll be relieved to know that the last member of your team, Captain Hugh McAlister, has been captured alive."

Jorge struggled to keep his emotions in check, but he heard Inez let out her breath. That small, involuntary response seemed to satisfy Black, because his smile reappeared. "He was injured while resisting capture by our marines, but he's receiving medical attention in separate quarters. Your spacecraft, of course, has been impounded. So if you were expecting to be rescued"—he shook his head—"then you should know that is no longer an option."

Once more, Black waited for either Jorge or Inez to say something. When neither of them spoke, he shook his head. "Please . . . there's no reason to be silent. It won't get you anywhere, and it'll only make your situation worse." He cocked his head toward the door. "It's locked and guarded at all times, and this location is very secure, so don't even consider trying to escape. We will make you as comfortable as possible, and I promise that none of you will be harmed in any way. But your cooperation will have a lot to do with how long you and Captain McAlister remain here, and the first step toward that cooperation is your speaking with me."

Jorge looked over at Inez. She said nothing but only gave an indifferent shrug. Jorge was proud of her willingness to tough it out; however, he was also all too aware of the fact that, as prisoners, they were vulnerable to Black's every whim. And he didn't trust the man to keep his word not to harm them or McAlister.

He hesitated, then spoke. "So . . . how do you want us to cooperate with you?"

Pleased that one of his prisoners had finally decided to talk, Black nodded. "We just have one small thing we want you to do. It'll help us achieve our goal, and once that's accomplished, you'll be released."

Black was doing his best to present himself as an affable host, but Jorge wasn't fooled for a moment. One look at him, and he instinctively knew that Black wasn't someone to be taken lightly. He had to approach the situation carefully, so as not to arouse his ire. "I'll . . . do what I can," Jorge said, "but there are a few things I'd like to know. Like why . . ."

"Why you were captured, and even why my people took such an immediate interest in you." Black nodded. "Of course, and the answer to that is simple . . . we knew you were coming." His smile became a broad grin. "In fact, we've been waiting for you for quite some time now."

Although Jorge had already deduced that Vargas had betrayed them, what Black said rattled him more thoroughly than he had expected. He felt a shiver that had little to do with the chill of the room, and when he glanced at Inez again, he saw that her mouth had drawn into a taut line.

"You're saying that this was a trap?" he asked.

"Yes. That's exactly what it is . . . a trap." Then Black shook his head. "You're not the prey, though, but rather the bait. My people are after much bigger game than any of you."

"The *chaaz'maha*." When Inez finally spoke, her voice was little more than a whisper. "That's who you're really after, isn't it?"

Black favored her with a wink. "Correct, Corporal. The *chaaz'maha* . . . or Hawk Thompson, as we prefer to call him . . . is who we want to meet, not you. You're just the means to an end."

"Then why . . . ?" Jorge was baffled. "I mean, how did you . . . ?"

"'Why' isn't important, really. At least not to you. But 'how' . . . ah, that's quite interesting, indeed." Black shifted in his chair, making himself more comfortable. "Let's start at the beginning . . . your friend and mine, Mr. Sergio Vargas."

Jorge moved upon the mattress until his back was against the wall; he noted that Black watched him carefully, wary for any surprises on his part. Instead, Jorge crossed his feet together and folded his arms across his chest. "I figured that he was mixed up in this somehow. He's been one of your people all along, hasn't he?"

"Umm . . . no. Not really." Black shook his head. "Fact is, he didn't even know that he was working on behalf of the Provisional Army, or even the United Republic of America. So you shouldn't blame him too much, Lieutenant. In his own way, he's just as much part of the bait as you are."

Jorge started to open his mouth, but Black held up a hand. "Let me explain. When the Provisional Army decided that we wanted to . . . shall we say, arrange a meeting with Thompson . . . we knew that we'd have to find a way to lure him to a place and time that would be of our choosing. When he's visited Boston in the past, it's always been where his followers have been able to protect him. We wanted to change that, and it occurred to us that the best way of doing so was to provide him with a reason to come here that he couldn't easily ignore. And the answer to that was . . ."

"Getting someone from Coyote to return to Earth, with the purpose of finding him as well."

"Excellent." An enthusiastic nod. "Well done, Lieutenant. Yes, Thompson wouldn't have done this if we'd captured or intimidated any of his followers here. We've tried that already, but they're remarkably loyal to their messiah, and vice versa. But while we knew that luring someone from Coyote wouldn't be easy, nevertheless there was a remote possibility that it could be done . . . we just knew that having someone from his homeworld return to Earth was something that he couldn't ignore."

Jorge gave a noncommittal shrug, and Black went on. "Using Starbridge Earth was out of the question, of course. Nothing has come through it in years. But we also knew that there was another functional starbridge out in the Kuiper Belt, so it was just a matter of finding someone who'd know how to activate it and would be willing and able to pilot a ship through hyperspace to 47 Uma. We didn't have anyone like that in our own ranks, unfortunately, but after a long search by our people, we found Captain Vargas."

"And so you recruited him," Inez said.

"Again . . . no, not exactly." A wry smile. "'Recruited' implies that Vargas was a volunteer, or at least that he knowingly went along with this. But we were careful not to let him know that the Provisional

Army was involved, or that he was serving the goals of the URA. And can you guess why?"

Black waited for a response. When neither Jorge nor Inez replied, he continued. "Not long after Thompson came here and set himself up to be the savior of mankind"—his tone was heavy with sarcasm—"he revealed that he was a telepath and that there were others like him back home. So it was not unreasonable to expect that whoever went to Coyote would have their minds read, and if so, that our plans would be discovered. So it was important that whoever went there didn't know that he was working for us, but instead truly believed that he was acting on his own. Do you understand?"

"Yes . . ." Then Jorge shook his head. "No, I don't. When he arrived on Coyote, Sergio told us that he'd stolen the freighter himself and that no one else had helped him."

"Good." Black grinned. "That was exactly what we wanted him to think. But the truth of the matter is that it had all been carefully arranged. Our agents located a decommissioned freighter in the lunar shipyard and made sure that it was in good operating condition, with a working biostasis cell, even that its fuel tanks were refilled . . ."

"And then made sure Sergio would have no trouble stealing it," Jorge finished. "So you manipulated him from the beginning."

"It wasn't hard." Black shrugged. "Sergio wasn't very fond of Thompson. I don't think he'd liked the man the moment he first laid eyes on him, when he rescued him from that lifeboat. Certainly, we lucked out by finding a former UA pilot with a starbridge key, but we didn't need to motivate him. He did that himself. A little nudge in the right direction was all that was required."

Black laced his fingers together. "Once Sergio was on his way, we instructed our loyalists to remain on the lookout for anyone coming into Boston who didn't look like they belonged here, and to alert the Provisional Army if and when they saw someone like that. We've also had people watching Port Logan for a couple of months now, figuring that it would be the most likely place a spacecraft might try to land."

Again, the self-satisfied smile. "All we had to do after that, really, was sit back and wait. It took a while, but we were patient. We knew someone would show up . . . eventually."

"Very cunning." Inez slowly nodded. "I'll have to give you that." She paused. "I hope you're planning to reward Sergio for his efforts. It's the least you can do."

The smile flickered, and it seemed to Jorge that, for the first time since Black walked into the room, he didn't have a ready answer. "He will be, yes," he replied. "We haven't seen him since . . . well, doesn't matter. His role in this is done, and we have no use for him anymore. If he comes to us, that's fine. If not . . . well, he has the gratitude of the United Republic of America."

"I've been wondering about that." Jorge glanced up at the flag above his head. "Your people . . . the Provisional Army, I mean . . . they're really trying to put this together again? No offense, but the URA has been dead and gone for . . . how long? Almost three hundred years?"

Black's expression darkened, and his hands fell to his sides. "The URA was America's finest moment. When the Liberty Party was in control, our great nation enjoyed a time of peace and prosperity unlike any before or since. Now that the Western Hemisphere Union is gone, we're returning to take back our country."

Oh, my god, Jorge thought. *The man's a fanatic.* Not only that, but delusional as well. Like everyone else born and raised on Coyote, Jorge had learned in school about the events leading up to Captain Lee's hijacking of the URSS *Alabama*. The Liberty Party had presided over one of the ugliest periods in American history, with nearly one-third of the population living in squalor and political dissidents being sent to government reeducation camps. Any peace and prosperity there might have been during that time had been enjoyed only by a few, and was enforced at the barrel of a gun. Apparently Black hadn't realized that one of his prisoners had the same name as one of the key figures in the *Alabama* conspiracy; if he learned that Jorge was the great-grandson of a D.I., though . . .

Jorge decided to change the subject, fast. "So I take it that the *chaaz'maha* . . . Thompson, I mean . . . represents a threat to your new order. Is that what the TC is?"

Black raised an eyebrow. "Who told you about the TC? Vargas?"

"No," Inez said. "Sam's son asked us if we belonged to it, when we met them at the dock. Does it stand for something?"

"Terra Concorde . . . and that's all I'm going to say about them." Abruptly, Black stood up from his chair. "That's enough. You've learned everything you need to know. Time for you to do a little favor for us."

He walked over to the door, banged a fist against it. The door opened, and Black said something to the guard standing outside. The door closed again, and Black stood beside it, saying nothing to either Jorge or Inez. A couple of minutes later, the door reopened, and another Provisional Army soldier walked in, carrying a folded metal tripod with a small vidcam mounted on it.

"We intend to send a message to the *chaaz'maha*," Black explained, as the soldier set up the tripod in front of the mattresses, "telling him that you're here and that you'll be given to him once he agrees to a meeting on our terms. That means, of course, that we need to supply proof that we actually have you in our custody. So I'd appreciate it if you'd state your names and say where you're from." He paused, then added, "And that's all you're going to say. If you make an attempt to pass any messages of your own . . . cryptic slogans, hand signals . . . I assure you that your stay here will be less comfortable."

Jorge suddenly realized why the crude URA flag had been hung from the wall behind them. It was to serve as a backdrop for the vid the *chaaz'maha* would see. He glanced at Inez, and she slowly nodded. "We understand," he said. "Just one more thing . . . where are you planning to have this meeting of yours?"

Black shook his head. "You don't need to know that," he replied. "Just do your part, and everything will work out fine." He looked at the soldier. "Ready?"

The other man nodded as he bent over the vidcam. He touched a stud on top, and a small red light glimmered next to its lens. "All right, now," Black said. "Talk."

Jorge faced the lens. "I'm Jorge Montero, of the Coyote Federation Corps of Exploration."

Obeying Black's order to say nothing else, he looked over at Inez. She remained quiet for a couple of seconds, just long enough to earn a scowl from Black, before she finally opened her mouth. "I'm . . . Inez," she said slowly, looking straight at the vidcam. "I'm also from Coyote."

She fell silent again, continuing to stare at the lens until Black finally nodded. "That'll do," he said. He tapped the cam operator on the shoulder, and the other man shut off the unit. "Thank you," Black went on, as the soldier refolded the tripod and carried it out of the room. "You'll be brought food and water soon. If you need to relieve yourselves, all you have to do is knock on the door and someone will escort you to the facilities. Until then"—a shrug and a smile—"just rest and wait. This should not take long. And after that, you'll be free to go."

Without another word, Black picked up the chair. Carrying it under his arm, he turned and walked out the door. It slammed shut behind him, leaving Jorge and Inez alone in the room.

Inez let out her breath in a long, shuddering sigh, then raised her knees to her chest and closed her arms around them. "Don't be frightened," Jorge said. "I'm sure everything's going to be all right."

Inez shook her head, not looking up at him. "No," she said, so softly that he could barely hear her. "No, it's not."

Seeing that she was trembling, he moved over to her mattress, draping his blanket around her shoulders. "We'll get out of this," he said, trying to comfort her. "They're not going to . . ."

"Everything he said was true," she went on, "except one thing." When she turned her face to him, Jorge saw tears glistening at the corners of her eyes. "He was lying when he said that we'll be let go. I could feel it. When my father comes to them, they'll kill him . . . and then us, too."

Black did keep his word about their treatment, though. Shortly after he left, the same soldier who'd operated the vidcam brought them a couple of liters of water and two bowls of chicken broth. When Inez asked for more blankets, those were brought as well, although Jorge's request to have their boots returned was ignored; apparently someone believed that depriving them of their footwear would interfere with any escape attempts. And at no time were they physically or verbally abused; it appeared that Black had instructed the guards to treat them as war prisoners, not criminals.

Yet without their watches or pads, they had almost no way of judging the passage of time. It was only when Jorge knocked on the door and told the guard that he needed to relieve himself that he had a clue as to when and where they were. Outside their room was a long, concrete-walled corridor; at one end was a stairwell, guarded by another soldier, and at the other end a narrow window at shoulder height. Sunlight streamed through its dusty panes, but Jorge's guard didn't let him get close enough to look out. Halfway down the corridor, past several closed doors, was a pair of restrooms, their doors marked with faded gender symbols; inside the men's room were several urinals and toilets, each of them as dry and waterless as the sinks. The guard waited patiently while Jorge visited one of the stalls, then marched him back to his room. From the looks of things, Jorge determined that he and Inez were in the basement of an abandoned office building. Yet it could be anywhere in Boston; without access to the window, he had no idea exactly where they were. When Inez made the same trip a little while later, she learned no more than he had.

Time passed slowly, marked only by another meal they were brought several hours later: again, chicken broth and water. The room gradually became colder; the wall vent supplied no heat, and the extra blankets did little to keep them warm. They pushed the mattresses together and huddled beside each other; Inez suggested pulling down the flag and using it as a bedspread, but Jorge immediately rejected this. Their captors would doubtless be offended, and he didn't want to do anything that might put him and Inez further at risk.

In whispered tones, they discussed trying to escape, yet none of the schemes they concocted seemed viable. Even if they were able to trick the guard into opening the door for both of them—unlikely, since he always checked to make sure that one of them was still on the other side of the room before opening the door more than a crack—there was nothing that could be used as a weapon except the lantern, which wasn't heavy enough to serve as a bludgeon. When they were brought dinner, one person stood watch with gun in hand while the other delivered the meal. And even if they were able to overpower two armed men, they had no idea how many others were in the building. Besides, they'd also have to rescue McAlister; they didn't know where he was, though, or even if he was in any condition to make a run for it.

After a while, the topic of conversation shifted to what Black had told them about the Provisional Army of the United Republic of America. "You know," Jorge murmured, "I've got a feeling that these people aren't quite the force he made them out to be."

Inez nodded. She'd calmed down a little, but Jorge knew that she was still afraid; he could see it in her eyes every time she looked at him. He figured that, so long as he kept her talking, she wouldn't slide into depression.

"I've been thinking the same thing," she replied, keeping her voice low. They had no idea whether anyone was listening at the door or if the room was bugged, but they didn't want to risk speaking out loud. "We didn't see any of their flags on the streets, and there was no one wearing those armbands." She paused. "But when we were in the alley, Sam said that no one would come to help us, so . . ."

"That doesn't mean much." One of blankets they'd pulled up around them was falling off; he pulled it over their shoulders again and moved a little closer to her. "Maybe they're sort of a street gang. Big enough to intimidate a neighborhood but not so much that they have any sort of real political power."

"It's hard to imagine that, yes." Inez considered the thought for a moment. "Did you see the look on Black's face when you said that the URA has been gone for three hundred years? That really got under his skin . . . and I can tell you, he came close to losing his temper just then."

"Uh-huh." Jorge sighed. "Any other time, I would've loved to give him a history lesson. Like about how Massachusetts belonged to the Commonwealth of New England, not the URA, and how the URA used bioweapons against Boston just before it collapsed."

A wan smile crossed Inez's face. "I would have liked to see him respond to that." The smile vanished as quickly as it had appeared. "But people like him have an answer to everything, and it usually doesn't have much to do with facts. Only their beliefs matter . . . and he really seems to believe that the world would be a better place if only they could bring back something that ceased to exist long before he was born."

"Maybe." Jorge remembered something he'd once read. "A long

time ago, here on Earth, there were groups of people who shared
a hobby of re-creating historical times. They'd dress up in medi-
eval clothes and fight with fake swords, or wear the uniforms of
soldiers from past wars and stage mock battles. They did this just for
fun, but now and then someone would take it too seriously and start
wishing that they actually lived back then, and conveniently forget the more unpleasant aspects." He shrugged. "Maybe that's how
Black and his people got started. They became interested in the
URA, then . . . well, one day they decided that they wanted to *become*
the URA."

"It's possible, I suppose. It would explain a lot, if it were . . ." Inez
suddenly yawned, cupping her mouth as she did so. "Sorry. I guess
I'm more tired than I thought."

"It's been a long day, yeah." It occurred to Jorge that the last time
either of them had slept was when they were on the *Mercator*. Although he had little idea of what time it was, it had been many hours
since they'd been brought dinner. Probably the middle of the night,
perhaps even later. "Want to get some sleep?"

"Uh-huh." Inez hesitated. "Should one of us stand watch, or . . . ?"

"I don't think it matters." Now that she'd mentioned it, Jorge realized that he was exhausted, too. "If anyone comes in, I'm sure we'll
both wake up."

"You're probably right." Inez lay back upon the mattresses, pulling
the topmost blanket over herself. Jorge crawled on hands and knees
to the lantern and switched it off, then he returned to the mattresses
and curled up beside her, sharing body warmth as they'd learned during Corps winter survival training. She yawned again as he pulled the
rest of the blankets around them, then mumbled, "G'night."

"G'night. Sleep well." Jorge stayed awake for a minute or two longer, feeling her breath against the side of his neck, until his eyes closed
of their own accord.

*   *   *

He had no idea how long he slept, only that he was abruptly awakened by the touch of a hand upon his shoulder. Jerked out of a dreamless slumber, thinking that he was being attacked by one of the guards, he grabbed at the hand . . . and heard Inez yelp in surprise.

"What . . . ?" Letting go of her, Jorge realized that she was very close to him, her body touching his own. "I'm . . . sorry, I . . ."

"Shh," she whispered, her mouth near to his ear. "It's okay."

He couldn't see her, but he was aware of her hands upon him. Before he could say anything more, he felt her lips close upon his, soft and warm in the cold night. "Don't say anything," she whispered again, lifting her face away. "Just . . . please . . . I don't want to be alone right now."

There were a dozen reasons why it was wrong for them to do what she wanted, but also one that mattered more than the others: she was frightened, and desperate for solace in any way that she could find it. Or so Jorge thought as he reached for her. Inez had already taken off her tunic and trousers, and the front zipper of her unitard opened with only the slightest sound. Beneath it was her body, her skin deliciously warm, the muscles beneath it tense with desire. He gently stroked her left breast, feeling its nipple become erect beneath his fingers, as her hands found the fastenings of his clothes and impatiently yanked them apart.

In the pitch darkness of the basement room, with the blankets keeping away the chill of night and an uncertain fate, their bodies came together, their hands and mouths exploring, searching, grasping. After a time, Inez gently pushed Jorge flat on his back, then straddled him between her sleek bare thighs. She sighed deeply as he entered her, and cried out ever so softly as, if only for a few seconds, they found a place where there was no fear, no loneliness, no thoughts of death.

And it was in that instant that Jorge remembered something that he'd tried to force from his mind: he loved her, and he always would.

They had fallen asleep in each other's arms, having put on their clothes again once their lovemaking was over, when Jorge was awakened a second time. Not by Inez, though, but by the rapid succession of gunshots just outside the room.

Inez's head was tucked into the crook of his left arm. He didn't need to rouse her, though, because she woke up on her own. "What . . . Jorge, did you hear . . . ?"

"Uh-huh." He sat up, trying to listen harder. "But I . . ."

The door banged open, and someone charged into the room. The corridor outside was dark, so he couldn't see who it was, but in the next instant a flashlight beam found them. "Are you Jorge and Inez?" demanded the vague silhouette backlit by its glow.

"Yes . . . yes, we are." Squinting and confused, Jorge raised a hand against the sudden glare. "Who . . . ?"

"Never mind that now." A young man's voice, calm yet insistent. "Hustle. We're getting you out of here."

Jorge and Inez glanced at each other, bewildered by what was happening. "C'mon, move!" the young man snapped, then his voice lowered slightly. "Shadow Three to Shadow Leader . . . I've found Coyote One and Two, both unhurt."

Throwing aside the blankets, Jorge staggered to his feet. He reached down to help Inez up from the mattress, but she was already out of bed. "Are you Terra Concorde?" she asked.

Shadow Three, whoever he was, ignored the question. Instead, he reached down to the floor to snatch up the lantern. Switching it on, he revealed himself as a figure dressed in black, a mask hiding his face save for a thin slit for his eyes. He wore a wireless headset over the mask; a pair of night goggles dangled around his neck, and a dark grey carbine nestled in his arms.

"Take this," he said, as he handed the lantern to Jorge. "You'll need it . . . we've knocked out their generator." From somewhere nearby, more gunshots; Shadow Three whipped around, raising his weapon to his shoulder. He waited a moment, then spoke again. "Copy that, Shadow Two. We're clear." Then he looked over his shoulder at Jorge and Inez. "C'mon, let's go."

Just outside the door, one of the guards was sprawled facedown across the corridor floor, his pistol at his side. In the pale light of the lantern, Jorge saw that he appeared to still be breathing, and that there was no blood on his body. "Is he . . . ?" Jorge started to ask.

"No," Shadow Three said. "We used darts." Jorge started to reach down to pick up the guard's weapon, but his rescuer kicked it away. "Don't worry about that," he added, stepping over the guard to lead the way down the hall. "He's out of it for the next few hours."

Another black-clad figure—apparently a woman, although it was hard to tell—emerged from an open doorway halfway to the stairs. She held a carbine in her right hand, and with her left arm she supported what appeared to be a wounded man. It wasn't until Jorge got closer that he realized that it was Hugh McAlister.

"Fancy meeting you here." McAlister's face twisted into a wry grin. "Did you enjoy the accommodations, too?"

"Very nice, yes." Jorge saw that his left leg was stiffly wrapped in bloodstained bandages from the thigh down. "What happened to . . . ?"

"Caught a bullet while trying to protect the shuttle." The pilot winced as, held up by the woman at his side, he limped forward on his good leg. "Should've paid more attention to the guys on those boats. They . . ."

"Be quiet." The woman stopped, glanced down the corridor. "Shadow Two to Shadow Leader. I'm with Shadow Three, and I've got Coyote Three. Gunshot wound to left thigh but otherwise unharmed and mobile." Without waiting for a response, she turned to her colleague. "Ready?"

"Wait a sec," Jorge said before Shadow Three could respond. "I don't know if you've noticed, but we're barefoot. We can't . . ."

"Your stuff's upstairs." Shadow Two turned to head down the corridor, McAlister's arm still draped across her shoulders. "We'll get it before we leave. Hurry, now . . ."

Another Provisional Army soldier lay at the foot of the stairs; Jorge recognized him as Sam. He was tempted to kick their former native guide in the ribs, but they were in too much of a rush for him to exact petty revenge. Instead, they hurried up the stairs, Inez taking over from Shadow Two to help McAlister manage the steps. They reached a landing, where Jorge saw an outside door that stood ajar. Dangling from its hinges, its outer panel was blackened and had been dented; the lingering, acrid scent of explosives testified that it had been blown open. It was night outside, and Jorge caught a glimpse of another figure in black running past; he thought they were going to leave that way, but Shadow Three continued the rest of the way up the stairs, beckoning for him and Inez to follow.

Another landing, then they went through a door into what appeared to be the building's ground floor. Glowing lightsticks lay upon the black-marble floor of a long, wide hallway; more Provisional Army soldiers were scattered across the corridor, all apparently unconscious. Figures in black darted from room to room, kicking open battered oak doors to aim their rifle barrels inside before entering. The gunfire had largely stopped, but every few moments they heard another loud report from somewhere.

Shadow Three led the group to what appeared to be a conference room. Leather armchairs, their upholstery long since chewed up by rats and mice, were arranged around a long mahogany table. Jorge found their parkas, caps, and boots lying in a heap upon it, but that wasn't the first thing he noticed. At the far end of the table, slumped back in a chair and staring up at the high ceiling with sightless eyes, was Major General Roland Black. The wet, gaping hole in the back of his skull told what had happened in this room.

"Shot himself when we came through the door," another raider said as they walked in. "Crazy bastard." Then he turned away. "Shadow Leader to all units," he said quietly. "All hostages located. Shadows Two and Three commencing evac operation. All other units, continue sweep of premises. Detain any suspects, but don't use fatal measures if it can be helped."

Jorge stared at Black, wondering at the mind-set of a man who'd rather kill himself than be taken alive by adversaries carrying non-lethal weapons. "C'mon, hurry up," Shadow Three growled. "We're not out of this yet."

Jorge needed no further urging. He pulled on his boots and yanked on his parka and cap, then helped Inez do the same for McAlister. There didn't seem to be anything handy for the pilot to use as a crutch, so he and Inez supported McAlister between them. The rest of their equipment—datapads, weapons, watches, and headsets—were no-where to be seen, but there was no time to search for them; Jorge figured that they must have been taken by the Provisional Army, with only their clothes left unclaimed. Probably because Black had decided that his prisoners would need to be wearing them when the *chaaz'maha* showed up.

"Just tell us one thing," he asked Shadow Leader before they left the room. "You *are* with the Terra Concorde, aren't you?"

Shadow Leader was distracted by reports coming in through the headset beneath his mask, but he managed to give Jorge a withering look. No answer was necessary. Jorge nodded, then extended his hand. "Thank you."

Shadow Leader hesitated, then grasped his hand. "You're welcome, Lieutenant. *Sa'Tong qo.*"

Jorge felt his jaw drop. He'd heard this *Sa'Tong*ian expression all his adult life, but the last thing he'd ever expected was to hear it said on Earth. He was still grappling with this when Inez came to his assistance.

"*Sa'Tong qo,*" she responded, bowing slightly. Shadow Leader nodded and turned away again, then Shadow Three motioned for her, McAlister, and Jorge to follow him.

"He's a *Sa'Tong*ian?" Jorge whispered to Inez as they hurried down the darkened corridor, Shadow Two guarding their rear flank. "I didn't see that coming." Inez didn't reply, but he didn't miss the knowing smile that briefly appeared on her face.

The corridor intersected with another from the right. Shadow Three paused at the corner; he peered around it, his gun at the ready, then silently waved for the others to follow him. Passing a Terra Concorde raider standing watch on two captured Provisional Army soldiers who knelt on the floor with their hands laced together behind their heads, they hurried down the corridor until they reached a large hall, two stories in height, with a bronze statue at its center. Jorge realized that they were in some sort of public building, but it wasn't until they passed a pair of raiders guarding the front doors and exited the building through a row of brick arches that he saw where they were.

Stopping on the veranda just past the arches, he let go of McAlister so that he could turn around and look up at the building. A gold dome rose from the third-floor roof; having seen it only yesterday morning from the Charles River and Revere Street, he immediately knew where they were. The Massachusetts State House. They weren't far from where they had been captured on Beacon Hill.

Jorge didn't get a chance to remark on the irony, though, before Shadow Three and Shadow Two ushered them down a flight of cracked granite steps into a broad, fenced-in courtyard that lay in front of the capitol building. "We're going to wait here," Shadow Three said, coming to a halt and turning to the freed prisoners. "Your ride is on the way."

Jorge looked up again. A pair of gyros was orbiting the State House, their searchlights trained on the grounds below; another had landed only a dozen yards away. In the far distance, he could see a reddish orange haze just above the rooftops of the nearby buildings, the first light of dawn. It occurred to him that it had been almost exactly twenty-four hours earlier that the *Mercator* had touched down at Port Logan. A lot had happened since then . . .

"You came in by gyro?" McAlister asked. He leaned upon Inez's shoulder, left leg raised a few inches above the ground. "It's a miracle those guys didn't see you before . . ."

"Not by gyro," Shadow Two said. Her back was turned to them as she continued to watch the building's front entrance. "On foot, from all sides of the hill. We didn't bring in the gyros until after we secured the premises." She paused, then added, "Our inside man told us where you were being held. All we had to do was get to this location, and wait until . . ."

She was interrupted by an abrupt roar from somewhere above. Jorge thought at first that it was another gyro coming in, until he realized that the noise was too loud. A second later, from just beyond the State House dome, a dark form swept into view, the twin beams of its floodlights traveling across the building's slanted roof. As the craft came closer, stopping to hover in midair above the courtyard, Jorge suddenly realized what it was.

"What the hell?" McAlister shouted. "That's my ship!"

The *Mercator* made a slow, gradual descent, its landing thrusters causing a miniature whirlwind to whip across the State House grounds. Raising a hand to his face, Jorge watched as the shuttle's landing gear lowered from beneath its fuselage. McAlister was yelling something, and it sounded as if he was angry, but Jorge couldn't make out the words. All he knew was that the shuttle was the last thing he had expected to see.

The *Mercator* settled upon its wheels, but its engines didn't throttle down all the way before its belly hatch opened, and its ladder unfolded. "What are you waiting for?" Shadow Three shouted. "Go, go . . . get out of here!"

Jorge helped Inez carry McAlister again as the three of them hurried to the shuttle. "Who the hell is flying my ship?" the pilot demanded, as they ducked beneath its starboard wing. "That was the worst landing I've ever—"

"Never mind." Jorge glanced up at the cockpit, but it was too dark to make out who was at the controls. "Let's just go while we can."

Shadow Three and Shadow Two remained behind, but when Jorge assisted McAlister up the ladder, he found two more Shadows waiting for them in the passenger compartment. He stayed long enough to put McAlister into a seat and make sure that Inez was aboard, then trotted down the center aisle and scrambled up the ladder to the cockpit.

Sergio Vargas was strapped into the pilot's chair, his hands upon the yoke. He turned his head to look up at Jorge, and grinned when he saw the astonishment on the lieutenant's face.

"I know, I know . . . this is going to take a lot of explaining," he said. "But right now, we've got somewhere else we need to be." Before Jorge could respond, he reached up to nudge his headset's mike wand. "Secure aft hatch and prepare for takeoff," he murmured, then nodded toward the right seat. "Strap in, Lieutenant. We're lifting wheels."

From behind him, Jorge heard the belly hatch slam shut. McAlister was still protesting, and Jorge fervently hoped that Inez would prevent him from entering the cockpit; the last thing anyone needed just then was to have McAlister see who was flying the shuttle. Jorge had a lot of questions of his own, but he kept them to himself as he climbed over the center control board to the copilot's seat.

"Where are we going?" he finally asked as he buckled the seat harness.

"Where do you think?" A sly smile from Vargas as he rested a hand on the thruster bars. "We're going to see the *chaaz'maha*."

And then he slowly pushed the bars forward, and the *Mercator* rose into the dawn sky of Boston.

Part 6

KING PHILIP'S LIGHTHOUSE
(from the memoirs of Sawyer Lee)

Late afternoon of the day after Chris Levin was murdered, I reached Navajo.

From a passenger cabin porthole of a Corps skiff, I watched as the suborbital transport reentered the atmosphere over Coyote's eastern hemisphere. The captain and copilot were not very happy with me, nor were the three blueshirts also aboard; no one had said as much, but I could see it from the look in their eyes. Bad enough that I'd ordered the skiff to fly down from Fort Lopez to Defiance, picking me up shortly after noon at the airfield. Or that I'd also mustered the soldiers from the local Militia garrison out of their warm bunkhouse when they would have rather spent a lazy Orifiel playing poker and drinking ale. No, I'd gone further than that; I'd also demanded to be flown to the other side of the world, and didn't explain why until we'd left Midland.

Captain Hansbach had done his best to try to reason with me, but I let him know that this wasn't a request but rather a direct order that wasn't open to negotiation. He'd calmed down a bit when I told him what it was all about. Nonetheless, I had little doubt that, once this was over, he'd lodge a formal complaint with President Edgar. An official reprimand was probably coming my way, yet I couldn't have cared less what the president or Hansbach or three irate soldiers thought of my actions. There was a man in Manuelito I wanted to find, and when the day was done, he'd either be in handcuffs or lying dead at my feet.

So I sat alone in the back of the cabin as the skiff made the long descent that shed the rest of its airspeed. Through the porthole, I could see the icy blue waters of the Narragansett Channel pass beneath us. A brief glimpse of King Philip, the large island off the west coast of Navajo where the Providence Straits flowed into the channel, then the transport cruised over the confluence on its final approach to the fishing village of Manuelito.

A recent settlement, Manuelito was not much more than a collection of cabins, shops, and warehouses nestled beside the wharf where the whaling fleet was anchored. This time of year, the ships were anchored at harbor, its crews waiting for the coming of spring, when the North Sea would break up and the catwhales would begin swimming south from their winter spawning grounds to the warmer waters of the Great Equatorial River. Until then, few boats would venture into the Straits; the fishermen stayed at home, temporarily becoming greenhouse farmers by helping their families raise the crops that would get them through winter. Like many such places on Coyote, Manuelito was a town whose residents preferred the isolation of the frontier. No doubt they'd be surprised to see a Corps spacecraft coming in for an unscheduled visit.

Which was exactly what I wanted. If David Laird, a.k.a. Peter Desilitz, was in Manuelito, I didn't want him to get any advance warning. That was why I'd ordered Captain Hansbach to pick me up in Defiance as soon as possible and fly me straight to Navajo. Although I hadn't had any problems explaining Chris's death to Defiance's chief proctor or the reason why we'd been in town in the first place, I didn't want to risk having one of Desilitz's pals learn what had happened and, putting two and two together, send word to Manuelito. Laird had already proven himself to be slippery; the sooner I made it to Navajo with a squad of blueshirts, the better my chances of nabbing him before he made another getaway.

I was no longer pretending to be a traveling salesman. I'd tried subtlety, and it had cost me the life of someone I respected. So once again I was General Sawyer Lee, commandant of the Coyote Federation Corps of Exploration. But what I was doing was barely legal; the Corps wasn't in the business of tracking down fugitives, and my rank and uniform gave me scant authority to recruit Militia soldiers in pursuit of what amounted to a personal vendetta. Edgar might well demand my resignation once this was all over. No doubt he would. There was no love between us, and he'd probably use this incident as an excuse to get rid of me.

I didn't care. To hell with protocol. I was out for revenge.

The skiff touched down on a small airstrip on the outskirts of Manuelito, not far from the waterfront. The townspeople hadn't failed to notice our arrival; by the time Captain Hansbach shut down the engines and his copilot cranked open the side hatch, a couple of local officials had driven a shag wagon out to greet us. That, too, was something I'd expected, and even hoped for; it would save me the effort of having to find them instead.

A tall, thin-faced man watched as the blueshirts came down the ladder. His eyes widened when he saw them, and it was obvious that armed soldiers were the last people he thought he'd see. But there was a flash of recognition in his eyes when I emerged from the skiff, and although it occurred to me that I'd met him before, I couldn't quite remember where or when.

"General Lee," he said, stepping forward to extend a hand. "What a surprise."

I shook his hand. "Yes, I imagine it is, umm . . ."

"You don't remember me, do you?" A trace of disappointment in his reedy voice. "Gerald Copperfield, the mayor of Manuelito. We met . . . oh, I think it was four, maybe four and a half years ago, when the Corps surveyed this area. I was one of the original settlers. We had dinner together, talked about the prospects of establishing a catwhaling station."

Even after he reminded me, I barely recollected our previous encounter. The Corps of Exploration was still new back then, and I'd spent its formative years going from one survey mission to the next. I met a lot of settlers during that time, most of whom I never saw again.

"Yes, of course," I said, doing my best to pretend recognition. "It's been a while. You looked a little different back then."

"Umm . . . yes, perhaps." Copperfield continued to smile, but I could tell from the look in his eyes that he knew I was faking it. "And this is our chief proctor, Emma Stanley," he went on, motioning to the heavyset and unsmiling woman standing beside him. "A more recent resident . . . I don't think you've met her before."

"No, but it's a pleasure," I said, offering my hand.

Chief Stanley nodded, but didn't accept my handshake. Instead, she regarded the blueshirts with suspicion, like they were invaders from another world. "All mine," she murmured, her voice as cold and dry as the northern breeze that whipped up snow from the airfield. "So what brings you out here, General? This can't be a courtesy call."

She was direct and to the point, with little patience for niceties. Fine with me; I wasn't in the mood, either. "No, it isn't. Official business. I'm searching for someone who I have reason to believe now lives here . . . a suspect in an ongoing criminal investigation."

Her eyes narrowed. "If this is a criminal investigation, then why wasn't I informed?"

From the corner of my eye, I caught a glimpse of Captain Hansbach disembarking from his craft. Although he'd apparently overheard this part of the conversation, he didn't come over to join us but lingered near the ladder. He was trying to distance himself from me as much as possible, if only for the sake of deniability. The blueshirts stamped their boots against the snow, clutching their rifle straps and obviously wishing they were anywhere but here.

"It's a classified matter," I said, using the half-truthful excuse I'd concocted during the flight. "The federal government has been keeping it as quiet as possible, so as not to tip off our quarry. That's why no one here was informed that we were coming." I paused. "Sorry, but we've had to be careful."

This didn't seem to satisfy Stanley, but before she could respond, Copperfield stepped in. "Of course we understand. Whatever assistance we can give . . ." He gave Stanley a sidelong look, and although the frown didn't leave her face, she nodded reluctantly. However, it was clear that she didn't like having blueshirts or generals stomping into town unannounced; I hoped that I wouldn't have any trouble from her.

"Who is it that you're looking for?" she asked.

I reached into my parka, pulled out a pad. "His name is David Laird. He's also gone by the name of Peter Desilitz, but . . ."

"There's no one here by that name." Stanley glanced at Copperfield. "There *is* no one here with that name, is there, Gerald?"

The mayor reluctantly shook his head; he appeared to defer to his chief proctor, and I wondered whether she was Manuelito's real power. But I didn't have time or inclination to deal with small-town politics. "As I was saying," I continued, "it's possible that he may have assumed another identity. Our information leads us to believe that he came here about three years ago from Defiance. I realize that Manuelito is small enough that you know everyone here . . ."

"Our population is only 152," Copperfield said. "We pretty much know everyone by sight."

"Then perhaps you'd recognize his face." Opening the pad, I fumbled at its keyboard with my gloved hand until I accessed the menu. "Here, take a look . . ."

David Laird's mug shots, the ones taken of him by New Brighton proctors when he was arrested at the spaceport in c.y. 16, appeared on the screen. I touched another button, and they coalesced to form a hologram that rose above the pad. The image was old, though, and I could only pray that Laird hadn't changed so much in the last seven years that he'd be utterly unrecognizable.

But I didn't need to worry. The moment Copperfield and Stanley saw the holo, their expressions changed. The mayor's mouth fell open, and even the chief proctor looked as if she'd just received the shock of her life. Neither of them said anything for a moment, though, but simply stared at Laird's image in dumbstruck surprise.

"I take it that you know him," I said.

"Yes . . . yes, we do." Copperfield struggled to recover himself. "But there must be some sort of mistake."

"That's Joe Ross," Stanley said. "He moved here from Midland about three years ago. But . . ." She shook her head, no longer quite as obstinate as she'd been only moments earlier. "Are you sure this is the man you're looking for?"

"His real name is David Laird," I repeated, "and, yes, I'm sure." I hesitated, then decided that they needed to know the rest. "He was a member of Living Earth, who may have participated in the bombing of the New Guinea space elevator. He escaped to Coyote almost seven years ago but was arrested by the New Brighton proctors on charges of attempted assault with a deadly weapon. The authorities couldn't deport him, though, so they put a control patch on him and released him on probation, and it was during that time that he built the bomb that destroyed the *Robert E. Lee*."

Stanley gave me a querulous look. "I thought it was Alberto Cosenza who blew up the *Lee*." She glanced at Copperfield; the mayor's face had become grim, but he said nothing.

"Cosenza carried the bomb aboard the *Lee*, yes . . . but it was Laird who actually put it together for him. The authorities suspected that he might have had something to do with the bombing, but since they didn't have any evidence, in the end they were forced to let him go." I paused. "I can't tell you how or why, but we know better now. He was responsible for the *Lee* disaster . . . of that, we're more than reasonably certain."

Copperfield slowly let out his breath. When I looked at him again, I saw that his fists were clenched at his sides. "My older brother was aboard the *Lee*. We'd moved to Coyote only a few months earlier, and he was on his way back to Earth to fetch the rest of our family." His voice trembled with repressed anger as he said this, and there was cold fury in his eyes when he turned to Stanley. "We trusted him, Emma. Damn it, we . . ."

"I know, Gerry. I know." She laid a comforting hand upon his arm as she looked at me again. "General, I appreciate what you're trying to tell us, but there's something you need to know. Joe Ross . . . or whoever you say he is . . . is one of the most respected members of our community. And believe me, that's saying a lot. Many people here came to Manuelito in the first place because something had gone wrong with their lives, and they wanted a fresh start. We . . ."

"Look, I don't care . . ."

"Let me finish, please." Her expression hardened; once again, she became the chief proctor. "One thing that's unique about this town is that nearly everyone here has converted to *Sa'Tong*. It's not mandatory, of course . . . there's a small nonsectarian church for those who've chosen not to do so . . . but, all the same, every person who's moved here has agreed to abide by the Codicils, regardless of whether they've read the *Sa'Tong-tas* or not." A faint smile. "Believe me, I've got the easiest job of any proctor in the Federation. I could count on one hand the number of arrests I've made since I've been here, and maybe have a finger or two left over."

"She's not exaggerating." Copperfield calmed down a bit; his right hand was no longer clenched into a fist as he reached up to absently brush back his hair. "Manuelito is a decent community. We trust each other so much that no one ever bothers to lock their doors. So when we tell you that Joe is someone who's . . ." He stopped, shook his head. "No. There's got to be a mistake."

"Sorry, sir . . . no mistake." I nodded toward Laird's holo, still floating above my pad. "This is definitely the man I'm looking for, and you've identified him as a local resident. Now where do I find him?"

The mayor and the chief proctor didn't reply at once. They gave each other an uncertain glance, almost as if silently debating whether or not to tell me. "Joe Ross doesn't live here in town," Copperfield said at last. "Fact is, it's what he does that makes him one of the most trusted people we have. That's why . . ."

"Where is he?" I was quickly losing patience.

Chief Stanley sighed, then stepped away from me. "Here . . . I'll show you."

I followed her as she walked around from behind the skiff. On the other side of the spacecraft were the ice-covered breakwaters that had been built along the shoreline. Beyond them were the Providence Straits, and in the distance, several miles away, lay King Philip.

She pointed toward the island, and at first I didn't see what she was trying to get me to see. Then I realized that it was a tiny spire rising from the southernmost tip of King Philip: a lighthouse, erected at the mouth of the Straits to help fishing boats find their way home.

"Joe lives out there, at the lighthouse," Stanley said. "With his wife and baby."

Of the dozens of islands that dot Coyote's global maze of rivers, channels, bays, and straits, King Philip is the oddest, if in name only. Many people have asked why one landmass would bear the name of a monarch, while nearly all others—with the exception of those first explored and settled by Coyote's original colonists—had been christened after Native American tribes and historical figures. So why is this single island different?

Yet King Philip is not the exception that it seems. It was named after the seventeenth-century Pokanoket leader Philip, whose father, the tribal sachem Massasoit, had given him an Anglo-Saxon name out of fondness for the English settlers of the Plymouth colony. But Philip had no love for the white man; once he came to power among the Pokanokets, he proclaimed himself to be a king, then united the other tribes of New England to launch a bloody war against the European invaders that came close to wiping out the first American colonies.

Perhaps it was fitting that David Laird sought refuge on an island named after someone who'd caused such widespread death and destruction.

Chief Stanley took me out there herself, on a small wooden boat that she and her husband Paul used for sport fishing during the warm seasons. It had an outboard motor, and there was enough room for the three blueshirts I'd brought with me. Mayor Copperfield could have joined us as well, but he decided not to; he was heartsick at what he'd been told, and I don't think he wanted to see a trusted member of his little community put under arrest and taken away. I wish I could say that I didn't blame him, but his feelings or Stanley's were none of my concern.

It took about an hour for the boat to make the short journey across the Providence Straits to King Philip. It was almost dusk by then, with dark grey clouds obscuring the setting sun. Buoys floated in a ragged line down the center of the Straits, marking the safe passage through its reefs and shoals. The frigid waters were choppy, a harsh wind out of the northeast kicking salt spray against our faces. While the blueshirts huddled together in the bow, their heads lowered beneath the raised hoods of their parkas, Stanley and I sat next to each other in the stern, and she passed the time by telling me a little more about the man she'd known as Joe Ross.

Laird had come to Navajo aboard a freighter carrying livestock from Defiance. By then, he'd apparently decided to ditch his Peter Desilitz identity and create a new one. As Joe Ross, he was a down-on-his-luck drifter who'd decided to make his way to Manuelito in search of work. He found a job as a longshoreman, hauling cargo to and from ships that docked at the town's commercial wharf, while living in a boardinghouse near the waterfront. During this time, he was something of a loner; rarely seen in the taverns, he kept to himself and didn't have many friends.

It appeared that loneliness finally got to him, though, because after a while he joined a *Sa'Tong-tas* study group that convened once a week at the town hall. It was there that he met Amy Atkins, a recent widow whose late husband had been the lighthouse keeper on King Philip. George Atkins's boat had disappeared in a storm while returning home from Manuelito, and Amy had assumed the task of maintaining the lighthouse on her own. She had also recently converted to *Sa'Tong*, and it was while studying its teachings that she met and fell in love with Joe Ross.

The two were married six months later, in a civil ceremony presided over by the local justice of the peace. Joe Ross quit his job as a longshoreman and moved out to King Philip, where he took over the role of lighthouse keeper. That came as no surprise to anyone; Amy was pregnant by then, and she'd never been as good at maintaining the light as her first husband had been. What was a revelation was how well Joe learned to handle his new line of work. No evening went by without the light coming on, and no fog rolled in upon the Providence Straits that wasn't heralded by the King Philip horn. The buoys were kept in good condition, and marine weather reports from the lighthouse were prompt and accurate.

But that wasn't all. Last summer, a catwhaling ship on its way home from the Great Equatorial River lost its bearings due to an inexperienced pilot's error and foundered on the reefs off the east coast of Narragansett, twelve miles south of King Philip. This happened in the early hours of the morning, and the proctor on duty in Manuelito wasn't awake to hear the distress signal transmitted by the stricken ship (Chief Stanley later fired him for sleeping on the job). But Joe Ross had been up late, reading in the den, when he heard the ship's SOS come over the wireless, which he kept switched on at all times. He immediately woke up Amy and told her what had happened, but while she was on the phone with the chief, Joe himself took action. He ran down to the lighthouse dock, untied the family's boat, and set out on his own for the ship, which he knew to be taking on water and sinking fast.

"Joe saved seven men that night," Emma Stanley told me as she guided her boat toward King Philip. "He got there on his own, with nothing more than GPS coordinates and his knowledge of the area to help him find his way. The crew was already in the water by the time he got to them, floating around in their life jackets and about to be swept away by the channel current. He hauled them all aboard even though it put him at risk himself . . . his boat isn't any bigger than mine, and believe me, eight men will capsize you if you're not careful . . . and managed to get them back to King Philip while I was still getting our search-and-rescue team out of bed."

"So you're saying he's a hero," I replied.

"Damn right, he's a hero." She didn't look at me, but instead stared straight ahead. By then, the lighthouse dock was only a few hundred yards away. "He earned the respect of every person in town that night. And he didn't have to do this, either. He could've just sat back and waited until the SAR team got there. But if he had, I don't think those guys would still be alive."

I didn't reply. There was little I could say that wouldn't offend her. The chief seemed to realize this, for after a moment she went on. "I know what you've told me, and I have no choice but to believe you. But sometimes, y'know, a man gets a chance to make up for the bad things he's done in the past, and maybe that's what Joe . . . or David, or Peter, or whatever you say his real name is . . . has been trying to do with his life. You ought to remember that when you and your boys take him away."

A silence fell between us, one that lasted long after Stanley pulled her boat alongside the floating dock and one of the soldiers climbed out to tie us up. A long flight of wooden steps led up the steep, rocky point to a small wood-frame house perched at its top. The lighthouse, a white-painted concrete cone sixty feet tall, rose beside the house, connected to it by an enclosed walkway.

Not much grew on this side of King Philip, but when we reached the top of the stairs and walked toward the house, I spotted what appeared to be a tidy little garden, buried beneath the snow but marked by tomato stakes and a trellis, which had been cultivated just below the porch that wrapped around the channel side of the house. Steps led to the front door, and above it was an awning from which a small, hand-painted sign swung in the evening breeze: WELCOME, FRIEND. SA'TONG QO. Lights gleamed from within the windows; the odor of woodsmoke told of logs burning in the fireplace. All very warm and inviting.

"Let me go first," Chief Stanley said quietly, when we reached the porch steps. "Might make things easier." She glanced back at the blueshirts. "And I'd appreciate it, too, if you'd tell your men to wait outside."

I hesitated. I hadn't brought a Militia squad all the way from Midland just for show; they had a duty to perform, as distasteful as it might be to the chief. But I'd have to do things her way if I wanted any cooperation from her. Besides, I wasn't unarmed; my gun was in its holster, hidden by my parka.

So I reluctantly nodded and left the blueshirts standing at the bottom of the steps while I followed her onto the porch. The chief had barely touched the brass doorknocker, though, when the door opened from within, and a woman peered out at us.

"Hello?" she asked. "Who's . . . ? Oh, Emma! What a surprise!"

"Hello, Amy." Emma Stanley tried to make her tone pleasant, but it wasn't working. "Sorry to disturb you, but . . . well, something's come up, I'm afraid."

Amy Atkins was one of those petite, trim ladies whose age couldn't easily be determined: older than she looked, yet not quite as young as she seemed. She wore her dark hair long, with bangs that she constantly brushed out of lively brown eyes. From somewhere behind her, I heard a child's voice pipe up. "Whoizzit, Mommy?"

"Just Ms. Stanley, Erin." Yet as she said this, Amy caught sight of me. An instant later, she looked past the chief proctor and me, and her eyes widened when she spotted the blueshirts standing at the bottom of the steps.

"What's going on, Emma?" she asked. "Why are they . . . ?"

"This is General Sawyer Lee, of the Corps of Exploration." Chief Stanley spoke my name as if it were a curse. "The men with him are . . ."

"Militia. I can see that." Amy stood in the doorway as if to bar our way into her house. "What's going on?" she repeated. "Is there some sort of problem?"

"I'm afraid there is." Stanley hesitated. "Amy, General Lee says . . ."

"Ma'am," I said, interrupting the chief proctor as I stepped forward, "I apologize for the intrusion, but I've come to see your husband. Will you tell me where he is, please?"

Amy stared at us in confusion. In that second, I saw myself as she saw me: a stranger in a uniform, abruptly showing up on her doorstep with three armed soldiers and demanding to see her husband. Every wife's worst nightmare. I hated myself for what I was about to do to her, but there was no way I could stop what had to be done.

"He's . . . upstairs," she said at last. "In the tower. Getting ready to turn on the light." She looked at Stanley again. "Emma, please tell me . . . what's going on?"

"Amy, I'm sorry, but . . ." Stanley let out her breath. "These men have come to put Joe under arrest."

"What?" Amy's mouth fell open. "I . . . what did he . . . ?"

"I'll explain it to you in a minute." The chief turned to give me a quick nod. Moving past her, I stepped through the door. Yet Amy stood her ground, silently refusing to allow me into her home.

"Amy, please . . ." Stanley began.

"How do I get upstairs, ma'am?" I found that I was having a hard time looking her in the eye.

"To the right," she said, the words falling from her lips as if they were deadweights. "But you can't . . ."

She wouldn't budge from the door, so I laid a hand on her arm and, as gently as I could, pushed her out of the way. At first she resisted, but then she seemed to realize that I was coming in whether she liked it or not and reluctantly let me pass.

The living room was small, comfortable, and immaculately clean: blackwood beams across a low ceiling, old but well-kept furniture, a clothbound copy of the *Sa'Tong-tas* lying open on a coffee table in front of a sofa. On the wool rug before the fieldstone fireplace, a little girl—no older than one Coyote year, as beautiful as a child could be—looked up from the wooden blocks she'd been using to build a castle. As I marched through the room, heading for a closed door to the right, her mother immediately rushed over to plant herself between me and her daughter. I tried to ignore the astonished look on the little girl's face as I opened the door, but I knew that I would be permanently engraved in her memory.

The door led me into a short, unheated walkway in which firewood had been stacked. I went down it, passing shelves containing neatly labeled jars of preserves, until I reached another door. Unlatching it, I found myself inside the bottom of a hollow shaft fifty feet in height. The inside of the lighthouse was as cold as it was outside, with fluorescent lamps along its concrete walls lighting a cast-iron spiral staircase that led up the interior to a ceiling hatch at the top of the tower.

An electrical generator hummed as I began to climb the stairs, but not so loudly that it muffled Emma's and Amy's voices behind me. I couldn't make out what Stanley was saying, but I had little doubt that the chief was explaining the situation to Joe Ross's wife. My boots clanged against the risers; looking up, I saw that the hatch was shut. No one had followed me into the lighthouse, but I knew that I wasn't alone. David Laird was up there.

Halfway up the stairs, I paused to open my parka, pull out my gun. Not an airpulse pistol this time—I'd seen where trying to use a nonlethal weapon would get me when it came to dealing with dangerous men—but an old-style fléchette gun of the type used by the Militia. Making sure that its safety was disengaged, I raised it in my right hand as I continued up the spiral staircase, never letting my gaze leave the hatch, ready to open fire at the first sign of trouble.

But the hatch remained shut until I reached it. With my left hand,

I pushed down the lock lever, then shoved the hatch open. Pointing the gun at the opening, I waited, carefully listening for any sound. Nothing but a steady mechanical grind, though, and the only thing I saw was a bright glow that rhythmically pulsed like the silent beating of a luminescent heart. After a few seconds, I slowly climbed the rest of the way through the open hatch.

The top floor of the lighthouse was a small, circular cupola, its broad windows facing in all directions. At the center of the room was the light itself, an immense quartz iodine lamp contained within a ribbed metal drum that slowly revolved upon a rotary pedestal. At the base of the light was a small control panel; lying on a table next to it was a loose-leaf logbook, a pen resting upon its open pages. A so-called dumb compass—not magnetic, but fitted instead with an arrow that could be manually moved to calculate the correct latitudes and longitudes of the offshore buoys—stood upon another table, a radio transceiver just below it.

The sun was down, and so the lamp had been lit, along with the buoy lights. It slowly revolved in a clockwise direction, throwing a brilliant beam through the windows that threatened to blind me every time it turned in my direction. Careful not to look straight at the light, I glanced around the cupola. There was no one in sight, but I saw that, to my right, a small door was open, leading to an outside balcony.

The light turned to the southeast, capturing a solitary figure standing at the railing not far from the door. His back was turned to me, and he didn't look my way as I slowly crossed the cupola. Gun gripped in both hands and raised to shoulder height, I stepped out onto the balcony.

"Are you David Laird?" I asked.

"Yes, I'm David Laird," he said. "Hello. I've been expecting you."

The lighthouse beam swept past Laird again, and it was then that I was able to see him clearly. He'd aged a bit in the last seven years—

his body was thicker, his face a little more wide, his hair short and becoming thin at the top of his head—but he was unmistakably the same person. The lapels of his long wool coat were turned up against the cold, and he held on to the railing with both hands, still not looking at me but instead out at the Straits.

"I'm General Sawyer Lee," I began, pointing my gun straight at him, "and I'm . . ."

"I know who you are and why you're here." Laird nodded toward the ground below. "I saw you and the others coming. This time of evening, it gets quiet enough up here that you can hear just about everything . . . including what's being said on the front porch."

It hadn't occurred to me to look up at the lighthouse to see if anyone up there was watching and listening. A quick glance over the railing confirmed what he'd said; from this side of the tower, we were almost directly above the front door. The blueshirts stood below, murmuring to each other, apparently unaware of our presence.

"That makes things easier," I replied, looking back at Laird. "Unless you're going to give me any trouble, that is."

"If you're asking whether I'm armed . . ." Turning toward me, Laird slowly raised his hands so I could see that they were empty. "We don't even have a gun in the house. Amy won't allow it . . . and even if she did, I wouldn't carry one anyway. I gave that up a long time ago." He looked at my pistol. "Might as well put that away, General. You're not going to get a fight from me."

I wasn't about to trust him. We were standing on a narrow balcony sixty feet above the ground, and he knew this place much better than I did. "All right, then," I said, keeping the gun trained on him, "since you've been waiting for me, let's . . ."

"That's not what I said." Lowering his hands, Laird turned toward the railing again. "When I said that I've been expecting you, I didn't mean you personally . . . just the day when someone like you would come for me." He closed his eyes, shook his head. "I was hoping that it wouldn't be quite so soon. At least not until Erin grew up a little more, so she'd understand who her father really was . . . but I suppose that can't be helped, can it?"

He didn't seem to be disturbed at all by my arrival, or the fact that there was a gun pointed at him. Instead, he gazed out at the flashing lights of the buoys, as if studying them to make sure that they were lit and in the correct position. "If you think you can beg me to leave you alone," I said, "you're talking to the wrong man. You're responsible for the deaths of everyone who was on the *Lee* . . . including someone very close to me. No way I'm leaving this island without you." I paused, then added, "Dead or alive . . . your choice. Doesn't make much difference to me."

"Is that why you're here? To kill me?" He barely glanced at me. "If that's what you'd really like to do, then go ahead. Shoot." The light flashed by us again, this time revealing a sad smile upon his face. "You can always say that I tried to throw you over the side and that you acted in self-defense. I'm sure your men will back up whatever claim you make."

I'd be lying if I said I wasn't tempted to do just that. It wasn't just Lynn who called out for vengeance; it was also Chris, who'd died trying to find this man. But there was something about the placid detachment with which Laird was willing to accept his fate, whatever it might be, that made me curious.

"You're awful calm about this," I said. "Not what I was expecting from someone who spent the last six years or so covering his tracks. Or do you think that, just because you call yourself another name and have a family now, that I'm going to give you a break?"

"No, I don't." Again, Laird shook his head. "You're not a follower of *Sa'Tong*, are you?" When I didn't reply, he went on. "Well, I am . . . or at least I have been, ever since I met Amy. One of the things we believe is the Fifth Codicil . . . that wrongful acts must be atoned for with righteous acts of equal or greater proportion." He let out a sigh. "I can't do anything for your friend or anyone else who was aboard the *Lee*. I didn't kill them myself, but that's only a minor point, isn't it? I built the bomb that Alberto used to destroy the ship, and that makes me just as culpable as he. And to make matters worse, one of those aboard was the *chaaz'maha*, whose teachings I've come to embrace." A reflective pause. "I regret every death I caused, but that . . . that has weighed upon me the hardest."

I had an urge to tell him that the *chaaz'maha* was still alive, no thanks to him, and his death need not be on his conscience any longer. But I wasn't about to allow him even that small mercy. In fact, I was still undecided whether or not to shoot him on the spot. "Don't you dare play the spiritual card with me," I said, sounding angrier than I intended. "I'm not buying the idea that converting to *Sa'Tong* makes you a better man."

"I'm not claiming anything of the kind," Laird said. "What I'm trying to tell you is that, in the years that I've been waiting for someone like you to find me, I've tried to atone for what I did. Amy showed me the way, when I moved out here with her. I once ended lives. Now I do my best to save them."

He nodded toward the offshore buoys. "Every night, I come up to turn on the light and the buoys. I issue weather reports, sound the foghorn when I need to, listen for distress signals. Last year, I was even able to help rescue several men . . ."

"I know. Chief Stanley told me all about that." I shook my head. "It's not enough. It'll never be enough."

"No . . . no, I suppose it isn't." He looked at me again. "But you're wrong about one thing. I *am* a different person now. David Laird was an angry young man who hated the world, and everyone he met, for reasons he couldn't understand. So he made bombs, but since he was too cowardly to use them himself, he put them in the hands of those who would, then ran away while others died for . . . well, whatever infantile causes he happened to believe in. That's not who I am anymore. I'm Joe Ross, and I'm a lighthouse keeper. Nothing more, nothing less."

"Yeah, you're breaking my heart." I wasn't accepting anything he said. "You didn't let your wife know the truth, did you? To her, you've always been just some guy who drifted into town?"

"No . . . and I'm afraid that it's her heart that's going to broken, not yours. Erin's, too." He continued to gaze at me, his face once more cast in shadow. "So . . . are you going to shoot me now? I rather wish that you would. It would be a kindness, really."

As soon as he said this, I made up my mind. "No," I said, "I'm not going to kill you." I cocked my head toward the door. "You're going downstairs with me, and after you say good-bye to your family, you're getting on the chief's boat, and we're taking you with us."

"To jail?"

"Uh-huh, but not in Manuelito. You've got too many friends there, and I'm not giving you a chance to get off easy." I couldn't help but smile. "I've got a skiff waiting. You and me are going to Liberty, where you're going to be put on trial in federal court. I don't know what the maggies will do with you, but I do know that, before this is over, everyone will know you for who you really are."

"I see." Laird took a deep breath, slowly let it out. He looked out at the Straits, perhaps as if he knew that would be the last time he'd see them from that place, then he turned away from the railing. "Very well, then . . . let's go."

When we returned to the living room, we found Amy seated on the couch, her shoulders slumped forward and her head hanging low. Erin was curled up in a tight little ball at the end of the couch, her feet on the cushions and her arms wrapped around her knees. Emma Stanley stood near the door; she was quiet, but I knew what had happened while I was upstairs with Laird. She'd told his wife and daughter who Joe Ross really was, and the things he'd done when he'd called himself by another name.

Amy looked up as we walked into the room. Her eyes were red-rimmed and puffy, her face wet with tears. She stared at her husband,

and it was as if she were seeing a doppelganger who'd taken over the body of the man she'd married.

"Is it true?" she asked, her voice so low that it was almost a whisper.

Laird regarded her for a moment, then he looked down at the floor. "It's true. I'm sorry. I'm . . . I'm so sorry."

For a few seconds, neither of them said anything. It was as if the two of them were trying to find the right words but simply couldn't. The silence was broken when, from her corner of the couch, Erin let out a quiet sob that could just as well have been a scream. Hearing this, Laird started toward his daughter. He meant to comfort her, but before he could reach her, Amy jumped up and, with the urgency of a mother protecting a threatened child, swept the little girl into her arms.

"No!" she snapped. "Stay away from her!"

Laird's face went pale. He halted in midstep, hands still extended toward his daughter. "Amy . . . honey, please. You can't . . ."

"Just go." Hugging the weeping girl tight against her chest, Amy recoiled from him. She almost tripped over the coffee table as she retreated from her husband; their copy of the *Sa'Tong-tas* fell off the table and onto the floor, but she didn't seem to notice or care. "There's nothing you can say that's going to make anything better, so just . . ."

"Amy, please . . ."

"Get out of here!"

Footsteps pounded up the porch steps. An instant later, the front door was flung open and one of the blueshirts rushed into the house, his rifle half-raised. Stanley turned toward him, holding up a hand. "It's all right," she said quietly. "No problem here." Perhaps realizing the terrible absurdity of what she'd just said, her face blanched. "Go back outside," she added. "We'll be along shortly."

The blueshirt cast a wary glance around the room, then nodded once before stepping backward through the open door. Stanley watched him go, then moved toward Laird. "We need to go now," she murmured, almost apologetic as she laid a hand upon his arm. "Amy . . . Erin . . . if there's anything you need . . ."

Amy shook her head. She refused to look at her husband, but instead gazed at the *Sa'Tong-tas* as if deliberating whether to pick it up from the floor or leave it where it had fallen. I couldn't see Erin's face except for her eyes, peering over her mother's shoulder. She stared at Laird with something like longing mixed with horror, then she buried her face within her mother's hair, unable to bear the sight of her father.

Laird stood there for another few seconds. He'd let his hands fall to his sides, and he looked at his wife and daughter, as if waiting for them to say something more to him. When they didn't, he reluctantly backed away from his family.

"I'm sorry," he said again, more quietly this time. "And whatever else happens, just . . . just know that I love you both." He turned to Chief Stanley. "All right, Emma . . . I'm ready to go now."

I closed the front door behind us and followed Stanley and Laird down the stairs to where the blueshirts were waiting. The chief reached within her coat pocket; when her hand reappeared, within it was a pair of magnetic handcuffs.

When Laird saw them, he shook his head. "You're not going to need those," he said softly. "I'll go quietly." Stanley gave him a questioning look, and he added, "I promise. Just . . . please don't take me away like this."

I thought she was making a mistake, but it was her decision. Stanley looked him straight in the eye, then nodded. "All right, then," she said, putting the cuffs back where they'd come from, then she looked at the blueshirts. "Follow us, please."

We went down the stairs, our way illuminated by the passing beams from the lighthouse; no one said anything as we returned to the dock. Laird walked beside Stanley, the three soldiers behind them. I brought up the rear; halfway to the dock, I paused to look back at the house. Amy was standing at the window, still holding Erin in her arms. We were too far away for me to see their faces, and I was glad that I couldn't.

We climbed aboard the chief's boat, with Laird sitting in the bow between two of the soldiers and the third seated directly across from him. Emma Stanley and I resumed our places in the stern. After the chief started up the engine, the third soldier stood up to cast off the lines. Once he was seated across from Laird again, so close that their knees touched each other's, Stanley throated up the engine, and the boat purred away from the dock.

The wind had settled down a bit now that the sun was down; the water was still, with very little chop. Stanley had the buoys to guide her way, but after a few minutes she switched on the boat's floodlight and aimed it straight ahead. The Straits were as black as the night; off in the distance were the lights of Manuelito, low upon the horizon and gleaming against the cold darkness.

Laird said nothing. He sat between the blueshirts, hands on his knees, his eyes never leaving King Philip. Every few seconds the lighthouse beam swept over us. When it did, it briefly illuminated his face: an unemotional mask, devoid of expression.

It wasn't long before we'd passed the first buoy and were halfway across the Straits. By then, the silence had become unsettling. Figuring that I had to say something, I turned to Chief Stanley, started to ask her about . . . well, I don't remember. Maybe the weather, or the fishing season, or something neutral and inconsequential like that. But whatever I was about to say was lost in the next instant when one of the soldiers yelled, and I looked around to see that Laird was on his feet and that there was a rifle in his hands.

How he had managed to get it away from the blueshirt seated across from him, I'm still not sure. Perhaps he'd been watching the soldier from the corner of his eye while only pretending to look at the island, waiting for the blueshirt to relax his guard just long enough so that he could make a grab for his weapon. Or perhaps the soldier himself was at fault; he later told me that he'd been looking at Manuelito when Laird snatched the rifle from his hands. Whatever the reason, though, it happened fast enough that no one had time to react. One second, Laird was sitting quietly between the blueshirts. The next, he was standing up in the boat, the gun cradled in his arms, its barrel aimed at the startled soldiers.

"Joe . . ." Chief Stanley stared at him in horror. "Joe, settle down. Just take it easy."

He ignored her. The soldier who'd been deprived of his gun started to move toward him, but Laird quickly took two deft steps back, putting himself most of the way to the prow of the boat so that he could cover us all.

From where he stood, I realized, he easily could shoot everyone aboard. He must have realized this, too, because when the lighthouse beam fell across the boat again, I caught a glimpse of his face and saw a cunning expression that I could only imagine had been there the day he'd delivered the suitcase bomb he'd made for Alberto Cosenza. Joe Ross was gone, and David Laird had returned.

"Don't do it," I said, fighting the urge to try to tackle him. He was too far away for me to do so before he put a fléchette in my chest.

"Joe, stop it," Emma said. "Please . . . just stop."

The lighthouse beam disappeared from his face, but I could still see him against the backglow of the boat's floodlight. His gaze shifted toward me and Chief Stanley, and as it did, it seemed as if there was an instant in which two men were fighting for control of one man's soul.

"I'm sorry." When he spoke, his voice was little more than a dry croak. "I'm sorry," he said again. "Tell Amy and Erin that I love them."

And then he turned around and, without another word, leaped over the side of the boat.

"Joe, *no!*" Stanley screamed.

A loud splash, then he was gone. Weighed down by the gun and his heavy clothes, he vanished beneath the black and icy waters, leaving behind only a brief spurt of bubbles that disappeared as soon as the lighthouse beam touched them.

His body was never found. We could only assume that it was caught by the undertow of the Providence Straits and washed downstream to the Great Equatorial River, never to be seen again. But I knew that it wasn't David Laird who died that night, but Joe Ross.

In the end, he'd found a way of reconciling himself with the sins of his past, in accordance with the Fifth Codicil of the *Sa'Tong-tas*.

Part 7

TERRA CONCORDE

Feeling the bump of the *Mercator*'s wheels settling upon concrete, Jorge looked away from the cockpit windows to watch Vargas as he throttled down the landing thrusters. The pilot reached forward to shut off the jets; the engines slowly died, and he turned to Jorge.

"Well . . . here we are," he said.

"And where is that, exactly?" Again, Jorge peered out the windows. The sun was still coming up, but this time there wasn't a dense fog to hide their surroundings. The shuttle had touched down on what appeared to be a rural airstrip outside a small town. Past a row of hangars was a recently harvested farm field, its dark brown soil covered by fallen cornstalks, a barn and grain silo not far away.

"Amherst." Vargas finished switching off the control panels, then began to unbuckle his seat harness. "End of the road, such as it is."

Jorge waited for Vargas to explain further. When he didn't, he scowled at him. "You're still not going to tell me what's going on, are you?"

It had been about a half hour since the *Mercator* had lifted off from Beacon Hill. During the short flight from Boston, Jorge had seen little more than hills, rivers, small towns, and an abandoned four-lane highway. Vargas had maintained a cryptic silence the entire time, giving only monosyllabic responses to Jorge's questions as he flew the shuttle westward across Massachusetts.

"I could," Vargas replied, "but I think you ought to get it from someone else." A reflective pause. "Considering all we've been through, you probably wouldn't believe me. Better that you—"

"Will you open the damn hatch?" From the back of the shuttle, McAlister's voice was an irate demand for attention. "And who the hell said you can fly my ship?"

Vargas rolled his eyes, smiled slightly. "Not exactly grateful, is he?"

Jorge wasn't amused. "I think we'd all be a little more grateful if we knew why you—"

"Later." Vargas rose from the left seat, stepped over the center console. "Just be patient," he added as he headed for the passenger compartment. "You'll learn the answers soon enough."

Jorge unclasped his harness, followed Vargas from the cockpit. One of the Shadows was already unsealing the belly hatch; he lowered the ladder, then turned to assist Inez in helping McAlister out of his seat. The pilot winced and swore as the two of them carried him down the ladder; the indignity of having to be helped off his own ship didn't improve his foul mood, and the sight of Vargas emerging from the cockpit hadn't made him any less cranky.

Two small, three-wheeled vans were waiting at the edge of the airstrip. Vargas raised a hand to their drivers, and the vans approached the shuttle, their electric motors emitting no more than a soft whine. One of the vans was marked with a red cross; it came to a halt, and a young woman in a white tunic climbed out of the rear, carrying a collapsible stretcher under her arm. She unfolded it on the ground, then she helped the Shadow carefully place McAlister on it.

"There's a hospital in town where we can take care of him," Vargas said, as McAlister was lifted into the ambulance. "You'll see him again soon, I promise."

"I think I remember Black saying the same thing," Jorge murmured.

Vargas gave him a sidelong look. "We're not the Provos. Trust me, you're among friends."

Jorge said nothing. Vargas might have rescued them, but lacking any explanation, Jorge wasn't inclined to trust him any more than he had before. Yet when Inez turned toward them, he noticed that she seemed relaxed. She walked over to Jorge, and he was surprised when she took his hand.

"It's all right," she said quietly. "We'll be okay." A glance at Vargas. "He's . . . different now. Something about him has changed."

Jorge wanted to ask what she'd sensed but refrained from doing so. The ambulance purred away, and the other van moved in to take its place. "C'mon," Vargas said, holding open the rear passenger door for them. "There's someone I think you'll want to meet."

Without hesitation, Inez climbed into the rear seat. Jorge followed her, and Vargas shut the door behind them before taking a seat beside the driver. The van sped away from the *Mercator*, its wheels bumping ever so slightly against the battered concrete. Its broad windows gave them a good view of where it was going. Once the vehicle reached the end of the airfield's narrow dirt road, it turned left onto a paved road that led toward town. Just ahead was the ambulance, red lights on its roof silently flashing.

"Amherst got through the hard times a lot better than most other towns," Vargas said, as they passed farms and small, wood-frame houses. "Pretty much all of western Massachusetts did, really, but that's largely because people here have always been rather self-reliant. But this town had a particular advantage, though, in that it has three schools . . . the state university, Amherst College, and Hampshire College. That meant that it had an advantage that other places lacked . . . mainly, more than the usual number of educated people who knew how to use the resources they had."

Jorge gazed through the windows. The houses appeared to be well kept; most had rooftop solar arrays, and every so often he spotted small greenhouses in their backyards. "I'm surprised Black and his people didn't try to take over. You're not that far from Boston."

"Yeah, well . . . we did have to worry about them." Vargas glanced over the front seat at him. "Even though the Provisional Army wasn't much of a threat to anyone outside Boston, Black had great ambitions. He wanted to . . ."

"I know. He told us that he wanted to bring back the United Republic of America."

"Uh-huh." Vargas smiled. "Thanks to you, though . . . whether you know it or not . . . they're no longer a threat to anyone. The raid we made on their hideout pretty much put an end to them."

That remark gave Jorge a clue as to what was going on. "By 'we,' I take it you mean the Terra Concorde. I assume you belong to them . . . whoever they are."

Vargas looked away, becoming quiet once more. Ahead of them, the ambulance turned left onto a side street; Jorge caught a glimpse of a road sign marked HOSPITAL, and knew that this was where McAlister was being taken. He thought that Vargas was going to revert to his earlier reticence, but then he looked back at him and Inez again.

"I'm with the TC, yes," he said. "I'm sorry I didn't tell you this earlier, but . . . well, to tell the truth, I didn't know it myself."

Jorge stared at him. "How could you not . . . ?"

"I think I know." Inez's voice was very quiet. "You were memory-blocked, weren't you?"

At first, Vargas didn't respond, but then he reluctantly nodded. "I guess you've figured that out. Yeah, I was."

"Memory-blocked?" Jorge peered at him. "What . . . you mean you were brainwashed or something?"

"That's something else that another person should explain to you," Vargas said. "To be honest, I barely understand it myself." A rueful smile that quickly disappeared. "Believe me, though, it was necessary for this whole plan to work . . . and, yes, there was a plan behind all this. Nothing . . . ah, well, *almost* nothing . . . that happened was by accident." He turned back around again but continued speaking.

"Anyway, Amherst is also the location for the New England satrapy of the Terra Concorde . . ."

"Which is what, exactly?" Jorge leaned forward in his seat. "C'mon, Sergio, enough with the mystery already. You owe us an explanation."

"I'm getting to that." An annoyed glance, then Vargas went on. "The Terra Concorde was formed about twelve years ago in Canada, with the goal of restoring civilization under a global government."

Jorge raised an eyebrow. "Not thinking small, are you?"

"No, we're not. But when all the major superpowers collapsed, beginning with the Western Hemisphere Union and continuing with the European Alliance and the Pacific Coalition, there wasn't any other choice. Even the United Nations was in a shambles. Something has to fill the void, or else there'd be nothing but chaos." Vargas looked back at Inez. "We have your father to thank for that. The *chaaz'maha* showed us the way."

Her eyes widened. "But you said you hated . . ." Then she stopped herself, and smiled. "Oh. Now I get it."

Get what? Jorge started to ask, but Vargas was already going on. "The TC got started at a conference in Montreal . . . one of the few cities in North America that didn't fall apart entirely . . . and since then has grown into a worldwide organization. We now have chapters, or satrapies, in just about every country, where we're working to do everything that needs to be done to bring about a global democratic coalition. But instead of adhering to the old ideologies, the Terra Concorde took the best of what's worked in the past and tailored it according to our needs, while adopting the teachings of *Sa'Tong* as its guiding principles."

"So my father is . . . ?"

"Our leader?" Vargas shook his head. "No. Oh, he was offered the job, all right. During the founding conference in Montreal, quite a few delegates wanted to elect him General Secretary. But he refused, saying that being *chaaz'maha* precluded his taking any sort of formal position within the government." He shrugged. "So he's something of a spiritual advisor, and pretty much operates out of the Amherst satrapy."

Remembering something else that Charles Black had said in the State House basement, Jorge slowly nodded. "That's why the Provisional Army wanted to get their hands on him. Black saw the TC as a threat to his own plans to restore the URA. If they'd killed him . . ."

"Again, that's something which ought to be explained to you by someone else." Vargas looked away from them again. "Be patient. Your questions will be answered soon enough."

Realizing that he'd get nothing more from him, Jorge reluctantly turned his attention to the van windows. By then, the vehicle had entered the Amherst town center, and he couldn't help but notice its contrast with downtown Boston. Pedestrians strolled along clean and well-maintained sidewalks, walking past shops and cafes that were beginning to open their doors for business, while small electric cars moved along streets that looked as if they'd been recently resurfaced. The van passed the town commons, and Jorge caught a glimpse of the library, the fire station, the city hall. Nothing was boarded up; there were no armed men in sight. It was as if the meltdown of the Western Hemisphere Union had never affected this small New England borough; the citizens of Amherst had refused to let their home collapse into ruins.

Turning left, the van followed another side street through a residential neighborhood until it reached a large granite sign: THE UNIVERSITY OF MASSACHUSETTS. "Welcome to UMass," Vargas said, as the van entered a sprawling, tree-lined campus. "That's not all it is now, though. It's also the Terra Concorde's New England headquarters."

Jorge gazed out at ivy-covered classroom buildings, high-rise dormitories, sleek glass-walled laboratories; some were relatively new, others obviously several centuries old. A left turn, then a right; the van passed two enormous geodesic domes built in what had once been an athletic field, the tall, slender pylons of wind turbines rising behind them. "Guess it makes sense to put it here," he said. "If you've got a university in a safe place . . ."

"Uh-huh. Amherst had already done the hard work of providing a stable environment. As I said, it comes from having so many teachers, students, and intellectuals living in one place . . . they didn't want their town to go to hell, so they got together and did something about it. So when the time came, the Terra Concorde only had to move in and set up their regional headquarters here . . . in fact, there it is."

Turning in to a driveway, the van headed up a small hill toward a tall, slender building rising above the campus center. Twenty-six stories in height, it was built of red brick, with narrow, slotlike windows along its sides. The van circled the tower before gliding to a halt beside the elevated plaza surrounding it.

Vargas climbed out of the van, then opened the passenger door for Jorge and Inez. Jorge noticed an inscription above the building's front entrance: W.E.B. DUBOIS LIBRARY. "The TC took over the school library?" he asked. "I'm sure the university must have loved that."

"Actually, they didn't mind at all." Vargas led them up the plaza's concrete steps. "It was built in the late twentieth century, when the faculty and students still relied mainly on printed material. After everything went digital, though, it wasn't used for much more than storing old textbooks." He grinned as they approached the front door. "The irony is . . . well, you'll see."

They entered the library through a ground-floor lobby, then walked down a flight of stairs to a spacious mezzanine located in an underground sublevel. A few dozen men and women—most of them Inez's age or younger; Jorge assumed they were students—were seated at carrels surrounded by stacks of crates and cartons. A few of the boxes were open, revealing books of every description: history volumes, science references, novels, poetry collections, atlases. The students barely glanced up as Vargas ushered Jorge and Inez through the mezzanine;

opening one book at a time, they briefly inspected their title pages and contents, then typed the information into the keypads of their desk comps before carefully placing the books on nearby library carts.

"One of the principal tasks of the New England satrapy is gathering and preserving published material." Vargas spoke softly as they paused to look around the room. "Not everything was digitized before the collapse, and there are still a lot of libraries and private collections scattered around the world that have paper books. A lot of them were used for firewood, or burned by extremist groups like the Provisional Army, before the TC made it a goal to save as many books as possible. The students here are processing the ones we've been able to gather before they're sent upstairs to be scanned."

"What happens then?" Inez asked. "I mean, what becomes of the books you've scanned?"

"They're being preserved for future generations. A lot of electronic databases were lost in the collapse, too. No one wants to have that happen again, so this time we're saving the books as well." Vargas raised a hand toward the ceiling. "This is why it's terrific that we've been able to acquire a library of this size. Once the cities are rebuilt, we'll be able to send our collection to local libraries around the world."

Turning away from the carrels, he led them to the center of the library, where a row of elevators was located. Vargas moved a palm across a lighted arrow, and the doors of one of the lifts slid open. He raised a finger above a button marked 26; the doors shut, and the lift began to rise. "There's more here than just books, of course," he continued. "Data storage and retrieval, intelligence analysis, administrative offices . . ."

"Never mind that." Jorge was unable to keep the impatience from his voice. "You said we were going to find the *chaaz'maha*. So where . . . ?"

"Soon." A sly smile as Vargas gazed at the flashing numbers of the floor indicator.

The elevator reached the top floor. A quiet chime, then the doors slid open again. Walking out into a short corridor, Vargas escorted them to a small, glass-walled anteroom. A young woman behind a desk looked up as they came in. She didn't ask who they were or why they were there, but instead rose from her chair and turned toward a mahogany door behind her. Not bothering to knock, she opened the door, then stepped aside and, a soft smile upon her face, bowed ever so slightly.

"*Sa'Tong qo*," she said. "Please, go in . . . he's waiting for you."

They entered a large conference room, with an oval, oak-surfaced table dominating its center and high-backed armchairs placed around it. Bright morning sunlight streamed through floor-to-ceiling plate-glass windows that looked out over the campus; in the distance to the west lay a range of low mountains.

At the far end of the table, a lone figure seated in an armchair gazed out the foothills of the Berkshires. At the sound of the door opening, he turned about in his chair. In his middle years, tall and slender, with long, dark hair becoming grey, he had a face that was both young and old at the same time.

For a moment, he said nothing, but simply gazed at the three people who'd just come in. Then he stood up and walked around the table. He wore a long, white robe, its front and sides embroidered with *hjadd* symbols. Its hood was pulled back; as the robed figure came closer, Jorge saw a tattoo on his forehead, between his eyebrows and just above the bridge of his nose. Resembling an upside-down *pi*, with one leg a little higher than the other, it was a *hjadd* symbol Jorge recognized from photos he'd seen countless times.

Ignoring both Jorge and Vargas, the man approached Inez. He regarded her for a second or two, as if studying the young woman who stood nervously before him, then a smile slowly appeared.

"Hello, Inez," he said quietly. "I'm your father."

* * *

There was a timeless instant in which it seemed as if neither Inez nor the *chaaz'maha* knew what to say or do.

By Gregorian reckoning, nineteen years had passed since Hawk Thompson had last seen his daughter, and then she'd been only a baby held in her mother's arms the day he'd left for Earth. And she had no memory of him; indeed, she'd grown up believing that he was dead. They were practically strangers, separated not only by years but also light-years.

But then the *chaaz'maha* held open his arms to her, and with a soft cry Inez fell into them. Jorge felt something catch in his throat. Despite everything he and Inez had endured, the hardships and moments of terror, this single moment made it all worthwhile.

Deciding to give them some privacy, he started to turn away, but then he felt a hand on his arm. "You're Jorge, right?" the *chaaz'maha* said. Jorge nodded, and he went on. "We've never met before, but . . . thank you. Thank you for bringing her back to me."

Inez was still in her father's arms, but beneath her tears there was a grateful smile on her face. "My pleasure, *chaaz'maha*," Jorge said.

The *chaaz'maha* shook his head. "That's my formal title. You're my cousin . . . and among family, I prefer to be known as Hawk."

Jorge swallowed. He wasn't ready to be on a first-name basis with a legend. "I'm sorry," he murmured, "but I'm afraid I'm going to have a hard time with that."

"Well . . . whatever makes you comfortable." The *chaaz'maha* grinned. "I couldn't have been more surprised when I saw you and Inez in the vid Black sent us. Of all the people I expected to come from Coyote, you two were the very last I thought I'd see."

Jorge was unable to keep the shocked expression from his face. "You knew someone was coming?" He turned to Vargas. "So that's what you meant when you said there was a plan."

Leaning against the back of the nearest armchair, Vargas folded his arms across his chest. "A lot had to do with my bringing someone from Coyote, yes. But as the *chaaz'maha* says, we didn't think it would be either of you." An offhand shrug. "Luck of the draw, I suppose."

Jorge looked back at the *chaaz'maha*. "I can see how you'd know it was me when you saw the vid. I identified myself by my name and rank. But Inez . . ."

"All she had to do was say her first name." The *chaaz'maha* gave his daughter a querulous look. "That *is* what you were trying to do, wasn't it? Tell me who you were without tipping off Roland Black?"

Inez smiled as she wiped away her tears with one hand. "I figured that if I only said that my name was Inez and that I was from Coyote, you'd know who I was."

Remembering the vid Black had made of him and Inez, and the way Inez had spoken to the cam, Jorge suddenly realized that Inez had been trying to pass a subtle message to her father. "Indeed, I did," the *chaaz'maha* said. "Very clever . . . one look at you, and I knew exactly who you were." Letting go of his daughter, he stepped back to admire her. "You've grown up quite a bit, but you look almost exactly like Melissa when she was your age." He hesitated. "How is she, anyway?"

"She's fine, Papa," Inez replied, then her face paled. "I'm sorry . . . can I call you that?"

The *chaaz'maha* laughed out loud. "You can call me whatever you—"

"Wait just a minute." Jorge shook his head. "Look, I don't want to break this up, but . . . will someone please tell me exactly what's going on here?"

Inez's face darkened. "Jorge, don't you think that can wait? My father and I—"

"No." The *chaaz'maha* shook his head. "He's right. There's much you don't know about how you came to be here, and why." He gestured to the table. "Please sit down, all of you."

Jorge settled into the nearest armchair, with Sergio beside him and Inez and the *chaaz'maha* across the table from them. Clasping his hands together, the *chaaz'maha* took a deep breath. "Perhaps it's best that I start from the beginning," he said. "For the last nineteen years, ever since Sergio rescued me and brought me to Earth, I've been working to restore stability to this place." He glanced at Vargas. "I'll assume that Sergio has already told you about the Terra Concorde and my role in it."

"A little, yes." Jorge glanced at the man sitting beside him. "But when he showed up on Coyote, he led us to believe that he hated you. That you'd set yourself up to be some sort of messiah, and . . ."

"Uh-huh." Vargas nodded. "That I did . . . and I even believed it myself, or at least at the time." He cocked his head toward the *chaaz'maha*. "The truth of the matter, though, is that I've been with him almost the entire time since he came through the starbridge. In fact, I was one of the first people he converted to *Sa'Tong*."

Jorge stared at him. "But Melissa . . . Inez's mother . . . when she scanned your mind during that first meeting we had with you, she found nothing of the kind. She said that everything you'd told us about the *chaaz'maha* was true."

"And it was," Vargas said. "Or at least so I was made to believe."

"'Made to . . .'?" Jorge shook his head. "I don't understand."

The *chaaz'maha* raised a hand. "We're getting a little ahead of ourselves. Again, it's best that we take this back to the beginning." Jorge fell silent again, and he went on. "One of the first things the Terra Concorde accomplished was to persuade the remnants of the space-faring superpowers . . . the Western Hemisphere Union, the European Alliance, and the Pacific Coalition . . . that it was in their best interests to shut down Starbridge Earth and start bringing its offworld colonists back home. Earth had been losing many of its best people to Coyote even before the *Lee* was destroyed. Even after Starbridge Coyote went down, the lunar and Mars colonies continued to drain the world's resources. As things turned out, perhaps it was for the best that they no longer had hyperspace access to Coyote. It meant that people here had no choice but to confront their problems instead of trying to run away from them."

Jorge gestured toward Vargas. "He told us that you had something to do with this. Or is that something else that wasn't quite true?"

"No, Sergio is correct. The decision to shut down Starbridge Earth was made on my advice." The *chaaz'maha* smiled slightly. "Your grandfather and I were on a diplomatic mission to find a solution to the refugee crisis. What I did after I got here was in keeping with that objective . . . it's just that the solution wasn't quite what he or I thought it would be. I expected that Starbridge Coyote would eventually be rebuilt . . . after all, you had *hjadd* technology at your disposal . . . but I didn't want hyperspace travel between Earth and Coyote to resume until the situation here had been stabilized."

"So that's why we didn't get any ships from here," Inez said. "You could've reopened the starbridge at any time, but you chose not to."

"That's correct, yes."

"The *hjadd* imposed a similar condition on us," Jorge said. "For much the same reasons. We can travel to the other Talus homeworlds . . . just not our own."

"Ah-ha." The *chaaz'maha* slowly nodded. "That explains why no ships from Coyote ever came through the starbridge. Although it was shut down to outgoing spacecraft, the Terra Concorde decided to keep its gatehouse on standby, with its comps ready to admit any incoming ships. Nothing ever came through, though . . . and now we know why."

"But the Terra Concorde forgot about the second starbridge in orbit around Eris . . . or did you?"

"No, we didn't," Vargas said. "And, unfortunately, neither did the Provisional Army."

"Which brings us to the next part of the story." The *chaaz'maha* settled back in his chair. "We'd known about Roland Black and his Provisional Army for quite a while . . . how he'd managed to put together a group with the intent of overthrowing the Terra Concorde and eventually reviving the United Republic of America. A lot of it was big talk, of course . . . the Terra Concorde was pretty well established by then, and the Provos were never much of a threat to us . . . but nonetheless they'd succeeded in taking control of Boston while stamping out all our attempts to restore democratic order to the city, and it wasn't long before it became unsafe for me or anyone else from the TC to visit Beacon Hill."

"Let me pick it up from there, please," Vargas said, and the *chaaz'maha* agreed with a nod. "Besides being one of the *chaaz'maha's* aides, I also serve as chief of the New England satrapy's intelligence division. About a year or so ago, we learned that Black had devised a scheme to lure him to Boston . . ."

"He told us about that," Jorge said. "Get their hands on a starbridge key and a freighter, then use them to send someone through the Eris starbridge back to Coyote, with the intent of getting someone to come to Boston to find the *chaaz'maha*."

"That was the general idea, yes." A wry smile from Vargas. "Of course, that meant they'd first have to find a qualified pilot who still had his hands on a starbridge key . . ."

"And that was you."

"That was me, yes . . . because I deliberately planted myself in their way." Vargas's smile became a broad grin. "You see, they didn't find me . . . I found them."

"Sergio volunteered to allow the Provisional Army to learn that he was just the person they were looking for." There was no similar expression on the *chaaz'maha's* face as he gazed across the table at Vargas. "But it was an incredibly dangerous task. We'd already tried twice to plant an informant within Black's organization, but we were unsuccessful. Black suspected that the Terra Concorde would attempt to infiltrate his group, so any outsider who tried to get in was always interrogated, sometimes even tortured." He briefly closed his eyes, shook his head. "We lost two men that way. Black's methods were brutal, and after our people broke under questioning, Black had them executed."

Leaning forward in his chair, Vargas looked Jorge straight in the eye. "As it happens, the Terra Concorde had come to the conclusion that the time had come to make some sort of tentative contact with Coyote, if only to let the Federation know how things stood here. So we saw the Provisional Army plot as a way to accomplish two things at once." He raised a finger. "First, send someone to Coyote with the objective of letting them know that the *chaaz'maha* was still alive, and perhaps even bring someone back to Earth so that they could see the progress we were making." He raised another finger. "And second, take down Black and his people by turning their own scheme against them. Of course, that meant getting someone inside their organization. I decided that it would be me."

"Why you?" Jorge asked.

"I had the starbridge key, of course, but also . . ." Vargas paused, let out his breath. "Look, the last time I'd tried to take a ship through hyperspace was the day the *Lee* was destroyed. You may understand this, but . . . well, I felt like I owed it to everyone on the *Lee* to be the one to try and reach Coyote."

"So Sergio had an idea," the *chaaz'maha* said. "He'd let himself be recruited by the Provisional Army, but this time in a way that Black wouldn't be able to break him."

"You were memory-blocked," Inez said quietly.

"You said that before," Jorge said, "but you didn't explain what that means. What's . . . ?"

"A technique developed a long time ago by the Order of the Eye," the *chaaz'maha* said. "Some of our members came from very difficult circumstances . . . abuse from friends or family, or things they'd once done themselves, continued to haunt them. Since it's hard to share a telepathic rapport with someone who's carrying that much pain, the Order learned how to install psychic barriers that would block their memories so that they'd simply forget those things. After some experimentation, we also discovered that it was possible to implant false impressions, so that when they did try to recollect the past, all they'd find were pleasant memories."

"In other words, you'd brainwash them."

The *chaaz'maha* shook his head. "No, not exactly. Their essential personalities would remain intact. The only real difference was that their memories would be deleted or even altered." He glanced at Vargas. "The catch is, a person who undergoes memory blockage must want to do so. It can't be done involuntarily . . . he or she has to be willing to undergo this kind of therapy."

"The *chaaz'maha* had told me about this," Vargas said, "so I asked him to do the same for me . . . only this time, he'd remove any memories of our friendship and instead implant hate and distrust of him. To be on the safe side, I also asked that he remove any awareness of the Terra Concorde, so that if the Provos asked me anything about them, I'd be in a position to deny knowledge of its existence."

Jorge nodded. "Makes sense. If you were memory-blocked, you wouldn't break under interrogation."

"Uh-huh. That was the general idea." A thin smile. "As it turned out, Black didn't put me under the thumbscrews. He must have figured that, once I reached Coyote, my mind would probably be scanned by a member of the Order . . . the *chaaz'maha* had publicly spoken of them during his years here, so Black knew all about them . . . so he was careful to keep the Provisional Army at a safe distance. Everything was arranged for me through third-party contacts, without any direct involvement from him or the Provos."

"So that's why my mother didn't pick up on any of this when she searched you," Inez said. "You didn't know about Black or the Provisional Army because they'd never spoken to you, and you weren't aware of the Terra Concorde because your memories of it had been blocked."

"Right." Vargas grinned. "All I knew was that I loathed the *chaaz'maha* and that I was so desperate to get away from Earth that I was willing to steal a freighter. So I was carrying out Black's scheme, all right . . . but I was also carrying out my own as well, and just didn't know it."

"There's just one thing," Jorge said. "Sawyer Lee told me that, when Melissa . . . um, searched you . . . she discovered a mental image of the flag of the United Republic of America."

"That was my doing," the *chaaz'maha* said. "I, too, figured that Sergio would be searched once he made it to Coyote. Since his mission . . . Black's, that is . . . was to bring someone back here to find me, I didn't want them arriving in Boston without any advance warning of who might be waiting for them. On the other hand, we didn't know for certain whether Sergio would be making the trip alone or if one of the Provos would be with him, so the block would have to remain intact until he returned to Earth. So . . ."

"You placed a mental image of the URA flag in his mind as a subtle warning," Jorge said, and the *chaaz'maha* nodded. "Very sneaky . . . and, yeah, it worked, all right." Another thought occurred to him, and he turned to Vargas again. "But then we got to Boston, and you suddenly disappeared . . . what was that all about?"

"I'd hoped that, once we were actually in Boston, we'd able to make contact with the Terra Concorde underground without the Provos finding us first. But in case that didn't happen . . . that is, if I received any indication that we were in danger of being caught by them . . . my unconscious mind would snap the block, and I'd recall what I was really supposed to be doing."

"I think I remember now," Inez said. "You were very nervous when we were on the Charles River, and utterly insistent about going ashore as soon as we saw the first signs of life in the city."

The *chaaz'maha* looked at her. "You're telepathic?"

A slight smile as Inez shook her head. "Only empathic, Papa . . . something I inherited from you and Mama." She paused, then added, "I was raised by the Order, but no, I haven't joined them. I'll explain it later."

"Anyway"—Vargas politely coughed into his hand—"the block began to crumble once we reached the city. It hadn't fallen yet, but . . ." He shrugged. "I just knew that I had a very strong urge to get to Beacon Hill and find someone who'd lead us to the *chaaz'maha*. When Sam took off, though . . ."

"That's when the block collapsed," the *chaaz'maha* said. "That was in keeping with what I'd planted in his mind. If Sergio received any visual indication that something was wrong once he reached Boston, he'd remember everything, then go find someone in the underground who, in turn, would get in touch with the New England satrapy."

"I'm sorry, but . . ." Jorge was confused. "Look, I've been following you so far, but how could just seeing something break his memory block?"

The *chaaz'maha* smiled. "Maybe I could demonstrate. Would you allow me to place a memory block on you? Don't worry. It'll be harmless, and last only a minute or two." Jorge hesitated, then slowly nodded. "Relax. Just look at me, and don't try to resist."

Jorge took a deep breath, tried to relax as much as possible. Resting his elbows on the table, the *chaaz'maha* stared straight at him, solemnly peering into his eyes. For a moment, Jorge felt an odd tickle at the back of his skull, almost as if a gnat had nestled within his hair. He started to reach back to scratch at it, then the *chaaz'maha* smiled again.

"All right, it's done," he said, then he glanced at Inez. "Would you go stand behind him, please?" Without a word, Inez rose from her chair and walked around the table to stand behind Jorge's chair. "Don't look at her," the *chaaz'maha* continued. "Just look at me. Now, tell me, please . . . what are your parents' first names?"

Jorge opened his mouth . . . and suddenly found that he was unable to respond. In his mind's eye, he could see their faces very clearly, yet as hard as he tried, he could not recall their names. He winced, struggling to remember . . .

"Can't do it, can you?" the *chaaz'maha* asked, and Jorge shook his head. "Now . . . look at Inez."

Jorge turned his head. Inez was standing behind him, a smile upon her face. "What are your parents' first names?" the *chaaz'maha* asked again.

"Jonathan and Susan," Jorge said, with no effort at all. Inez grinned and gently patted his shoulder. "I'll be damned," he murmured, stunned by what had just happened. "It was like . . . like . . ."

"You couldn't remember their names until you saw my daughter." When Jorge looked at the *chaaz'maha* again, he noticed that he was regarding them thoughtfully. "I had her become the visual trigger that would break the memory block . . . someone who'd make a very strong visual impression on you."

Jorge felt his face grow warm. How much had the *chaaz'maha* learned about his feelings for Inez while he was placing the block? He tried not to look at her as she returned to her seat beside her father. "So . . . ah, that's how Sergio remembered what he was supposed to be doing."

"Right." Vargas nodded. "When Sam ran off, I realized we were in danger." He hesitated. "I'm sorry I didn't tell you, but it would've taken too long to explain, and I wasn't sure if you would've believed me anyway. So I disappeared while you and Greg were studying the map . . ."

"And allowed us to be captured by the Provos." Jorge glared at him. "Nice thinking."

"I'm sorry, but there wasn't anything I could've done to stop that." Vargas shook his head. "But I did keep the three of you in sight from a discreet distance . . . believe me, I didn't abandon you entirely . . . until

I saw where you were being taken. Then I found our contact on Beacon Hill, whom you'd just met . . ."

"The old bookseller?" Inez asked.

"That's him, yes." Vargas nodded. "He'd been watching the Provos on his own, and by then he'd learned that they were holed up in the State House and that they'd begun keeping their prisoners in the basement. So it wasn't hard for us to figure out where you'd been taken. And . . . well, you know the rest. The Terra Concorde brought in its paramilitary units. One team staged the rescue operation while I led another team to Port Logan, where we recaptured the *Mercator.*" He smiled. "And just in case you're wondering . . . yes, the starbridge key is safe. That was the first thing I checked. Black's people hadn't gotten around to removing it yet."

"So we'll still be able to use the shuttle to get back home." Jorge let out his breath. "That's a relief."

"Sergio's plan worked . . . with two exceptions." The *chaaz'maha's* face became grim, his voice subdued. "One was Sergeant Dillon's death and Captain McAlister's becoming wounded. I apologize for this, and hope that you'll understand that neither could be helped. The other was your personal involvement. I never expected, in all my dreams, that the people who'd come to find me would belong to my own family . . . or that my own daughter's life would be put at risk."

Inez didn't respond, but instead laid a hand upon her father's. The *chaaz'maha* smiled as he looked at her, then his expression became serious again as he turned to Jorge. "Now . . . I'm sure you're very tired, and I'd like to have some time alone with her. Sergio . . . ?"

Vargas pushed back his chair, stood up. "We have a room for you at the student union, Lieutenant. If you'll come with me . . . ?"

"Sure." Jorge's legs were rubbery as he rose from his seat. It wasn't just exhaustion he felt, though. He needed rest, but also time to absorb all that he'd learned. He started to let Vargas lead him from the room, then stopped to look back at Inez. "Are you . . . ?"

"I'm fine." She didn't look away from her father. "I'll talk to you later."

Jorge nodded and left them with each other.

The university's guest quarters were located on the third floor of the student union, not far from the library. Jorge's room was small, with only the most basic furniture, but it did have its own bathroom; seeing this, he realized that he needed a bath just as much as sleep. Vargas promised him a meal and a fresh change of clothes, then he left Jorge alone, closing the door behind him.

Jorge peeled off his Corps uniform, then stood beneath the shower for a long time, letting the hot water rinse away the grime and sweat. When he emerged from the bathroom, he discovered that someone had visited his quarters while he was in the shower; his uniform was missing from where he'd dropped it on the floor, and a clean outfit had been placed on top of the dresser, along with a covered tray. His hosts were nothing if not efficient. Breakfast consisted of scrambled eggs, toast, a bowl of mixed fruit, and a small pot of coffee. He devoured everything while he was still wrapped in his bath towel but ignored the coffee; the last thing he needed just then was something that would keep him awake. Feeling clean and well fed, Jorge closed the window blinds, then crawled beneath the bedcovers. He was asleep almost as soon as his head touched the pillow.

Daylight was still visible through cracks in the blinds when he finally woke up. A small clock on the bedside table told him that it was only a quarter after three, but he had to remind himself that Earth days were two hours shorter than those on Coyote. Which meant that it was late afternoon, and he'd been asleep a little more than six hours. That was enough; time to get up, perhaps see a little more of where he'd found himself.

The clothes he'd been brought were plain but fitted him well enough:

brown denim slacks and a matching shirt, underwear and socks, a heavy wool sweater. His parka and boots had been left behind, though, so he wouldn't get cold if he left the building. And it was a relief to find that the door wasn't locked, nor was there a guard posted outside. Yet he'd barely pulled on his boots when there was a knock at the door, and a young man stuck his head in.

"Oh, good . . . you're already up." Jorge nodded, and he went on. "The *chaaz'maha* would like to see you if you're not too busy."

"Not at all," Jorge replied.

"Great." The student smiled and nodded. "If you're ready, I'll take you to him."

Jorge thought at first that they would return to the library. Instead, the young man escorted him across the campus, past the library, and down the hill, until they reached the geodomes he'd spotted earlier. In the waning light of the day, the translucent hemispheres glowed from within, looking like a pair of blisters that had grown up in the middle of the former athletic field. A concrete walkway led them to the one on the left; an airlock door opened to a small anteroom, where the student told him he could leave his parka. After Jorge hung up his coat, the kid opened the inner door and took him the rest of the way into the dome.

Jorge found himself in a large greenhouse, with row upon row of elevated racks arranged beneath a gridlike ceiling of ultraviolet lamps. Upon the racks were long trays filled with dark, rich soil; spray-heads above the racks watered the plants being cultivated in the trays. The air within the dome was warm and humid; Jorge was glad that he had left his parka outside and found himself wishing he'd done the same with his sweater. Nonetheless, the dome was a pleasant relief from the autumn chill outside; it was as if there was a little bit of summertime in the place.

The student left him then, making a slight bow before turning to walk back the way they'd come. So far as Jorge could tell, there was no one else in the dome. Hands clasped behind his back, he strolled down the aisles between the racks, casually inspecting what was being grown in that part of the greenhouse: herbs, for the most part, although none he immediately recognized.

He'd just bent over to look more closely at what appeared to be a bed of grass when he heard the airlock door open. Looking up, he saw the *chaaz'maha* come in. No longer dressed in the long white robe, he wore an ordinary sweatshirt and jeans; were it not for the *hjadd* symbol on his forehead, he could have been a university botanist, dropping by to check on the gardens.

Spotting Jorge, the *chaaz'maha* smiled. "Oh, excellent . . . you're already here." He carefully shut the door behind him, then sauntered down the center aisle. "Thought you might prefer to meet here," he went on. "This is one of my favorite places, especially when it's cold outside. I can't get here often enough."

"Yes, it's . . . it's pretty nice." Jorge found that he was having trouble speaking. He wasn't a *Sa'Tong*ian, but nonetheless he was still overawed to find himself in the presence of the *chaaz'maha*. "Are these . . . I mean, is this being grown as food, or . . . ?"

"These species? Oh, no . . . or at least, not exactly. Most of what's here are exotic species, some of them very nearly extinct until the Terra Concorde undertook its horticultural revival program. The herbs in this part of the dome were often used as folk remedies, way back when." Coming closer, the *chaaz'maha* nodded toward the rack Jorge had been inspecting. "That's couch grass, for instance . . . sometimes used in witchcraft, or so it was said. Placed under the bed, it could break evil spells."

Jorge raised an eyebrow. "You don't believe that, do you?"

The *chaaz'maha* chuckled. "Not at all. Still, it's fun, knowing the lore behind some of these species." He pointed to another tray. "That's horny goat weed . . . yes, that's really what it's called . . . and it's supposed to increase the libido. Quite a few of the herbs here have that purpose, it seems. Blood root for sexual enhancement, parsley for fertility . . ." A salacious wink. "I suppose the old-timers needed a little help now and then."

Suddenly nervous about the direction this casual conversation had taken, Jorge decided to change the subject. "How did you find them? You said they were nearly extinct."

"Good question. Glad you asked." The *chaaz'maha* gazed around the greenhouse. "The Terra Concorde isn't without precedent. As long ago as the early twenty-first century, various organizations recognized the inevitability of global climate change and began to take measures to assure the long-term survival of endangered species. One of those was the Svalbard Global Seed Bank, which the U.N. established on a Norwegian island just south of the Arctic Circle. It served as a repository for seeds of various plants . . . particularly agricultural species . . . that naturalists figured might disappear unless an effort was made to save them."

"And the specimens here . . . they're from that seed bank?"

The *chaaz'maha* nodded. "About eight years ago, the Terra Concorde recovered the seeds from the vault and began disseminating them to facilities much like this one. We have similar greenhouses all over the world now, raising plants that were once thought to have been wiped out. In some areas, we've already begun widespread farming. A little like what we're doing at the library, only this time it's rare herbs instead of books we're trying to preserve."

"So eventually these plants will be . . . ?"

"Put back in the world? Yes, that's the objective." The *chaaz'maha* shook his head. "It's going to take some time, though, I'm afraid. First, we have to restore social stability, and there are still too many places like Boston, too many groups like the Provisional Army. But that's how we're saving the world . . . incrementally, one step at a time."

"Makes sense," Jorge said. "Still, as you say . . . you've taken on a lot."

"Yes, we have . . . and that's what I wanted to speak to you about."

The *chaaz'maha* raised a hand, gestured toward the middle of the greenhouse. "Come with me. Let's talk."

Jorge followed him to the dome's center. A couple of wooden benches had been placed there as a place for gardeners to take a break; ivy-covered trellises concealed it from the rest of the greenhouse. Taking a seat, the *chaaz'maha* motioned for Jorge to sit down across from him. "I've asked Inez to join us," he began, "but before she gets here, I'd like to speak with you alone about . . . well, your involvement with her."

Jorge felt his face burn. "I guess she must have told you about . . . ah, what happened."

"She did, yes . . . but she didn't need to." Now it was the *chaaz'maha's* turn to be embarrassed; Jorge was surprised to see that he seemed to be having trouble meeting his gaze. "I picked up on your feelings for her almost as soon as I saw the two of you, but I didn't know for sure until I searched your mind in order to block your memory. Inez confirmed what I'd found . . . you love her very much, and last night . . ."

He stopped, took a deep breath. "Well . . . much of that is none of my business. I may be her father, but the fact remains that, even if Inez hadn't grown up without me, the decisions she makes are entirely her own, as they should be." He hesitated. "But both of you are having to deal with your feelings for each other, and in your case, there's quite a bit of guilt as well."

Jorge nodded. "Her mother made it clear to me that I'm to stay away from her." He hesitated. "Our relationship is also illegal . . . or at least it is in the Federation."

"I think Melissa is being overprotective. From what Inez has told me about the way she was raised in The Sanctuary, that's the impression I get." A wry smile. "As for the latter . . . you know why the law against relatives having sexual relations is in place? Even among second cousins?"

"It goes back to the early days of the colonies, when there were concerns about . . ." Reluctant to complete the rest, Jorge's voice trailed off.

"Inbreeding, yes," the *chaaz'maha* said, and slowly nodded. "Not really a concern now, though, especially since Coyote's population has become so large. I'm a little surprised that it hasn't been repealed, but I suppose old laws and the social concerns behind them take a long time to change. Still, it's not like she's your sister. You shouldn't have to apologize for the way you feel about her."

"Then you don't object?" Jorge was stunned.

The *chaaz'maha* shrugged. "Here on Earth, there have been many famous men who married their cousins. Edgar Allan Poe, Albert Einstein . . . in terms of bloodlines, you're separated from Inez even more than they were from the women they took as their wives."

The subject had taken an uncomfortable turn. Jorge cleared his throat. "I don't think marriage is something either of us has in mind. As for what happened last night . . . look, she was frightened, and needed to . . ."

"She wanted comfort." The *chaaz'maha* raised a hand. "I understand . . . and I'm glad you were there for her. And the last thing I want to do is tell you or Inez what you should or should not do. I only want to point out that you're on Earth, not Coyote. Here, at least, you don't need to worry about an obsolete old statute."

"Thank you." Jorge felt himself relax a little. "I'm glad you aren't—"

"Let me finish, please. You two are still going to have to work things out between you. However, there's something else you should know . . . something that may have some bearing on your situation." He paused, slowly let out his breath. "I'm not going back with you."

Jorge stared at him. "You're not?"

The *chaaz'maha* shook his head. "I know that's the objective of your mission. Inez also told me that my returning to Coyote was a stipulation imposed upon you by the High Council for their permission to permanently reopen Starbridge Coyote to Earth. However, my role as spiritual advisor to the Terra Concorde is more important than either of those things. I shouldn't leave . . . in fact, I can't."

"But . . . but Coyote needs you . . ."

"Does it?" The *chaaz'maha* raised a skeptical eyebrow. "Judging from what both my daughter and Sergio have told me, my homeworld . . . my former homeworld, really . . . has gotten along just fine without me. Earth needs a *chaaz'maha* to help it discover the wisdom of *Sa'Tong*. Back there I'd be little more than a figurehead." A wry smile. "And I never wanted to be a messiah, regardless of what Sergio said while he was memory-blocked."

The smile vanished, and again he shook his head. "So I'm staying here. You'll be able to report that I'm alive and well but have opted to remain on Earth . . . or at least for the time being, until the Terra Concorde has finished its work. When that happens, I have little doubt the High Council will be willing to allow Coyote to resume direct contact with Earth. I'll even make the trip to *Talus qua'spah* myself to make the case for doing so. Until then, though . . ."

The *chaaz'maha* spread his hands apart. "Earth and Coyote must pursue separate destinies. For Earth, it's to recover from the foolish mistakes of the past. For Coyote, it's to continue its present course of becoming a member of the galactic community."

"I think I see your point." Jorge slowly nodded. "It'll be hard for Inez and me to explain why you haven't come back with us, but . . ."

"Well . . ." Gazing past him, the *chaaz'maha* paused. "Perhaps this is something my daughter should explain for herself. Inez . . . ?"

Jorge turned to look over his shoulder and found Inez standing behind him.

So involved had he been in conversation with her father, Jorge hadn't heard her enter the greenhouse. Like Jorge, she no longer wore her Corps uniform, apparently also having found a fresh change of clothes in her quarters. Even dressed in loose trousers and a baggy woolen sweater, though, she was as attractive as she'd ever been. Seeing her, Jorge felt his heart skip a beat.

"Hello, Papa." She didn't seem to notice Jorge as she strolled through the trellises; instead, she walked over to the *chaaz'maha* and bent low to give him a kiss on the cheek. "Sorry . . . am I interrupting?"

"Not at all." The *chaaz'maha* grinned as he accepted the kiss. "I'm done here, so"—he stood up from the bench—"I'll leave you two alone. I think you have some things to talk about."

Inez watched her father walk away, but said nothing until they heard the greenhouse door open and shut. "How long have you been there?" Jorge asked.

"Only a few minutes." Inez sat down on the bench beside him. "Of course, my father knew I was there long before you did." An amused smile. "It's almost impossible to sneak up on a telepath, you know."

"I suppose." For the first time, Jorge felt wary in her presence. "So . . . um . . . you must have heard us talking about you. About the two of us, I mean."

"Uh-huh. I hope you realize that I couldn't have hidden that from him either, even if I'd wanted to. Oh, I could have shielded my thoughts . . . you can't grow up in The Sanctuary without learning how to . . . but as soon as I saw him . . ." She looked down at the floor. "Well, that wasn't something I'd considered. I'm sorry if I caused you any embarrassment."

"Don't apologize. He learned it from me, not you." Jorge let out his breath. "So you also know he's refusing to come back with us."

"He's already told me. I don't think it was ever an option . . . not for him, at least." Inez looked up at Jorge again. "If you're wondering . . . yes, I support his decision. His work here is too important to leave behind. Coyote doesn't need him anymore, but Earth does."

"Yeah, well . . ." Jorge couldn't help but frown. "We're going to have a hard time explaining this once we get back home. Our mission . . ."

"Jorge . . ." She hesitated, then reached out to lay a hand upon his. "I'm not going back either. I'm staying here, with my father."

For the second time in as many minutes, Jorge felt as if his heart had suddenly stopped beating. His mouth fell open as he stared at her in mute surprise. "You're not?" he finally managed to say.

"No." Inez looked him straight in the eye. "And that's my choice, not his. He and I have talked it over, but . . . really, I think I'd made my decision the second I saw him."

"What . . . why?" Jorge struggled to find the right words. "How could you . . . ?"

"Because I need him, and I think he needs me, too." Inez sighed, shook her head again. "Maybe it's hard for you to understand, but . . . look, you grew up with both of your parents, so you've never known what it's like, going through your whole life believing that one of them is dead. I had my mother, sure, and I love her very much, but . . ."

"Now that you've met your father, you want to spend time with him."

"That's it, yes. We've got a lot of catching up to do, and we can't do that in just a day or two." Turning her head, Inez gazed around the greenhouse. "Also, I think he could use my help. You said it yourself . . . he's taken on a big job. Perhaps he could use someone by his side."

"But back home . . ."

"What's there for me? The Corps of Exploration?" She looked back at him again. "Do you remember what we talked about, that night when we were flying back to Liberty? About how I'd joined the Corps partly because everyone who knew that I was the *chaaz'maha's* daughter expected me to follow in his footsteps?"

Jorge nodded, and she went on. "Here, I won't have that problem.

Oh, I'll still be his daughter, all right . . . but there won't be quite the same degree of expectation. I won't have to call myself by another name, or spend my life telling people that I don't want to be a spiritual leader. And I can use the skills I learned in the Corps. There are a lot of places on Earth that need to be reexplored. Maybe the Terra Concorde has more room for me than the Corps ever did."

"I have a hard time believing that."

"Maybe, but . . . well, there it is." Inez paused, a slight frown appearing on her face. "Now, there's something else I want to say to you, and this is going to be a little hard for you to hear, so . . . just wait until I get it all out, all right?"

"Okay." Sensing that this was bad news, Jorge braced himself.

"All right, then . . ." She took a deep breath. "Look, I know how you feel about me. I've known that for a long time. And, to be honest, I love you, too . . . but not the way you want me to." She slowly let out her breath. "We can be friends, even close ones, but . . . we can never be lovers."

A cold stone settled itself in the pit of Jorge's stomach. It was almost the very same thing her mother had said to him; hearing it again, he felt a surge of anger and sought to put a clamp on it. "Great. So last night . . ."

"Please, no . . . don't be angry." Her hand tightened upon his as she moved a little closer to him. "Try to understand . . . last night, I thought we were about to die. I needed to reach out to someone, and you were there. I'm glad you were. I have no regrets about what we did, and I hope you don't either. But . . ."

Inez looked away again. She seemed to be trying to find the right words. "That was last night, and this is today. I simply don't share the same feelings for you as you do for me, and that's never going to change."

"If you gave it a chance, maybe . . ."

"You don't follow the Codicils of the *Sa'Tong-tas*, but I do . . . and the Second Codicil holds that I must never do anything that will cause harm to myself or to others around me." When she looked at him again, Jorge was surprised to see tears glimmering in the corners of her eyes. "Jorge, if I tried to love you the way you want me to, I'd only hurt myself . . . and in the end, the situation I'd put you in would inevitably hurt you, too. So I have no choice, really. We can be friends . . . but only that. Do you understand?"

Jorge wanted to argue with her, yet deep inside, he knew that Inez was right. And the last thing he ever wanted to do was hurt her. "Yeah . . . yeah, I guess I do."

He started to withdraw his hand from hers, but she refused to let it go. "All right, then," she continued. "Now here's the other thing I have to say to you. You need to go home. Back to Coyote."

"I wasn't . . . I mean, I wasn't planning to do otherwise." He shook his head. "Why are you telling me this?"

"You need to go home not because it's part of your mission, but for the same reason that I'm staying." Inez hesitated, then went on. "That night on the *Monroe*, when we were talking on the observation deck . . . you said something about knowing what it's like to have a famous father. Remember?"

"No." Jorge shook his head. "Your memory must be better than mine."

"It probably is. I don't forget conversations like that." A quick grin that promptly faded. "I don't know for sure, but I think you were trying to tell me that you've also had to deal with the expectations of those around you. Your family, friends, the Corps . . . everyone believing that you should be like your parents, your grandfather and grandmother, even our great-grandfather." She paused. "It's always been something of a burden to you, hasn't it?"

Jorge stared at her, astonished to hear this. "Are you sure you don't know how to read minds?"

Inez didn't laugh. "It's not hard to tell. Even before we became . . .

um, close . . . you were my commanding officer. I could see how you were having trouble, trying to live up to the family name and all that." A slight frown. "Just between you and me . . . did you ever really want to belong to the Corps?"

Now it was Jorge's turn to look away. "Not really, no. You're right . . . it's something that seemed forced on me, from the very beginning. I don't think I ever had a choice."

"You always have a choice. But . . . what else would you have done with your life, if not become an explorer?"

Jorge shrugged. "I don't know. Maybe become a writer, like my grandmother . . ."

"Your grandmother wrote her memoirs because she was an explorer, not the other way around." Inez impatiently shook her head. "Don't you see? Maybe this isn't what you wanted to do . . . but all the same, perhaps it's what you were meant to do. Just as I was meant to be here, by my father's side."

"Are you trying to tell me that I . . . ?"

"I'm not trying to tell you anything that you don't already know yourself." Inez smiled at him again. "I've watched you over the last few days, and what I saw was someone who was much stronger than he himself realized. Anyone less strong would've given up trying to get here, to this place, long before you did. But you didn't, and that's why you need to go home." Again, she paused. "But it's still your life and your choice of what to do with it."

Jorge didn't quite know how to respond, yet he knew that what she'd said was true . . . all of it. He could be her friend, but their relationship would never be more than that. And his place wasn't on Earth, but on Coyote.

"Maybe you're right," he murmured.

"Think about it awhile. You'll know I am." Letting go of his hand, Inez stood up. "That's enough for now. I think Papa is waiting for us to have dinner together . . . and I've been told that Hugh will be there, too."

Jorge realized that he hadn't thought about McAlister in many hours. "He's okay? They've let him out of the hospital?"

Inez nodded, and grinned. "Still upset about finding Sergio at the controls, but . . . well, he'll have his ship back soon enough." The grin faded. "Sooner than he thinks. Jorge, you've done everything you can do here. It's almost time for you to go home."

Without asking why, Jorge slowly nodded. She was right about that, too, whether he liked to admit it or not. There was no place for him on Earth, and the time was coming for him to return to Coyote.

Standing up from the bench, he let her slip her arm inside the crook of his elbow. Then they walked down the center aisle of the green-house, two friends going in search of others with whom to have dinner.

Part 8

SHALL WE GATHER BY THE RIVER?

On the bright winter morning of Anael, Gabriel 30, Wendy Gunther passed away.

As usual, she woke up shortly after sunrise, getting out of bed with the assistance of her aide, Tomas Conseco. Her dog Campy watched from his place on the bedroom rug as Tomas helped her put on a robe, and once she was seated in her wheelchair, he pushed her across the house to a small dining nook adjacent to the kitchen, where he'd already prepared a breakfast of oatmeal and strawberries. Tomas put Campy outside, then he and Wendy sat down at the nook table and had breakfast together while listening to the morning newscast from Liberty.

Wendy wasn't very hungry that morning, but she ate a little bit of her oatmeal while she and Tomas chatted about politics; even after retirement, Wendy hadn't lost interest in affairs of state. Tomas then wheeled her into the living room, where he left her at the desk comp with a cup of hot tea. As she went about reading and answering the day's mail, he returned to the kitchen to clean up.

Campy returned shortly after that, scratching at the kitchen door to be let back in. By then, Tomas had already put out a bowl of kibble for him, yet he noticed that the dog didn't go straight to it but instead hurried to the living room. Tomas didn't think much of this; he finished washing the dishes, then began an inventory of the pantry, preparing a grocery list that he planned to take with him when he went shopping in Bridgeton later in the day. He'd just finished writing the list when he heard Campy barking from the other side of the house. A second later, there was a faint crash, and Tomas dashed from the kitchen to the living room.

He found Wendy collapsed in her wheelchair, her face ashen as she struggled to breathe. The crash he'd heard was her knocking the teacup off the desk; Campy was standing beside the wheelchair, barking frantically at his mistress. Tomas quickly picked her up from the wheelchair and gently laid her on the carpeted floor. Discovering her pulse to be weak and erratic, he proceeded to administer mouth-to-mouth resuscitation. Her pulse didn't get any stronger, though, so he placed his hands together upon her breastbone and compressed her chest, repeating this a dozen times in quick succession before planting his mouth against hers again to force air into her lungs.

Despite his best efforts, Wendy didn't regain consciousness. Tomas took a moment to stab at the Vox button on the desk comp and make a call for help, but by the time a gyro from the university hospital landed on the ridgetop near Traveler's Rest, she had slipped into a coma. As Campy frantically ran back and forth, barking the entire time, Tomas helped the paramedics load Wendy onto a stretcher and carry her to the waiting aircraft. Leaving the dog behind to fend for himself, he rode with her to the hospital. Tomas held Wendy's hands in his own as he quietly spoke to her, begging her to please not leave.

It was no use. A few minutes before the gyro touched down on the hospital's landing pad, the electrocardiograph flatlined, and stayed that way. Wendy Gunther died within sight of the very hospital she herself had helped found. Doctors would later pronounce the cause of death to be a severe coronary seizure.

Within the hour, local news media issued the first reports of the death of the second president of the Coyote Federation. To the end, Tomas acted as Wendy's aide; borrowing a suit from a hospital administrator, he dried his tears and composed himself, then walked into a reception area crowded with reporters and, calmly and deliberately, issued a public statement. His voice cracked at one point, and it seemed for an instant that he'd break down, yet he managed to perform this one last official duty to the woman he'd served for so many years.

Wendy's family was quickly informed of what had happened. Her daughter Susan and son-in-law Jonathan were in Liberty; Susan would later blame herself for not being with her mother at the time, having instead decided to return to the city for a few days. She and Jon arrived at the hospital just as Tomas was preparing to meet the press. They didn't join him, though, going instead to the room where Wendy's body lay. The doctors closed the door behind them, allowing them a few minutes of privacy.

Marie Montero was told about her sister-in-law's death a short time later, yet it barely registered upon her. From deep within the abyss of her senescence, Marie's only visible response was a flickering frown, the slightest batting of an eyelid. Her caretakers at the hospice where she lived said that it was probably just as well that she wasn't fully aware of what had happened. Nonetheless, it was lost on no one that Marie was now the last surviving member of the *Alabama* party; it had only been a couple of days earlier that Chris Levin had been murdered in Defiance.

As significant as Wendy Gunther's death was, the importance of the life she'd spent was not overlooked. Long aware that she was dying, the editors of the *Liberty Post* had already researched and written a long obituary for her, which they issued as part of a special report. Her place in Coyote history couldn't be understated. One of the small handful of children who'd traveled to 47 Ursae Majoris aboard the URSS *Alabama*, the daughter of a Liberty Party loyalist who'd attempted to kill Captain Lee shortly after arrival. Wife of legendary Carlos Montero, and mother of the first child born on Coyote. Member of the first major expedition to leave New Florida and explore the Great Equatorial River. Participant in the resistance movement that revolted against the Western Hemisphere Union and eventually succeeded in expelling its occupation forces from Coyote. Doctor, diplomat, former Federation president, author of the memoirs that became the first and, in many ways, most reliable account of the colonies' early years . . . there seemed to be no aspect of life on this world that she hadn't touched.

By noon, President Edgar issued a statement of his own from Government House, expressing regret on behalf of the Federation and ordering all flags to be flown at half-mast. He also stated that President Gunther would be honored by an official state funeral, details of which would soon be made public. It was noticed by some in the press that her family didn't respond in kind, instead maintaining a neutral silence. No one said anything about it, yet a few political observers had already taken notice of the fact that there had never been any great affection between the current president and the former one, and that Wendy's family reportedly didn't like President Edgar very much either.

In the midst of all this, almost no one paid attention to the return of a Federation Navy shuttle, the CFS *Mercator*, through Starbridge Coyote.

A cold wind from the north was whipping across the concrete field of Liberty's municipal aerodrome as Sawyer Lee watched the government gyro from New Brighton come in for a landing. Its rotors were still in motion when the side passenger hatch opened and Jorge Montero climbed out. Sawyer raised his hand as Jorge ducked beneath the spinning blades to trot toward him, his duffel bag slung over his shoulder.

"Welcome home, Lieutenant." Ignoring the perfunctory salute from the younger man, Sawyer extended a gloved hand instead. "I'm just sorry that the circumstances couldn't be better."

"Same here, General . . . but thanks anyway." As Jorge shook his hand, Sawyer noticed that he wasn't wearing his Corps uniform. Which was just as well; neither was Sawyer, although most likely for different reasons. Jorge glanced around the airfield, looked back at Sawyer again. "Not that I'm unhappy to see you, sir, but . . . where's my father?"

"Still at the hospital, last time I checked." Sawyer grimaced. "I'm afraid your mother isn't taking this very well. She had to . . . well, rest awhile." He wanted to avoid telling Jorge that Susan had broken down at Wendy's bedside; Sawyer was reluctant to let Jorge know about this, or at least so soon after he'd returned. Things were hard enough already. "I think your family plans to eventually get together at your grandmother's house, but right now . . ."

"Yes, sir. I imagine everything is pretty much a mess." Jorge glanced past Sawyer at the coupe parked nearby. "Is that for us?"

"Uh-huh. I'll take you to the hospital . . . or wherever you want to go." Sawyer turned to lead Jorge to the waiting coupe; he hoped that Jorge wouldn't immediately notice that it wasn't a government vehicle but a private cab instead. "Hospital? Or maybe you'd like to get a drink first?"

Jorge gave him a sidelong look. "Pardon me for saying so, General, but the last time you offered me a drink, it was just before you dropped a bombshell on me." A grim smile. "And I thought that I'd already received the bad news."

Damn, Sawyer thought. *The kid doesn't miss a trick.* "A couple of things happened while you were gone," he said, opening the cab's rear door for Jorge and climbing in after him. "For starters, you can knock off the 'general' and 'sir' bit. Looks like I'm about to become a civilian again."

Jorge stared at him for a moment, as if not quite believing what he'd just heard. "I may need that drink after all," he said at last, then turned to the driver. "The Laughing Boid, please."

The driver smiled and nodded, then pulled away from the gyro and headed toward the aerodrome gates. For the first time, Jorge seemed to notice that he wasn't in an official vehicle. Before he had a chance to ask why, though, Sawyer reached forward to close the window between the front seat and the rear.

"There . . . we can talk now." Sawyer settled back in his seat, crossed his legs. "It's a long story, but to make it short, things haven't gone well for me lately."

"You were planning to find David Laird . . ."

"And I did, but . . ." Sawyer sighed, shook his head. "It didn't work out quite the way I expected. He's dead, and so is . . . well, an old friend of your mother's who went along to help me. I also twisted a few rules, and because of all that, the president isn't very happy with me just now." He paused. "Anyway, word came down from Government House that I could quit or be fired, so I've decided that I'd rather leave headfirst than feetfirst. Just this morning, before the news about your grandmother broke, I submitted my resignation letter. I haven't heard from Edgar yet . . . he's likely been too busy to read it . . . but no doubt he'll accept it." A short, humorless laugh. "In fact, it'll probably make his day."

Jorge didn't say anything for a moment. He appeared to be taking it all in. "Sir, I . . ."

"Like I said, there's no point in calling me 'sir' anymore." Sawyer gazed out at the houses passing by. "I appreciate the courtesy, but save it for your father. He probably doesn't know it yet, but he's up for a major promotion." He glanced at Jorge again. "And I imagine you'll be, too."

"I doubt that." Jorge shook his head. "I found the *chaaz'maha*, all right, but I didn't come back with him. And Inez . . ."

"Stayed behind to be with her father." Seeing the surprised look on Jorge's face, Sawyer smiled. "Just because I'm no longer the Corps CO doesn't mean I'm entirely out of the loop. I saw the preliminary report you sent while in transit from the starbridge. I'm sorry that you lost a man and that Corporal Sanchez has elected to remain on Earth, but otherwise it appears that you achieved most of your mission's objectives."

"Sir? I mean . . ." Jorge's mouth fell open; he appeared to be struggling for words. "With all due respect, but . . . that's not the way I see it. I didn't bring back the *chaaz'maha* . . ."

"You ascertained that he's still alive." Again, Sawyer smiled. "That alone is enough for the president to claim that your mission was a success. Believe me, once Edgar learns this, he'll waste no time trumpeting it from the Government House rooftops."

"But . . . our access to Earth is still closed. The Terra Concorde reopened Starbridge Earth only long enough for McAlister and me to make the jump home, and the *chaaz'maha* told me . . ."

"He wouldn't reopen it until his people have stabilized things back there." Sawyer nodded. "I read that part of your report, too. The president might not like it very much, but he can leave it to Manny to explain things to the Talus . . . and I bet that the *hjadd*, for one, will be pleased to know that the *chaaz'maha* has a firm hand on things back there and won't allow any more vessels from Coyote to visit Earth until he's good and ready." He favored Jorge with a wink. "It all comes down to politics, Lieutenant. In politics, anything that maintains the status quo is usually perceived as a victory."

Jorge scowled. "That's a rather cynical way of looking at it."

"Sorry." Sawyer let out his breath, gazed out the window again. The coupe was approaching Liberty's city center; as it passed an elementary school, he noticed that the Federation flag hanging from its front post had been lowered to half-mast. "It's been a rough day," he murmured, "and there's not a lot for me to be happy about."

Jorge didn't reply. He was quiet for a couple of minutes, apparently lost in thought. "If you don't mind," he said finally, "maybe we should have that drink later. Right now . . ."

"You need to see your family. I understand." Sawyer reopened the window. "Change of plan, driver," he said. "Take us to the university hospital, please." The driver quietly nodded, then took the next right, heading for the University of New Florida campus. "But I'd still like to have that drink," he added. "Maybe tonight, once everything has calmed down . . . ?"

"Yes, sir. I'd like that very much." Then Jorge smiled for the first time. "And I'm sorry, General, but you're just going to have to get used to me calling you that. Some things shouldn't change."

Sawyer wanted to return the smile but found that he couldn't. "Don't count on it," he said.

Lew's Cantina stood at the edge of Liberty's historic district, where it had been ever since the early days of the colony. Built by Lew and Carrie Geary, the *Alabama*'s agricultural specialists, it was Coyote's oldest tavern, and had remained open after both the Gearys passed away. Over the years, a few changes had been made—the cloverweed-thatch roof replaced with mountain briar, the goat pen that had once been out back finally torn down—but the new proprietors continued to brew their own sourgrass ale, and the blackwood-log main room was still heated by a stone hearth. Nonetheless, it had been decades since the tavern was the center of Liberty's social life; it had remained largely as a piece of history, its patrons mainly nearby residents and a handful of curious tourists.

It wasn't Jorge's first choice as a place to go for a drink; his favorite pub was on the other side of the city. But his father had insisted upon going to Lew's Cantina. After all, it was a place where Jorge's grandparents had spent a lot of time during their youth; perhaps it was appropriate that the family pick this location for a small, private wake.

Susan had refused to come along, though. She was still upset, and President Edgar's announcement that afternoon hadn't helped matters at all. Jorge missed having his mother join him and his father, but when the front door opened and Sawyer Lee walked in, he was relieved that she wasn't there.

The cantina wasn't crowded that evening, and the few people who were there paid little attention as Sawyer hung up his jacket by the door and strolled across the room. Jorge and his father had taken a table near the hearth; they looked up as Sawyer came over, and Jon waved him to a vacant chair.

"Good to see you, General. Welcome." He turned to raise a hand to the bartender. "Another round, please." Looking back at Sawyer, he tapped a finger against the nearly empty pitcher on the table. "We're drinking ale tonight, if it's all the same with you."

"Ale's fine . . . although I might start with a shot of bearshine." Sawyer pulled back the chair and settled into it. "Looks like you've already got a head start on me. I'll have to catch up."

"No need to rush," Jon said. "Take your time . . . we're in no hurry." Jorge noticed that his father's voice was slightly slurred. It had been a long time since he'd gone out drinking with his old man; Jonathan Parson had never been a lightweight, though, and Jorge knew that he could hold his liquor. "We're catching a cab home after this, so . . ."

"You're going back to Traveler's Rest tonight?"

"No." Jorge shook his head as he reached for the pitcher. "We're staying at our place in the city." He poured the rest of the ale into his mug. "My mother is . . . um, kinda busy just now."

Sawyer didn't say anything as a waiter came by with another pitcher and a mug for him. Jorge was vaguely aware that it was the third pitcher he'd brought to the table. Sawyer took the opportunity to ask for a shot of bearshine. "How's she doing?" he asked, once the waiter was gone. "Better, I hope."

"She's no longer crying all the time, if that's what you're asking." Jon poured ale into the fresh mug, placed it in front of his old friend, then refilled his own glass. "Now she's just mad."

"What about?" Sawyer didn't pick up his mug; he was waiting for his bearshine.

Jorge sighed. "I take it that you didn't hear the president's announcement this afternoon."

"Sorry, no. I've been"—an uncomfortable glance at Jon, who calmly gazed back at him—"working out the details for the change of command," he finished, his voice low. "A lot of stuff needs to be done before, y'know . . ."

"General . . ." Jon slowly let out his breath. "I can't tell you how sorry I am about this. The last thing I ever wanted was . . ."

"I know, I know." Sawyer shook his head. "Don't worry about it. I'm sure you're going to do fine." A wry smile briefly crossed his face. "But like I told your boy, stop calling me 'General.' I'm a civilian again, for better or worse."

"What are you going to do now?" Jorge asked.

An offhand shrug, but Sawyer didn't say anything until after the waiter returned to the table with a small glass of bearshine. "I dunno," he replied, once they were alone again. "Maybe go back to being a wilderness guide. Good money in that." A reflective pause, then he scowled. "Sure as hell won't be a bounty hunter, though," he quietly added. "I think I've had enough of tracking down wanted men. It's not worth it."

No one spoke as he lifted the shot glass to his lips, flung back the bearshine. He hissed between his teeth. "That's for Wendy," he murmured, then he looked at Jorge again. "So . . . you were saying something about our wonderful president?"

Jorge started to speak, but his father beat him to it. "Our wonderful president, once again proving that he always has the best interests of the Federation at heart, announced this afternoon the details of Wendy's funeral. In accordance with her standing as a former president, her body will lie in state at the Grange . . ."

"Say *what*?" Sawyer's mouth fell open as his eyes involuntarily turned in the general direction of what was now the historical museum. "Where?"

"You heard me right." Jon nodded. "The Grange Hall. In fact, she's already there. A squad of blueshirts in full-dress uniform showed up at the hospital and took her away before we had a chance to object."

"For the love of . . ." Sawyer shook his head. "And you didn't . . . I mean, Edgar didn't ask if you . . ."

"No, he didn't." Jorge's tongue was becoming thick with alcohol, but he picked up his mug anyway. "Her body will be on display in an open casket at the Grange for the next two days, so that the public will have a chance to visit her one last time. Then the casket will be placed on a horse-drawn carriage and be carried . . ."

"In a full military cortege," his father added.

"In a full military cortege through the city until it returns to Government House, where the president will preside over the official memorial service." Jorge took a drink, then went on. "After that, she'll be buried in front of the building, right beside Captain Lee's statue, where a bronze plaque will be . . ."

"Stop." His face writhing with disgust, Sawyer raised an impatient hand. "I got the picture. And I take it that this isn't what you . . . the family, I mean . . . wants."

"No. Not at all." Jon angrily shook his head. "And we don't think this is what Wendy would have wanted, either. Problem is, she never really told anyone . . . not me, not Susan, not even Tomas . . . what she wanted to be done with her after her death. She left behind a will, all right, but it didn't specify any funeral arrangements." He let out his breath, shrugged. "She was always like that. 'Just throw my body in the river and be done with it,' she'd say. 'I really don't care one way or another.'"

"But if the family doesn't want it this way, then why can't you stop it?"

"It's not about what we want," Jorge said. "It's about what Edgar wants. And if what he wants is a full-dress state funeral for a former president that'll make him look good, then he can make it stick."

"Susan's over at Government House right now," Jon said. "She and Tomas are trying to argue with the Chief Magistrate." He reached for the pitcher; his hand shook slightly as he poured himself another drink, slopping ale across the table. "I doubt they're going to get anywhere. He's one of Edgar's appointees, so he's not going to want to do anything that'll piss off . . ."

"It's like what you told me," Jorge murmured, remembering something Sawyer had said earlier in the day. "In the end, it's all about politics."

"The hell with politics . . . and the hell with Edgar." Sawyer slammed a hand down on the table. "If Wendy didn't want to go out this way, then it's not his right to say otherwise."

"Oh, I agree . . . but what can we do?" Jon shrugged. "I don't think we're being given a choice."

Jorge had fallen silent. Perhaps it was the ale taking control of his thoughts, but he found his mind was not turning to his grandmother, or President Edgar, or his parents, or Sawyer, but rather to something that Inez had said to him. Back on Earth, in the greenhouse dome when they'd shared their last moments alone together.

"It's your life," he muttered. "It's your choice of what to do with it."

His father peered at him. "What did you say?"

But Sawyer had heard him. "You're right," he said quietly. "We *do* have a choice." He paused. "Why, do you have something in mind?"

Jorge hesitated. "Did you get around to returning the keys to the Grange?" he asked.

Jon's eyes widened as a crafty smile spread across Sawyer's face. "Y'know," he said, "come to think of it . . . I don't think I ever did."

Bear had fully risen in the cloudless night sky by the time they left Lew's Cantina and walked across the historic district to the Grange. The windows of the historical museum were dark, but the light above the front door revealed the two Militiamen standing guard outside. They looked bored and cold, and no wonder; not only had they been given a thankless task, but someone had also insisted that they wear their dress uniforms, which were appropriate for official ceremonies but were hardly warm enough for a Gabriel night.

Sawyer was counting on that. "Evening, gentlemen," he said, careful to keep his distance so that the blueshirts couldn't smell the bearshine on his breath. "Keeping busy?"

The soldiers peered at the three men walking toward them; it took a moment for either of them to recognize Sawyer. "Hello, General," the master sergeant on the right said as they snapped to attention, their rifles at their sides. "We're doing fine, sir."

Sawyer nodded, trying not to smile. Apparently they had not heard that he'd just resigned from the Corps; he'd been counting on that, too. "I'm sure you are," he said drily as he fished his key ring from his coat pocket. "Just paying a little visit, if you don't mind . . ."

"Sir?" A querulous expression crossed the face of the corporal on the left. "We weren't informed that you were planning to drop by."

Neither he nor the sergeant moved away from the steps, but instead regarded Sawyer and the other two men with bewildered expressions. A quick glance at Jonathan and Jorge, then Sawyer stepped a little closer to the guards.

"I realize that, but . . ." His voice dropped to a conspiratorial whisper. "Look, I don't know if you recognize these two, but they belong to President Gunther's family. That's her son-in-law and grandson, and the kid just returned from an important offworld mission, so he wasn't here when she died. I'd take it as a personal favor if you'd let us in, then make yourselves scarce so he can pay his respects in private."

The corporal nodded, but the master sergeant was reluctant. "I understand that, sir," he said, keeping his voice low as well, "but we have orders to . . ."

"Remain on duty until relieved. Sure." Sawyer smiled. "When does your shift end, Sergeant?"

"Zero-dark hours, sir."

Sawyer made a show of checking his watch, even though he already knew what time it was. "It's 2502 now. Your relief is due in about two hours." He gave them a wink. "I think you've got better things to do between now and then than stand around in the cold. In fact, I've already taken the liberty of paying your bar tab at Lew's Cantina."

The sergeant stared at him. "Sir?"

"Go get a drink, Sarge. You, too, Corporal. Consider that an order." Sawyer jingled the keys in his hand. "I'll lock up behind us. So long as you're back by midnight, no one will be the wiser."

The two blueshirts gave each other an uncertain glance, then the sergeant looked back and forth along the street. There was no one else in sight; this time of night, the historic district was deserted, with only a few lights glimmering in the windows of Government House to show that anyone was around. "Yes, sir," he said at last. "Thank you."

The two men slung their rifles across their soldiers and walked down the street, heading for the cantina. Jonathan watched them go, then moved to Sawyer's side. "You realize, of course, they're going to get in a lot of trouble for this," he murmured.

"I know . . . but not half as much as we will." Sawyer shifted through the keys until he found the ones for the Grange's front door. "If you want to change your mind, now's the time."

Jon hesitated, then slowly let out his breath. "I got to Coyote in the first place by disobeying orders. Might as well end my second military career the same way." He looked at his son. "You? This was your idea. Still want to go through with it?"

Jorge grinned as he teetered back and forth on his feet. *The kid's plastered,* Sawyer thought. *In the morning, he'll probably regret this.* Again, he found himself wondering why Jorge had said so little about what had happened on Earth. He didn't know for certain, but he had a distinct feeling that there was another reason, besides his grandmother's death, that he'd put away so much ale at the cantina. Maybe it had something to do with Inez's decision to stay with her father . . . ?

"Why not?" Jorge shrugged. "Far as I'm concerned, I'm just carrying on a family tradition."

"Defying authority." Sawyer chuckled as he marched up the steps.

"Your grandfather would be proud." Jorge gave him a sharp look; although he didn't respond, Sawyer realized that he'd hit a nerve with that remark.

The front door opened with a soft creak, and Sawyer felt around until he located the light switch. The museum was much the way he'd last seen it only a couple of weeks ago, only this time the display tables had been moved aside to make room for an ornately carved blackwood casket that rested upon a low pedestal. The casket lid was shut, and it had been draped with the Federation flag, with two more flags hangings from posts at each end of the pedestal. A red carpet had been laid down the center of the floor; gilded ropes separated the casket from the rest of the room. As a final touch, Wendy Gunther's official presidential portrait had been placed on an easel behind the casket.

"Oh, god," Jon muttered. "She always hated that picture." He paused, then added, "In fact, she would've hated all of this."

"Well, let's see that she doesn't have to endure it any longer," Sawyer said. "Call Susan and Tomas, tell them we're ready."

Turning away from the casket, Jon pulled a phone from his pocket. He'd already spoken with his wife, calling her from the cantina to tell her of the plan. By then, Sawyer figured, Susan and Tomas would have returned home to fetch the lorry she and Jon still owned from the days they'd operated a wilderness trekking company and had used the vehicle to transport canoes and kayaks.

As Jon talked to Susan, Sawyer pulled out his own phone. He had friends in the Corps who owed him a favor or two; time to call in his markers. He had little doubt that he could have a Corps gyro fueled and ready to fly from the aerodrome within the hour, no questions asked. There would be hell to pay later, of course, but . . .

Looking around, he realized that Jorge was no longer beside them. The young man had walked across the room; his back turned to Sawyer, he was gazing at one of the display cases. And quietly chuckling to himself.

Curious, Sawyer delayed making the call. He strolled over to Jorge, and saw what the lieutenant was studying. Within the glass sarcophagus was the cat-skin kayak that his grandparents had used to explore the Great Equatorial River, long before he was born.

"What's so funny?" Sawyer asked.

Jorge looked at him, and Sawyer saw that his cheeks were wet with tears. Yet there was a smile on his face, and there was no sadness in his eyes.

"I just . . ." Still grinning, Jorge reached up to wipe away the tears. "I just thought of something." He nodded to the kayak. "If we're going to send my grandmother away, she might as well go in style."

For a moment, Sawyer didn't know what he was talking about. Then he understood, and laughed out loud.

It was still dark when a Corps gyro landed on a sandy beach on New Florida's southern coast. There were no settlements on this part of the island, just above the equator, a few miles west of Miller Creek. So no one observed the aircraft as it touched down a few dozen yards from the Great Equatorial River, or saw the figures who emerged from its rear cargo compartment.

Jorge took a moment to look around. Bear was beginning to set upon the western horizon, its silver rings touching the dark expanse of the river. To the east, the first light of the new day had tinted the sky with hues of red and orange. The tide would be receding soon, but he still had a few minutes in which to savor the predawn morning.

"This is where your grandmother said good-bye to your grandfather." Susan had come up behind him; she, too, was looking out at the river. "They'd eventually see each other again, of course, but all the same, it was the moment in their lives when they parted from each other." She paused. "You picked a good place to do this."

Jorge nodded as he turned to look back at the gyro. He'd sobered up over the last few hours, but there wasn't much that he felt like saying. Instead, he watched as his father and Sawyer unloaded his grandparents' kayak from the gyro. They carried it to the river's edge and put it down, its bow in the shallows and its stern on the sand.

"I sort of thought it was appropriate," he said at last. "Besides, no one ever comes down here. No one will know." Then he smiled. "You were here, too, weren't you?"

"I suppose you could say that. I just hadn't made my grand entrance yet." Susan absently nudged a piece of driftwood with her foot, then bent down to pick it up. "C'mon, let's build a fire. It'll help keep us warm . . . and we'll need it for the rest, too."

By then, Tomas had come over from the gyro, along with its pilot. As the four of them began gathering dry wood that had washed up on the beach, Jonathan and Sawyer went about erecting the kayak mast and raising its sail. Before long, a small heap of driftwood lay upon the shore; Sawyer found a firestarter in the gyro, and he used it to set the stack ablaze.

The six of them—Jorge, his parents, Sawyer, Tomas, and the Corps lieutenant whom Sawyer had sworn to secrecy—stood around the bonfire, quietly passing a jug of bearshine as they watched Bear go down. The sky was still full of stars, but it wouldn't be long before the sun would make its appearance. They finished the jug, then Jonathan dropped it on the ground next to the fire.

"All right, then," he said. "Let's do this."

They walked together back to the gyro, and as Susan, Sawyer, Tomas, and the pilot stood on both sides of its cargo hatch, Jorge and his father climbed into the aircraft. Wendy's body was no longer in the casket; it wasn't needed, so they'd left it behind, instead using the flag that had been draped over it as her funeral shroud. Carefully, with Jonathan nestling her head and shoulders within his hands and Jorge carrying her feet, they lifted Wendy from the floor of the aircraft and gently unloaded her from the gyro. Once she was out of the aircraft, the others came forward and, placing their hands beneath her, helped Jorge and Jonathan carry the body to the beach.

No one spoke as they laid Wendy within the kayak, making sure that she was in the center of the small boat, with her head toward the bow and her feet to the stern. They stepped back from the boat and stood silently for a few minutes. On the way there, they'd agreed that no speeches would be made. Wendy wouldn't have wanted any last words; the presence of her family and friends was sufficient testimonial.

After a little while, Susan turned away from them. Walking over to the bonfire, she bent down and pulled a burning branch from the embers. Bringing it back to the kayak, she started to lower it . . . then she hesitated and turned to Jorge.

"Here," she whispered, offering the branch to him. "You should be the one."

Jorge hesitated. He looked at his father; Jonathan quietly nodded, as did Tomas and Sawyer. So he took the branch from his mother and, stepping closer to the kayak, let its flame touch the edge of the flag near Wendy's feet.

The flag caught fire at once. Jorge dropped the branch into the water, then he and his parents bent down and pushed the kayak into the water. The morning breeze caught the sail, billowed it outward; as the fire reached for Wendy's body, the kayak floated out into the Great Equatorial River.

Jorge silently watched as the small boat moved away from the shore, the body it carried becoming a funeral pyre upon the water. Her remains would soon become one with the Great Equatorial River, flowing forever around the world, a minute-yet-significant contribution to its long seasonal cycle of life, death, and rebirth. In this way, Wendy Gunther would become Coyote.

Tiny sparks rose from the kayak, carried upward by the breeze to meet with the fading stars. Looking up at them, Jorge sought out a small point of light. There it was, low on the horizon, just below Vega. He couldn't see Earth, but he knew that it was there.

He found himself smiling. He, too, had come home.

Somewhere out in the marshes, a boid cried out, a chilling cry against the darkness that soon became quiet. As Wendy's ashes were lifted into the morning sky, a new day came to Coyote.

COYOTE CALENDAR

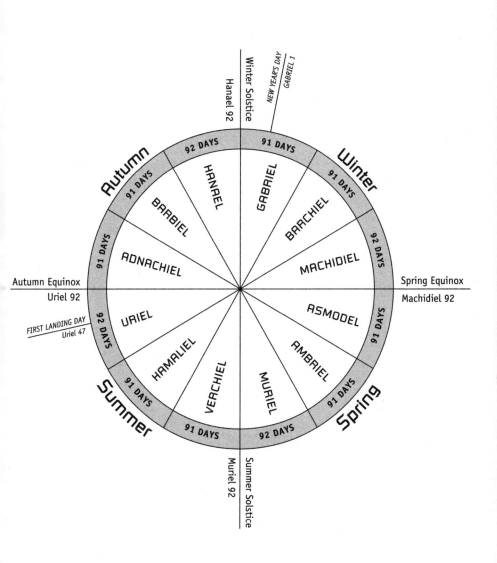

TIMELINE: COYOTE HISTORY

Earth Events:

JULY 5, 2070—URSS *Alabama* departs from Earth for 47 Ursae Majoris and Coyote.

APRIL–DECEMBER 2096—United Republic of America falls. Treaty of Havana cedes control of North America to the Western Hemisphere Union.

JUNE 16, 2256—WHSS *Seeking Glorious Destiny Among the Stars for Greater Good of Social Collectivism* leaves Earth for Coyote.

JANUARY 4, 2258—WHSS *Traveling Forth to Spread Social Collectivism to New Frontiers* leaves Earth for Coyote.

DECEMBER 10, 2258—WHSS *Long Journey to the Galaxy in the Spirit of Social Collectivism* leaves Earth for Coyote.

AUGUST 23, 2259—WHSS *Magnificent Voyage to the Stars in Search of Social Collectivism* leaves Earth for Coyote.

MARCH 4, 2260—WHSS *Spirit of Social Collectivism Carried to the Stars* leaves Earth for Coyote.

AUGUST 2270–JULY 2279—The Savant Genocide; 35,000 on Earth killed; mass extermination of Savants, with the survivors fleeing the inner solar system.

APRIL 2288—First sighting of Spindrift by telescope array on the lunar farside.

JUNE 1, 2288—EASS *Galileo* leaves Earth for rendezvous with Spindrift; contact lost with Earth soon thereafter.

JANUARY 2291—EASS *Galileo* reaches Spindrift. First contact.

SEPTEMBER 18, 2291—EASS *Columbus* leaves for Coyote.

FEBRUARY 1, 2344—CFSS *Robert E. Lee* returns to Earth, transporting survivors of the *Galileo* expedition.

APRIL–JULY 2352—Collapse of Western Hemisphere Union; mass exodus of refugees from Earth, halted by destruction of Starbridge Coyote.

Coyote Events:

AUGUST 5, 2300—URSS *Alabama* arrives at 47 Ursae Majoris system.

SEPTEMBER 7, 2300 / URIEL 47, C.Y. 01—Colonists arrive on Coyote; later known as "First Landing Day."

URIEL 52, C.Y. 02—First child born on Coyote: Susan Gunther Montero.

GABRIEL 18, C.Y. 03—WHSS *Glorious Destiny* arrives. Original colonists flee Liberty; Western Hemisphere Union occupation of Coyote begins.

AMBRIEL 32, C.Y. 03—WHSS *New Frontiers* arrives.

HAMALIEL 2, C.Y. 04—WHSS *Long Journey* arrives.

BARCHIEL 6, C.Y. 05—WHSS *Magnificent Voyage* arrives.

BARBIEL 30, C.Y. 05—Thompson's Ferry Massacre; beginning of the Revolution.

GABRIEL 75, C.Y. 06—WHSS *Spirit* arrives.

ASMODEL 5, C.Y. 06—Liberty retaken by colonial rebels, Union forces evicted from Coyote; later known as "Liberation Day."

HAMALIEL C.Y. 13—EASS *Columbus* arrives; construction of starbridge begins.

NOVEMBER 2340 / HANAEL C.Y. 13—*Columbus* shuttle EAS *Isabella* returns to Earth via Starbridge Coyote; United Nations recognition of Coyote Federation.

MURIEL 45, C.Y. 15—*Galileo* shuttle EAS *Maria Celeste* returns to Coyote via alien starbridge.

ASMODEL 54, C.Y. 16—Hjadd cultural ambassador arrives on Coyote.

HAMALIEL 25, C.Y. 16—CFS *Pride of Cucamonga* departs for Rho Coronae Borealis via *hjadd* starbridge.

HAMALIEL 1, C.Y. 17—Exploratory Expedition departs Bridgeton for first circumnavigation of the Great Equatorial River.

URIEL 2, C.Y. 17—Destruction of the CFSS *Robert E. Lee* and Starbridge Coyote; later known as "Black Anael."

GABRIEL 10, C.Y. 23—Arrival of WHS *The Heroism of Che Guevara* through rebuilt Starbridge Coyote.

ACKNOWLEDGMENTS

The author wishes to thank his editor, Ginjer Buchanan, and his agent, Martha Millard, for their continuing support for his work. The Coyote series, including the spin-off novels set in the same universe, is now ten years old; none of these books could have been written or published without their encouragement.

I'd also like to thank Rob Caswell, Patrick O'Conner, Ron Miller, Horace "Ace" Marchant, and Bob and Sara Schwager for their aid and advice during the writing of this novel.

Sources consulted for this book include *The World Without Us*, by Alan Weisman (St. Martin's Press, 2007); *Boston Architecture*, edited by Donald Freeman (MIT Press, 1970); and "Goat House Lighthouse" by Jeff Bonney, published in *The Salt Book*, edited by Pamela Wood (Anchor Press/ Doubleday, 1977). The polar cows and medusas described in Part One were inspired by the ceramic *Little Monsters* sculptures of artist Holly Fox and are used with her permission; the originals can be seen at http:// mmmmonsters.blogspot.com. I'd also like to commend Boston Harbor Tours for their guided excursion of Boston's inner harbor and the Charles River, which played a key role in the research for this novel.

And finally, last but never least, my greatest appreciation goes to my wife, Linda, for keeping me sane during this long expedition to 47 Ursae Majoris.

August 2008–March 2009
Whately, Massachusetts